LEAVE NO TRACE

LEAVE NO TRACE

Jay Warton

OLEANDER

The Oleander Press
16 Orchard Street
Cambridge
CB1 1JT

www.oleanderpress.com

First published in 2019 by The Oleander Press

ISBN 9781999900465

For my mum who always made me
feel I could do anything and my dad who
made me feel safe enough to try.

LEAVE NO TRACE

ONE

It was just a whim. Nothing more. Doe was interested to see if it could be done; if he could do it. He had a little vacation time to fill and nothing much that interested him was going on at work, so he figured that rather than continue to wonder, he would find out.

He knew that most people would think it was odd but it was part of who he was. It was part of why he had his job. He wasn't the kind of guy who would sit on a beach or the kind that would climb a mountain. If Doe climbed a mountain he would expect to find something at the top. Probably a criminal. Probably one that no one else even knew existed.

His bosses gave him a lot of autonomy. It was a big part of his role. He had the freedom to investigate anything that he thought was strange. Anything at all, however big or small. If Doe thought there was something there worth investigating then his bosses let him get on with it. Although that didn't really cover it, because he never had to ask. His bosses didn't expect him to ask for permission. They expected him to tell them and they expected results but they didn't ask for regular meetings or written proposals and they certainly didn't care whether he took all of his vacation time.

Doe looked idly through the window of a travel agency and decided to go for it. He didn't care what people thought was strange and he really did want to know. Now all he needed to do was work out the parameters of the experiment. Something that would make it a meaningful test, but something that would give him a chance.

*

He wanted to find out if it was possible to visit a place, to live there relatively normally for a while and then leave without anyone remembering that you had been there. To do that and have it as a meaningful test he needed to pick somewhere in a 'Goldilocks' zone of populations.

Location would be important. If the place was too small it would be too easy. Or perhaps it would be too difficult. He would either find somewhere sheltered and stay hidden away from the locals, or he would go into town and then everyone he met would remember him. The first would be way too easy and the second would be impossible. The obverse was equally true. If he chose somewhere too big then the whole thing would be a waste of time. Doe figured he could spend a couple of years living perfectly normally in LA or New York without anyone remembering anything about him.

As well as population, he had to consider the type of place. America was littered with towns. Plenty of them were in the right population range but most of them were on the way to somewhere. Or on the way back from somewhere. America had its big system of interstate highways. Huge freeways. Two or more lanes of black top. Criss-crossing the country. Passing close to the bigger places and further away from the smaller ones. Always heading onwards. Roads leaked off the highways and into the towns and other roads spread out from the towns, seeking out the unrelenting black top. Thousands and thousands of miles of asphalt, always heading on and on. Never stopping until they hit the sea or an international border. And between the interstates there was another system of roads connecting the smaller places. Roads that were still huge. Some running exactly parallel to the interstates. Smaller two and three lane roads connecting regional centers. Roads thinning down as the importance or the size of the towns along it decrease, but all linking up. All taking people from A to B via C.

Doe needed an A or a B, not a C. In Cs there are always people passing through. That would make the test easier. Even in the smallest places people would stop off on their way down the road. On their way down to the next even smaller place. Or on their way back up the road to the brighter lights of the cities. Maybe they would have mechanical problems or maybe it would be biological. Maybe their muffler falls off or maybe they just get tired and decide to stay overnight. Doe figured that in C-type places people would take less notice of people who didn't stay long. Even if they were patrons or tourists. In transitory places people wouldn't be programmed to take much notice of people. Their attention would just slide over him.

In the As and Bs people would be more interested. Their culture would be different. They would look to find out about people a little, even if they were only passing through. It would give the experiment a chance. It would make it a proper test.

The trouble was, there weren't many As or Bs. The roads looped around the bigger towns and passed right through the smaller places. If they hit the ocean they bent and followed the coast hunting out other places, other towns. If they hit a border, they branched, funnelling people to the crossing points and away again. At the borders Doe figured people would pay even less attention. The people passing through those C-type towns could be from anywhere, heading anywhere. You might not even share a language.

*

Chronology was going to be important too. In most places folks would be expecting tourists to come at the weekend, so at the weekend he might be ignored or forgotten. Conversely, on a weekday, working locals would be likely to be busier. They might not notice a newcomer as readily as they might on the slower, weekend days. Doe decided that to be fair he would arrive early on a Friday and stay until the Tuesday morning. Two full busy working days and a full lazy weekend.

The final planning issue was arrival. Jet pack or private helicopter would be sure to be remembered but he had a hunch that if he arrived on foot, either through the woods or by the side of the road, then that would prove equally memorable. People would talk. For most places, a bus or train wouldn't even be an option. Even in the places where there was a railroad or bus station, he figured that arriving that way would probably destroy his chances before he even reached town. In the USA, and especially in rural USA, people just don't take the bus. Anyone who does has absolutely no choice. In towns the size and type Doe was looking for he was willing to bet that everyone knew who they were. Anyone riding the bus, anyone that hadn't sat on that bus before, was going to be remembered by the driver. Any stranger getting off a bus would be noticed by the locals. They would be likely to be undesirables. Drifters, panhandlers, thieves. People to keep your eye on. People to remember.

By far the most likely scenario was that there wouldn't be a bus at all. There would be a handful of taxis in town and a railroad station a hundred-miles away. The taxis would have drivers full of curiosity about a stranger without a car and there would be two hours of journey time for them to ask all the questions they wanted. Afterwards, when he had left, they would find the taxi driver. Even if Doe risked the driver's wrath and said nothing for the whole ride, they would get a good description. Then he would have been doubly memorable. He would have been the guy who didn't have a car and the guy who didn't say a single word for two whole hours.

And there would be a 'they'. Doe had reached out to a buddy at Quantico. His buddy was an instructor and nine days after he left town, six of Doe's buddy's Basic Field Training Course New Agent Trainees would breeze in and try to find out who he was. Doe's buddy was going to use it as a fugitive tracking simulation. The trainees would be told that an active fugitive may or may not have spent time in the town a few days or weeks earlier. All they had to do was find out if he had. Obviously, it would be unfair to them if Doe kept his own identity during his stay. Doe had by necessity pruned and hidden his public identity. He had also obscured and deleted almost all the information that would show up on even a relatively well-connected, classified, access search. To use his own identity would completely skew the experiment. The recruits could discover a huge amount of information from the time he was in town and still be unable to find out anything at all about him.

So Doe had spent an afternoon setting up a fake identity. It was pretty good. It had a back story and documentation. The back story was good enough to survive casual interest. The documentation was good enough to cover him if he got into a bar fight or got pulled over for speeding, but the trip was whim, not a work thing. He wasn't going to spend a week of department time developing something fireproof. It would be a waste of time and somehow, it didn't feel to be in the spirit of the endeavor.

Anyway, an adequate but breakable alias worked perfectly for both him and his buddy. If the recruits could find out enough about him from his four-day stay to be able to pull the threads and work out that there was something dodgy going on, then they had won. His question would be answered. The answer would be 'no, he couldn't'.

*

Doe turned his attention back to location. He didn't have as many places to choose from as he had expected. With as little research as possible he chose Seal Harbor on Briel Island - way up at the top of Washington State. It was right out in the straits between the USA and Canada, closer to Vancouver Island than to the American mainland. Up there he found himself a town of nine hundred and twenty-eight souls at the western edge of a horseshoe-shaped island. Seal Harbor was incontrovertibly an A or B type of town. The road petered out at the southern edge of town. Single lane blacktop went in at the north and a rutted, muddy logging trial went out at the south. The trail led nowhere and no one ever drove through. If you found yourself in Seal Harbor you either stayed or you turned around and drove back out the way you came. There were boats in the harbor and there was some hiking in the forests around town, but it was eighteen miles through open water back to Heath Haven or a tough, forty-mile hike. Doe guessed that at some point, in this century or the last, someone had arrived at Seal Harbor on his way to somewhere else, but not more than twice and probably not successfully.

Next, he tackled the transport issue. He was going to have to drive. It wasn't just a practical thing, it was cultural. He had to have a vehicle, but that provided a whole raft of additional problems. If he stayed in a motel he would have to enter the license plate in the register. If he stayed somewhere else or hid behind the dumpsters at the local diner, he would have to park the car somewhere. Doe figured that the residents of a town like Seal Harbor were likely to notice a strange car parked on their streets. Even if it was only for a day or two. They would walk past it on their way to the grocery and look at each other. They would say, 'whose car is that Agnes? Note down its license plate, it might be one of those bang-ganger gangs.' They would fall over themselves to tell Doe's buddy's recruits.

There weren't any convenient twenty-four-hour service operations with huge parking lots. No airports or retail parks with hundred-room business hotels. Nowhere to hide the vehicle in plain sight. He considered fake number plates. The recruits would uncover them, but it wouldn't necessarily tell them that their fugitive had been there. They would probably assume the car was stolen or try to chase down an insurance fraud. They would chase it down just in case - and Doe's biggest problem was that he couldn't tell how determined they would be. He had to assume that they would be good at their jobs and that they would work eighteen-hour days trying to find him.

Once they had his license tags, real or fake, they would be able to use the surveillance cameras on the highway to trace his journey. He didn't want to drive in all the way from Tijuana, but he couldn't be sure how far back they would be able to go in the time they had. If they were fast enough they could work out where he joined the highway system and track him even further. They could use local police cameras and private security cameras. If they were good they might even locate where he picked up the car or changed the plates. He would use underground garages and switch cars in the rush hour. He could disable cameras or use airports or dark farm roads to change plates. Whatever he did, given enough time, if the investigator was determined enough and well-enough resourced, there was always a chance they would track him down.

His buddy's recruits wouldn't have unlimited time or resources. He figured that made it a fair test. Their lack of time was balanced by the fact that they had been tipped off to the fact that he might be there. It would still be a major pain in the ass. To eliminate the risk, he would have to start his journey a long way south and spend a lot of time confusing the cameras. Even then, his victory would be muted. They might find his car but not have the time to work out whether or not it was significant. If that happened he would know that the only reason he had succeeded was because of their lack of time, not their lack of expertise. Maybe he would have to call that a tie. It would be a lot easier if he could find a way to hide the vehicle from them.

Doe spent another couple of hours on the internet. He restricted himself to the kind of searches a determined criminal or extremely-paranoid private citizen might make.

*

Doe reached out to another colleague at the D.E.A. He picked up an impounded pickup truck with clean tags from a short stay, covered parking lot at Seattle-Tacoma International Airport. He had flown to Portland and arrived in Tacoma by train. The subterfuge was probably pointless. He decided that, if the students managed to track him to the parking lot, then he would consider the experiment to have failed. He could have driven there grinning into every camera. Once you have failed, you have failed. It was good field craft though and Doe had a plan. He was certain that they weren't going to know the truck had ever been in Seal Harbor. They couldn't track what they never saw.

The interstate took him up past Seattle, paralleling the pacific coast and wiggling a bit as the coastline changed or the towns of economic value moved further toward the coast or further inland. About ninety miles north of Seattle he turned west onto a two-lane highway and headed toward the coast. After another fifteen miles, the road stayed the same size, but the towns started to get smaller. He passed plenty of towns that were the right size for his experiment, but they were all

Cs. He sped past them all and after another ten miles even the road started to get smaller. First the lanes got narrower. Then the second lane disappeared altogether.

Fifty minutes later Doe was on a ferry. He figured ports would be as bad as borders. Soukous wasn't a big place, but it was too big for Doe. Ferries came in right through the day. There were four-story hotels by the dock and big motels on the road out of town. Doe rolled on through and took the only route out of town, one of the island-hopping ferries that left six times a day for a slow crawl around five ports on four islands. There were cameras and tickets to buy. Doe had no doubt that his car would be remembered, but there were other cars on the ferry and his buddy's trainees would have no reason to pick on his rather than any of the others. If his plan worked, no one in Seal Harbor was going to remember his pickup.

After a choppy two hour crossing he drove the truck onto a single-track, wood and steel pier and on into the town of Heath Haven. Population five hundred and forty-two. Heath Haven was perfect. Except that it was still a C. Not much of a C, but nevertheless, there was a road out of town. Folks got off the ferry at Heath Haven and drove across the island to the state park, or to the wilderness preserve, or to any one of a dozen fishing spots and lodges. Doe drove out of town and headed north in a big loop around Rooster State Park and a huge bay that almost cut the island in half. After eighteen miles the road turned back toward the south, down the western coast of the island and into Seal Harbor.

Seal Harbor might have been bigger than Heath Haven, and therefore not as good for Doe's experiment, but it was most definitely the end of the line.

*

He drove into Seal Harbor in the dark-blue pickup truck. The license tags were from in-state and they were real, but they weren't the same tags he had used on the interstate. He drove to the speed limit and to the laws of the state. He pulled up at the second diner he saw within the town limits and parked nose in, tight to the wall of the diner. There was barely enough space to walk in front of the cab. He arrived forty minutes before the main morning rush. He knew when the morning rush started from the social media accounts of patrons and staff and by looking at commercially available aerial and satellite images of the diner's parking lot.

He was dressed in a light-blue button-down shirt and faded blue denims secured with a wide belt. The belt had a small emblem buckle. The buckle could have been a purchase from a sports franchise or a giveaway from a muffler shop. There was a bright red cap stuffed in the rear pocket of his jeans with the very edge of an embroidered logo visible. He ordered breakfast and coffee and took forty-five minutes and two coffee refills before he finished. It was no chore, he had been traveling since midnight and the food was good. When he walked out of the diner the parking lot was full and he had to squeeze around the front of his pickup to get to the driver's door. He got into the cab and then got back out. He walked to the load bed and pulled out a jacket and carried it back to the cab. The morning was warm but maybe he was heading back north or maybe he was planning to use a chainsaw wherever he next stopped.

Doe started the motor and reversed slowly though the busy lot. He turned left onto the road heading into town. His license plate was still showing in-state tags, but the license number had changed again.

Doe drove the full length of the town. Main Street paralleled the coast, a couple of streets inland. To Doe's left, the touristy part of town covered the few streets running down to the sea. To his right the residential spread covered another few streets before the trees crowded in. Driving north to south, he passed through a prosperous-looking commercial district. There were diners and a small strip mall. A block further south was the municipal district. A concrete police department. Another small mall with an M.D.'s office and a dentist's practice. A few showier stores and some lawyer's offices. Less than a block further and he was back into a slightly-seedier commercial district before he finally reached his motel. A few blocks further south the road petered out and turned into the abandoned logging road. The tourist sector was thicker further north, but Doe had chosen somewhere he thought he might be noticed but where he thought he might not stand out.

He turned off the road and into the motel parking lot late, driving quickly enough to surprise anyone who was looking and slowly enough not to scatter the gravel and alert anyone who wasn't. He pulled up hard against the plate glass of the office window. His front license plate was below the sill and the rear tag was hidden by twelve feet of dark blue pickup. He signed a name in the register and wrote the license plate number of a brown pickup that he had spotted waiting to get on to the ferry at Heath Haven. If they got this far the recruits would have to assume the discrepancy could be down to poor memory or faulty filing. They might think it was suspicious, but all they would be able to trace it back to would be an innocent local guy who was off the island at the time.

Doe checked with the clerk that there was parking around the back of the accommodation block. He knew perfectly well that there was parking back there. He asked because he wanted the guy to remember. He wanted him to think that was where Doe's truck was probably parked. He took his key and said he had a few errands to run and got back into the pickup and pulled out of the lot.

He headed back north and took the first left and then a right. Into the residential zone. Seal Harbor wasn't a large town. Doe parked by the curb a hundred yards down a long, curving street outside a low-slung, four-bedroom ranch-style house with a twin garage. Inside that garage there was an identical dark-blue pickup with license tags that exactly matched the ones that were now on Doe's pickup.

Social media had told Doe that the family were going on holiday. Common sense told him they would take her sedan rather than his pickup. More of those commercially-available satellite images told him that they usually kept their vehicles in the garage. Doe knew that there was a risk. Their neighbors might notice that the pickup was out on the street when it should have been in the garage, but the family had left less than twelve hours earlier. He doubted anyone would notice, and if they did, by the time the recruits arrived and started asking questions the timeline would be blurred. 'No Janice, you're wrong, they left on the Monday and you saw the truck on Friday.' Or 'I think they left on the Friday and Jimmy saw their truck there, let me see... was it Tuesday?'

Doe, now wearing the jacket, walked two blocks back into town and sat in the coffee shop opposite the motel.

*

A couple of coffees later Doe walked around the block, hopped the wall at the back of the motel and let himself into his room. He ran the shower and put the TV on and then he rang reception and asked if there was anything special he had to do to get an out-of-state phone line. He figured it was a reasonable question. One that the guy would get asked pretty often with all the weird 'dial nine' type rules there were for using phones in motels. He didn't care. It just needed to be plausible. The only reason he made the call was to let the clerk, and through him any later investigators, know that Doe was in his room.

Maybe it would put a seed of doubt in the guy's mind as well. He wouldn't have seen Doe walk or drive past reception because Doe had climbed the back wall, but Doe was clearly in his room. Maybe the guy would get to thinking that he had missed Doe when he went past. Maybe he would work it up into a little story so that it made sense. Maybe Doe would have been in his room most of the day, because the guy hadn't seen him arrive or leave, but he had made that out of state call, right? If he played it right, maybe Doe would spend most of the weekend in his room without actually spending much time there at all.

And that was important to Doe. He had decided that he couldn't stay holed up in his motel room the whole time. He wasn't sure that doing that would seem particularly unusual, he just figured it was too easy. His experiment was to find out if he could live in a place for a couple of days, not just stay there. Doe was a proactive man. He figured the best way to confuse his pursuers was to be several people. If Doe was the guy with the blue, or possibly brown, pickup who spent all his time in his motel room, then he couldn't be the guy who had sat in the diner across the street. Just before he hung up on the clerk he asked him if there was a decent pizza place in town. One that did takeaway to the motel.

Doe didn't make any phone calls from the motel. He didn't want to leave any phone numbers to be traced even if they were only to the local pizza joint. It was his aim to leave absolutely no trace that he had ever even been in Seal Harbor. Instead, he jumped the back wall again and headed to a call box on, what the map told him, should be a busy residential street. Doe had bought a burner, an off-the-shelf pay-as-you-go cell phone. It was a cheap thing specifically for the trip. A sealed pay-as-you-go phone is as close to anonymous as you can get and if you buy them in the right way then Doe knew of no way they could be traced back to the user. Their usage could still be traced however, and it could offer an investigator plenty of information. They didn't only record when a call was made and who it was made to. By triangulating the cell towers, it could tell you where the call was made from. If the caller was moving when they made the call, it could tell you in which direction they were moving and how fast.

Doe didn't want to leave any breadcrumbs, so he wasn't planning to use the burner at all. It was there for emergencies and as a prop. These days people seem odd if they don't have a cell phone and a dozen credit cards. Doe didn't want to look odd, so he had the burner and a couple of usable credit cards and a bulging wallet full of real-looking but non-active cards. More practically, he had a few hundred dollars in cash and he had memorized the location of every public phone booth in the town.

He guessed the kid on reception would have some kind of deal with the pizza place that he had recommended. Maybe it was a full kick-back. If it was, it was more likely they were giving him food, not cash. Doe figured the kid might have something in place that meant that, any time they delivered to the motel, they dropped him a free pie. Or maybe it was more innocent. Maybe he just knew the owner or the delivery guy. Maybe, whenever he dropped off there, he would stop off and chew the fat for a while. It would help to pass a dull evening shift. The motel wasn't busy and the kid hadn't looked like the kind of guy that took much initiative. Either way, it could screw up Doe's plan. He had an unusual request for the delivery guy and he didn't need him sharing it with the motel clerk, so he had already picked out the newest pizza joint in town and he called them from the pay phone. He asked them to deliver to the motel but leave his order at his room door. He said he was having a couple of beers and watching the game at a bar and he would pick up the pizza when he got back. He paid over the phone with one of the credit cards.

He hoped the clerk would shrug his shoulders when he saw a guy in a different uniform delivering. He would assume that Doe had forgotten his recommendation and looked someone up on the internet or gone old-school and used the directory. He also figured that the guys from the newest place in town probably hadn't made the social or commercial connections yet. They wouldn't feel the need to drop into the motel reception and tell the clerk about the pizza boxes resting on the doorstep. It was a low-risk strategy anyway. If the clerk found out he would shrug his shoulders. He would assume he had just missed Doe leaving again and revise his testimony. Doe would go from being the guy who never left the room, to the guy that was out all the time. It wouldn't cripple Doe's plans if it failed and if it worked the clerk would mentally file Doe as having been in his room all evening eating pizza. It was worth the risk.

*

Doe walked to the third and final diner in town. It was across the road from one of the quieter bars. He sat down in a booth and ordered dinner and then headed for the rest room. The rest rooms were in a corridor. At the end of the corridor was the building's rear exit. Doe walked straight out of the back door, round through the side alley and over the street to the bar. He sat on a stool at the bar and ordered a draught beer. A couple of minutes later his cell rang. He looked apologetically at the bartender and answered the call. As he stepped out front of the bar he reset the alarm on his phone. He crossed the street and a few minutes later, in the diner, he pulled the same trick with the phone.

An hour later he was pretty sure that both his waitress and the bartender would remember him and swear that he had been in their establishment all night. They would probably describe him as a bit of a jerk, but they would both remember him. They would probably describe him pretty accurately, but the investigator would need to be very alert to make any connection and very paranoid to give the connection any credence. If the questions were asked as a matter of routine, then the similarity between the two patrons would just get smothered in the rest of the data. It would add to the noise that would cover the reality of his stay. Just to be sure he flirted with the waitress in the diner and the barman in the bar.

He left exactly the average tip for that part of the country in each place, walked a different route back to the motel, and hopped the back wall yet again. He picked up the pizza boxes from outside his room and took a bite from each pie. He didn't expect to be asked whether he had enjoyed the takeaway but just in case he was, he wanted to be able to give an accurate answer. He took one pizza and tipped it into the other box. He skipped the wall again and walked two blocks before dumping both pizzas in an alleyway. He felt sure that long before morning the local scavengers, human or animal, would remove all evidence that they had ever been there. He took the empty box back to the motel, opened his door and squashed both empty boxes into the trash can before showering and going to sleep.

TWO

They picked him up mid-morning on the second day, Saturday. He was back at the diner he had visited when he first rolled into town. He was hoping that his return visit would either establish some kind of commuter invisibility or lead to some confusion about when exactly he had been there. Either he would blur into a sea of semi-regular faces or there would be some disagreement about which days he had been there. A single event is easy to remember, two or three can start to run in to each other or contradict.

He chose a different booth from his first meal. That meant a different waitress. He ordered an identical breakfast hoping that a few weeks later the waitresses would start to contradict each other; "no, that was the Saturday..." "yes, that's the guy, that's what he ate, but it was Friday." "He sat over here...", "no, he sat over there..."

It was a different booth, but it had a virtually identical view. Doe had selected it carefully to make sure that it would. The building was at right angles to the street. Short frontage and a long parking lot. Big windows that ran the whole way down the long side. He could see the parking lot through the windows and some of the street through the plate glass customer entrance. On the other side of the building he could see the short corridor which led to the restrooms and then on, past the storeroom door, to the rear entrance. It was mostly habit that had made him pick his seat so carefully, but Doe much preferred habits over rules. Rules could be broken but good habits would last a lifetime and the right habits could extend that lifetime by a good long way.

He saw the two cruisers crawl past the street entrance. He saw a blur of faces turned toward the diner door. A few seconds later he saw them enter the parking lot and he knew right there that something was going down. One cop car entering a diner parking lot was almost comically unremarkable, two of them at the same time might mean a meet up. Maybe a shift handover. The worry wasn't the number of cars. It was the number of cops. There were three cops in each car. Whatever was going down, it was serious. Cops hate riding in the back of their own cars, that's where the perps sit and, as well as the fact that it messed with their idea of natural hierarchy, there was a more practical issue. People often, either inadvertently or through malice, made the backs of patrol cars unpleasant places to be. The cops didn't own the vehicles. They would hose the interiors out to a degree that would satisfy their sergeants but not to a point whereby they would choose to ride back there unless they absolutely had to.

However unlikely it was that a cop would chose to ride in back of a cruiser, it was even more rare for them to be deployed in a way that would require it. Cops work in pairs. It's a tried and tested formula and one that their bosses are loath to mess with. They work in even numbers and cars fit two people comfortably in the front. If you need four cops you send two cars. If you need six, you send three. It's very simple math and it rarely fails. When Doe saw that there were six cops in two cars he knew two things. First, that they felt that there was a reasonable chance that the suspect they were there to apprehend would prove dangerous, and second, that they didn't want to let him know that they were coming. Two cop cars entering a diner parking lot wasn't going to raise any eyebrows. Three might.

He could tell that they were worried about their suspect because six people meant three teams. Three teams meant that, as well as the arrest team, they wanted to have two guys at the front door and someone out back. That meant that they thought it was possible that the suspect might be able to get past their best guys and head for a door. Anyone who they thought might be willing and able to get past a trained, armed and wary arrest team deserved to be considered dangerous. Really dangerous.

As Doe watched the two cars split up in the diner's parking lot the only question he had was whether they were there for him or for someone else. One of the cruisers slowed and the cop in the back seat got out and then it accelerated in a stupid, noisy hurry that caused even a few of the late-morning locals to look up from their meals. Doe watched it disappear around the corner of the building, heading around to the back.

*

Doe figured the odds were about fifty-fifty, or more accurately he guessed that he had so little information that he couldn't make an objective decision. The fact that they feared the person they were there to arrest suggested to him that they were looking for someone from out of town, but he couldn't be sure. He figured the police department in a small town would know most of the major players on their patch. They would know who was dangerous and who wasn't. He thought that they would know everything about the most dangerous guys, right down to what kind of whiskey they bought and whether or not they were running low.

He guessed that an experienced chief of police would have strategies for arresting all the crazies on his watch and he couldn't imagine any of those plans involving cornering the guy in a public diner. Not if he had been the chief of police. Not if he had been planning the arrest of a guy that he knew all about. Not if he suspected that guy of having both the hardware and intent to go through six cops in order to get away from people who knew who he was and where he lived. If Doe was that cop then he figured he would take the guy out in public, but that he would do it somewhere where there was lots of space and not many actual people.

He guessed he would do it as a traffic stop. They could have done it with the two cars they had come to the diner in. Wait somewhere

where the guy's pickup had to slow down and then drive one car out in front of him and the other one up behind. If you had the other two cops as well they could step out with weapons drawn and catch the guy with at least one hand on the wheel and any potential weapons in plain sight.

The only reason Doe could see for them making the arrest at the diner was if they didn't know where the guy was going to be, but they knew where he was right then. If they had a tip-off or a sighting but they didn't know where their guy was going to go after the diner and they didn't want to run the risk of losing him - in that case they would be willing to make the arrest around civilians and take the risk of someone getting hurt. It would be a matter of balancing the risks. The risk of the arrest going wrong against the risk of losing their suspect.

Doe looked around the diner. There wasn't another person in the place that looked as though they hadn't sat in the same seat every Saturday for the last twenty years. There was a young couple who couldn't have been coming down for that long, but they were chatting with the younger waitress about some mutual friends. Doe doubted that they were new in town. There were a few other couples, mostly the wrong side of fifty, but they all had weekend clothes on, not vacation clothes. Not one of them looked like they had driven more than a few miles to be there. There was no rumpled clothing; no tired eyes from getting up early and driving for miles in the early morning darkness.

There was another single man, but he looked about eighty and was actually wearing denim coveralls. He looked like he could have posed for the brochure of whatever work-clothing outfitters his denims and checks had come from. Looking around the room Doe knew that he was the only obvious stranger in the place.

*

The odds nudged upward. Maybe three or four to one now. What he still didn't have was local knowledge. He couldn't tell whether the local police department had recently lost their chief. Maybe there was a new guy in the big seat now. One who didn't know the local guys.

One who hadn't worked out all the scenarios over beers on the back porch. Or maybe there was a new bad guy in town. One who would look local to Doe but would be unknown to the chief. A cousin maybe, or a long-lost uncle of a local rowdy. Someone who would look at home but would mess with the well-established plans of the experienced cops.

Doe just couldn't tell and, if he couldn't tell, then he had no reason to react. Plus, he had no real skin in the game. If they were there for him then it should be a pretty minor problem. He hadn't done anything wrong and it didn't seem likely that anyone meeting his description had caused an outrage in the small town in the last few hours. He had listened to the local FM station as he took his shower and the biggest news story had been about a storm rolling up the coast. The waitress had taken his order with barely a glance and the rest of the diners still didn't seem at all interested in him. If something major had happened, then it would have been on the news. If it hadn't made the news yet, then you could bet your bottom dollar the waitresses at the local diner would know about it. If the cops were there for him, it would be a minor problem and his cobbled-together ID would hold up.

The six-man response still worried him though. That didn't look like a minor issue, but maybe the chief was real paranoid, or maybe they were taking the opportunity to do a little training. Maybe he had told them to treat the routine apprehension as if it was a really serious arrest. Maybe he wanted to give his guys a run out. Give them some experience in almost, but not quite, real circumstances.

It didn't ring true but, even if it was more serious, Doe still didn't have much to lose. Things might get tough for a couple of hours. When they saw through the fake identity they would start to implement all sorts or weird procedures. At best he would spend the whole time alone and locked up. If they got really scared they might leave him shackled. He would certainly lose the bet with his buddy and the recruits, but it wouldn't be awful. Nothing he hadn't experienced before. If the shit hit the proverbial he had numbers he could call. His real ID, or a suitably edited version of it, could be proven in a variety of ways and would lead to his immediate release and a massively disproportionate apology. It would be annoying, possibly briefly painful, but definitely not a reason to flee from officially-deployed, and more importantly armed, local law enforcement.

So, Doe drained his coffee and finished his meal. There was a newspaper lying unattended on the next table. He picked it up and slipped it into his back pocket, just in case. He studiously ignored his pre-planned contingency for exiting the building in a hurry. Possible plans for moving through the arrest team and out of the diner were already running through his head but, unless someone started shooting, Doe was going to wait and see what happened. If they took him in and his ID broke down, he hoped that they wouldn't leave him shackled. It hurt his shoulders and the newspaper in his back pocket wouldn't be much use for killing the time if his hands were cuffed behind his back.

Unless someone started shooting, the most likely scenario was that he would be back out on the street in a couple of hours. It would provide an interesting sidebar to his experiment. If the recruits dug deeper than the cops and decided that he was their man, then he hoped that he would be magnanimous enough to accept that his experiment had failed. If they didn't then he would know that it had not only been tested, it had been tried in battle and found to stand. The answer would be, 'yes, he most certainly could'.

Unless someone started shooting.

*

Doe counted the seconds that it would take for the arrest team to circle the building and he took a last look around the diner. If they weren't there for him then whoever they were there for might be just as good as Doe. In a place like Seal Harbor it seemed extremely unlikely and, having checked out the rest of the clientele, it seemed nearly impossible, but Doe was not arrogant enough to believe that it was actually impossible. One or more of the other diners might also have seen the two cruisers come into the parking lot. They might know exactly what it meant. They might be counting down the same seconds that Doe was. They might be clicking off the safeties on well-maintained and powerful hand guns.

Doe waited until he was sure that the cops were just behind the connecting door and then he looked around the room one more time. He looked for slight increases in alertness. He looked for people whose body posture had shifted a little to put them squarer to the door. He looked for jackets that were a little more open, shirts that were rucked-up at the back. He saw nothing, so he turned back to look at the door.

He could see the street, the parking lot and the rear entrance. The view of the street and the parking lot was perfect. His view of the corridor and the back entrance was through a refection in a mirror over the cash desk. On his first visit, he had chosen a seat with a better view of the room and where the rear exit was pretty much directly behind him. That had given him a decent view of the back door in the reflection in the windows that lined the side of the building.

He liked the first position, but he couldn't predict the weather. Changes in the intensity of the sunlight could mess with his view of the door. He would have to wait on occasion while his eyesight adjusted to the changing light levels. It was possible that at a crucial moment his perception would be compromised. The second position was better. The degradation of the view of the room was minor and the mirror would behave pretty much consistently throughout the day. Ordinarily, Doe would have used the same booth on both days, but he was trying to leave false trails to cover his tracks. He had liked the first position well enough to think it was worth the risk.

He had decided that the second day would be riskier than the first. He wasn't expecting trouble, but he had decided that if it was going to happen, it was more likely to happen on day two rather than within hours of him hitting town. He wasn't planning to have breakfast at the same place on the Sunday, so he had only needed two different seats. He had used his least favorite position when he felt safest and the best position a day later when he figured he was technically more exposed.

*

He watched the mirror image of the first cop enter through the rear door. The guy came in fast and quiet and did a quick sweep of the room. To the cop's eyes Doe was facing away from him at an oblique angle. He didn't spot Doe's eyes watching him in the mirror. He looked right at Doe's booth and then did a full sweep of the rest of the room. He then stood to one side and let the second cop walk in. Doe watched the second guy step into the room and move to the opposite side of the door. Doe didn't wait to see the third guy. He knew what was happening. The first and second guys were holding handguns and they both moved easily and confidently. They both looked like they knew what they were doing. That meant the third guy would be very good indeed.

It was always tricky deciding in which order to deploy a team like the one that was coming in through the rear door of the diner. In management speak, all your staff were well trained and skilled, but in practice some officers were more experienced, more talented or had temperaments that better suited extremely dangerous situations.

The first guy had to be good. Maybe he had to be the best. He was going to be out front and he was going to be talking to the suspect. If there was going to be trouble he was the one who was most likely to be able to avoid it, but he was also going to be the one who got hit hardest by any repercussions. You wanted your best guy out there. The second guy had to be very good too. If the first guy was generating any rapport the second guy had to be rock steady.

The third guy was the clincher. The third guy wouldn't be carrying a handgun. He would have a big shot gun. His job was to make it impossible to escape. If the suspect took out the first two cops, then the third guy would just cut him in half. The third guy had to be steady enough and imposing enough that the suspect knew it was hopeless. He also had to be skilled enough and reliable enough that the two guys in front of him could concentrate on their jobs. They needed to be able to do their jobs without worrying that the guy behind them was going to trip or panic and blow them both to hell with a pump-action, riot shotgun.

In Doe's experience, commanders played around with the first and third guy positions, but never with the second guy. The second guy was the least skilled, least experienced guy. If he looked good then the team was good. Doe didn't need to see the third guy. The second guy was good enough to tell him everything he needed to know.

Doe took yet another look around the diner. The way that the first guy had looked directly at Doe's booth before moving his eyes around the rest of the room had made it look likely that they were there for him, but he still wasn't certain. If they weren't there for him then whoever they were there for might be trigger happy. They might also be dumb or complacent. They might not have noticed that the cops were coming. They might be sitting there with loaded Glocks and when the cops got close enough to catch their attention they might react by blasting away at anything that moved. Doe couldn't allow that. He couldn't put the civilians or the cops at risk. Not just for an experiment. If it looked like there was going to be shooting he would have to step up and stop it before people got hurt. Once he got involved his cover would be blown. He would have to tell the cops who he was and he would have to tell his buddy to call off the trainees. He would lose a few afternoons worth of work and he might never get the time to repeat the experiment, but hopefully no one would die.

There was also the chance that there might be an entirely-unconnected individual in the room. Someone the cops had no interest in but who had a serious interest in the cops, or a serious mental or political problem. Doe knew that there were places in the world where he wouldn't have to worry about it. Places where the response of a room full of innocent civilians to a legal police arrest team would never include someone, who had nothing whatsoever to do with it, standing up and unloading an illegal fully-automatic weapon. Such places were commonplace but rural America was not one of them. Doe checked the room again.

There was still nothing that looked out of place.

*

Now Doe looked back at the cops again. The third guy was in the room, holding his shotgun rock steady behind his two colleagues. The three of them were making a direct line to Doe's booth. Doe had one last thing to check. Six dirty local cops in an out of the way place was statistically very unlikely, but Doe had read popular fiction just like everyone else and he figured it was worth considering.

In all his years in police enforcement he had never heard of a single plausible example of an organized police hit squad. There had been plenty of dirty cops who had been willing to off the right guy in an arrest for the right money. Some who would do it just for kicks or because they thought someone deserved it. He knew of racist, sexist and just plain stupid cops who had killed people on the spur of the moment because they got angry or scared or felt like gods in the crucial moment. What he had never heard of was six cops from the same small department all acting in concert to kill a suspect during a routine arrest. He just didn't think it could happen.

He didn't think it could happen, but he wasn't sure that it couldn't. So, he checked. First, he checked for dishevelment in the officers, for ruffled hair, torn clothes, evidence that they would later rely on to assert that he resisted arrest. He looked for other weapons or objects they were carrying which they could jettison and later reclaim. Items they brought with them but that they would claim belonged to him. Things they would use as evidence that he had posed a danger. He saw nothing.

He watched them get closer in the mirror and when they got to a point three booths away from him, he stood up, turned around and placed his palms, face down on the table in front of him.

*

He studied them more closely now. Not looking for danger but collecting information. He was going to jail and at the very least he was going to be questioned. He was going to need all information he could get. He wasn't going to have many advantages and his captors were going to have plenty. Anything he could do at this stage to even that up was going to help immensely.

The first thing he did was memorize all their names. Their names were embroidered in gold thread on little cloth panels stitched onto their uniforms. Just above the right shirt pocket. The lead guy was called Eugene, the second guy was Mathers and the guy with the shotgun was Mayfield. Next, Doe looked at the state of their equipment. It was neatly stowed and looked well maintained. Mayfield and Mathers were wearing level two holsters. Mayfield's was full and locked closed, Mathers was empty, his pistol was in his hand. Eugene's holster looked like a level three holster. That would mean it was personally owned. He would have needed to get it passed by the departmental armorer before he could use if for official business. Their belts were all uniform nylon. Their vests looked clean and were correctly worn. They carried their weapons, handcuffs and pepper spray and nothing else. It told Doe that they were a well-run department. They did things well and by the book. Where they had access to additional experience or improved equipment, like Eugene's holster, they allowed it.

They walked confidently, their weapons held ready but safe. They had stopped when he stood up, a little surprised. There was some miscommunication, some lack of control, lack of training. The gaps between them shrank. The guns of the guys behind Eugene got hidden for a second. If he had been desperate he would have had a vital second to make his move. He wasn't desperate.

They were all roughly the same age, mid-to-late twenties but to Doe's practiced eyes they fell into two groups. Mathers and Mayfield had fresh buzz cuts, neat but not as neat as Eugene's. His hair was a fraction longer but also smarter. It looked like it had been cut longer rather than having grown out, cut longer but with more care. Their uniforms and equipment were the same. Mathers' and Mayfield's equipment were proficiently carried and looked well maintained but Eugene's had the little tweaks and additions that come from having been used, not just carried. Used regularly and for a long time. He moved differently too. Mathers and Mayfield were a little tense. They looked excited, like young soldiers on a live-fire exercise. Eugene was smooth, careful. Full of purpose.

*

Doe looked around the room again and shuffled his feet further back, placing more of his weight over his hands. It was a posture of submission well understood in police circles. It said to the cops approaching him 'I am now unable to straighten up quickly or to use my arms'. It usually meant that you were making yourself harmless. The cops acted as if nothing had happened but the eyes of everyone else in the room were now drawn to Doe and from him to the three cops creeping their way down the aisle.

Doe's position was anything but submissive. He was still playing the odds. By standing and leaning his weight on the table he appeared to be complying, but he also kept a good view of the room in his peripheral vision, and he could watch the cops directly through the last few feet of their approach. The booth table was a four-seater with two scuffed chrome legs bolted to a plastic-topped, chipboard table. Doe had spent the whole time he had been waiting for the cops to circle the building and reach his booth loosening the bolts on the table leg with his pocket knife. By the time he stood up they were loose enough for the table top to pivot a little when he leaned on it. By moving his feet backwards, he had increased the length of that pivot and that stressed the bolts further.

He was as sure as he could be that if he pushed down on his side of the table top, the bolts would rip out of the old, soft wood and the opposite side of the table would shoot upwards and catapult his cutlery and crockery into the air. Doe inched his fingers toward the edge of the table and ran through his plan in his mind. Holding the edge of the table he would step forward, between the two, now unattached, chrome legs and push the table top forwards at the cops. The hand guns would go off but even at that distance, with their view blocked by the table top, Doe figured they would be extremely lucky to hit him. He could get behind them and if he got behind them he could put them down. Guns only fire in one direction, if they are pointing away from you then they are no threat to you. If they are no threat to you then they are an advantage, an encumbrance to your enemy.

Even if he got past the two hand guns there would still be Mayfield standing safely, further back with the shotgun. He would be reluctant to fire in such an enclosed space with civilians all around, but Doe knew that he would still fire, despite the reluctance. They were a good team and the first rule of carrying a weapon professionally is, don't carry it unless you're willing to use it. The very fact that Mayfield had carried the shotgun through the door told Doe that he would fire.

Doe figured Mayfield would expect him to go upward. To step up onto the bench seats and then step over the booths and head for the back door. It had to be the back door. There was no percentage in heading for the front doors. If he stepped out into the isle and headed for the front he would be covered for the first few steps by the table top but once that fell to the floor he would be running with his back to three armed cops. He would still have a long way to go and he would have two more cops ahead of him watching the whole thing through the glass front doors. Waiting for him with drawn handguns.

His only option would be the back door. Past the first two cops in the initial move and getting closer to the third just by moving. If he got to the shotgun he could put it out of action and then he would be free to get to the rear exit. Unlike his colleagues at the front door who were watching the whole thing, the guy at the back wouldn't be sure what was going on. He would hear shooting and then he would hear silence and then, some indeterminable number of seconds later, Doe would explode through the door at him. If he could reach the door, Doe knew from experience that he could make it out of the diner and melt away into town. After that, it wouldn't be easy, but he would be able to find his way home.

The first two guns could be done. The fourth would be simple. It was the shotgun that would be the problem. Doe figured that if Mayfield was going to guess that he would go high, over the back of the booths then he would have to go low. High was the natural option and subliminally, with the table top and the cutlery and the crockery all flying up into the air Mayfield's attention would follow them. It was like a magician leading your eye with one hand and then moving the other way. Doe would dive across the aisle and under the opposite table. If he was quick, and if the wood on that table was as weak as the wood on his table then he thought he might be able to stand up, splintering the table top. He could jump Mayfield from below and to the left while his shotgun had moved fractionally right and up.

It would be difficult, but it was possible. But most of all Doe hoped that it would be unnecessary. So, he watched the room and he watched the cops and hoped that there would be nothing that would spook him. There wasn't. When they got close enough to feel safe they yelled at him to turn around and then they cuffed him and took him outside to the cruiser.

THREE

Eugene and Mayfield put him in the back of the second cruiser and drove him back to the police department. They drove fast with the lights and siren flashing and blaring. They left no one in the back of the car with him, just two up front and everyone else crammed into the other cruiser. No one said anything. The roads were empty and the little town was quiet, so the sirens and lights didn't make much sense to Doe. He was hunting for extra information but getting nothing. These guys were pretty good, but he already knew that. They didn't make any mistakes on the journey. It was a short trip, but he had resorted to old counting games to keep himself alert by the time they arrived at the Police Department.

The Department building covered an entire block. Doe figured that land was still cheap around there and the lack of neighbors certainly made the building more secure. The Department building was huge for the size of the town. It had worried Doe at the planning stage.

The USA had an average deployment of around three hundred law enforcement officers per ten thousand head of population. By that math Seal Harbor should have had two cops. Obviously, no town would have a department that constituted just two cops. There might be tiny places with just a cop or two, but they would theoretically work out of an office someplace else. The smallest possible workable department would probably comprise five people. It would need to cover shifts and vacations and a hierarchy. They needed people to cover one hundred and sixty-eight hours in each and every week and they would need to do it with roughly forty-hour contracts. That alone would require four people. Then they needed to cover vacations and provide some overlap for briefings and allow for some occasions where two officers were required at the same time. Then you needed a boss and a clerk and some time for training. Five people would be bare bones.

What happened was places got swept together. Some departments covered hundreds of miles and dozens of isolated communities. Call the cops to tell them you had an intruder on the premises, and in plenty of rural locations and you would be told that someone would be with you in a couple of hours. Doe could understand why people in those communities might want to keep a handgun for personal protection. Although, on the other hand, those places were so remote that the only people likely to be invading your home were your neighbors. Maybe you should be able to sort it all out over a beer on the porch or a fight in the yard.

Seal Harbor housed the Police Department for the whole of Briel Island and the specialist support for the local island chain. It had border patrol and homeland security funding. Wealthy second-homers from Seattle lobbied hard for state funding and the town had a Department that would be the envy of a town ten times its size. Doe looked hard, but he couldn't find a sinister reason for the seemingly bloated deployment.

As they approached the Department building he peered out through the windshield. He saw blank walls along the northern end of the building. Hard up against the sidewalk. Then they got alongside the building itself. He turned his head and watched through the side window. He had seen photos on the internet, but he wanted to see it for real. He needed to make sure nothing had changed. There was lots of glass and windows along the front of the building, all set back from the road behind a long, thin parking lot. They drove the length of the building and then pulled in through a chain link gate at the south. They followed the side wall of the building for the entire width of the block and then turned right and drove almost all the way back down the block before stopping the vehicles. There was a blank two-story wall in front of them. No windows and just a single door. Doe had craned his neck and peered up at the walls as they had passed. The ground floor was a uniform concrete, uninterrupted by doors or windows. On the second story there were windows. There was no third floor.

Eugene and Mayfield got out of the front of the cruiser. The second cruiser pulled in behind. Two of the occupants of the second car got out and pulled Doe off his seat and out of the car. Eugene and Mayfield were looking around the yard. Not at the building or the fence, but up at the skyline and out at the yards beyond. Doe matched them and did a quick look around the yard. He hoped he had covered it with a slack-jawed, "this can't be happening to me" expression. He noted the thick, fortified, external walls of the Police Department building, the empty two-story wall in front of him and the twelve-foot chain-link fence topped with razor wire that extended all the way around the yard. The yard was narrow, and a lot of Doe's view was obstructed by the two police cruisers parked nose to tail. He needed a better look at the layout, he needed a different perspective.

Doe somehow slipped out of the supporting officer's grip and fell heavily, just managing to twist himself to the side so that he fell on his shoulder rather than on his face. The two cops dragged him back to his feet and pulled him through the armored door into the main body of the Department building, but not before he had a good look around the rest of the yard.

*

One of the cops was a good match for Doe's height and he counted the guy's steps as they passed through a short corridor into the main building. Doe could accurately pace his own walk to within a few meters in every hundred but not when he was being dragged along with his hands handcuffed behind his back after a tough fall. He figured the cop's pace looked similar enough to work in an emergency.

They passed through a second, thick steel door and into the main building. For some reason Doe had never been able to comprehend, municipal architects were allowed to produce large, uncluttered working spaces for law enforcement operations. If Doe had his way every Department building in the country would be part labyrinth. The cops would find their way around and no one else would. Dominance through terrain.

Here, the entire uniformed services part of the building was essentially one big square room. Between the yard and the main building there was the short corridor that ended in the huge steel door and inside there was a large open plan space with the double glass doors and big plate-glass windows looking out over the narrow parking lot. Along the wall to Doe's right, fifty yards away at the other side of the room, a staircase led up to the second story. Offices lined the other two walls and rows and rows of desks filled the middle of the room. The offices even had helpful nameplates screwed to each door and Doe noted each one as he was shoved past.

The cells were at the back corner of the building. From there, even if you made it out of the cell, you would still have to cross the entire squad room before you made it to the front doors and freedom. Doe passed an empty office and the rec room, both with their doors wide open, then there were the bathrooms and three or four closed offices. There was no door into the cells area. Just a big, brightly lit hole where any civilized room would have a door.

There were three cells. Doe's captors shoved him towards the first of them. The third was already occupied. Doe noted the discipline and practice. The first prisoner gets put furthest from the door. The second gets put furthest from him. The cell door clanged shut behind him and his entourage left. Doe looked over towards his fellow prisoner. Their eyes locked. If there had been a film director in the room, cartoon sparks would have flown briefly before they both feigned disinterest and Doe settled back to read his paper.

*

Doe expected to be stuck there for a while. It was a well-run department, but something was going on. There was a nervous energy to the place. He didn't know if there were other suspects to be rounded up. He didn't even know what he had been picked up for. All he was sure of was that, whatever it was that they had arrested him for, they thought it was serious. He lay on the thin mattress on the bunk and read the paper.

While he read he kept a very close eye on the guy in the other cell. The guy was tall. He looked fit in the way that the boss of a sports franchise is fit. Fit because he wants to be fit, because it's easy to be fit and because he needs to prove to other people that he isn't a fool. Not fit because that was the way his life made him. He was also dressed the way the head of a sports franchise might dress - if he was going under cover as a sailor.

It was an odd outfit. Whoever had dressed him hadn't screwed up in any major way. They hadn't picked a designer knock-off of a working man's garment and tried to distress it to make it look authentic, and they hadn't bought the stuff straight off the back of an entirely different guy. The elbows and shoulders sagged in the right places. It could have been the guy in the cell that had worn the blue cord Jersey for five or ten years.

It was more the way the clothing fitted together. The t-shirt was more faded than the jersey. The jeans were old but wrinkle-free and slim-fit. Doe guessed the t-shirt could be an old favorite and the jersey newer but still first choice, but if that was true then the jeans were wrong. The jersey and shirt may have come out of a kit bag as the guy got off a fishing boat, but the jeans hadn't. No one wore slim-fit at sea and nothing comes off a working boat unwrinkled. If he had gone home after he left the boat then he would have changed the shirt and if he hadn't, then he wouldn't have had access to the jeans.

To Doe, it set all kinds of alarm bells ringing and coupled with the unexpected, proficient and completely overblown arrest it threw his natural paranoia into overdrive. He was still on the hunt for information, so he read his paper and he fidgeted and struggled to get comfortable on the thin, plastic-coated foam mattress. Doe had only a passing interest in the local news and had long ago learned to make himself comfortable in far less hospitable environments for far longer periods of time, but by staring through the paper, defocusing his eyes and then shifting his position as if in discomfort, he was able to get a good view of his cellmate every two or three minutes.

By the time the cops came back in to see him thirty minutes later, his paranoia had turned into something that was as close to dread as he had ever felt.

*

It wasn't so much the fact that the guy in the other cell had never stopped watching him that filled Doe with such unease. It was more the fact that he had never once tried to hide it. Every time that Doe's apparently disinterested, unfocused gaze had passed over his cellmate's face the other guy was staring straight at him. There was no fear, no disguise and, if anything, a certain degree of recognition. This was not the look of a man who was uncertain of his future and every man in a jail cell, even Doe to a degree, was uncertain of his future.

It comes with the territory, or rather the lack of it. The thing that anyone does when they lock you up is they deprive you of control. The degree to which they deprive you of that control depends primarily upon your resources, then upon their mood and finally upon your innocence. Rich people get treated better than bums, angry cops would treat you more harshly than content ones and on average, in general terms, innocent people have a better time of it than those who are obviously guilty.

Doe wasn't rich, but he had huge resources at his disposal. He was reasonably sure of his captor's motives and he was completely innocent. Altogether, that meant that he felt relatively safe, but the guy in the other cell was showing a degree of confidence that bordered on insanity.

As a stranger, he couldn't be any surer of his captors than Doe was, and Doe doubted that he was stupid enough to think that greater innocence would protect him. So, the unnatural confidence had to come from a belief in a truly supreme resource. Here was a man, unconvincingly dressed as a commercial fisherman, sitting in a police cell, calmly awaiting his future while the local cops rounded up strangers with a caution bordering on the paranoid. Meanwhile Doe was far from his own sources of support and trapped in an unprepared community. All in all, it worried Doe to a degree he wasn't sure he had ever felt before.

*

They took the first guy out for interview first. That slowed Doe down a little. He couldn't risk doing what he was planning to do until the guy was safely locked back up in his cell again. In the absence of any other sensible options, he sat and thought and tried to read the newspaper until the fake fisherman was led, quiet but unbowed back into his cell.

"I need to make my phone call sergeant."

The cop walked straight past Doe, playing deaf, then he turned back at the hole leading to the squad room.

He paused for a second then said,

"I'll see what I can do."

It was the second cop from the arrest team. Mathers. He was sullen and unfriendly. Resentful even. Doe could understand him being unfriendly. They were on opposite sides of the bars and Doe wasn't some local tear-away or stupid motorist. Whatever they had brought him in for it was serious. Unfriendly was exactly how Doe expected him to behave. Sullen might not be out of the bounds of understanding either. The cop wasn't a young man, he had shown himself competent and yet he had been given the second position during Doe's arrest and now he was on prisoner escort duty. Maybe he was just pissed at his superiors for not giving him a more active role. It didn't feel like it though. Doe's experience told him that the prisoner interview had gone badly, and his instinct seemed to be borne out when Eugene stormed into the cell block a few minutes later.

"You're just going to have to wait!" Where his colleague had been sullen and unfriendly, Eugene was angry and, at least in Doe's opinion, scared. "You'll have a chance to make your call after you're interviewed."

Doe took the opportunity gratefully, but he had to shift his projected persona a little to accommodate it. He had been planning to present himself as respectable and innocent, but in order to lever the door that the cop had opened he would have to come closer to disreputable but uninvolved.

"I understand that, sir. That's why I want to make my call." He squirmed a little in his seat as if he was about to do something unpleasant, "I'm not unfamiliar with this process and I never say anything to you guys without word from my counsel, but I ain't done nothing here and I want out. So, if you can put me through to my lawyer and he says it's OK, then I'll talk to you at that interview."

He sat back on the thin bench, arms crossed, belligerent now and seemingly, much more comfortable.

"If not, I'm stuck here anyway. You can ask anything you want for the hours and days that it's gonna take for my representation to get here. I won't say a fucking word."

Doe had seen people glower before and this cop glowered. He left without saying a word and Doe returned to his newspaper and his intermittent but constant observation of his cellmate. The prisoner was still unashamed in his staring at Doe, but now his previously deadpan face had a small smile and a distinct quizzical expression. He seemed to be asking "Well now, who are you and what are you up to."

*

Eugene was back inside of five minutes.

"You can have your call but it's gonna be a while before we have anyone free to supervise. You're gonna have to wait."

Doe shrugged like he didn't care but it was exactly what he had expected. They were going to trace his call and they needed a little time to set it up. It was the smart move. They couldn't record the conversation or use it in evidence, but if they really weren't sure whether he was involved or not then the location and identity of the guy he called might tell them a lot.

Doe settled back again. His cellmate's quizzical expression had taken on a distinctly amused air.

Doe wasn't planning on coming back to his cell once he was taken out to make his phone call. He figured he had nothing to lose by talking to his cellmate.

"You seem pretty relaxed. I guess that must mean you're innocent, right?" Accompanied by a wry smile it was a pretty standard, comradely prison opening. Like moving a pawn to the center of the board in chess. The fisherman just smiled, a pawn reply.

"What're you in for? Jaywalking?" Still nothing controversial but also nothing the guy could reasonably ignore. Pawn to D-three. At the very least he would need to provide a 'Yes' or a 'No'.

"Vagrancy." The smile was still there. He looked like a CEO in front of a congressional committee. One who knew he had done it, but also knew that they couldn't prove anything.

"You could be here a while then."

The fisherman couldn't resist a little shake of his head at that.

"Oh, friends nearby huh? Someone's going to spring you."

The guy's involuntary gesture stopped with a jerk and his eyes narrowed.

"Spring me?"

"You know. Get you a lawyer. Stand bail."

His smile came back, sly and full of teeth. Like a cartoon cat.

"No, nothing like that." He seemed to be relaxed again, but he changed the subject. "What about you, pal? What did they pull you up for?"

Doe noted the odd phrasing, filed it away.

"Fucked if I know. They're scared about something."

The cartoon sparks flew again.

"It's a dangerous world."

They went back to their silence for a spell.

"Where's the holding tank around here anyway?" Doe feigned interest, "Will they move you all the way down to Seattle?"

The fisherman was gnomic again. Nothing more than a shrug. Then he sprang to life.

“What about you Mister ‘ain’t’. Will you be heading down to Seattle?”

Doe nodded to the ‘ain’t’ comment but stayed in character.

“I guess so. I was just eating breakfast and they bundle in mob-handed and bring me down here.” He moved slightly on the hard bunk to look more directly through the bars, “Something must have them scared.”

The fisherman smiled and laid back.

“It’s a small town. Anything could scare them.”

“No. Quite the opposite. These are self-sufficient people. Takes a lot to scare them.”

Lying down hadn’t been an affectation. The guy was starting to relax. Cracks were starting to appear.

“Self-sufficiency isn’t always a virtue and virtue is rarely a defense.”

It was all a bit cryptic for Doe, but it was progress. He tried to think back. The change had come when the guy had changed the subject. Up until then he had given nothing away. He hadn’t entered into the conversation. Once he had asked Doe the question he was involved. Doe thought back. He tried to remember what he had said to spark the change.

“So, might your friends know a good bondsman?”

The fisherman shook his head slowly, his eyes indicating that Doe had spoiled it again. That they were skimming over their public personae, fencing. Doe had made a gauche move. He had moved a bishop too near to a pawn. Doe filed the affectation away as a future means of attack and looked for another opening.

If you waste a move then you have to attack.

“There’s no alibi for vagrancy. Your friends can’t get you out that way.”

His eyes were narrowing again. The grin changing from cartoon cat to cartoon shark.

“What are they going to do? Roll up at the back door with some dynamite? Send you a cake with a file in it?”

He couldn't tell if he was getting anywhere. He felt like he was chasing the other guys King around the board. On the attack but getting nowhere. It was time to ramp it up.

"You don't look like a fisherman."

Nothing.

"Who bought you those jeans?"

The guy shifted a little. Trying to stay untroubled but becoming irritated.

"Only, they don't look like they'd be much good on a trawler. If it was me, I wouldn't want to rely on any people who had bought me them. They look like people who make mistakes to me."

The guy was bristling now. Angry but still not scared. He had tried to resist but he had the bully's tendency. If you're attacked, attack back.

"And how about you, Mister phone call? Feeling good about your chances? Going to call in the cavalry?"

It was an odd thing to say. Doe had to think about his next move. While he did so, Eugene came in to tell him his phone call was ready.

*

It had taken them a fraction under ten minutes to set up the trace. It was an interesting amount of time. Doe thought that it told him a lot about the state of their technology and the level of their outside support. Ten minutes was pretty quick for a rural department. Either they were even better equipped than he had been led to believe or else they were lying. Either they had access to some equipment they shouldn't have or they were lying.

Eugene brought Mayfield with him, not Mathers. Doe filed the information away in that growing folder of departmental loyalties and possible tensions. Whatever happened once Doe left the cell it was going to be embarrassing for the cops in front of him. Doe tried one more time to find a reason to go easy on them.

"Whatever you're looking for, it isn't me." He turned and looked at his cellmate as he said "isn't" instead of "ain't". Eugene's brow furrowed like he was trying to remember something important, but

Mayfield just took his handcuffs off his belt with that annoying swish that cops use when want to prove they are in charge.

"I can help. You should tell me what's going on."

Eugene shook his head like he was clearing it. Doe figured he had gone too far. The man had been thinking but Doe had overreached himself and now Eugene was back to being a cop. To be fair, Doe had heard similar shit from prisoners in the past. It had been a long shot, but Doe had to try.

Eugene nodded to Mayfield and left the cell block leaving the two of them alone with the man in the cell. Mayfield stepped over to the bars and motioned to Doe to put his arms through the gap in the cell door so that he could cuff him. Doe turned his back on the officer and backed towards the bars. His hands slipped through a gap in the bars and Mayfield cuffed him. Mayfield unlocked the cell door and marched Doe from the room. As they left the room Doe's cellmate gave him a little wave and a faux salute.

"Good luck."

FOUR

Mayfield walked him out of the cell block and into the main squad room. Doe had the floorplan of the building pretty well mapped out in his head from when they had brought him in. The cell block was at the extreme back and extreme left of the building as seen from the street. It was a good location for them, equidistant between the two entrances and therefore equidistant from the two exits. To get to it from the road you had to drive right around the building and in through the yard door and then walk back along the rear wall of the building. The only other in way was to walk through the front doors, the public entrance, past the desk sergeant and fight your way through a room full of cops. A whole room full of cops who could watch you arrive through the big, glass windows and doors that fronted the building. They could pick you up pretty much as soon as you got onto the block and then follow you right along the sidewalk, across the little parking lot and up to the door. If you were carrying anything bigger than a handgun they would notice and they would be ready for you before you even got off the street.

To get out you had to pick one of those doors and do the exact same thing but in reverse. Fight your way through the squad room and out through the doors, across the little parking lot and away or out through the back and all the way around the building.

The squad room itself was a large, square building with twenty-one desks, three rows of seven, filling most of the floor space. Doe paused for a moment at the entrance of the cell block, looking across the room to the civilian entrance and the empty street beyond. To his left there were the restrooms and locker rooms and then a coffee room. Doors stretching out in a row from the cell block to the yard door. Beyond the yard door were the Patrol offices, places for the higher-ranking uniformed cops and administration. They ran the entire width of the building. The guy in the far end office probably got a nice big window looking out onto Main Street.

The squad room was half empty. The same way it had been an hour earlier when they had brought him in. It was late morning, mid-shift, either the department was under-strength, or it was overstretched. There were a couple of civilian employees riding desks up by the main entrance and a couple of uniformed officers leaning against the wall to the coffee room on Doe's left. Six or seven of the desks were full and Doe had no way of telling how many people were upstairs or in the closed Patrol offices.

To Doe's right were the stairs to the second story. Up there would be the offices for the very high-ranking officers and the plainclothesmen. The detectives would be up there and the Sheriff, and probably some conference rooms, maybe someplace for the press to work when they were in the building. The positioning of the stairway made the same kind of sense as the positioning of the cells. Anyone who wanted to get up there would have to make it through a cop filled room first. If they had started in the corner nearest the street, then it would be pretty easy to walk in through the front doors with a couple of hand guns in your pockets and then charge up the stairs and take some hostages before anyone could stop you.

They were well-positioned unless, of course, you were already standing at the bottom of the stairs because you had just been brought out of the cell block. Mayfield shoved Doe in the back to get him moving and steered him to the left, heading for an interview room or one of the offices where they would have an ordinary-looking phone waiting for him. An ordinary-looking phone ready to trace and possibly even record his call.

The first two doors in front of Doe were firmly closed. The third door, the last of the locker rooms, was partially ajar. Doe sped up and got a pace or two ahead of Mayfield who lengthened his stride to catch up. The floor of the squad room was smooth. Low pile, commercial flooring tiles worn down by lots of foot traffic. The building had clearly been built at a time when it was expected that each desk would only require a small number of electrical outlets. Each desk had a couple of outlets recessed into the floor with the older equipment still plugged in - PC, monitor, printer - but modern life and modern policing had already caught up with a building that was probably not more than twenty years old. Now the desks were cluttered with technology that didn't stay where it was put. Technology that needed a plethora of cables and chargers and an equal number of outlets, Mobile phones and tablets and DUI test machines and battery-charging units were scattered across the desks. To accommodate these devices the officers had littered the otherwise smooth floor with extension leads and because health and safety demanded it they snaked them all through cable tidies and walk-on cable trenches.

Doe waited for Mayfield to catch him up and then stumbled on one of the cable tidies. As he fell he reached out with the hands Mayfield had cuffed behind his back and grabbed the officer's belt. He kicked backwards with his left foot to take Mayfield's legs out from under him and then used the momentum of his fall to throw the guy over his back and face first into the door jamb of the partially-open interview room door.

Doe fell heavily onto his right knee and rolled over onto the unconscious body of his escort. His hands were already gripping the guy's belt so it didn't take him long to feel along it and locate and detach his keys. Doe rolled himself to his feet and took off, not across the squad room but up the staircase to the second floor.

*

There was a solitary shot as Doe reached the top of the staircase and it went very high and well to the left of him. The layout at the top of the stairs was new to Doe. He had never been up there before. The staircase turned at the top and opened out into a large reception room that looked like it doubled up as a secretary pen. There were potted plants and comfortable-looking chairs and magazines on low tables for the people who had to wait for their meetings. There were four desks in a space almost the same size as the squad room below and right in front of Doe there was a big reception desk with a very startled-looking young woman behind it. The wall to Doe's right, the wall overlooking Main Street and the public entrance to the building, was clear but offices lined the other three walls. The empty wall had three windows overlooking the street. The second of the windows was open.

The window wasn't open very wide. It was on a sort of latch that allowed it to open a few inches but not swing wide open. The latch looked pretty flimsy and Doe figured he could get the window open far enough to squeeze through and he figured that even with his hands cuffed behind his back he could make the jump down to the street and get up and run. But, if he did that, he would land almost directly in front of the main doors to the Department building. Cops would be out of that door and chasing him in seconds. They might even react quickly enough to catch him before he had recovered from the jump. He would be marched back through the squad room and back into his cell before he had even made it off the block.

Doe ignored the open window and he ignored the young women sitting at the desks and he turned left and ducked through the first closed door he saw. Very few doors are locked inside a police department. The evidence store and the cells are obvious exceptions but mostly the other doors are left unlocked. It isn't really a matter of cops being more trustworthy or even that petty theft is any less likely. Generally, people don't lock office doors and beat cops usually have a locker to store their valuables in and their superiors have safes. So, Doe wasn't worried that the door would be locked but he was more than a little worried that there would be an angry mob with guns waiting behind it.

He picked the first closed door rather than an open one, despite the fact that it posed a practical problem for a man with his hands cuffed behind his back. He picked a closed door because it was more likely to be empty. In modern management, it was seen as extremely poor practice to close your door unless you were involved in life-changing discussions and those discussions were usually of such an important or sensitive nature that they couldn't be conducted in a normal office at all. They required a relocation to the HR department or to neutral space. On the other hand, when people left their offices it was almost impossible to avoid the impulse to pull the door closed as they left. Closed doors usually meant the occupants had left, open ones that they were in there and available.

Doe got lucky. He needed an empty office on the left-hand side of the building with a window and he found one on his first try. The doors were all wood-framed with a frosted glass insert. As he ran he aimed his shoulder at the wood nearest the door jamb and the latch gave way – he was into the room. He took another risk and paused to unlock the cuffs. He had practised unlocking handcuffs behind his back many times and he came away a few seconds later with blood coursing down his left hand but no significant damage. A few seconds wasn't always of great importance in Doe's life but right now he was trying to assess the reaction time of a dozen or so cops. A few seconds could make a big difference.

He guessed that they would spend a couple of seconds working out what had happened and then a couple more trying to work out what he was up to. He was handcuffed and he had run into the building rather than towards the exits, so he hoped that they would assume he was headed for a hostage situation. That he planned to threaten the secretaries or one of the top guys up there and try to negotiate his release. He hoped that no one down there would start thinking creatively because as long as they thought he was staying in the building, and that there may be hostages in the way, they would approach the staircase slowly and with care. If any of the cops were thinking quickly they would probably figure that it didn't hurt any to get some people outside of the department and get some eyes on the street. If they did that then Doe was in a serious race against time.

He walked over to the window and looked down at the street. He couldn't see any cops. He inspected the window frame looking for locks and finding none. Doe pulled the sash up to its furthest extent. The chain-link fence surrounding the vehicle yard was ten feet high and topped with razor wire. The Department building filled the entire block. Beyond the fence there was a neat little strip of grass and then the sidewalk. Doe cleared the fence from the window sill of the second story office and rolled through the impact with the ground on the sidewalk beyond. Three minutes later he was lost in the back streets and looking for a bike.

*

In his later, anonymous report Doe suggested that the Police Department had made just two avoidable mistakes that facilitated his escape. The first was hardly their mistake at all, more that of the original architect who designed the building, but he recommended that they move the staircase through ninety degrees so that it started by the reinforced steel door from the vehicle yard. With that single change Doe figured his escape would have proved virtually impossible.

His other recommendation was of such long-standing that his bosses didn't even bother to pass it on. Doe recommended the immediate banning of Velcro and press studs in all police equipment, excluding any equipment specifically designed for quick deployment. Doe was certain that if Wallace's keys had been securely attached to his belt, with a fabric loop or a metal chain, then he would have failed to escape or would have been picked up in a couple of hours at most due to the fact that he would have been blundering around town with his hands cuffed behind his back.

*

Doe was out and he was free, but he was alone. He was in his own clothes but that was about the best that anyone could say. He had no phone, no money and no information. The first two had been taken away from him by the police when he was processed. They had taken everything right down to the change in his pockets. The third of those items however, had never been taken from him and rarely denied.

Doe prioritized his requirements. The first thing he needed was a bike and the second was a quarter. He walked three streets before he found the first and four more before he found the second. The bike was chained to a picket fence. A lock is only ever as strong as the thing it's chained to and, although the lock on the bike was strong, the wood of the fence came away at Doe's first tug. The owner had locked the bike to the fence through the frame rather than the wheel so once Doe had broken it free of the fence he just rode the thing away with the lock still swinging from the frame.

The second thing he needed, the quarter, was just lying in the gutter. Doe walked those first few blocks using a well-honed evidence gathering technique, quartering the street, low, mid, high. It was a technique that he had used many, many times except that at that time he wasn't looking for evidence. When he was looking low he was looking for dropped coins, when he was looking at street level he was looking for the bike and when he was looking further afield he was looking for the cops or for a concerned citizen, anything that would cause him to need to run. Once he had what he needed he rode to the extreme southern edge of the built-up area of town, to a phone box, and he used the quarter to place a call to officer Eugene at the Police Department. He spent a little time debating to whom he should place the call. Mayfield was probably still unconscious, and almost certainly unable to talk, but Mathers and Eugene were still both around and Doe had interacted with both of them during the arrest. He could try to use his knowledge of either of them to further the conversation and both of them would have that innate, human reaction: the compulsion not to completely ignore someone with whom they had spoken. Even if they thought that Doe was the devil himself they would find it difficult to completely ignore him. In the end Doe chose Eugene because he had seemed far more in control throughout. He had looked like he was a lot more capable and to Doe he seemed to have some natural authority.

His call was picked up by a different officer whose name Doe didn't recognize. It sounded like there was chaos in the background, but the guy said he would find Eugene and bring him to the phone. There was a long delay during which Doe worried that his quarter wouldn't last but at last Eugene picked up.

"You just lost a prisoner," Doe said, "but believe me your day is only going to get worse."

"Who is this?" Eugene's anger transmitted itself through the telephone line as clearly as if Doe was standing right next to him. "Are you threatening me?"

"No, I'm not. I'm a friend. The threat isn't coming from me." Doe paused to let the guy get properly worked up, "I'm the guy that just walked out of a second-floor window at your department. I'm the guy that you dragged in with no evidence because you're scared of that guy in your cells. I'm the reason Mayfield will be eating through a straw for a couple of weeks." He stopped again, hearing angry noisy breathing from the other end of the line.

"But I have nothing to do with the guy you have holed up in your cells, nothing to do with whatever he is planning and nothing to do with the trouble you're about to get into."

Doe's quarter was running low. Eugene's breathing was getting ragged. Doe figured that anything that was breakable on his desk would be lying in pieces on the floor within a couple of seconds.

"I'm going to call back in a few minutes and reverse the charges. If you want to talk you're going to accept the charges. Call it a show of faith."

Doe hung up.

*

He didn't want Eugene to know he had no money and no phone. He didn't want him to know that he was on his own, unsupported and clueless so he turned his biggest weakness into a strength and made up the line about reversing the charges as a show of faith. There was another reason for the delay. Doe felt that it was perfectly natural for Eugene to be mad and equally natural for him to be mad at Doe. He wanted to give Eugene a little time to smash the desk furniture and calm down, so he waited nearly five minutes before calling back.

"Hello!" Eugene sounded pretty much furious.

"I'll say it again," Doe was looking to move on past his possible involvement and get Eugene thinking about the future. If possible, Doe wanted to get Eugene working with him on stopping whatever the confident guy in the cell had planned. "the guy in the cell has nothing to do with me. I escaped because I can help with this, but I can't do that unless you believe that I'm unconnected and I certainly can't do it from the inside of a jail cell."

"Yeah right. Two strangers in town, one of whom just walks out of our Department building while handcuffed and under escort. You sound real 'unconnected'."

"I didn't say I was untrained or even innocent, just that I was unconnected."

There was silence on the other end of the line. Not a sign of acceptance, but maybe the beginnings. Faint signs of progress that Doe could work with.

"Think about it. If I was connected wouldn't I have found a way to get him out of there too? Why would I leave him there?"

There was more silence.

"And more importantly, why would I call you back? I could be doing anything right now. I could be in a stolen boat heading for Canada, I could be in a stolen car heading for the ferry. I'm not, I'm calling you, trying to warn you that there is trouble coming and offering to help."

Doe wasn't worried about Eugene tracking the call. They had already told him how long they expected it to take to set up something like that when they had made him wait for his 'phone call' back before his escape. Plus, even if they did manage to trace the call they would end up at a public payphone that he had no intention of ever using again. On the other hand, things were urgent. He needed to move the situation on. He had things to do and he was pretty sure they all were on a tight timescale.

"I'm not connected to this, but I do know what I'm talking about. The guy you have in your cells is very dangerous and he is not at all worried about the fact that you caught him. I think you already know that. You need to call for all the backup you can get and you need to do it right away."

It was Doe's turn to stand in silence. He waited as long as he could, fighting to control the frustration he was beginning to feel, but in the end, it was Doe who broke the silence, not Eugene.

"Listen, I will stick around and I will do everything I can, but you need to make that call and you need to make it right now. We are going to need every bit of help we can get."

Eugene finally snapped.

"We can't do that." There seemed to be a little acceptance and a little fear mixed in with the policeman's anger, "We can't call for help because all communication in and out of the town has been dead since four am this morning."

*

"We tried to call out for help shortly after we picked the guys up, but the phone lines were down. That's not all that unusual around here. But then the radio didn't work either and well... that would have been worrying even if picking this guy up hadn't been so weird."

Eugene told Doe that as soon as they were sure that the radio wasn't working they had dispatched a cruiser to drive to Heath Haven but that they hadn't heard from the driver for nearly five hours. He should have been in Heath Haven by now, but they figured that, if there was a problem with the phones, he wouldn't be able to call them to let them know. They couldn't work out what was going on with the radios but if Heath Haven had a problem with theirs as well, then the deputy had been told to take the next ferry to the mainland and then drive through to the next Police Department and call it in from there. Depending on the timing of the ferries and any delays on route the guy might even have to stay overnight on the mainland and drive back the following day.

Doe could tell that Eugene was troubled. Doe was still a little raw himself. His wrist was still bleeding and he was breathing heavily. He should have been more considerate, broken the news more gently but he just came right out and told Eugene that he had to assume that their Deputy was dead.

"Or maybe a hostage. Either way he isn't going to be any help." Doe looked up at the sun, trying to assess the time. The things he had to do were even more urgent now, but he had to get the cops to realize the danger they were in, the danger the entire town might be in. "This guy is expecting friends and based on his confidence I don't think you're going to be a match for them. Send a boat, send a flare, draw a pentagram and try to summon the undead, I don't care what you do but you have to get some support."

If he had been talking to a homeowner about the loss of communications Doe would have told them to turn everything off and turn it back on again. He had heard computer people saying that and he figured that they must say it so often because a lot of the time that actually worked, but this wasn't someone's home it was a prosperous little police department. Doe figured that before they sent a guy away on a journey that would cost them an entire shift in each direction, they would have done everything obvious to get their communications working again. He glanced up at the sky again and got ready to leave the phone booth.

"It isn't all that strange." it sounded like Eugene was biting his lip, "The phones go out now and again and the radio can get screwed up by the weather."

"But not both at the same time, right?" Doe could sense the shrug.

"I don't see why not."

There was something that Doe was missing. He tried to work out what it was.

"Do you have mobile signal?"

Eugene was still reluctant.

"Yep, that is weird."

Doe was getting frustrated.

"Everything is fine in town, landlines, mobile, everything. It's just out of town where we can't get through."

*

Doe tried one more time. He knew that Eugene was worried, it was just a natural optimism that was keeping him hoping for the best rather than planning for the worst.

"Listen, you have a stranger in your cells who is supremely confident and you pick him up at exactly the same time as you lose all communications with the outside world. There's no way that you lose mobile, landline and radio communications all at once. Even if you did, you'd lose everything, not just calls out of town. They've completely cut you off. They must be jamming the signals or something. They're going to come and get him and they've made damn sure that you can't get any help or let anyone know what's going on."

Doe was already hanging up.

"You need to find a way to get more back up and you need to start fortifying your department house and warning the public. Sometime today they're going to walk into your Department and take him away from you and unless the way the cops work is very different up here, that's going to mean that a lot of you die."

*

Doe cursed himself. He had made a huge tactical error. He had underestimated the strength of his enemy. He had assumed that the guy was confident because he had a band of friends with a few sticks of dynamite or an anti-tank weapon. A gang that were planning to blow a hole in the back wall of the Police Department and make a run for it. A group that Doe could track down and neutralize before dark, before they could attack. A group that Doe could stop with the limited resources at his disposal leaving an increasingly bewildered prisoner to while away the long, escape-free hours until dawn.

The communications blackout screwed that up completely. Doe guessed that a determined group with the high-tech equivalent of a big pair of bolt cutters could probably cut the phone lines to somewhere as isolated as Briel island. He figured that with the telephone line, or with a little bit of extra work, internet and mobile phones would probably go too. Police radio was another thing altogether. Blocking radio signals required equipment. It required commitment and it required planning. Cutting all communication to a town of nearly one thousand people just of the coast of, and well under the protection of the United States of America, was a huge and difficult undertaking. That put the friends of guy in the cells firmly in the camp of people that worried Doe, and people that worried Doe were scary people indeed.

Doe was cursing himself because he should have made his escape attempt while his cellmate was also out of his cell. In the interrogation room or wherever they had taken him. If he had managed to cause enough confusion during his escape, then there was every chance that the guy would have taken his opportunity and escaped too. If the guy was out and free, then there would have been no reason for his friends to attack the Police Department and all that Doe would have had to do was to track him down and bring him back in. Instead he had to worry about foiling what would indubitably prove to be a deadly attack. Judging by the sun it was nearly noon. The latest they would wait before attacking would be until just before dawn and that couldn't be much more than eighteen hours away.

*

Doe had transport and he had a method of communication, but both were woefully inadequate for his requirements and he still had no real information. He was on a tight timescale, so he decided to solve all three problems with a single act and to deny the enemy of some of its strength at the same time. He collected the bike and cycled back toward the Police Department building.

FIVE

Doe cycled past the front of the Police Department and risked a glance through the window. The place was half empty but everyone in the squad room was moving. It didn't look like panic yet, but panic didn't look very far away. Nobody even glanced his way as he cycled past. Doe was pretty sure they would have some kind of plan in place. He guessed that if he actually cycled up to one of their cruisers and tapped on the windshield, then they would recognize him and arrest him. What they weren't expecting was for him to be right outside their front door, and what they definitely weren't expecting was for him to be on a bicycle. They would likely have cars quartering the streets and they might even send someone out on the road to Heath Haven hoping to catch him trying to leave town, but they didn't have anyone keeping a watch outside their own department.

Doe hoped they hadn't sent anyone to Heath Haven because he was pretty sure that if they did, those officers would wind up dead. Someone had gone to a lot of trouble to isolate the town. Whoever they were, Doe was sure that they wouldn't just let the cops drive out of town on the only available road. He hoped that he had done enough on the phone to convince Eugene that something serious was going on and that his colleagues were at deadly risk. At the same time,

Doe really wished that they would post someone outside the department building to watch the street. There was plenty going on out there that should interest them.

He cycled a couple of blocks past the Police Department and took two quick lefts. He got off the bike by the service entrance at the back of the small mall and hid it behind a dumpster. The staff entrance was unlocked, wedged open. Doe left the outside door open and slipped into the building. He tried every door he came to. His third attempt put him in an access stairwell. It was just an unpainted cinder-block shaft heading up through three stories. It was designed for staff use. Maybe only for emergency use. There were no frills. The fancy customer entrances would be out front, in the public part of the mall.

The cinder-block shaft had no decoration of any kind. No pictures, no windows, not even a plant. Just plain cinder-block walls for three flights and then a double fire door with a push bar but no alarm. Doe checked the door carefully before he touched it. He pushed the bar and stepped out onto the long, flat roof of the mall. He took off one sock and used it to jam the fire door open. The sock kept the door open just enough to make sure that Doe would be able to open it easily and leave, but not so much that a casual observer from a floor below would notice the open door and investigate. A shoe would have done the trick pretty well, but Doe didn't want to take off a shoe. Doe knew that if he had to run it was much easier to run with only one sock than with only one shoe. His shirt or his pants would have worked too, but if you have to run from the police it's best not to do it without pants. That was a really good way to draw attention.

There was a low wall around the roof. It was there to make the mall look neat and tidy from the street. It hid the peeling felt that covered the roof and the battered air-conditioning units and the rusting vents that sprouted from it. Doe crouched down by the door. Staying low he moved to the edge of the roof and settled in behind the wall. He was worried that someone might be watching the rooftops. If any spotters were high up he would be pretty exposed. He peered over the concrete plinth on top of the little wall and quartered the nearby rooftops. He couldn't see anything that looked like an observation point.

He skirted the wall and did a full circuit of the roof. His was the tallest building he could see. If the guy in the cell's pals did have a static observation post, then the mall itself was the most likely location. He had come out of the door ready for a fight but there was no one up there. The roof was empty. There were no telltale little piles of food wrappers or cigarette butts that would suggest that someone had spent a lot of time up there. Doe found himself a point where he could see both the Department building and Main Street stretching away beyond it and he settled down behind the three-foot wall and made himself as comfortable as he could.

*

It took him about five minutes to make the first positive ID and about as long again until he could be sure of the second. After an hour, he had watched them though two full circuits and he had their pattern firmly mapped out in his mind. There were two pickup trucks maintaining a rolling watch on the Department building. Each of the pickups contained two men. Doe spent another fifteen minutes making sure that he hadn't missed pedestrian surveillance teams or other vehicles and then he took another trip around the perimeter of the roof rechecking the higher windows, ledges and even parked cars. He was looking for fixed observation points where someone could be keeping a static watch. He still thought that the best position for a static observation post was precisely where he was standing, but he liked to be thorough and he knew that he could be wrong, so he checked everything. As far as he could tell the two pickup trucks were the extent of the surveillance.

It made sense to Doe. There was no need for anyone else. All they really wanted to know was if their guy was being moved or if significant preparations were being made to protect the building from attack. They had one or other of the pickups rolling past the building every few minutes and they were changing route and appearance after every few passes. They would approach from the south and then switch it up and approach from the north, sometimes they barreled straight down Main Street and past the building, sometimes they turned onto the road from one of the side streets or parked up for a little while at some point before or after the Department building.

They changed the appearance of the vehicles too. They had picked two late model, crew-cab pickups and they had avoided the simple mistake of picking vehicles that were too similar. It amazed Doe how often criminals made the mistake of buying a fleet of identical vehicles. That made observation so much easier. In any given location identical vehicles stand out, even popular models of common vehicle types. These two were different makes and different colors and sizes but the guys were still working hard to disguise them. They would roll past with the load-bed of the truck completely empty and then come back with it fully loaded. They had some kind of stick on decals that they would peel off so that they looked like private citizens and then they would reattach the decals to look like workmen. Doe saw them roll past in trucks that purported to belong to construction crews, auto mechanics and even an attorney at law. They didn't stop there. Every now and again they went somewhere and got the whole truck muddy and dusty and then took someplace else and got it cleaned up and drove back. Doe almost felt sorry for them. They were going to so much trouble and the Police Department didn't even have a guy out front who might have noticed. That guy could have earned himself a commendation that morning if he had kept his eyes open.

They were trying for a random pattern but after the hour Doe had what he needed and he reclaimed his sock. He closed the fire escape carefully and quietly, climbed back down the staircase and slipped out of the back of the mall. He took the stolen bicycle from behind the dumpster and headed off down Main Street, passing the non-existent deputy on the Police Departments steps for the second time.

*

Whenever the trucks were clean, they approached the department building from the same direction. From the south. Heading into town. Doe cycled north, along the busy street, looking out for car wash places. He figured they would be using an automatic place rather than a hand-wash because taking the same truck into a hand wash a couple of times an hour would start to look suspicious however much you tried to dress the thing up. They had probably spent days amassing a heap of the little tokens that the automatic places used. They would buy a few at a time and send different people to make the purchases. They probably even staked the place out so they could take advantage of the different shifts that the operators worked.

He spotted the place about a half mile past the Department building. There were suds everywhere. The machine was getting a lot of action and there wasn't enough time for the soap to drain away completely before the next wash topped the suds up. Doe guessed that on a usual Saturday morning there would be a few cars an hour through the little corrugated plastic shed. Maybe there would be a little rush at ten or eleven o'clock as folks got all dutiful and did their weekend chores. Maybe the rush would come earlier, at eight or nine because this was a rural setting and people tended to get up earlier in the country. Or maybe people got up late in the towns. Doe guessed it depended on your perspective. Either way, he estimated that the machine was getting near to double its usual peak business, and it showed. The suds were starting to blow around the forecourt.

Doe hid the stolen bike and walked up to the side of the machine. It was in a yard behind and to the side of a filling station. It wasn't in use and no one seemed to be watching so he slipped inside the plastic shed that housed the washing equipment. He took a quick look around, trying to work out what was dangerous and what would be sturdy enough and wide enough to hide him. There were plenty of moving parts that could catch a limb and crush or break it. There were belts and wheels that could snag on fabric and drag you in to get chewed up or pulped. He tried to remember the last time he had used one of these machines. He tended to use rentals or pool cars from a variety of different agencies. You don't clean either of that type of car. You log your mileage, you are supposed to report any damage, but it's always someone else's job to clean them. From what he recalled everything seemed to move quite slowly when you were sitting inside your vehicle. The machinery seemed to move with almost balletic precision, but Doe bet there were some pretty hefty bits of metal flying about ready to hit you on the head if you happened to be out there in the real world.

He took up a position behind the big fabric rollers that slapped and rubbed the dirt off of the vehicles. Space was tight but there was enough for him to keep some distance from the wall and from the machinery and at least the rollers were a little padded. Doe knew that wouldn't save him if he got caught between them and something solid, but it looked like his best option. He settled down to wait and hoped he wouldn't have to go through many cycles before one of his trucks arrived.

He got lucky. After ten uneventful minutes he saw the grill of a pickup poke its way into the shed. He moved forward a little to double-check that it was one of the surveillance trucks and then he backed away, out of sight, back behind the big, blue roller. He was starting to worry about what kind of chemicals the machine used. The metal trucks wouldn't care how astringent the detergents were and the paintwork and underside metalwork could get caked with all sorts of difficult to shift crap. The machine only had a few minutes to get the whole thing sparking and Doe guessed that would mean that whatever they were spraying wasn't going to be good for his skin. To get in there he had walked past a whole heap of warning signs posted on the side of the shed. There had been a row of stylized images like the badges down a boy scout's arms. They all had different little triangle emblems but most of them also showed a stick figure in a circle with a diagonal bar though the middle.

He decided that he would wait as little as possible and then make a break from his hiding place and run over to the truck. He could hit it while the water was just getting going. He needn't have worried. The detergents were clearly expensive and not much was wasted. The nozzles directed it carefully onto the vehicle and the rollers spread it around, but they didn't fling the stuff all around the inside of the shed. Doe watched the machine start up and decided to wait until the scrub cycle when the big, blue rollers would march down the side of the truck. They would give him perfect cover right up to the doors.

All he would need to do would be walk along, behind the rollers, moving around slightly to keep hidden from the windshield as the angle changed.

*

He stayed pretty dry right up to the spin-cycle, but water was obviously less costly than the detergents and since the vehicles being cleaned couldn't feel the cold the machine didn't bother to heat it. Icy water filled the little building and Doe had to wait until almost the very end of the cycle before the rollers moved sufficiently to allow him to open the passenger side door of the crew cab.

He pulled the door open, put one foot up on the door sill and grabbed the guy in the passenger seat by the collar. He straightened his legs, stepping right up, onto the sill and leaned backwards, pulling hard and using his weight to add to his leverage. He wrenched the guy right out of the truck and used his arms to pull himself past the guy and inside the cab of the truck. He straightened his knees and drove himself across the center console and rammed his forehead into the nose of the driver. The guy had half turned in his seat and was reaching inside his jacket. The impact of Doe's forehead into the center of his face slammed his head back into the glass in the driver's side door.

The driver tried to sit back up, his hand still fumbling inside his jacket. Doe's right arm was close up to the truck seats. He couldn't do much with his right hand except push it forward under his body, but his left arm was free and the crew cab was big. He swung his elbow in a vicious circle, catching the guy in the driver's seat on the nose for a second time. The guy's head hit the toughened glass window for a second time. This time his body went limp and his hand fell out of his jacket and a black handgun thudded to the floor of the truck.

Doe spun around and ended up sitting in the passenger seat with his legs sticking out of the door. He looked down for the first guy, expecting to see him getting to his feet and pulling a weapon. The guy was gone. Doe fought an urge to pull himself further into the truck. There was an armed, mobile opponent in an unknown position out there and Doe's first instinct was to find himself a nice safe spot inside the truck. There was no percentage in that. The crew cab was big, but he couldn't hide in it and the construction was tough, but the windows wouldn't stop bullets. He stayed where he was for a second and scanned the area.

The guy was lying on his back a few feet further into car wash. Doe had reacted the moment rollers had cleared the passenger door and he had pulled the guy out and past him in the direction the roller was moving. Somehow the man had got tangled up in the roller and it had dragged him three or four feet and left him lying next to the load bed of the truck.

*

Doe stepped out of the truck's cab and over to the figure lying in the suds. He checked for a pulse, but he could tell from the angle of his neck that the guy was dead. There were strands of the blue fabric of the car wash roller wrapped around his neck. His eyes had bulged slightly and he had gone a little red. Somehow, the roller had broken his neck. Doe had seen people who had been strangled. There was a lot more drama. The victims clawed at the ligatures and foamed at the mouth. Little blood vessels broke in their eyes and on their skin. This guy looked almost peaceful. He had died quickly when his neck snapped, not slowly as his throat was crushed.

The driver was breathing but there was a lot of blood around his nose and mouth and the blood was already beginning to thicken. His breath was blowing little bubbles in the blood around his nose and the bubbles were starting to tremble before they burst. Doe picked the gun up from the floor of the truck and reached under the guy's jacket and unbuckled his shoulder holster. It was a strong, nylon webbing holster. Doe put the gun on the passenger's seat and used the webbing of the holster to tie the guy's arms behind his back. Then he cracked the back of the man's head on the driver's side window again and manhandled him into the rear seat of the cab. He pulled and twisted him around to get him into the recovery position and to keep his airways from filling up with blood and drowning him. Then he stepped back out of the cab, heaved the body of the second guy onto his shoulder and dumped him into the load bed.

Doe walked all the way around the truck, looking carefully for anything he or the dead passenger might have dropped or disturbed. When he saw nothing unusual he stepped around to the driver's door, got in and pulled the truck out of the car wash.

*

Doe stopped the truck as soon as the tailgate cleared the car wash. He figured that from the outside, the guy on the back seat didn't look too suspicious, but as he was already a fugitive from justice it wouldn't be wise to drive around town with a fresh corpse on public display in the load bed. He searched the truck and found a tarp in a little locker behind the back seats.

He took a quick look around the yard. He wanted to search both men. It wouldn't be a quick job. He needed somewhere where he would have a little time without being interrupted. Dead or unconscious bodies aren't easy to search. They don't co-operate. Jacket pockets are usually OK, it's easy enough to get your hands into jacket pockets. Pants pockets were tougher. Even quite loose-fitting pants can be a bitch to get your hand into at the best of times, even if you're the one wearing the pants. They're made so that it's easy for the person wearing them to slide his or her hand in from the top and a little to the side but the opening faces away from you if you're looking into the face of the person you want to search.

The easiest way with a live, conscious suspect is to get them to take the garment off and then search it on a table. The second-best way is to get around behind them, have them hold up their arms and then slide your hand in from behind, like you are hugging them. There was no way Doe could do that with a corpse lying down in the back of a pickup load bed. Even if he could, it would arouse all sorts of suspicions.

Doe would have to go with the worst way. He would have to push his hands in from the front. He would need to put the backs of his hands flat against the guys hips and slide them into the pocket with his palms facing outwards and then he would have to feel around with his finger tips and pull out what he found as best he could.

Then he would have to check the rest of the body, under the arms, inside the shoes around the ankles and neck. After that he would have to roll the guy over and check the rear pockets and his belt and the small of his back. The he would have to do it all over again with the guy on the back seat, but then he would be inside the truck, a roomy enough spot for a fight but not great for a search.

The guy in the load bed was clean. He had no real injuries except the broken neck which had killed him, but the guy inside was covered in his own blood and added to that he might come around or move while Doe had his hands stuck in the guy's pants pockets. Doe would need to be careful to avoid getting the guy's blood all over his clothes and he would have to watch the guy the whole time. It was all going to take some time so Doe looked carefully around the yard before he started.

He was in a small gravel courtyard at the back of the car wash. The filling station was in front of him and to his left, close to the street. He was facing the back of the building and there were no windows at the back. A big grass mound at the back of the yard screened the property from the businesses on the next block. There was a blank wall to the left and an empty lot to the right. Between the filling station and the empty lot there was a wide entrance that would take three or four cars. Doe guessed that it was that wide so that one car could ride up to the entrance to the car wash while another drove alongside into the yard. Big country, big cars. A little foot and road traffic passed along the street and they had three full cars widths of entrance through which they could see into the yard.

Doe looked around, inside the yard. There was a single car parked up and empty. He figured it would belong to the cashier working in the filling station. There was a little litter blowing right to left across the yard and there was a bird sitting on the wire fence overlooking the vacant lot. He decided to risk it. The sides of the pickup were two feet high and the dead guy was lying still and on his back. The body was less than a foot high. Anyone looking up from the street would just spot a guy messing about in the back of his truck, maybe reorganizing some tools or tying down some loose cargo.

The only way that someone might get close enough to see what was in the back of the truck would be if they drove right into the yard, or worst case, if they drove up to use the car wash. If the car wash got a customer then Doe would have the driver and any passengers, sitting bored in the car wash hut, staring directly at him from about nine feet away for however long the wash cycle took. Doe decided that if anyone came into the parking lot, or into the car wash, then he would still have time to pull his hands out of the guy's pocket, cover him up and leave before they got close enough to see that something was wrong. He checked the corpse's jacket pockets first.

*

The two guys had good operational discipline. Neither was carrying any identification, just a cheap cell phone and some cash. The dead guy had a handgun in a shoulder holster. Just like the driver. Doe took the two guns and a couple of spare clips and the two phones and all the cash. Then he covered the corpse with the tarp and placed the bicycle on top of the tarp and he drove a little further down the road toward the town limits. He pulled over at a closed down diner.

His transport problem was temporarily solved. He had money, but he still had very little information. He switched on both phones. They were password protected. He tried one - two - three-four. He tried zero - zero - zero - zero. He tried a half dozen of the more common combinations, but the phones stayed stubbornly locked. Doe turned and looked at the guy on the back seat. He tried to find something about him that might give him a hint about his password. Doe shrugged. There was nothing. If either of them had been carrying ID he might have got something, a birthday or social security number or something, but there was nothing. By just looking at the guys he couldn't even work out what he was supposed to be looking for. It wasn't likely that one of them would have a four-digit number tattooed on his forearm and nothing else was likely to help. The password probably wasn't even personal. Doe could imagine some Quarter Master type handing out the cellphones to the mobile members of the crew. Issuing them the phone with a password already programmed in. Telling them the password, telling them to memorize it and to never write it down.

He toyed with the idea of waking the guy up and making him tell him the code, but he doubted whether the phones would tell him anything anyway and he would have to put the guy back to sleep again afterwards. There was a limit to the number of times you could concuss the same person in the space of a few minutes without risking serious brain injury. The cellphones were burners. Pay-As-You-Go phones picked up at convenience stores or pharmacies or Walmarts. He figured they would have made and received calls from at most two or three cellphones and that those phones would also turn out to be burners. There would be no real names, no text messages, nothing that he could use without sophisticated technical support, and probably very little even then.

He took the backs off the phones ready to remove the SIM cards. Unless Doe was very wrong about what was going on, then at some point there would be an investigation and Doe would have to pass on as much evidence as he could. His evidence would be anonymous of course, but if he was right, then whatever was going down was going to be serious enough to warrant a big investigation. If he was right, then what was going on would be important enough that he would need to pass on everything he could. His little experiment was going to be blown out of the water. He had his fingers around one of the batteries but then he stopped when one of the phones started to ring. The locked phone wouldn't let him answer the call, but it did, helpfully, display the number of the caller and the name that the owner of the phone had assigned to that number. Nine digits along the top of the screen and midway down a little image of a ringing phone and the word "Mill".

Doe paused a beat and then took out the batteries anyway. He took the SIM cards and slipped them into his pockets. He knew people who would be able to wring the very last drops of information out of them. He took the two batteries, opened the truck door, walked over toward the diner swinging his arms and kicking his legs out in front of him. He walked like a man who has been driving for a long time and needs to stretch his legs. He stopped by the tall weeds near the peeling, disused steps up into the derelict diner. He dropped the two batteries into the long grass and walked back to the pickup.

Doe picked up the two identical, battery-less phones and slipped the covers back on, then he reached across and opened the glove compartment. He stopped dead. There was a machine pistol and four spare clips concealed in the compartment on top of the usual map and owner's manual. He took the gun and ammunition out of the glove box and threw the two phones in and closed the compartment. He stowed the machine pistol in the pocket on the driver's side door. It made sense for the two sentries to hide the big gun in the dashboard. A routine traffic stop probably wouldn't notice the two hand guns in their shoulder holsters and depending who the cop was, they probably wouldn't have cared even if they did notice. An automatic weapon was a different matter. That was a vehicle check and a night in the cells all by itself.

The sentries were hoping to stay under the radar, but that concern didn't apply to Doe. If the cops stopped him they were taking him in on sight. The gun might as well sit where he could get at it and free up space in the glove box for the phones. Doe checked the rear view and side mirrors and then he turned his attention to the Sat Nav in its little holster attached to the windshield.

He clicked one of the little buttons on the side of the screen and tutted to himself as it powered itself up. No passwords on this device and almost certainly a hell of a lot more useful information than there would have been on the phones. He took a couple of minutes to familiarize himself with the Sat Nav's menus then went into its history. There was a page of distances and times and average speeds and then he scrolled through to the map. The elaborate surveillance pattern was laid out for him in little red lines on a street map of the town. There were a couple of trips out to what looked like a vacant lot. Doe figured that was where they got the truck muddy and put on or took off the fake business decals.

The longest journeys were two long spikes out of town. The first spike took the truck north, about four miles out of town on the road by which Doe had arrived the previous day. The second followed the old logging trail south for about ten miles. The truck had taken the first trip a couple of times but only one red line led south down the logging trail. It looked to Doe as if the truck had started out down there, in the middle of nowhere, then it had come into town. It had done an hour or so of observation and then scooted back out of town on Main Street and come back in and resumed the sentry duty around the police department.

Doe turned around in his seat and looked at the unconscious man on the back seat. The blood around his nose was starting to crust again and little white smears of spittle were hardening at the corners of his mouth. Doe half stood in the tall cab, one foot on the drive shaft housing, and the other up on the seat. He leaned over the curled figure and rolled him over onto his back. His breathing immediately became labored. Doe pulled back his arm and punched him hard on the nose. Fresh blood started to pour from his nose, washing away clumps of semi-congealed blood from around and within his battered nose. Doe rolled him back into the recovery position and pulled the truck out of the weed filled parking lot. He turned a big u-turn through the middle of the street and drove back into town.

*

Doe's biggest problem now was the guy on the back seat. He wasn't overly worried about the fact that he had killed the guy who was lying in the load bed. The guy was planning something seriously bad and Doe hadn't set out to kill him. The guy had been unlucky. If he hadn't gotten tangled up in the car wash mechanism then he would still be alive. If Doe's plan had worked out he would have been lying on the backseat alongside his colleague. Tied up and probably unconscious or in pain, but alive. Doe wasn't overly concerned about the well-being of the surviving guy either, but he had to at least consider ways of getting him some medical attention sometime in the next few hours. Doe knew that there was no emergency medical facility in the town. He couldn't drive they guy up to the doctor's office and leave him at the door. That was way too public and it wouldn't help the guy much anyway. He was likely to need a hospital and the nearest one was hours away.

Doe took another look in the rear-view mirror. His prisoner was breathing comfortably again. The flow of blood was already slowing. His nose was swelling but still working. Doe shelved the problem. He would wait until the guy started to look like he was in serious trouble before he went out of his way to help him. He started looking for the entrance to the logging road.

His priorities were still transport and communications. He was armed and funded now, but he was still Seal Harbor's most wanted man and although the cops wouldn't be looking for the pickup, the bad guys would be. He couldn't drive around in it for long. Whoever the friends of the guy in the police cells were, they could have already noticed the disappearance of the truck and they would stop him on sight. Doe would be back to using the bicycle sometime in the near future. That was OK for a few miles along well-maintained blacktop, but it was way too slow for a trip that would be ten miles along a rutted logging road and then ten miles back.

Doe decided that while he still had access to the truck he would check out wherever the pickup had started its journey. After that he could drive back into town and work out where to dump the pickup and what to do with the injured guy in the back seat and the corpse in the load bed.

SIX

The logging road had been easy to find but it was deeply rutted. Even the high suspension on the pickup struggled and Doe was working hard to average much over ten miles an hour. There were deep tracks through the dried mud and the tires that had made them looked to have been over a foot in diameter. That was almost twice the width of the chunky, all-weather tires on Doe's truck. The tracks were deep, sometimes they looked to drop away a foot and a half into the ground. A man could hide in those tracks. The gap between them was only slightly wider than Doe's truck. He estimated that there were a couple of inches on either side between the edge of his tire and the axle-snapping drop. If he increased his speed he could just about drive keep himself on the raised hump in the middle of the track, but every now and again he would fall off into the ruts. It was worth the risk when the tracks were shallow, but when they looked deeper he had to slow right down. If he fell in there he could ground the big pickup. If that happened he would have to abandon the truck and the injured man in the back and walk out of the woods, all the way back into town.

Trees crowded the little track on both sides. Doe was no expert but the trees all looked different. There were long stands of what he knew to be firs or pine trees. They were huge things with big trunks soaring up to improbable heights and letting his truck pass well below their lowest branches. Then there were other, very different but almost equally vast trees. They had trunks that looked like someone had tied a bundle of smaller trees together, and there was nothing green anywhere on them until you got to the very top. There were places where there was nothing between the big red trunks except for dried brown needles and dead branches, but there were other places where smaller trees had sneaked in and sometimes they had formed into large thickets.

It was the smaller trees that slowed him down almost as much as the ruts. Occasional stray branches whipped out and smacked the windshield with a sound that worried Doe. The trees were small in comparison to the giants that they nestled between, but they were still full-sized trees. The branches hit the truck like drainage pipes. There was nothing Doe could do to avoid them without running off the center of the road and into the suspension snapping tracks on either side. He couldn't avoid them and he couldn't slow down much more than he already had, but if the windshield shattered it would be even worse. Then he would have to stop and remove the crazed glass and afterwards he would have to push on with the branches whipping directly into the cab and threatening to break his nose.

It made no sense to Doe. If the track led to the camp where the pickup drivers and their bosses were based, (then) he would have expected a much better track. He would have expected it to be better maintained and better laid out. Sure enough after fifteen minutes of bouncing and rocking across the ruts the road widened out. Someone had trimmed the trees back to the edge of the track and smoothed it out into a wide, graded pavement. Doe pushed the truck up through the gears and did a further six, fast miles before he saw the house.

*

He killed the truck's engine and braked gently, pulling over as far as he could get to the side of the road. He wanted to offer the worst possible angle to anyone watching from the small front windows. The building was a squat little two-story thing with a porch and a smaller one-story phase on the southern side. The lower story had two tall, narrow windows facing forwards and none at all on the side facing Doe. The upper story had one forward-facing window high up towards the eaves. Doe imagined that the corners of the upper room would slope where the angle of the roof met the walls. Maybe the room was open up right into the roof space.

It looked to Doe like a three-room place, possibly four in the summer when the porch doubled up as a lounge. Behind the porch there would be a kitchen and to the side of that a dining room slash lounge. Upstairs was the bedroom and maybe tacked on to the back or maybe twenty yards away from the back door, there would be an outhouse. The bathroom would be the sink in the kitchen or a hose in the yard. The trees crowded in on three sides and the road ran past it on the other. Doe glanced at the Sat Nav, but he knew this wasn't the place. There was nowhere to park any vehicles. The guy in the police cell was confident and that confidence was bred of the understanding that major resources were being brought in to play to release him. Doe doubted that all they had was two pickups. Somewhere there was a well-stocked vehicle park. Somewhere there was flattened earth and trucks parked tail in.

There was a gap at the side of the house. Doe could imagine some kind of yard out back, but it was all too small for their needs. They would need vehicles for troop movement and they would need vehicles for exfiltration. They would need trucks to get everyone to the Police Department for the attack and they would need trucks to get everyone, including the guy in the unconvincing fisherman's outfit, out of town afterwards. They would keep those vehicles nearby in case they had to move quickly, either for attack or retreat. If the bad guys were here then their trucks would be here, and they weren't.

The Sat Nav told him that the place his pickup had started its journey was still a couple of miles down the road. This wasn't the place, but it would still make an excellent sentry post. Doe checked on his prisoner. He was still out cold, or at least pretending to be. His hands were secured and he would be disoriented for a while even after he did come around. Doe pulled the key from the ignition, took the machine pistol from the door pocket beside him, slipped out of the passenger side and locked the cab.

*

He took the magazine from the machine pistol and placed it on the roof of the truck. It was a nice gun, a Steyr TMP with a twenty-round clip. He checked to make sure that there wasn't still a bullet in the chamber. It was empty. He took the pistol to the edge of the forest and stowed it behind a tree, out of sight of the pickup. He was pretty sure that his prisoner was still unconscious, but Doe didn't want to come back to the truck to find him waiting for him with a fully loaded automatic weapon. Doe figured that if the guy could get out of a locked truck with his hands tied behind his back, if he could then find and reload the weapon and either free his hands or fire the gun accurately from behind his back, then faced with a gang of such supermen, Doe was likely to be dead soon anyway. He didn't think there was much danger of that though, not after the ease with which he had taken the two of them at the car wash.

He didn't want to take the Steyr with him on the recce of the house. Unless there was an army in there it wouldn't be much more use than the two handguns, and it was bulkier and it would make a loud and very distinctive noise. Doe guessed that the sound of a pistol might be mistaken for a rifle shot at a distance of a couple of miles. In the woods a rifle shot wouldn't elicit undue concern, but the sound of something firing fifteen rounds a second ought to alert even the dopiest of sentries. He looked at the captured hand guns. They were very nice weapons. Heckler and Koch USP Compact Tacticals. A lighter compact version of the USP Tactical which was in turn designed as a lighter but equally effective version of a weapon used by US Special Forces Units. Doe was pleased to have the two guns but worried about what it told him about his enemy. They were thousand-dollar weapons, hard to come by and not widely used. Someone had a lot of money to spend and people who liked to carry specialist weapons were usually good at using them.

Doe took the clip out of the first gun and slipped it into his back pocket then he checked the chamber and pushed the empty weapon into his waistband at the small of his back. He checked the second weapon and set off, along the tree line toward the house.

*

He moved carefully but he didn't creep. He had seen the house late and braked a fraction later than that. He had been running at reasonable speed all the way from the rutted track and the pickup wasn't an especially quiet vehicle. If there was anyone in the house, they would have needed to have been in a coma not to already know that he was here. He moved in close to the side wall of the house. In its lea but not tight up against the wooden boards. He wanted it to protect himself from casual observers, but he didn't expect the wall to protect him from attack.

The house was old and tired but not especially run down. It was built from overlapping wooden slats. The planks started up under the roof-line and sloped gently outward until they covered the top of the plank underneath, then the next slat started from underneath the first and sloped down over the third. It meant that rain couldn't get into the cracks between the wood without running down the first plank, along its width and back up the inside, fighting against gravity. Water doesn't flow uphill and it doesn't flow up the inside of walls.

The slats had been painted white at one point, but the paint was peeling now. Here and there Doe could see where new sections of hard, seasoned wood had been nailed in to replace rotten or damaged sections, but whoever had made the repair hadn't bothered to match the paintwork. Either the new wood had been left unpainted or whatever color was close to hand had been used. Doe figured that whoever lived here valued performance over appearance but, whoever he was, he also clearly didn't put much faith in preventative maintenance. There were sections where the edges of the boards were starting to crumble from the damp. The powdery wood looked grayer than the healthy boards. From where he was standing Doe could see entire slats that would need replacing before the winter.

Doe figured that the interior structure would be framed with big timber beams and that they would have arranged the slats on the outside and nailed big sheets of wood to the inside wall. The whole thing would keep the weather out and with a little bit of care it could last a hundred years but there was nothing behind him that would protect him from bullets. Doe doubted whether the rotten sections would even slow down a big knife. If someone knew he was there, then the only protection the wall was giving him was by hiding him.

He walked around the edge of the building, ducking under the tall front windows and hurrying up the steps to the porch. He walked in the shade of the walls but far enough away to allow him to walk normally and to keep his hands and arms free. The porch had a rickety old rocker, a small side table and a footstool. There was blank wooden siding on the left and a small window and door in the back wall. Doe avoided the window as best he could and reached over from the side and tried the door. It was unlocked.

*

Doe turned the handle and pushed the door slowly open. As expected, the room beyond was a kitchen. There was a plain pine dining table in the middle of the room and a small, oil fired stove with a couple of gas rings. A work bench at the back of the room suggested that it doubled up as a work-shop but the dresser and the shelves were tidy and clean. On the right-hand wall, there was a small window above a thick ceramic sink half full of water. A cast iron skillet sat on the drainer alongside a single white plate and cutlery for one. There was a clunky transistor radio plugged into the outlet on the counter and the window was open a few inches on a sash. On the left-hand wall, there was an empty doorway.

Doe stepped across the room and through the doorway. There were no screw marks in the frame. The gap had never held a door. It was a simple opening between the kitchen and the main room of the house. The room beyond had been decorated with an attempt at homeliness but it had happened many years before. Pale blue wallpaper with little yellow flowers covered the walls but it was peeling at the corners. Revealed beneath was carefully applied, yellow backing paper. Thick backing paper to smooth out the cracks and defects in the sheet wood walls. A big, polished imported dining table dominated the room, but it had been pushed right over to the side of the room and it was piled with papers and boxes and small tools. The space that was left held a single armchair, a small side table and an old TV. The TV was sitting on one of the dining chairs from the table. The rear door of the house opened directly from the back of the room, but it was completely blocked by the big dining table. Doe could see the hinges on the inside of the door. He knew it would open inward. The hinges were painted over with several layers of paint and anyone wanting to enter the room from outside to surprise him would have to push the door against the heavy wooden table. They would need to somehow shove the whole thing into the room, breaking the dried paint on the hinges as they did it. Even opening the rear door a crack and squeezing through would take immense strength and cause a hell of a racket.

To Doe's left a staircase ran to the upper story. The underside of the stairs was blocked in and there was a small door opening into a closet. Doe steeled himself and opened the door. There were coats and gum boots and hats in the closet and at the very back a couple of rifles and shotgun.

Doe checked his own guns one more time and turned to the first step and started to climb up to the second story.

*

There was no ceiling in the stairwell. The stairs just climbed up through a hole in the floor of the bedroom, but someone had put a rail of painted wooden posts against the edge of the gap. The posts were thick but nicely turned. Thinner in the middle and a bigger diameter at the tops and at the bottom. Doe imagined some proud young father working a lathe to craft the posts and planing and sanding the rail. Crafting it all to stop some new addition to the family from falling through the hole in the bedroom floor and breaking its neck on the stairs below.

He went up the stairs in a crouch and then stood up suddenly, at a point further up the stairs than anyone who was watching from up there would expect. There was a big wooden bed in the middle of the room, a small electric lamp and a candle in a stand on the bedside table. Windows let in light from both the front and back walls and a faded green rug covered the floor. As Doe had guessed, there was no ceiling. The room extended through the rafters and up to the white painted boards that covered the shingles. On the back wall, crammed into a space between the window and the corner of the room there was a carved oak closet.

Doe climbed the rest of the stairs and checked the closet. He did it carefully because it would have been stupid not to, but he wasn't really worried. He couldn't think of a single reason why a sentry of any kind would position himself inside a closet at the furthest corner of the highest room at the extreme rear of a building. Doe had known that the building wasn't being used as an observation post as soon as he had seen the dining table pushed up against the rear door. The first thing Doe would have done, if he had been planning to stay in the place, would have been to pull the table away from the wall and open the door a few times to get it running freely. He would have wanted to give himself a second exit and a faster route out to the back of the property. If anybody came calling at the front, anything that Doe wasn't happy that he could deal with, he would have been out through the back door and into the trees before they could make it across the tiny wooden porch.

The closet held a lot of winter clothing and another, newer shotgun but nothing else. Doe wandered over to the window and looked out over the small clearing hacked out of the forest at the back of the house. Only one more place to check.

*

Doe pushed the sash window until it was fully open and then he walked back down the stairs. He passed through the parlor and back into the kitchen. He walked over to the sink and pulled the cable attached to the radio from the outlet in the wall. He looked at the wire for a moment or two and then pushed the kitchen window closed. He walked back out the front door, across the porch and down the steps. He walked around the house toward the outhouse at the back wondering the whole way why the owner had blocked the back door with the big, heavy dining table and forced himself into this long walk every time he needed to use his own facilities. The only thing Doe could imagine with was that the dining table was a treasured heirloom. Too precious to get rid of or store outside, but no longer needed and taking up too much space in the center of the room. Doe still wondered why the guy hadn't pushed the table over to the front of the house and stood it under the window instead. It would have made it tricky to squeeze past and reach the stairs, but there would have had the same amount of room for the TV and the chair and the guy would have been able to step out of the back door and across the yard when wanted a pee rather than having to walk all the way around the house. Doe shook his head. Some things you just never got to understand.

Out back there was an old veranda, more dilapidated than the rest of the building and seemingly only used for storage. There was a chest freezer, and a pile of dining chairs, and a lot of fire wood. The yard floor was packed dirt and it looked like it got swept clear of needles and leaves every now and again. There were no remnants of the trees that must have filled the space before the house was built. The trunks were all long gone, rotted out or pulled up and dragged away. The holes they had left had filled up and the dirt had packed down so that you couldn't even tell where they had been. There were no dips or hollows. The house had been built a long time ago, but it was empty now. The whole place was quiet. It was the quiet that Doe associated with recently vacated, isolated places. When people are around there are always a few sounds, even if the people are trying to stay silent. There are odd creaks or tickings. The sounds of recently switched off equipment spinning down or cooling off, of stepped-on boards slowly relaxing back into shape. There are rustlings or flutterings as a breeze catches some abandoned scrap of material or as a recently-opened door settles into its new position. There was none of that here. Everything had cooled down. Everything had sprung back into shape. The wind had pushed everything that it could move into a stable position.

The place was empty but it still held the taint of man. There were hardly any birds and no larger animals at all. In time, hours or days or weeks, if the place stayed empty, the animals would come back.

They would be tentative at first. They would snuffle around furtively or fly in quickly and nervously. The birds would peck around with one eye on the building and then take fright and take flight in sudden, whirring flashes of color. The mammals would creep up to the porch and topple over the trashcan and scurry away, amazed by their own bravery, and then return after minuted of breathless hiding to dig around for their prize. The animals would come. They always came, but for the moment the place was still, quiet and empty. It hadn't yet reverted to nature, but it was empty of man.

Doe was still careful. He approached the outhouse from the side, hooked the toe of his boot under the door, swung it open and stepped inside. There was a newspaper on an upturned wooden box beside the john and a small chest with a pack of thirty-two rolls of toilet tissue on top, part empty. There was a small sink with an old-fashioned shower attachment hanging on a hook by the side. Otherwise the hut was empty. Doe walked around the little building to make sure no one was hiding behind it then looked closely at the tree-line around the yard before completing his circuit of the house and walking back to his truck.

*

He reclaimed the Steyr from behind the tree and reassembled it before getting back into the truck. He opened the rear door first. He opened the door by his prisoner's head, the one furthest away from his feet and any attempt at a kick. The guy had moved. Doe could tell by the way his arms were folded behind him that he was in a different position from the way Doe had left him. He had moved, but he was still quiet, so Doe checked his breathing and then ducked around the truck, into the driver's seat and he pulled back onto the road. According to the Sat Nav he had another couple of miles before he would run across whatever was sitting where the pickup had started its journey.

Doe couldn't see them setting their sentries more than half a mile from the base. Half a mile would give them plenty of warning on a road like this and if they were any further out it would take them too long to move between the sentry positions and the base. He figured that they would put a sentry post on the road and send patrols out from there. The patrols would move off the road and around the base. They might occasionally cross the road, but it wouldn't be often. They might widen their perimeter out in the woods. They might head out to three quarters of a mile or more depending on the reliability of their radios.

If he was right, Doe could drive as far as a mile short of the spot on his Sat Nav screen without being in any danger of running across a sentry or a patrol. After that he would have to hike the rest of the way through the trees.

The road wound around plenty. It didn't seem to be following the terrain and the trees on either side kept changing so Doe guessed that the road was moving to keep on top of the best ground. Some of the dirt looked pretty soft and in other places Grey rock was exposed. Doe thought that the builders would have wanted to keep a little dirt under the road, but that they would have wanted to stay well away from the boggy spots. Rock is difficult to grade but wet ground slips and running water would erode the edges of road surface. All in all, it meant that the road was rarely straight for more than a couple of hundred feet.

Doe watched the 'distance to destination' tick down on the Sat Nav and pulled onto the shoulder a little after it fell below one mile. From the tiny screen, it looked as though the road took a pretty smooth dog-leg around some unseen obstacle before reaching the pickup's starting point. It looked to Doe as if on foot he would be able to cut the corner. The direct route through the trees looked to be just over half the distance along the road. Doe had no way of knowing how accurate the little device was or what the terrain up ahead would be like. On the screen it was just a plain Grey, empty expanse, but up ahead it was all greens and browns and he couldn't see more than thirty feet.

Doe checked on his prisoner once again and took the clip out of the Steyr and hid it behind a tree. He locked the pickup and then he oriented himself by the little Sat Nav screen and the sun and set off into the trees.

SEVEN

It was old-growth forest. The trees were tall and well-spaced. There were saplings and ferns and lush rubbery plants in between them, but there was still enough light-brown, dusty soil left exposed to make it easy walking. The trees weren't densely packed, but they seemed to go on forever and they didn't grow in neat lines. In the gaps between two trees there were other trees a few yards deeper into the forest. The width of the trunks was such that it only took two or three of them to completely block his view. A dozen or so paces after leaving the road he couldn't see more than fifteen or twenty feet in any direction.

He made good progress. He walked at a pace that was slow by his city street standards, but he walked upright and paused occasionally to check the position of the sun. He didn't need to creep through the undergrowth or dodge from tree to tree for cover. There would be patrols out circling the camp, but they were covering a big area and until very recently, they had had no reason to believe that they needed any kind of serious security. There was absolutely no reason why anyone would know that they were there. No one was coming to look for them. They hadn't done anything. Not yet. There was a guy in a prison cell in Seal Harbor who knew exactly where they were and what they were up to, but they could be absolutely certain that he wouldn't have said diddly-squat about them to the cops. He was relying on them to spring him. There was no way he would give them up short of being tortured, and small-town cops don't torture people.

That could have changed in the last hour. They would be getting worried about their missing pickup and the two guys who had been driving it. They would have a communications check protocol. The guys would be expected to call home periodically. There would be a prearranged schedule and by now the guys lying in the back of his liberated truck should have missed at least one of those calls. Other than the mobile phones, Doe had found no other communications equipment in the truck. He had no idea how they had managed to block phone and radio signals in and out of the town without affecting their use within the town itself, but he didn't think it would be impossible and it made a kind of sense. Not only would it leave their own internal communications unaffected, it would also mean that the local population were unlikely to panic. Being unable to call your aunt in Los Angeles or your dentist in Heath Haven would be annoying but not especially worrying. On the other hand, if the townsfolk couldn't even call their neighbors, half of them would get in their trucks and head for civilization and the other half would head for the Police Department. The bad guys would have a traffic jam on the road out of town and a human shield around their guy in the cell. Far better to leave people their local communication and let them spend the time bitching to each other about their service provider, secretly grateful that they didn't have to call Aunt Sarah or arrange that visit to the hygienist.

The missed comms check would change things, but Doe doubted that it would change things radically. They would be upping their security, but they wouldn't be scrambling every able man. It had been an hour since he had taken out the guys in the pickup. They wouldn't have headed for the car wash shortly before their planned call-in time. They wouldn't have risked getting held up and missing the call or having to make it over the noise of the water jets and the spinning brushes.

Doe put their call at a maximum of fifty minutes overdue, probably more like thirty. These guys seemed slick, so he guessed they would put their contingency plan into action quickly and they would put it into action regardless of what they privately thought might have happened to their two colleagues. There would be no time at all spent working out what to do, just the briefest of queries up and down the command chain and then orders issued. Unless the operational side of their mission was imminent, unless they were loading up the trucks to head into town and break their guy out of jail, then one of those orders would be to increase the number of patrols around their base.

They would consider the possibility that the comms check had been missed because of some mechanical failure or due to human error. Maybe the guys had dropped both phones down the toilet simultaneously. Maybe they had been involved in an accident or picked up by the cops for a broken tail light. Maybe they would call in twenty minutes later and explain it all, but maybe they wouldn't. If they didn't then maybe someone now knew where the camp was. Maybe someone knew exactly what was going on. They wouldn't take the risk. They were too professional. The minute the call was missed they would react.

*

That reaction wouldn't be instantaneous. The extra patrols would have to assemble and then head out into the trees. If Doe was right about the half mile perimeter then the walk out to their existing picket line would take them ten minutes. His expectation was that at the same time they were increasing the number of patrols they would also widen the perimeter. That would mean they would be moving outward, away from the camp at the same time as he was inward, toward it. They would be moving for longer, alert, but not yet in their patrol pattern. There would be gaps.

Doe moved quietly but he didn't hide. He was wearing a dark plaid work shirt, black denims and a Grey baseball cap that he had found on the back seat of the truck. Spotting him against the greens and browns of the forest would be nearly impossible but hearing him would be a lot simpler. The big trunks and the soft pine covered dirt would soak up a lot of sound, but sound has a way of carrying even in the most muffled of environments. There were branches falling and creatures moving furtively out of sight but the sound of a biped moving across a terrain is something you can be taught to identify. Doe wasn't willing to bet that they didn't have someone who had taken those courses, so he varied his pace, he avoided any obvious dead branches and stepped on soft ground whenever he could. The patrols would be moving carefully too but there would be more of them and they were on their own territory. He was confident that he would hear them before they got close enough to see him. If he didn't, if they spotted him and he had to spend time evading them, then he would be of little use to the cops in the Police Department.

After about ten minutes, a lighter patch started to show in the dimness ahead. Doe slowed down and approached the upcoming tree line at a crouch. He pulled himself close to the last few trees and flitted from one to the next until he was staring out at a huge cleared area from the behind the trunk of the last big fir. Suddenly, being seen was much more of a worry than being heard.

The area that had been cleared covered a large, shallow bowl. The mature trees continued part way down each slope, stopping a dozen or so feet into the depression. There was no sign of exposed stumps where the cut down trees would have stood. Instead, wrist thick saplings continued down the slope for another dozen feet before petering out into another dozen feet of barren ground and then a nine-foot-high, barbed wire and chain-link fence that enclosed the main compound.

Doe didn't need to worry about the patrols any more. They would be further out, in the woods, trying to stop anyone making it as far as he already had. They didn't need to patrol the fence line. Doe's problem now came from within the camp itself. A couple of spotters with binoculars could cover the whole line of trees. The human eye is attuned to movement. If they were looking in exactly the right spot they would see him move. If they had their binoculars pointed in the right direction they would even see him crouched down in the last few meters of the tree-line. They would spot him right there in amongst the gloom and the big trees. It isn't easy to spot movement through binoculars whilst moving them in a sweep pattern, but it's a basic infantry skill and they wouldn't have to move especially quickly. The bowl covered a large area, but the perimeter was contained and uniform. Two spotters would be able to sweep the whole fence line in about two minutes. Doe imagined them, a story or two up in a tower, back to back, covering half the circle each. Covering a long slow one-hundred-and-eighty sweep and then reversing back through the same terrain and repeating the whole thing over and over until their shift ended.

If he stayed where he was and stayed completely still, then he should be safe. If he moved or tried to wriggle back into the deeper forest at the wrong time, then he might be spotted. Moving forward would pretty much guarantee it. There were nearly ten feet of open ground ahead of him before he even reached the fence. Ten feet of empty ground where if he moved quickly he would attract attention and if he moved slowly he would be spotted by the next sweep of the binoculars.

Then there was the fence itself. Even if it wasn't alarmed or electrified it would pose a substantial barrier. Even if he made it from the tree line to the fence between binocular sweeps and without moving quickly enough to draw the sentries' attention, even then he would still be spotted well before he could get over the fence. Doe wasn't planning to head through the wire, not yet, but he wanted to see what he was up against and he didn't want them to know he was there. He wanted time to check out the camp and he wanted to get back out and into town quickly. He wouldn't be able to do either if a sentry spotted him and raised the alarm. He also had an instinctive desire to keep them in the dark. He wanted them wondering whether there was a simple explanation for their missing truck. He wanted them to think that maybe they were still ghosts, that no one knew that they were there or what they were up to. Knowledge is power and these guys had way too much power already.

*

Doe crept carefully up to the edge of the trees. He crawled the last few yards on his belly and settled in close to the final tree trunk. Ahead of him, behind the wire, was what looked like an old logging camp. Doe cupped his hands around his eyes to eliminate peripheral vision and to improve his focus. He really wished he had a pair of binoculars, but he hadn't been able to think of a way to get hold of a pair. There was a single decent sized grocery store in Seal Harbor, the rest were mom and pop, local-type stores. Doe had guessed that the bigger market might sell binoculars for the tourist trade. Some low magnification items, cheap and probably sealed in a hard-plastic blister pack with a hole at the top so it could be hung on a rack. They would cost nineteen ninety-nine and include a tough nylon carry case with dodgy seams that would fray and unravel after a couple of months. They would have done the job though. The bowl was big, but ten or twenty times magnification would be plenty. He wanted to get a feel for what was going on down there, he didn't need to be able to read the labels in people's clothing.

He had the cash too. The money he had taken from the wallets of the guys in the pickup would have more than covered the cost. Doe hadn't been able to make himself take the risk. The cops had a missing prisoner. They would have started to canvass the local businesses. They might even have stationed someone at the grocery store on the off chance that he would try to rob the place. As far as the cops knew, Doe was broke. No cash, no wallet, no phone. Everything he had had in his pockets when they picked him up was still safely locked up in their evidence store and they would be watching his motel room so they knew hadn't been back there to resupply.

They would be expecting him to be wandering the streets. They wouldn't be expecting him to go shopping. But, they would know that if he was going to try to leave town he would need food and water and supplies. Even if he was planning to stick around and lay low for a day or two he would probably need something. It's not easy living off the land if all you have in your possession is a key, a pair of handcuffs and the clothes you're wearing. Petty theft or robbery would be the simplest, possibly the only, option available to a stranger in town.

Doe had toyed with the idea of scoping the market out. Driving past it in the pickup or cycling right up to the windows and checking the interior for obvious signs of the police. In the end, he had decided that he couldn't afford the time and that he didn't need to take the risk. He only wanted to find out roughly what was going on out where the pickups had started out. He just wanted to know what sort of numbers he was up against and how they were equipped but he needed to get the information quickly, before the guy in the back seat of the pickup started to cause trouble and before his comrades acted on whatever plan they had in mind. Doe had decided to head out and check out the camp before he did anything else. He could always source some equipment and go back later if he thought it was necessary.

*

He was regretting the decision now. Doe scanned the fence as far as he could see in either direction. There wasn't a lot to see. The absence of the tree stumps and the presence of the saplings in the cleared ground running up to the fence told him that the bowl had been cleared years earlier, but the fence was brand new. There was no rust, no breaks in the chain link and no vegetation clinging to the wire. Even the dirt under the pilings still looked freshly disturbed.

Beyond the fence the cleared ground continued for a hundred or a hundred and fifty yards to the center of the camp and then stretched away for a similar distance, back up the slope of the bowl until the fence curved around to meet it. All the way around there was the fence, then the cleared ground, then the saplings appeared and then, suddenly, the trees. Doe couldn't see a single spot where the cover of the trees looked to be any closer to the fence than the spot where he was now.

The whole depression was maybe twenty feet deep. If you were walking through the woods nearby the bowl was deep enough to completely hide a two-story building. Its large diameter meant that the sides sloped gently despite the depth. Looking down at the center of the camp, Doe's line of sight dropped a foot in elevation for every fifteen feet traveled. If he was walking into camp he would start off with a bit of a scramble out of the tree line and then the slope would gradually lessen until he reached the final thirty yards which were virtually flat.

Thirty yards to Doe's left, the town road entered the compound. The sides of the bowl had been dug or blasted away and the rubble had been piled up on the downhill slope to lessen the gradient. The track ran straight as an arrow in a gentle slope from the fence to the edge of the logging camp. The bowl bottomed out about seventy yards from the fence and that was where the buildings began. They lined the road, two or three deep all the way to the center of the camp and then petered out along with the track itself. Doe could see smaller shacks that he took to be bunk houses and offices and maybe a canteen. In amongst them there were bigger buildings. They were open sided and Doe guessed they were where the felled trees would have been stored, back when the camp was still in use.

Taking up the whole of one side of the track, right from the edge of town to the center of the bowl, was a massive two-story structure which had to have been the saw mill. The buildings were all timber-built and weathered to a light gray. Their roofs sagged and shafts of sunlight darted through rotten holes and lit up portions of the interiors. The windows were empty or smashed. Sunlight glinted on uneven rows surviving glass. Here and there stones had rolled out of the foundation plinths and planks has fallen out of the sidings leaving gaping holes in the walls. The whole place should have been empty, abandoned and quietly rotting away. But it wasn't.

At the front of the bowl tall grass and fast-growing shrubs covered the ground. They grew up to and into the old buildings. They pushed at the broken-down hulks and pulled at their foundations, trying to break them down and reclaim the ground they covered. The vegetation was lush and green or tough and dark brown but beyond the end of the road, in the shadow of the big sawmill, the ground had been re-cleared. Along the near edge of the newly cleared area, almost abutting the ruined side wall of the mill, a half dozen steel shipping containers were arrayed in a rough quarter circle. The sides of the containers were sparkling new, but the roofs were painted in mottled browns, whites and bright primary colors. It would give the effect, if seen from directly above, of discarded and rusting machinery. Doe figured that viewed from a plane or on satellite imagery they would fit perfectly with the surrounding buildings. The track had been recently extended as well. New gravel had been laid and tamped down where the original track petered out. On the opposite side of this new track to the shipping containers, there were four prefabricated huts. The huts were a little bigger than the shipping containers and they had proper windows and doors, but they still had the mottled brown camouflage painted onto their roofs.

Behind the new buildings, the ground was covered by a large expanse of camouflage netting that extended all the way over to the slope of the bowl. There were vehicles parked under the net. Big vehicles in neat rows. People were bustling in and out of the shipping containers and under and around the net. At the very back of the covered area, outside the netting, Doe could see a couple of dish antennae and from the center a forty-foot-tall radio mast poked up through a hole. The bottom twenty feet of mast were plain steel, but the top had been painted green and branches and foliage had been stuck to and through the steel tubing.

Doe took his hands away from his face and pulled his focus way out. He watched the entire camp for a few minutes, counting the people he saw, trying to get a feel for the strength of the company. Then he used his hands to compress his field of vision again and focused on the open side of the netted area. He was looking down on it from an angle and at a distance of three of four hundred feet. There was deep shade under the net. Doe couldn't make out much detail. He squinted and looked closely into the shadows. He could see what looked like the fronts of another two pickups and beside them there was another vehicle. He couldn't see much of it past the camouflage net and the deep shadows, but it clearly wasn't a pickup truck. It was much taller, much wider and it was painted a sandy yellow.

*

Ten minutes later he had learned all he was going to learn. The compound was huge. The natural geography and man-made additions gave it formidable protection. Doe had spotted their watch tower. They had a couple of guys with binoculars up on top of the old mill. They were at the extreme end of the roof, just above the top of the first shipping container. He had seen the glint in the lenses of their binoculars. The lenses flashed every few minutes as the sentries swept the perimeter. The position put them almost dead center of the bowl. They wouldn't need to refocus, just concentrate. He timed their sweep. They were consistent to about ten seconds. Every minute fifty-five seconds to two minutes five seconds he would spot a glint from their optics as they swept past him scanning the tree-line for movement. It was impressive discipline. Even if he had arrived just after a shift change, if these guys were fresh and not yet bored or tired, then their technique was good. They were doing a good job and it wasn't an easy task.

He had also roughly mapped out the camp. As far as he could tell the shipping containers were used for storage. He suspected that at least one of them was doubling up as a bunker office, possibly as a command and control center or as the communications hut. People went in or out of the other containers rarely and when they did, they came out carrying boxes. No one went in or out of the two furthest away from him during the whole time he was watching.

The prefabricated cabins were a different matter altogether. They were a hive of activity. Doe counted a couple of dozen people moving about the camp. It was difficult to get an accurate count because he was too far away to spot many identifying features and they were all dressed pretty much identically in military desert camouflage fatigues. He picked a point when the camp seemed to be at its busiest and he did a quick head count. The count came up at twenty-three. Most of the people he saw moved in or out of the prefabricated buildings at least once. Doe pegged the buildings as offices and sleeping blocks. The fourth hut in line, the one furthest from his position, he marked down as the canteen. There was a big white box bolted on the back. Doe figured they wouldn't want to have a chimney belching smoke and giving away their position, but every cook-house needs a refrigerator. The size of the refrigerator told him that there were either a lot of people in camp or that they were planning to stay there a long time.

The aerial in the middle of the cam-netting took up quite a lot of his time. It looked pretty unremarkable. There were a few bulges about two thirds of the way up but otherwise it could have been a film set prop made out of scaffolding poles. It emerged from the middle of the nets and rose another thirty feet, tapering to a point. It was anchored in place by six steel cables. The cables were attached to the scaffolding high up, near the top. The other ends were fixed into thick iron rings set deep into big concrete blocks dug or poured into the soil just outside the inner circle of the camp.

Doe finished his observation and squirmed his way back into the tree line and set off, not back to the pickup but clockwise, along the perimeter, towards the road and the gate into the compound.

*

He walked a good distance back into the forest. Far enough from the bowl to run no risk that the guys on the top of the mill would be able to spot him but close enough to the tree line to be able to see the sun lightening the gloom to his right. He followed the lighter ground all the way around until he came to a junction where the pine needles and ferns ahead of him were glinting in the same way as the ones to the side. The road was dead ahead, maybe twelve feet in front of him. The gate would be a further twelve feet down the road. Doe dropped to his belly and inched towards the light.

They had a fork truck parked up at the gateway. No stupid striped pole with a guy in an MP's helmet ready to push down on a cantilevered weight and raise the pole out of your way. The fork truck was massive. It looked as if it might be a relic of the time when the saw mill was still working. It sat in the gap in the fence with its exhaust belching smoke down the slope into the bowl and sixty cubic yards of concrete on its forks at the front. The concrete was a single huge block, probably poured on site for some inconceivable reason and now sitting on the forks of the truck. The driver of the fork truck wouldn't be able to see anything over or around it but that didn't matter. The truck was only there to make two, very brief journeys. Approach the gate as a friend and someone would back the truck out of the way. Once you were past they would drive the fork truck back into the gap. Approach as an enemy and you would be stuck in your vehicle on a narrow road, penned in by eight-foot-thick tree trunks on either side and four meters cubed of concrete and a mammoth, steel fork truck in front of you.

Try as you might, that would be a bad situation. Nothing short of a shaped charge was going to get through the concrete and you couldn't escape in your vehicle without reversing a quarter mile down the road. Meanwhile the guards could shoot at you through the fence, from the trees, from behind the fork truck, from anywhere they liked. You could abandon your vehicle and run for the trees but then you would need to exfiltrate through the forest while they hunted you. Even if you made it out, in no way could you claim it had been worth going in.

Doe melted back into the trees and headed back toward his stolen pickup.

*

Doe walked back along the edge of the forest again to the point from which he had observed the camp. He was pretty confident in his ability to cut across and make it back to the truck by dead reckoning but he wasn't absolutely certain. He knew how easy it is to take a curved path through trees when you are trying to walk in a straight line. On the way in it hadn't mattered much. He had been aiming for a huge target and if he had missed he would have still been in the woods, under cover. The pickup was a much smaller target and if he missed it he would meet the road. He would either be closer to town or closer to the camp than he wanted to be and he wouldn't know which. The way the track wound around there was a good chance that he wouldn't be able to see the truck from the point at which he emerged from the trees.

There was no way he was going to walk down the middle of the road with no idea whether he was heading toward his truck or away from it. He was going to make sure that he overshot the truck. He was going to aim for a point that he could be confident was further down the track in the direction of town. Then he could skirt the side of the road, walk just inside the tree line, facing his enemy, until he reached his truck.

He figured he had a better chance if he retraced his steps a few dozen yards further into the forest. There hadn't been anything much in the way of landmarks on the way in, but he had noted the occasional bigger or smaller trunk, some misshapen or leaning trees, one big, fallen log. If he walked with those on his right-hand side then he should come out on the road just behind his truck. As long as he didn't cross his own route in, then there would be no possibility of him coming out nearer to the camp.

He reached the tree from which he had observed the camp and used his hands to sweep the place where he had lain. If anyone was tracking him then the action would make it even more obvious that he had been there. It would leave obvious signs for anyone looking directly at the place, but it would make it more difficult to spot from a distance. He melted back into the trees and carried on along the periphery of the camp for fifteen paces. Then he turned through ninety degrees and set off back toward the road.

Doe knew when and how to go still and a couple of hundred feet back into the woods he froze. He didn't so much see the patrol as sense it. There was a little bit of sight, a flash of color in his peripheral vision, and a little bit of sound, a crack of a branch and a rustle of leaves. There might even have been what you might call touch, a slight tremor in the ground beneath him. Doe was happy with the sharpness of those three senses. He was sure that he had sensed the patrol before they could have noticed him. He quietly sniffed the air. He thought there was a possibility that he could work on his sense of smell. He had known a Special Forces guy once who had sworn he could tell the nationality of an unseen enemy by the odor that their food packs gave them. He even said he could tell between current and discontinued US military field rations. He said that it meant that he could tell whether he was smelling a US soldier or just someone whose quartermaster had bought some surplus equipment.

Doe had thought that the guy was exaggerating. He doubted whether the guy had conducted rigorous trials. Doe figured that the guy had just caught an odor on the wind once or twice and guessed correctly that he was smelling the enemy. That kind of thing could easily get built up into a legend. Still, even if Doe was right, the guy had been able to detect bad guys by smell. To Doe that meant he had an advantage. Doe couldn't smell anything other than pine needles and dirt. He had no interest in using his sense of taste.

The patrol was about twenty feet ahead of him, moving across Doe's path and slightly away from him. Doe didn't try to hide. He didn't move at all except to lower his head, letting the peak of his cap come down and cover his face. Dropping the peak of his cap was a hard thing to do. It felt counter-intuitive because it meant that he wouldn't be able to see what the enemy was doing, but it was necessary. The patrol was out there looking for people. They would be looking for flesh tones and movement. Even standing completely still, Doe's flesh tone stood out against a forest. In the snow, he would have been happy but out here he needed to cover his face. It took some discipline to stay that way. Doe could only see the lower legs and boots of the patrol. He couldn't see their faces, he didn't know which way they were looking. He couldn't see their weapons, he didn't know which way they were pointing them. Doe made himself stay still and watch their feet and continue to breath. The woods were quiet but not silent. They wouldn't hear him breathing any more than they could hear his heart beat. Holding his breath would only weaken him if he had to run or fight.

He ran his hands slowly alongside his body and behind his back letting them come to rest on the grips of the two pistols, his thumbs on the safety catches and his fingers on the triggers.

*

It was a five-man patrol. Staggered like a letter 'M'. Point man at the front on the left, second man a few feet to his right. The other three were a few feet behind and a little further apart. Doe watched the first man's feet moving carefully through the browning pine needles. He saw the second set of feet come into view and then the third. He saw the first pair of boots turn towards him and he tightened his grip on the pistols and then deliberately loosened it. He watched for the movement of the third pair of boots. The way the first man's boots were pointing didn't mean anything. He could have twisted at the knee or at the waist or at the shoulder. His eyes could still be pointing forwards. He could have changed his stance for a number of reasons. Maybe he spotted something ahead and wanted a firmer footing. Maybe he was preparing to crouch, to rest his gun on his thigh and bring his guys in for a huddle. Maybe his feet hurt. The guns were new, maybe he had new boots, sore insteps. One pair of feet pointing towards him didn't mean anything. If the feet of the third man turned as well, three steps behind the leader's, then he would worry, then he would move and bring out his guns.

The feet of the third man stayed pointing forwards. The lead man stepped carefully down into a shallow dip that was hidden to Doe's view by the flat brown carpet of the forest floor. Second and fourth in line skirted the dip and third and fifth crept forward normally until they got to the lip of the slope. Then number three turned his feet towards Doe and number five turned his away and they moved carefully down the little slope. Doe got it. They hadn't seen him. They had seen the dip. They had twisted at the waist to keep the guns pointing out in front of them and to ledge the boots into the soft dirt on the down slope. They were out of sight before they got to the up slope, but they wouldn't do the same there. There they would push the toes of their boots into the dirt and lever themselves up the slope. The physics were completely different. On the down-slope, they needed to lean back, make a solid ledge with as much contact area between their footwear and the dirt as they could manage. They needed a stable platform. They needed to avoid slipping and falling on their asses and sliding down the slope. On the way out of the dip they needed power. They could afford to slip a little. Their weight would be out in front of them. They could control it. A handful of seconds later he heard them slipping and scraping their way out of the hollow. They were good, stealthy and quiet but the sound was unmistakable.

He raised the peak of his cap slowly. He had seen one, two, three and five move off and he was sure they couldn't have circled around and come back, but he hadn't seen the fourth man's feet after he moved to the side to skirt the little dip. It would make no sense for the rest of them to move off and one of them to stay behind, but it didn't hurt to be careful. He was short of time, but he had the few seconds it took him to raise the peak of his cap slowly and look around the forest before he moved carefully and quietly off in search of his truck.

A couple of seconds later Doe was moving again, the patrol moving away from him to his left.

*

In the end Doe judged his direction well and came out onto the road close enough to the truck to be able to see it further up the track. He approached the pickup with care. There was still a chance that they had the logging road under electronic surveillance or that they had physical patrols out walking the road. Doe doubted it, but he didn't discount it. He guessed that there was a minimum of thirty men in the compound and they had all looked really busy. Doe figured they felt that the couple of miles of tough driving along the unmaintained track at the town end of the logging road was sufficient deterrent and camouflage to make direct observation unnecessary. It made the road unprofitable to the curious and unremarkable to the locals. In the unlikely event that anyone did take the road to nowhere, bump and scramble over the rutted section of logging road and then continue for another eight miles, all they would see would be the massive fork truck at the gate. They would be able to control the situation at the gate. They had no need to monitor the road.

Nevertheless, he approached the pickup with care and scouted both sides of the track before he approached it. There was a lot of banging and shouting coming from the truck. It made Doe pause for a second, but he recognized the dulled intonation of a man with a badly broken nose and the angry, ineffectual hammering of a man locked inside a vehicle. Before he had left the pickup and headed into the woods he had taken the extra precaution of loosening his prisoner's bonds for long enough to wrap them around the pillar that attached the driver's seat to the truck floor. The arrangement pulled the guy's arms way over to his right and wrenched his shoulders in a way that Doe knew would become agony in a very short space of time. It kept the guy in an uncomfortable position, but it also meant that even if the guy woke up, he would still be unable to sidle up to the truck's door, place his back to it and open the door with his fingers.

That prospect hadn't worried Doe at the empty house. They had still been a long way from the camp and Doe hadn't been planning to stay away from the vehicle for long. Even if the guy had gotten out of the truck Doe would have been able to round him up quickly enough. The second recce was different. He had been away from the truck for nearly an hour and the enemy camp was close. He couldn't picture the guy stumbling across the pine needles and fallen branches for the half mile through the trees, but he wouldn't have needed to. The guy could spend half an hour coming around and getting out of the truck and still have over fifteen minutes to walk up the center of the track hollering and yelling.

You can walk pretty quickly with your hands tied behind your back as long as you are on a flat, well-lit surface. You are a little inhibited because you know that if you trip you can't throw your arms out in front of yourself and break your fall. You know that you will hit the floor with your chin or your nose or at best your cheek. It makes you really focused on not falling and that slows you down a little, but not a lot. Fifteen minutes would be plenty long enough for the guy to get within sight of the gate house and the sentries. Or at least, close enough for them to hear his shouting. Close enough for them to come out and meet him and then to recognize him.

So, Doe had tied the guy to the seat pillar and he had wound all the windows fully closed. Outside of the vehicle, in the quiet of the forest, yelling would carry for a good distance, but the truck was a luxury vehicle. The engine was noisy and it was designed to work hard. The tires were big, with big treads. They would be noisy on highway surfaces. The truck would make a lot of noise whatever surface you were on, but the manufacturers needed you to be able to hear the CD player and use your cell phone while you were in there, so there was a lot of noise suppression in the fabric of the cab. If the noise of the big engine and the big tires couldn't get inside the cab, then the sound of his prisoner yelling couldn't get out. Doe's prisoner could scream and bang on the roof all he wanted. As long as he was inside the truck with the windows closed, then Doe would bet that he wouldn't attract attention.

Doe opened the driver's side rear door. The man was lying on the rear bench seat, his arms pulled way over to his right and his face a mess of clotted and dried blood. He was kicking at the opposite door with a ferocity that impressed Doe and there was a look in his eye of uncontrollable, injudicious rage.

Doe looked him in the eye, tilted his head slightly and gave him a half apologetic, half - 'what did you expect' - little smile, and then rammed his fist back into the man's battered and bloody nose.

EIGHT

Forty minutes later Doe was three miles out of town on the only road out of Seal Harbor. He had really pushed the little truck through the well-graded section of the logging track. He had driven hard, knowing that he was going to be slowed to a crawl for the last two miles. He had bounced his way back into town and then he had worked his way through the back streets, trying to avoid both the cops and the bad guys. He had made it through town without incident and was cruising at a steady fifty along the smooth blacktop that led from Seal Harbor to Heath Haven.

The Sat Nav on the dash gave a simplistic representation of a map. Just a basic, aerial view of the road. It showed a slow, mile long curve starting at a point three miles from the town limits. Doe did some pretty complicated three-dimensional geometry based on that map. The little red lines that traced the previous routes that the pickup truck had taken showed it stopping just after the bend straightened out. The truck had stopped there several times. Stopped and turned around and headed back into Seal Harbor. Just like at the camp, Doe thought that he could get to within half a mile of the place before anyone who was waiting there would be able to spot him. The long bend would hide him until almost the last moment.

On the little screen it looked simple. On the road it would be harder to judge. It was also entirely possible that the map was out of date or inaccurate. Doe stopped a full mile before the end of the red track and pulled the truck to the side of the road.

He had untied the guy in the back from the driver's seat pillar before he took the truck back through the rutted section of the logging road. He wasn't especially worried about the guy's welfare, but the man was unconscious and his hands were still tied behind his back. Doe didn't want to run the risk of dislocating both of his shoulders and leaving him dangling by them while he negotiated two agonizing miles of bouncing road. Amongst other things Doe thought that the noise the guy would make might distract him.

Doe pulled the truck as far off the road as he could and checked the guy and secured him to the bottom of the seat again. He took the stolen bicycle out of the back of the pickup and set off. The shoulder was lightly cambered and Doe cycled at a leisurely pace. The trees along the side of the road were big like the trees lining the logging road but they were set further back and they looked managed. The branches heading back into the forest were big and cankerous and twisted, but the branches on the road side were all small and straight and slightly green. The bike was capable of much more speed and Doe had plenty of space on the shoulder, but he kept the pace slow. He wanted to be able to stop quickly the moment he saw any sign of people up ahead.

Doe was sure that he would see anyone on the road ahead before they would be able to spot him. They would be set up to spot traffic in the road, not bikes on the shoulder. Maybe they just wanted to see what was going in and out of town. If that was all they wanted, then they would be parked on the shoulders of the road, facing downtown. Doe doubted that was all that was going on. If that was all they wanted, they would have set up much closer to town. The first three miles of the road were pretty much dead straight. They could have parked the truck a mile or a mile and a half from the last building and seen anything that was heading out of town. They could have picked the vehicles out while they were still a few blocks inside the town limits. They would be able to watch it crawl through the streets of the town, accelerate for half a mile or so after it hit the blacktop, and then cruise towards them at a steady sixty. They would have had it in sight for a good three or four minutes.

They would get less time with the vehicles coming from Heath Haven. The bend would hide the vehicles until they were a mile and a half or two miles away, but a mile and a half at a law-abiding speed of sixty would still give them a minute and a half before the vehicle passed them. A minute and a half is a long time and afterwards they would be able to watch the vehicles brake sharply before they hit the town and then crawl out of sight. If all the gang wanted to do was watch the road and know who was coming and going they would have plenty of time.

*

Doe didn't think that they would be just sitting there counting cars. From the end of the red lines on the GPS map they would get about a half a mile of visibility. Thirty seconds before the guys drew alongside. It was a lot less than they could get from the other side of the bend. The best reason Doe could see for them setting up further out of town was if they wanted to stay unseen or unheard.

Unseen because if they could see vehicles moving a few blocks inside the town limits, then the people moving around in town would be able to spot their trucks as well. They would be sitting there, big and suspicious on the shoulder a mile or so out of town for hour after hour. Sooner or later someone would come out to find out what they were doing. Possibly someone with a big neighborly grin on their face asking if everything was okay, or possibly someone in a Police Department cruiser asking to see some ID.

So maybe they moved further out, around the bend, just so that they would be less likely to be spotted. On the other hand, maybe it wasn't being seen that worried them. Maybe they were planning to make some noise and they wanted to be far enough from town that the sound wouldn't carry. Maybe they didn't want people asking different questions like, 'did that sound like a gunshot to you?'

Whatever their reasoning for moving around the bend, Doe didn't think that they would be parked on the shoulder. He didn't think they were there just to watch who was coming in and out of town. He thought they were there to control it. He expected them to be parked right across the road. Two cars would be stopped right out by the center-line, angled towards each other and facing into the traffic leaving town. They wouldn't be worried about how long they got to see the cars coming towards them, only about how long the drivers would have to spot them.

Half a mile is plenty of stopping distance, even for at a vehicle moving at a very *non*-law abiding ninety miles an hour. Maybe it was a perfect distance. It would give the oncoming traffic plenty of time to stop but it wouldn't give them much time to think about what was going on. It wouldn't give the drivers time to look at the situation up ahead and decide that they didn't much fancy going up there and asking what the hell they thought they were doing blocking the road like that. It would give them enough time to bring their vehicle to a stop but not long enough for them to decide to turn around and go back into town. To head home and drop a dime and let the cops come out and ask the questions. They could probably work it so that they had their roadblock set up twenty or thirty yards from where the vehicles would come to a halt.

Either way, Doc would be able to see their vehicles before they could see his bicycle. The only risk would be if they took their sentry duty so seriously that they had someone standing outside the vehicles, one at the very edge of each shoulder, looking across the road at the shoulder of the opposite carriage way. It would be the way Doe would do it if he was in hostile territory, but he didn't think there was much of a chance these guys would be doing it here. They didn't think they were in any danger. They weren't expecting people to come crawling through the trees or cycling up the shoulder of the road.

*

Doe was right. They weren't just watching the road and they didn't have any spotters out. The first thing he saw was the front corner of a pickup truck parked way out near the middle of the road. He grabbed hard at the brakes. The back wheel of the bike lifted up, nearly throwing him over the handle bars. He wrestled the bike back under the control of gravity and sat back down with a thump. He wheeled the bike over to the trees and put it gently on the ground. He stepped into the trees and crept along the shoulder until he could see a little more of the vehicles ahead. There were two pickups parked in a V-shape across the center of the road. It was a roadblock, not an observation point. There was a gap between the grills of the two trucks, but it was too small to drive through. There was a larger gap between the back of each truck and the edge of the shoulder. A small vehicle might have been able to drive along the shoulder between the back of the truck and the trees, but it would be precise work. You would have to slow right down to make it work.

He could see four guys. They were all heavily armed. It was a subliminal thing, like with the cops. They needed two vehicles to block the road. Each vehicle had to carry two people so that meant four of them to man the roadblock. It wasn't about how many people they needed. It was a consequence of the number of trucks. They could have done the job pretty well with two people and they had it nailed with three. The fourth guy was lying in the long grass at the edge of the shoulder. He looked like he was asleep.

The first of the working guys was behind the trucks, inside the V formed by their hoods. He was leaning across the hood of the left-hand truck and pointing a rifle down the center-line of the road. He had to stay alert because he only had a little under half a mile of blacktop in front of him before the road curved around and he lost sight of it. Half a mile was plenty, but only if he saw the vehicle early. Half a mile meant that he had to concentrate.

The second guy was sitting cross-legged in the load bed of the right-hand truck. He was facing in the opposite direction, following the road out of town as it headed to Heath Haven. He had a rifle across his knees and a cigarette on the go. His weapon wasn't an assault rifle like the first guy's. He had a sniper rifle with a big scope mounted on it. He had six miles of road stretching out in front of him. There were dips and a few small bends, he couldn't see every inch of the asphalt but there were no turn offs. Any approaching vehicle would be visible at the six-mile point and then it would spend five or six minutes going in and out of sight before hitting a last two-mile straight section directly in front of the guy. If anything came his way he would have plenty of time to put out the cigarette, get into position, raise his gun and then wait for the truck to come into sight.

The third guy was sitting in the front of the first truck. He was in the passenger seat, with his feet up on the dash and the seat ratcheted all the way back but he had the passenger side door open and had an assault rifle and a sniper rifle on the seat beside him. If either of his colleagues had a sighting he would be able to pick up a suitable weapon and step out of the cab to help.

Doe carefully retraced his steps for a hundred feet or so and then dodged back the woods. He went far enough into the trees to make himself difficult to spot and then he paced out the distance until he was certain that he was at least a quarter mile past the road block. He moved carefully, but he wasn't really worried about being spotted. They were all concentrating on the road. If he ran or waved his arms about they might spot him in their peripheral vision and if he made any obvious noise then they would look over or send the spare guys to check it out, but as long as he was quiet and didn't get too close to them, they weren't going to notice him.

Once he was certain that he was behind the roadblock he moved back towards the road and crept carefully through the trees to the edge of the shoulder. About fifty yards from the roadblock a vehicle was parked nose first across the shoulder. It was a police cruiser. As Doe got closer he could see that the car wasn't parked across the shoulder. It had crashed into the trees.

*

Doe inched up through the trees behind the cover of the crashed cruiser. The guy that was looking in his direction was the sniper. He was focused further out, at the six-mile point, and he wasn't concentrating that hard. All he had to do was check the road every few seconds to make sure that nothing was moving. The rest of the time he could scratch his balls, play with his cigarette, check his gun and think about home. Doe kept low and stayed near the trees and he moved very, very quietly. He kept a wary eye on the guy lying in the grass. He was pretty sure he was asleep and not a very cunning sentry, but he wasn't willing to bet his life on it.

They had left the cop strapped into the front of his cruiser and Doe thought that that was what annoyed him most. They had shot him through the windshield as he turned through the bend coming out of town. By the number of bullet holes in the outside and inside of the vehicle, Doe figured that both the guy leaning on the hood and the guy in the passenger seat had opened up in a totally indiscriminate manner. They cop had been hit multiple times. Doe figured that it would have happened so quickly that even if there had been enough left of his face to see, Doe doubted that there would have been time for his expression to register surprise.

They had left him strapped into the front of his cruiser and they had moved one of their trucks out of the way and then they had pushed his car through the roadblock and let him coast down the little incline behind them and crash off the road. It was the lack of respect that made Doe hate them, even more than the killing. They could have taken him out of the car. They could have moved the car into the shoulder and parked it. They did neither. As soon as they got the car behind the roadblock, where it wouldn't be in the way or act as a warning to anyone coming out of town, they forgot about him. They just let the car roll away and stop wherever it came to rest. If there had been more people leaving town that morning, Doe had no doubt he would be looking at a scene that resembled a highway pile up. They would unload on whoever tried to get out of town and then just wheel their corpses into a big auto graveyard at the bottom of the little dip.

He moved in close enough to read 'Burns' on the dead cop's name badge and then he crept to the front of the wrecked cruiser for a closer look at the guys manning the roadblock.

*

Doe watched them for a while. He was confused. The way they were deployed was professional. The design of the road block and its positioning was straight from the text book, but it wasn't put together in the way that an amateur would use a text book. It wasn't a to-the-letter recreation of a generic tactic. These guys had scouted the land. They would almost certainly have preferred a long straight stretch of road ahead of them as well as behind them. In the spot where they had been forced to set up they were susceptible to a determined attack from the direction of Seal Harbor. If the cops came out in force and knew where the road block was, then the roadblock would fall. There would be a mad half mile dash, some cops would die but there was no way the roadblock crew could hold out for long. The guys would be killed or captured and their mission would be compromised. The lock-down of Seal Harbor would be broken.

There was no such danger from the direction of Heath Haven. An armored division creeping around the bend six miles distant would probably make them pack up their gear and run for it, but even that wouldn't be able to overrun them. Anything lightweight and moving fast would be easy work for the sniper and anything heavily armored would be moving so slowly that they would be able to plan and deploy. Or to run. If they had been able to get a straight eight-or ten-mile stretch of road near enough to town they would have set up in the center and used sniper fire in both directions. It was what the text book would say but it hadn't been available. No such stretch of road existed. They had picked the bend because it was the best option available to them and they had modified their tactics because of the bend. It was good, creative technique suggesting that these guys were good professionals, not amateurs.

Then there was the way the two alert guys were behaving. The guy with the sniper rifle was checking his gear periodically and checking the road plenty often enough to get the job done. The guy leaning on the hood of the truck in the center of the blacktop was showing impressive concentration and good technique. He wasn't sprawled across the front of the truck and he wasn't standing rigid and uncomfortable behind it. He was using the truck to brace his weapon and take some of his weight. Again, it hinted at well trained personnel and a good, workman like military plan.

But the third guy wasn't well deployed and the fourth was so far off plan that it was crazy. He didn't look as if he was just relaxing between watches. He had put himself into a position whereby he would be useless if the shit hit the fan. If anything, he would be a liability. Doe could have crept up and slit his throat without the other guys even noticing. No soldier on active service should be so careless and the weirdest thing was that his colleagues didn't even seem to care. Doe would have been screaming at the guy to do something useful or at least to lie down somewhere where he would be able to easily get at the weapons in the truck.

It was puzzling Doe. There were perfectly good jobs for both of the other guys to do. The crew had the road well covered but there were miles and miles of trees surrounding them and no one was paying any attention to them. Doe had stood watch over a stationary target before. He knew the kind of concentration it took. He knew the spine-tingling feeling of being in a potentially dangerous position but looking only in one very specific direction. He knew the fear that creeps in over time. It was like the feeling you get when you are watching a scary movie with a crack of window showing through at the top of the drapes. It's the feeling that there is something bad coming to hurt you and you can't get up and look.

The two guys with the guns should have been worried that while they were concentrating on the road someone might come creeping out of the forest with a couple of liberated Heckler and Koch USP Compact Tacticals and shoot them both in the head. The other two guys should have been watching their pals' backs. They should have been standing, one on each side of the road, an assault rifle at the ready, watching the trees and the shoulder of the road.

Doe checked the two pistols tucked in the waist band of his pants and inched his way back into the woods, trying to make some sense of it all. They were using well-trained personnel, but they were unmotivated and overconfident. That was the only thing that made sense. In terms of gathered intel, it didn't add up to much, but it was something.

*

Doe wasn't much of a chess player. He tended to fall into the trap of taking every piece he could whenever he could and then trying to win the game with whatever pieces he had left. He knew that wasn't the best way to play chess, but it was the only way he had learned. He knew that he was capable of taking out one or two of the four-man crew and then melting back into the trees before they could organize and come after him. Their instinct would be to chase him into the trees, so he guessed that he would be able to loop around them and get back to the truck and take off before they figured out that he probably hadn't walked out from town, and that he certainly hadn't walked from Heath Haven. By the time they worked out that he had a vehicle parked up just around the bend he would be halfway back to town.

He had more than twenty rounds in the two guns and he was a good shot. He was less than forty yards from the roadblock and he could get a lot closer without giving up the cover of the trees. He would be able to get his gun right up against the temple of the guy asleep on the shoulder and then take the guy nearest him, the one with the sniper rifle, before he had a chance to react. The third guy would be tougher. Doe put the odds at less than fifty-fifty that he could take one of the other guys before he either took cover or returned fire. If he managed to put the third guy down then it would be one against one. Doe would always back himself in a one on one even if the other guy was considerably better armed than he was. It might kill him one day, but he wouldn't be able to live the life he lived if he started shying away from that kind of risk.

He did the math. Best case he took four pawns off the table and showed his opponent what he was up to. He spent a long couple of minutes trying to think of a way to convince himself that it was a good plan. He was desperate to punish them for their casual killing of Burns. He was also aware that the desperation meant that the longer he thought about the problem the more likely he was to convince himself that the obviously wrong course of action was actually right. Desperate men did stupid things because they convinced themselves that they would succeed.

Doe kept working on the problem. He really wanted to take four pieces off the board and he wasn't happy about what the guys had done to Deputy Burns, but his main worry was that he had no idea when some family of four were going to drive out of town to visit Auntie Jessica on the mainland. The thought of some truck smashed into the back of Burn's Police Cruiser with little bullet-riddled bodies still strapped into their car seats was horrific.

If Doe could have been sure of taking out that third man it would have been a close-run thing. His natural optimism would have combined with his desire for retribution and he might have given it a go, but it wouldn't help Aunt Jessica's nephews or nieces the slightest bit, if the road block just got reinforced with a bigger, more alert team. If Doe killed two of them and then had to run, the remaining guys would call up the logging camp and get reinforcements. They would know for certain that Doe was hunting them and the residents of Seal Harbor wouldn't be any safer.

More worrying than that, Doe couldn't be sure that the gang's response would be so conventional. He had counted nearly forty men at the logging camp. Maybe their response to being challenged would be to move into town. Maybe they would spring their guy early or take even more brutal measures to control the town. Maybe they would start rounding people up or picking off cops on the street. Doe was unsupported, pitted against a better-manned and better-equipped enemy and he was becoming ever more certain that it was vital that he stop them from springing their fake fisherman and spiriting him away into the heart of the USA. His country. Whoever he was, people were spending a lot of money and taking incredible risks in order to make sure he completed his journey.

If hitting the road block wouldn't protect the population of Seal Harbor and it would hurt his chances of stopping that man from making it onto the mainland, then hard as he found it, he would have to leave them be and head back into town.

*

Doe had been planning to get the guy in the back of his stolen crew-cab to a hospital as soon as he could. His plan had been to take the truck out along the road to Heath Haven. He would have driven until he was far enough out of town that any ambulance crew wouldn't be drawn into whatever the hell was going on and then he would have put the machine pistol back in the glove box. He would have put the driver and passenger back in the front seats and rigged the truck to drive into a tree. He would have left it there and cycled back into Seal Harbor and called nine-one-one as soon as the phones were working. He didn't think that his little tableau would fool the Police Department for long, but he was planning to be out of the state within a few days, so he didn't really care. The facial injuries would get the guy hospitalized and then the gun would get him institutionalized immediately afterwards. Doe had no doubt that the two guys would have records. Records which would probably get them some jail time just for being in a truck with an illegal weapon. All of which suited Doe's sense of justice.

The way the guys at the roadblock had treated the body of Deputy Burns had changed his plans both practically and morally. He couldn't get the truck out of town and he wouldn't risk calling an ambulance. He wouldn't ask anyone to drive that six long miles in cross-hairs of the sniper's scope. The driver from the car wash was going to have to take his chances until this was all over. Doe had lost all sympathy for the man. He wasn't overtly judgmental. He wanted to stop bad guys because of what they did, not because of who they were. He had met plenty of people who had committed crimes because their experience and personalities told them that it was an acceptable thing to do. He had apprehended people who stole because they wanted their children to have the benefit of the things that they saw other children enjoying. He had met people who thought the chaos and death they unleashed were necessary to change society for the better and men who felt they were being oppressed and that violence and destruction were the only ways to fight back. He had tracked and arrested criminals who had perpetrated the vilest of crimes but who thought that their victims were either willing participants or that they would benefit from or enjoy the experience. Then there were the rare individuals who were mentally incapable of caring, the people for whom their victims were no more worthy of consideration than the chairs they sat on or the clothes that they wore.

The vast majority, of course, knew exactly what they were doing and were doing it for personal gain, but Doe thought it was far too much trouble for him to bother trying to work out where the line fell. Were people fully responsible for their actions? Were they misguided, pitiable or evil? He would have had to research it and then use that knowledge in every single case. He would have needed to interview them once he had arrested them. He would have had to test them, treat them, test them again. He just wanted them to stop and once he had caught them, he knew that they would stop. At least for a while.

But the guys in this gang were angering him. In Doe's view they weren't just ruthless, they were also callous, and that made it easier for him to risk the fact that the guy in the back of the pickup might die a slow death before he made it to hospital. He picked a spot where he thought he might be able to inch the pickup deep into the woods and he carefully drove it off the shoulder and into the trees. He lost both mirrors, scraped and dented the side of the truck and blew one of the front tires before he felt that he was far enough into the trees to make the truck invisible from the road. He hadn't bothered to untie the guy from the seat pillar before heading into the woods. The man had slumped down into the foot well with one shoulder obviously dislocated. Doe untied him and heaved him back up onto the bench seat. He rolled him over so that he wouldn't choke and then Doe worked his way back towards the road and his stolen bike.

NINE

The bike was fast and Doe was back at the outskirts of town in a little under fifteen minutes. He needed coffee, water and food. In that order. He stopped on the shoulder a couple of hundred yards from the diner on the outskirts of town and threw the bike into the weeds at the side of the road. Heading back into the diner was dangerous. It was the place where he had been picked up earlier that day. Arrests tend to stick in people's minds but especially so if the arrest is carried out in a way that suggests extreme danger. If, for example, six cops walk the guy out in handcuffs and surrounded by pointed guns.

There was a call box right out front of the diner. Doe decided to take an extra risk. He sorted through the cash he had confiscated from the guys in the crew cab. It was mostly notes but there were a couple of coins and Doe used them to place a call to Sergeant Eugene at the Police Department.

Eugene didn't pick up the phone. Doe had to wait until the guy who had picked up the phone left to find Eugene and then he waited until the sound coming from the receiver changed from the low background noise of the office to a muffled, near silence. The change told him that someone had picked up the handset and put it to his ear. Doe gambled that it would be Eugene. He didn't wait for Eugene to speak.

"Have you had any luck finding me?"

There was a pause.

"We'll get to you."

Doe smiled. The first reason for his call was over. They hadn't put much effort into tracking him down yet. There was a decent chance that they hadn't canvassed the town. The local cops would be looking for him, but the townspeople probably didn't know he had escaped. Maybe it was pride, maybe the Sheriff was up for re-election and he didn't want the townsfolk to know that some guy had walked out of his shiny new Department building. Or maybe they were too busy.

"Don't trouble yourselves, I'm not planning on sticking around."

Doe took a long look up and down the street and around the parking lot. No one seemed to be taking any notice of him and there were no slow-moving patrol cars.

"Your guy, Burns is dead. It had nothing to do with me. I just found him." Doe gave him the dead cop's badge number.

Doe waited as long as he dared, then pushed the conversation along.

"I'm sorry. I hope he didn't have much family. If it's any consolation, he had no chance." Doe looked up into the windows of the diner. The waitress was peering out at him. He gave her a cheery wave. "They have a road block set up outside town and they're armed like an infantry unit. They cut him down before he could react."

Eugene paused again.

"OK. Anything else?"

"Yes, they're massed out at what looks like an old logging camp west of town. They have at least forty guys out there and as far as I can tell there are another six in and around town."

"At the road block?"

"Four at the road block and another two keeping watch on you." Doe heard the office noise come back on the line as Eugene moved to a window. He could almost see him peering out from behind the blinds, checking the street. "There were four of them watching you. They're are two men down and they almost certainly know it."

"You took the other two down?"

"Yep, I needed things they had."

"So, you killed them."

"No." Doe's coins were running out. He didn't want to explain what had happened to the dead guy in the car wash. "But they're out of the game. That will confuse their bosses. They have you under close observation. They know that you don't have their guys. They'll be wondering who does."

Another pause. Doe slipped his last quarter into the phone.

"That logging road is virtually impassable. We'll get some guys out there to watch the road. They can stop them there."

"No." Doe edged towards the door of the booth. "I've been out there, they have eight Humvees under camouflage netting. They look like military grade to me. They can do that road at twenty miles an hour with eight people in each truck and they won't even spill their coffees."

Doe counted five precious seconds.

"They are here for the guy I was sharing the cell block with and from the way they are equipped and what they did to Burns, they mean to get him. Fortify your station house and find a way to get help."

Doe waited through Eugene's last pause. Wondering if his money would run out and cut him off before the cop could respond.

"I still don't trust you, you know."

Doe put the phone down and walked into the diner.

*

It had been well over six hours since his arrest and he figured there would have been a shift change amongst the waitresses, but he was wrong. His waitress was still there. Maybe she had just got on shift when he had arrived that morning and she was nearing the end of her eight hours now. Maybe she was pulling a double, helping a colleague who was having child care problems or going on a hot date. Maybe she was the owner or proprietress saving a few bucks by working the long day-shifts herself. Doe didn't care, he just wondered a little about what her reaction to seeing him again would be. She hadn't liked it when he had waved to her from the phone booth and when he walked in through the front doors she turned straight towards the hatch where the fry-cook stood.

Doe walked over to the counter, taking the roll of confiscated cash from his pocket as he did so.

"I think I owe you for my breakfast ma'am. I had to leave before I could pay."

The waitress continued to stare at the chef. He shrugged a sullen little shrug and moved off into the back of the kitchen. The waitress turned back to Doe and took the proffered notes.

"That all sorted out now then, son?"

Doe shrugged a 'what can you do' kind of shrug and picked up the menu. He knew the kind of place. They were law abiding but self-sufficient. They would help the police if asked and they wouldn't tolerate anything illegal on the premises, but if the cops weren't involved and you kept your business outside of their business then they wouldn't ask and wouldn't tell.

"I'll have two burgers please ma'am. Fries and rings, no salad, coffee and a pitcher of water." He put some more notes on the counter. "It's been a long day."

*

Doe chose to sit in the same seat he had been using when he had been arrested. He figured it gave him a little subliminal respectability. He wouldn't sit there if he was embarrassed about the arrest and if he wasn't embarrassed then he couldn't have done anything wrong. The table was still a little wobbly from where he had loosened the bolts. Either the waitress and chef didn't care, or more likely, they hadn't noticed. The customers certainly would have. The slope wasn't enough for his plate or cups to slide to the edge but there was definite movement if you leaned on the tabletop. It was enough to make his coffee spill, but he figured it probably wasn't the kind of place where anyone would have complained. Maybe at some point in a few weeks' time some regular would sit there and notice and tell someone, but until then it would probably stay loose. Everyone would just work around it.

The booth still had the best view and Doe was no longer worried about the diner staff remembering him. He would be astounded if they didn't. Doe hadn't really had much time to think about his buddy at Quantico, but he didn't think that the guy's recruits were going to be getting their field exercise. However this thing worked out Doe didn't think there was going to be any doubt in anyone's mind that he had been in town on that particular weekend.

Doe sipped his coffee and ate his burgers slowly. He watched the windows and the street beyond. Every now and then his eyes flicked up to the mirror and the view of the rear door. After about twenty minutes he spotted Eugene slide in through the back door and head over to his booth. Doe nodded a hello in the mirror and saw Eugene's mouth tighten into a scowl. Eugene sat down, opposite Doe, obscuring but not obliterating his view.

"You found me then?"

Eugene narrowed his eyes.

"I figured it would be the last place you'd expect us to look."

"I figured it was the last place your colleagues would look." Doe took another sip of his coffee, "I figured you might just decide to check it out. Are you here to arrest me Sergeant Eugene?" Doe spoke quietly and kept one eye on the waitress.

Eugene shrugged.

"That depends."

Doe waited him out. Determined not to ask what it depended on.

"Did you really see Deputy Burns out there on the road?"

Doe nodded.

"I'm sorry." He put down what was left of his burger. "It really wasn't his fault. They have a killing field set up. You come out of a bend and into fully automatic fire. Two guns. Coming the other way, they have a sniper on you for six long, straight miles."

Eugene's mouth had become a very nearly invisible, just a white line across his face.

"So, what are you telling me? What's going on?"

Doe shrugged.

"I don't know. That guy you picked up is very, very important to some very well-equipped and very nasty people. Tell me about how you picked him up. Earlier, on the phone, you said something about it being weird or something."

Eugene looked around the diner. His eyes calm and determined but his fingers tapping restlessly on the chipped plastic counter top.

"You're going to have to tell me sometime." Doe finished the last of his coffee and started on the last glass of water. "You said that you would have been worried about losing the radio 'even if picking up this guy hadn't been so weird'. What was so weird about it? I guess you don't get a huge number of strangers around here, but you must have to pick up some tourists and stuff during the summer. Kids getting into fights, DUIs or speeding or something."

"I can't tell you anything. Not until you tell me who you are."

Doe shook his head.

"Here in this town this weekend, I'm nobody. I have no ID and no status, so even if I was willing to tell you who I was it would mean nothing." He drained the glass and looked up at Eugene. "But I can't anyway. Not here. Not now. Maybe another time on another investigation but not here and now. All I can tell you is that I'm from the same side of the fence as you are."

Eugene stopped tapping.

"Not from where I'm standing. From where I'm standing you're a fugitive who badly injured one of my colleagues while escaping custody and who claims detailed knowledge of the alleged killing of another of my colleagues."

"Hey!" Doe put down his water, causing the table to tip and surprising Eugene. "Don't even start down that path, we haven't got time. I'm sorry about Deputy Mayfield but I couldn't help you from inside one of your cells. As for Burns, I had nothing whatsoever to do with that and you know it. You must have sent him out early this morning, so there's no way I could have escaped your custody and still caught up with him and killed him."

"You could have killed him before we picked you up..."

"And then I came here for breakfast and just waited for you to arrest me? Come on Eugene, we don't have time for this!"

Eugene stared at Doe for a few seconds, his fingers still tapping on the table then he seemed to make a decision. Once it was made he relaxed.

"After all this is over we're going to have to work out what we're going to tell everyone about my meeting you here," He put both hands flat on the table, "but in the meantime, I guess I'll have to trust you because I know you can't have killed Burns. He was still in the Department building when you were arrested and he was well out of town by the time you escaped. I guess you could be lying about him being dead, but mostly I'm going to trust you because I think you're right. Something bad is coming and I can't get anyone at the station to take it seriously."

*

Doe signaled the waitress for more coffee.

"So, tell me about the arrest."

Eugene had been off shift when they had picked up the guy. A couple of cops had spotted him a little before dawn on a beach a couple of miles out of town. He had been dragging a black inflatable dinghy through the surf. The cops had been on their way back into town after dealing with a domestic disturbance. It had been dumb luck. The road they were driving was usually empty. It led nowhere except to a couple of isolated homes and it was very late and very dark. The guy's dingy had washed up on a stretch of beach near a small inlet. The river cut down through the trees, under the road and then across a couple of hundred feet of beach before the sea came in and collected it. The road followed the coast. It had to sweep inland to get around the inlet and then it turned back out to track the ocean shore again. The cruiser's lights had reflected off the sea and then quartered the beach as they made the turn inland. They had swept across the sand and had lit him up, out in the surf, trying to push the boat back out to sea.

The patrolmen thought that looked odd, so they had stopped to find out what was going on. As they got out of the car the man had turned briefly towards them and then thrown something that looked like a cellphone into the sea. The two cops had decided that was plenty enough of a reason to bring him in.

The guy had offered no resistance. He was carrying no ID and no money. It was strange, but no one could decide if it was a crime. By seven am, when Eugene came on shift, it had been decided that they would turn him over to the state troopers. He may or may not have committed a crime. They would hand him over and let someone else decide. It was then that they had discovered that they had no communications.

The phone lines worked fine in town. They could call their homes, they could call out for coffee, but they couldn't raise anyone at Heath Haven or the mainland. They didn't panic, didn't even break sweat. The phone lines had gone down before. Sometimes trees fell onto the cable out of town and snapped it. Sometimes electrical problems at one or other end of the line fried something crucial and they had to wait until it had been repaired or replaced. When it happened, they fell back onto the radio. It was annoying, but it wasn't worrying. Except, this time, when they tried to raise someone the old-fashioned way, all they got was static. They were used to losing the internet and email when the phones failed, but they had never lost the phone and the radio at the same time before. They couldn't raise anyone further away than three miles from the town limit. They had wasted over an hour trying to fix the problem in all the routine ways, but nothing worked. Fortunately, during that wasted time, Eugene had been thinking.

He had managed to persuade his superiors that the fact that they hadn't found any vehicles near the beach meant that the guy hadn't had any transport of his own. Except for the boat, and he had appeared to be trying to get rid that. He had no money either. He had to have been relying on someone local to shelter him or to get him out of town or to provide him with the means to do those things for himself. The shortest route from the beach to town was a hiker's trail a mile and a half long. It was poorly marked and tough walking even in daylight. Their prisoner wasn't likely to have been planning to walk it in the pitch dark. Either he had been planning to walk the two miles alongside the road or he was expecting to meet someone nearby. Someone with a truck or a boat.

Eugene's superiors had agreed with his assessment. They had sent a couple of guys out to stake out the beach in case the guy's contact turned up there and they had told Eugene and a small team of Deputies to set about trying to hunt out the contact. Doe had flashed up straight away. He was new in town, no one knew him, and he had a truck. It wasn't a certainty that Doe was their man but they all agreed that he was worth talking to. They had no idea what was going on, but their location near the Canadian border and the fact that their prisoner seemed to have arrived by sea, meant that there was a chance that they were looking at something with international or smuggling connections. 'International connections' was shorthand for 'Terrorism', so they had come for Doe hard.

The arrest had appeared to go smoothly but that hadn't calmed their nerves. They hadn't been able to re-establish landline or radio communications so they decided they needed to establish a physical connection. They sent the car to Heath Haven to report and get help. They had noticed with increasing unease the way that both of their prisoners in the cells watched all this with calm indifference.

They had interviewed the first guy a couple of times. He had sat in relaxed silence through each interview giving them nothing to work with. Then Doe had escaped and all hell had broken loose.

No one could work out what to do. All leave had been canceled. Every member of the department had been called in, but that was a smaller force than usual. A third of the department was out of town in Seattle. There was a protest against some banking conference and the cops on the mainland had reached out, asking for help. The overtime had been too good to turn down and the Department hadn't expected it to cause any problems. They still had more than enough manpower to deal with the usual rough and tumble of a Seal Harbor weekend.

They were left with twenty-nine Deputies, three detectives, the chief and a couple of support staff. One detective and two Deputies had proved impossible to contact. They were probably out of town for the day. That left thirty-two. The chief was worried that the town would panic if they found out that there was an escaped prisoner on the loose and that there was no way to call for help. Cops had quartered the town in the five remaining squad cars looking for Doe, but everyone had been told not to approach the local businesses. The civilian tech guy had opened up every piece of communications equipment the department had. He had used every spare part in the building, but by noon they had been no further forward and by one pm, almost half of the department was manning the phones taking calls from townspeople wanting to know why they couldn't get a phone call out of town.

*

"OK." Doe played with his empty coffee cup. "The guy comes ashore with a phone and a number to call to get picked up. He's in a little rubber boat so he can't control where he washes up but that's OK because all he has to do is call them when he lands. He makes the call and a small army will come out and pick him up, but then he bumps into your guys while he's still got his feet in the water. So, what does he do?"

Eugene signals to the waitress and orders two more coffees. Doe thought he looked like he needed something stronger than caffeine.

"He ditches the phone so that we can't use the data on it and then he comes along quietly."

"Very quietly. Like someone who knows he isn't going to be locked up for long."

Eugene nodded.

"Yep, I've seen it before. Jackasses who know that the way they were picked up looks suspicious, but also know they have a perfectly good reason for whatever they were doing. Sometimes they enjoy stringing us along. They think that making us look dumb makes them look smart."

Eugene took a swig of his coffee. Doe pushed his to the side and leaned carefully on the loosened table top.

"Except..."

“Except what?” Eugene was still sipping his coffee.

“Except he didn’t lawyer up. Dickheads who want to make your Department look foolish might clam up but not before they get their lawyer on the way. Without him they’re waiting for you guys to prove that they’re innocent and, not meaning to impugn your abilities, but that could take forever.”

Eugene’s eyes flashed but he conceded the point. He wasn’t about to argue that sitting around in a cell waiting for the cops to prove that you haven’t done anything wrong was a clever move. It’s not that if you are innocent it wouldn’t probably happen eventually, it’s just that cops aren’t really wired to work that way. They look for the things you have done, not at all the things you haven’t. Added to that they are usually very busy. From their point of view if you’re locked up, you’re safe, and if they don’t know what you did then it probably wasn’t that bad. They normally have lots of people to deal with who aren’t locked up and who are doing things that they consider to be bad. Sitting in your cell waiting for them to let you out you would fall a long way down in their list of priorities.

“Maybe he had time on his hands.”

Doe flashed a grudging smile. Eugene put down his coffee and continued.

“Or maybe he knew that when he didn’t turn up his friends would start looking for him. He knew that they’d send his lawyer and he knew that his lawyer would prove that however suspicious it all looked it was perfectly innocent. He didn’t lawyer up because he knew the guy was already on his way. He knew that he’d be straight out of jail grinning and calling us fools.”

Doe glanced at the window.

“Oh, he knew they were coming alright, but they aren’t sending his lawyer. My bet is that they got some kind of confirmation that he was on his way. A radio signal or something to say he was on the beach. You could do it with a torch or a lantern from the deck of the ship. Two flashes means he’s in the water. Three means he’s on the beach.

“He’s in a small boat and the currents are strong so they can’t be sure where he’ll wash up but that doesn’t matter. They know he’s on land. All they have to do is wait for his call and drive over and pick him up."

"Except he didn't call because he through his phone into the surf."

Doe nodded.

"To stop you guys getting hold of it."

Eugene shrugged and took another massive slug of coffee.

"So, when the call doesn't come in everyone moves onto plan B. They jam your communications and set up the roadblock to isolate the town. Getting him ashore was always going to be a risk. They knew it could go wrong and they put people in place to help him whatever happened."

Doe pushed his still half full coffee cup away and stood.

"I don't know who they are or why he is so important, but I do know that they are going to come for him. They aren't sending a lawyer. They're going to break into your Department building and take him and you and your colleagues are not going to stand by and let that happen. I'm sure you're all great at your jobs and committed and dedicated, but from what I've seen you're out-manned and hopelessly out-gunned. If you try to stop them there's going to be a bloodbath."

*

Eugene was shaking his head.

"I don't buy it. I can get with the idea that he's here illegally and that he's important enough for there to be some kind of reception committee. A group in place here to help him get out safely once he lands. But it's a big step from that to believing that they're willing to attack a whole Police Department and bust him out."

Doe sat back down. He had thought that the hard work was over.

"They already killed Burns."

"I only have your word for that, and you are the only one today who has incontrovertibly committed a serious crime."

Doe nodded.

"OK. There's the radio and phone blackout. That means they're stepping things up."

Eugene shook his head.

"They might have put that in place before he came ashore. It might be part of their exfiltration plan. It certainly doesn't have to be a change or an escalation."

Doe nodded and thought for a minute.

"OK. Treat me like a witness. Not one you believe, not one you disbelieve. Just a witness. Ask me the questions and make your own assessment based on my answers."

"You might lie about it all."

"We got past this. Something bad is happening. You decided to trust me. This isn't about whether I'm lying, it's about whether my assessment is right or not."

Doe didn't need any more coffee, but he reclaimed his cup and took a swig anyway.

"Plus, you're a cop. If you're a good one you should be able to tell whether I'm lying or not."

Eugene thought it over.

"OK. What was Burns vehicle plate number?"

Doe told him.

"But I could have watched him leave. I could have seen him through the Department windows or I could have memorized the plate numbers in the yard when you brought me in."

Eugene drummed his fingers on the table top again.

"Was there a beverage on the go? In Burns' car. Did he have a drink?"

Doe nodded.

"That's a better question. There was a Diet Coke on the floor of the cruiser. It looked like it was mostly full when it spilled."

Eugene nodded to himself.

"OK. The roadblock. Describe it."

Doe recounted his impressions of the roadblock in a bare-bones format. He explained the locations of the personnel and of the vehicles. He detailed the weapons, but he barely described the vehicles themselves or the appearance of the guys.

Eugene sucked it all up, looking more and more perplexed as Doe spoke. Doe figured he was a little torn. The description was puzzling.

The same details that had worried Doe were confusing Eugene. There were enough weird points about the way they had set up to make Eugene think that Doe must be telling the truth. But if Doe was telling the truth then the design and execution of the roadblock was professional, but half the crew were acting like amateurs.

There was the added layer. Once Eugene accepted that Doe was describing the roadblock accurately then it became obvious that they weren't out there just to watch what was going on. They were there to stop anyone leaving or entering town, and if Doe was telling the truth about Burns then they were there to stop people by killing them. Maybe by killing them regardless of who they were. Killing them just the same if they were cops or harmless civilians.

Doe finished up and waited, careful only to describe what he had seen, not to offer his interpretation.

"And what about the guys that you took prisoner?"

Doe started up again. He described their behavior, the way they had been watching the Police Department, their routes and the efforts they had made to stay unseen. Then he gave Eugene an edited version of his attack in the car wash. He described their weaponry and the phones and the Sat Nav device and explained how he had retained the SIM cards for future evidence. He told him about following the Sat Nav trail to their camp and then coming back through town and out to the road block.

Again, the detail confused Eugene. Doe could tell that the weapons had registered immediately. The guns were exactly the kind of thing that a well-financed group would buy if they were trying to offer generic weaponry to an extremely serious group of professionals. It would be way too tough to try to source and supply every individual's personal choice of equipment. Much easier to buy each item in bulk, but that meant they had needed to choose items that wouldn't be unacceptable to any of them. Those kinds of weapon suggested that the guys they had hired were ex-special forces at the least. You didn't hire that kind of mercenary in large numbers unless you were expecting trouble. Serious trouble.

Doe's retention of the SIM cards was a further corroboration of his good guy credentials. The actual SIM cards were wedged under the seat of Doe's stolen bike alongside the three guns. If Doe had been wrong and Eugene had decided to arrest him, Doe hadn't wanted to be taken into custody carrying two unexplained SIM cards and three guns. Doe didn't have physical evidence to prove his story, but if Eugene was trusting Doe then the SIM cards existed and if they existed then Doe was a good guy. It was a self-reinforcing circle but in the world of psychology even self-reinforcement is reinforcement.

Eugene nodded some more.

"OK. Now the camp."

Doe took a breath, glanced at his watch and started again. He described the road, the few miles of bumpy terrain and then the smooth, graded track. He walked Eugene into the woods and up to the clearing and he described the fence and the layout of the camp. He told him about the sentries in the tower and the camouflage on the roofs and the aerial and the cam-netting. He described the vehicles he saw and the people.

Then he walked Eugene up to the gate and described the sentries. He described the way they held their guns. He described their equipment and the desert camouflage fatigues they were wearing. He described the fork truck and the block of concrete and the way the slope on the track had been leveled.

He walked Eugene back out through the woods. He told him about the encounter with the foot patrol. He described the way they had moved, the way they had formed up and what he had seen of their equipment. The boots, the desert fatigues.

Eugene started to smile a little. He figured Doe was telling war stories. Most soldiers did it. Not exactly embellishment, usually not lying exactly, just making sure that if something serious happened it was included in the story. It didn't have to be relevant, didn't have to be germane. If it was cool and it was dangerous, it would make the cut. Doe noted the assumption, but he had a point to make. He carried on without correcting it.

He broke off after the patrol moved away and waited for Eugene to comment. Eugene made a little movement of his head, like an owl with a sore neck. Then he sat up straight and shook his head.

"Nope. It's still not there. They might have just come to escort the guy off the beach, to get him safely to the mainland. They could be sitting around up there waiting, wondering what to do now that their guy is locked up. They might be keeping everyone busy because everyone knows that idle soldiers cause trouble. It doesn't mean that they're going to bust him out."

"OK." Doe didn't agree but he had other points to make and other cards to play. "But you agree that if they were going to bust him out, then these aren't the kind of guys who will spirit him out in the dead of night or wait until you're moving him? These are the kind of guys who will come in through the front door and kill everyone they see?"

Eugene nodded.

"I guess so. But that's still a big step. Lots of dead cops, lots of publicity, big manhunt."

It was Doe's turn to nod.

"You understood the deployment at the roadblock?"

Eugene did the sick owl thing with his head again.

"Yep. They have a mile-long kill zone and they're set up to take out anything on the road."

"And they have proved themselves willing to use it. Willing to kill people leaving town."

Eugene shook his head.

"They've proved themselves willing to kill cops. Maybe they set up like that to stop us getting in or out. Maybe if they see a civilian they'll roll backwards out of the way at the last minute, make it look like they're playing some kind of prank, trying to freak people out. People would be pissed but probably not angry enough to report it. Probably not here and certainly not in Heath Haven after they've sat for the whole journey cooling down and getting less and less het up."

"And the guns? They're the guns you buy for elite professionals and you don't hire thirty of those just to walk someone off a beach."

Eugene was more certain here. His head shake was much more emphatic.

"No dice. There are plenty of terrorists out there with more money than sense. And the mercs are hardly likely to say, 'no thanks, that's fine, four of us will be plenty.'"

Doe glanced out of the window at the parking lot and then he swept his gaze around the room. If he couldn't convince Eugene within the next couple of sentences, then he was going to have to leave quickly. Eugene might trust him, but he wasn't going to let him out of sight. If Eugene wasn't going to help him, then Doe would have to ditch him and he would have to do it quickly. He couldn't sit around in the diner all afternoon, he needed to be out there stopping them.

"What about their uniforms?"

Eugene looked across at Doe.

"What about them?"

"You're ex-army, right?" It was in everything that Doe had observed about the man. The way he moved, the way he held himself, the haircut, the equipment, everything.

Eugene nodded.

"So, what would you be wearing in this environment? Lots of trees, temperate climate."

"Woodland battledress."

"And outside of the desert? Under what circumstances would you wear desert cam fatigues?"

Eugene's eyes widened a little.

"Only one thing I can think of. Urban warfare."

"Which means what?"

Eugene put down his coffee cup.

"You're right. They're going to attack the town."

*

Doe stood up again, impatient now. Eugene sat where he was, looking up at him.

"Come on!" Doe was sure he had convinced Eugene. He couldn't understand the delay. He turned away, heading for the door. Eugene picked up his coffee back up and stared after him. Doe stopped after a couple of paces and turned back towards the table.

"Come on! We have to move him. We need to get him out of your cells and we need to do it now."

Eugene looked back down at his coffee.

"He's safe enough."

"Listen. They want that man and they're willing to kill anyone they need to in order to get to him. If he stays in those cells they're going to get him out and take him back to their fortress in the hills and they're going to kill plenty of your people doing it."

Eugene put his coffee down.

"I believe you."

"So, you know that we have to move him. It's not just about not letting them win. It's about stopping them from attacking your Police Department. If we can get him out of there and let them know that we've moved him, then we might be able to save your colleagues." Doe turned to the door again. He was impatient to be active.

"Yes, we have to move him, but we have time, we have at least eight hours. We can make a plan."

Doe stopped and turned back once again. His eyes narrowed as he appraised the cop before him.

"What part of the Army were you in?"

Eugene smiled.

"The Rangers. This is what we do. Hostage recovery, all that shit. If these guys are ex-special forces, and I agree, everything seems to suggest they are, then they'll do it the way we would have done it. We literally wrote the field manual."

Eugene took another sip of his coffee. Doe walked over and sat back down beside him. Both men stared out of the diner window at the empty black top heading out of town.

"They'll wait 'til it's dark. Full dark, not twilight. It'll be midnight at the earliest. They'll want the darkness and they'll want to catch us on our least well-manned shift. Then they'll hit the power if they can, and these guys sound as if they can. If they can block our radio signals they can hit the power. They'll use the dark and some flash bangs and night vision to take the building with minimum resistance."

Doe started to nod, to settle back, then he stood up and grabbed Eugene's arm.

"You might be right about the field manual but you're wrong about their plan."

Eugene started to shake his arm free, but Doe pointed out of the diner window. Fifty yards down the street the two pickups from the road block were lined up on the shoulder.

"They're bringing in their perimeter. What would that mean in your book?"

Eugene stood quickly and headed for the door.

"It means they're preparing to attack."

TEN

They pulled out of the parking lot slowly. Doe was sitting in the back of Eugene's cruiser. They thought that would look less suspicious. The four guys in the pickup might not be manning a roadblock any more but they would still be watching. The sight of Eugene tearing out of the diner parking lot in a cloud of burnt rubber with an unknown civilian in the front seat of his cruiser was liable to tip them off that something odd was going on.

It made Doe a little nervous to be back there. There were no door handles, and there was no way to open the windows. A metal mesh separated him from the driver's compartment. If the car was attacked en route, or if Eugene changed his mind or got distracted, Doe would be trapped in there. It was uncomfortable, but he had endured worse. Once they were on Main Street Doe rapped on the mesh to get Eugene's attention.

"You need to drop me about three blocks from the department building."

He met Eugene's eyes in the rear-view mirror.

"Are you bailing on us?"

Doe shook his head.

"Drop me at a corner and then go to the Department and get our guy and drive back to the same corner. All being well I'll meet you there and we can drive him out somewhere and stash him."

Eugene glanced at the road and then looked back at Doe in the mirror.

"You are, you're bailing. You're gonna run while we're distracted and the roadblock is down. You're gonna leave us to it and I don't even know for sure that you're not involved. Even if you're not involved here you could be balls deep in something at least as bad as this somewhere else."

Doe was watching the side streets looking for the one nearest to the road where he had parked his pickup when he had first arrived in town.

"No. I'm not."

"So, come into the yard with me. I agree that you shouldn't come into the building. There are way too many people in there who want to arrest you, but you'll be safe enough in the car."

Doe shook his head again.

"You're not thinking. We need to get rid of the other sentry vehicle. We need them to know that we've moved him, but we can't let them follow us. If I don't stop them they'll just tail us to wherever we're going to stash the guy and radio in our new location. They'll attack us there instead. It might save your colleagues, but they'll still get their guy and the two of us will still end up dead."

Doe glanced out the side window. They were getting close to the Department building.

"Do you have any plastic restraints in the vehicle?" Doe looked uselessly around the interior of the cruiser. He was sitting where the prisoners sit. The last place you would store any equipment would be in the same place as you put your prisoners. Eugene glance up and nodded and passed him a couple of over-sized cable ties through the wire mesh.

"OK. Stop here. Drop me off and give me fifteen minutes and then come back and pick me up. Stop right here. Believe me. One way or another I will be here. You won't have to look for me."

Eugene looked back in the rear-view mirror again, but he looked past Doe and out of the rear of the car. He was looking back up the road, looking at the pickups parked on the shoulder in the distance. He pulled the cruiser over to the curb and scooted over the center console and got out of the passenger side door. He pulled the handle on the back door, letting Doe out of the car and then scooted back over the center console and pulled away. Doe was impressed. He had done it all quickly enough. The driver's door never opened. To the guys in the pickups it would have looked like the car slowed down, but the driver never got out.

*

Doe jogged the streets. He wasn't expecting any police patrols and he knew that the civilian population weren't looking for him, so he risked running in order to save some time. He was dressed in denim and plaid. Hardly sensible jogging attire. He guessed that even if he had been known in town, if someone had seen him they would have asked him what he was doing. They might have done it out of concern. A quiet, 'is everything OK?'. He was drawing attention to himself, but the streets were empty and he needed to get to his truck quickly. He turned into the road with the low-slung, four-bedroom, ranch style house with the twin garage and reclaimed his dark blue pickup. He might not be worried about attracting attention, but it wasn't something he was trying to achieve so he stuck the truck in reverse and pulled away as quickly as he thought he could manage without making the tires squeal. He pictured the nine-one-one call. Some harassed deputy at the Department building picking up a phone and getting a call from the neighbors, Janice and Jimmy. 'Someone is stealing his truck, we thought it was in the garage, but it wasn't and now someone is stealing it'.

Doe imagined the officer trying to sound interested, trying not to tell them that with everything they had going on at the moment, it would be days before they would get around to something as mundane as a possible auto-theft. He drove down to the junction with Main Street and parked facing away from it, the nose of his truck pointed back toward the street he had just left. He left the motor running and got out of the truck and walked around to the passenger side. He raised his boot and kicked at the door mirror until he snapped it off and fell to the ground. He picked it up, checked for damage to the mirrored surface and when he saw that it was intact he walked over to the opposite side of the street and propped it up against the curb.

Doe walked back to the truck and got back into the driver's seat. He looked through the passenger window at the mirror in the gutter on the other side of the street. He could see a portion of Main Street heading back into town, but the view wasn't good enough for his purposes. He got out and adjusted the mirror a couple of times before he was satisfied. He got back into the truck, sat down, put the pickup into reverse and waited.

It was seven minutes before he saw his first car and ten minutes before he spotted the pickup he was waiting for. The second sentry vehicle, on its regular patrol route. It turned out of a downtown side street and accelerated toward him. He had mapped the route while he was squatting behind the little wall on the mini-mall roof earlier in the day. He had known that fifteen minutes would be long enough to guarantee that he would get an opportunity, but even so he had been starting to get twitchy. The truck rolled past the Police Department building and headed towards Doe. It would pass his side street and make a left at the next turning. Doe sat and waited, trying to judge the speed of the oncoming vehicle.

*

The sentry truck picked up speed on the wide lanes of Main Street. Doe's eyes were glued to the mirror propped up against the curb on the opposite side of the street. He was counting under his breath. The sentry truck looked small in the mirror and the mirror looked small all the way over on the other side of the street. Doe's foot hovered over the gas pedal and the knuckles of his hand were white where he gripped the parking brake. The sentry truck crawled on, getting very slowly bigger and bigger in the mirror.

The pickup was about sixty feet from the junction when Doe released the parking brake and floored the gas. His pickup shot backwards, accelerating through the last ten yards of the side street and then across the width of Main Street before hitting the truck just at the point where the hood met the windshield.

Doe's truck came to a near instant stop. Ten miles an hour to a complete stop in a few inches. Doe was pushed backwards into the cushioning of the seat and his head sank into the foam of the seats headrest. The sentry truck was heavier, but it was moving forward and Doe hit it from the side. It spun sideways. The side and front airbags in the high spec'd vehicle deployed. The driver and passenger were thrown sideways and then backward by the impact.

Doe unbuckled his seat belt, got out of his truck and stepped over towards the stationery vehicle.

*

Doe approached the truck cautiously. It had side-impact protection and the passenger side window was obscured by the now deflated airbag. Doe thought that the person in the passenger seat would more likely be trying to work out what the hell was going on rather than waiting with a drawn weapon, but good habits save lives. He stepped up to the truck door and yanked it open while standing in the relative safety by the side of the rear doors. There were no shots so he stepped around, twisting into the doorway and using the momentum to throw a fast punch through white screen of the still flapping, deflating airbag. He felt the strange rubbery give of the airbag material. A dusting of powder transferred from the material to his knuckles and then he hit the side of the passenger's head. The door was still opening, pulling the airbag out of his way and giving Doe a clear view inside the cab. He used his forward momentum to push his fist through the punch and grabbed for some lose material around the guy's collar. Doe grabbed a handful of jacket and then he kicked his feet up in the air and fell backwards. All of his weight accelerated down towards the ground, traveling thirty-two feet per second faster for every second of the fall and pulling the passenger forward at precisely the same speed. The guy was wearing his safety belt. The mechanism rolled freely for a few inches, the way it was supposed to, and then it stopped hard, jerking the passenger cruelly but slowing

Doe's fall before he hit the floor. The passenger twisted inside the belt. The parts of him that could move, his head and one side of his body, moved towards the open door. He smacked his head face first into the corner of the glove-box console.

Doe stood and put a foot on the door sill. He stepped up onto the roof of the pickup. He gave the guy a quick kick to the jaw on the way past. It was a weak kick. The guy was already bouncing back into his seat, moving away from Doe and away from Doe's foot as he kicked out at him. It was weak, but the kick connected and Doe hauled himself across the pickup's roof without bothering to check whether the passenger was unconscious or not. It was easy math. He didn't think anyone could take a side-impact collision followed by a roundhouse to the jaw, and then his head bouncing off the dashboard a couple of seconds later. The kick to the chin, however weak, was just the coup de grace.

The driver of the truck was a whole extra ball of worry. Doe had been quick, but the guy had had four extra seconds to recover from the initial impact. Four seconds is a long time for a trained man. The surveillance team would not have expected such a violent collision of the quiet streets of Seal Harbor. They would have been driving carefully, checking for ambushes and stupid accidents. Doe had taken them by surprise, but well-trained men recovered from such surprises quickly. They learned that skill or they died. The guy in the driver's seat had a handgun in a shoulder holster and a machine pistol in the glove box. The crew would be equipped identically to the guys in the pickup that Doe had commandeered. Four seconds was plenty of time to recover and release a weapon.

Doe took a duplicitous route across the roof of the truck. He moved from the passenger's door towards the door to the rear of the driver and he made sure he stomped his way across the thin metal as he went. If the driver was still alert, Doe wanted him to react to the diagonal path. If he was going to be shooting, then Doe wanted him shooting blind through the roof of the truck. Doe wanted him to predict Doe sliding down alongside the rear window and coming at him from behind. Instead, Doe threw himself toward the front of the vehicle and slid down the windshield and off the side of the hood.

He stretched across and opened the driver's door and then he reached though the gap between the door and the windshield until he felt the fabric of the guy's shirt beyond the smooth, rubbery airbag. He repeated his earlier trick, grabbing a handful of shirt and falling backwards. Despite the awkward angles the guy was pulled forward and he smashed his face into the steering wheel. Doe stood up and stepped around the door and clubbed the guy a vicious jab to the side of the head to make sure he was out.

*

Doe took a second to glance up and down the street. Nothing was moving. The two trucks from the road block ambush were still sitting on the shoulder just outside of town. There was one parked on either side of the road, facing towards him. Neither was moving. He took the two cable ties from his belt and secured the wrist of each man to the truck's steering wheel. He did the driver first and then he walked the long way, around the back of the truck, away from the watching road block trucks, and secured the passenger. He bundled their wrists together and then looped a plastic strip around them and through the wheel. One cable tie for each guy. He left them sitting in the front seats of the pickup with no way to get out short of chewing off their own hands, and no chance to reach their phones unless they were double jointed and had pockets big enough to get their heads or feet into.

He frisked them, taking two more compact Tacticals from under their jackets and another Steyr from the glove box. He didn't need three more weapons, so he took the ammunition out of the guns, emptied their wallets of cash and ID and removed the SIM cards from their phones. He slipped the cash, the ID and the SIM cards into his pockets. He didn't see any way that the guys in the truck could get loose on their own, but if they did, he didn't want them to be able to use the guns, so he took the ammunition and then he threw the three guns, the empty wallets and the pieces of their cellphones into the load bed of the pickup.

Doe looked at his watch. Fourteen minutes thirty-seven seconds. He walked back to the driver's side door and peered in. He would have liked to take their shoulder holsters. Carrying handguns in the waist band of your pants is dangerous and uncomfortable. Dangerous not so much because they might go off but more because if you have to run or jump or even just twist around a little, they are liable to fall out. If they fall out at the wrong time they become useless, lost at the side of the road or down around your ankles when you want them accessible at waist level. Having a long chunky hunk of metal jammed into the waistband of your pants is just uncomfortable. No way to avoid that.

The holsters would make the guns much easier to carry, but Doe couldn't work out whether he could get them off with the guys hands tied to the steering wheel of the truck. There were some complicated looking buckles on the harnesses, but Doe couldn't tell if they were to tighten the things up or if they released them. He was about to reach in and mess about with them to find out when he spotted Eugene's cruiser.

*

Eugene swerved across the oncoming traffic lane and pulled up behind the wreck. He braked and leaned across the passenger seat and opened the door. Doe walked around the front of the cruiser and sat down on the passenger seat. He looked back through the grill between the front and rear seats of the car and nodded at the guy in the back. He was gratified to see that the guy in the fisherman's jumper was struggling to maintain his air of casual amusement. He had his hands cuffed behind his back and he seemed to be finding the jersey an uncomfortable fit. He kept squirming his arms up alongside his body and then trying to set them back down in a more comfortable position.

Eugene looked across at Doe.

"I figured if they didn't react to that," he nodded out through the passenger side rear window at the two wrecked pickups, "then they probably weren't going to rush into action when they saw me picking you up."

"Fair enough." Doe nodded. "Let's not test your hypothesis too rigorously though."

Eugene nodded and put the truck in reverse. He pulled gently away from the wrecked trucks, reversing all the way to the next junction and turning off Main Street shielded from the watching pickups by the two crashed trucks.

Doe turned back toward the guy on the rear seat, but Eugene was working at holding his gaze. Once he knew he had Doe's attention, Eugene raised an eyebrow. It seemed like he was going to be pretty prissy about procedure, but then Doe conceded, he was probably newly installed as a protector of law and order. Doe wondered what he had been like as a Ranger.

"No. I didn't kill them. They'll be fine. Probably. That's why I wanted the restraints." He continued his turn toward the back seat and made direct eye contact with its occupant, "They aren't going to be in any position to determine where we take him though, let alone to mount a rescue."

Eugene paused a beat like he was struggling to believe Doe and then he turned in his seat and looked back at the guy in the fisherman's sweater.

"So, do you think he's going to tell us what we want to know?"

Doe met Eugene's gaze. He wanted to believe that Eugene was trying to ratchet up the pressure on the guy. That he was acting a part. Trying to make them sound like two mavericks, off the leash, capable of anything. In truth, he didn't really know Eugene. For all he knew, Eugene was really suggesting they torture the guy. Or maybe he was dumb enough to think that now was a good time for a gentlemanly discussion of the situation, like it was an academic problem or something. Or worse still he was trying to set up some kind of 'good cop bad cop' kind of deal. Doe knew almost nothing about the guy in the back of the car, but he knew he wouldn't fall for that.

"I know a really quiet place we could use. It's got power and a generator and water and acres and acres of land."

Doe chose to assume that Eugene was attempting to convince their prisoner of their bad guy credentials. It was a simple choice. Making that assumption worked with Doe's preferred approach and he could always backtrack later if he was wrong. If Eugene turned out to be some kind of militia man or a part time fascist, then Doe could back right off and bring the situation back to somewhere safe.

"Well, that will give us plenty of time to find out how much Popeye the sailor man here has to tell us."

Doe saw his mistake immediately. The guy on the back-seat's eyes narrowed and he stopped fidgeting. It was like he saw a threat but one that he knew how to deal with. It confirmed some things for Doe, but it also told him that if they wanted information from the guy, they were going the wrong way about it. It told him the guy wasn't scared of torture. The guy's behavior had worried Doe up to that point, but way the he reacted to the threat of torture also told him that they weren't going to be able to threaten him.

"It doesn't matter anyway. We stash him somewhere. You lay low until the fireworks are over and then you take your truck cross-country, through the park and onto the ferry. He's just one guy. It's the other ten that did make it ashore safely that worry me - not this asshole."

It was a blatant ruse but Doe thought that it might work. Whoever the guy was, however skilled and trained he was, he had had one hell of a start to the day. He was stressed and tired and, most probably, scared. Doe felt like he had delivered the lines like the worst of the youngest, least talented daytime soap opera actors, but he figured they would be received as truth. He knew he was right when he saw the smile.

*

The other factor that Doe was relying on was the arrogance of talent. If a rapper gets a bad review they don't look at their product, they look at the reviewer. Doe figured there was a degree to which an artist needed to do that. You need to develop a thick skin to avoid agreeing with all the bad reviews and just stopping making new music. It made a kind of sense, but lots of people who thought of themselves as artists went a whole step further than that. The recognition became more important than the work. Any criticism became automatically imbecilic and intolerable in their minds. It was what made actors say, 'Do you know who I am?' at the entrances to restaurants. It was what made writers continue to churn out unpopular genre material and it was what Doe hoped to use to crack the guy in the backseat of the cruiser.

"He's worth keeping but we need to concentrate on the guys at the logging camp." Doe tried not to meet Eugene's eyes. He wanted it to look like they were partners and that they thought this was some kind of routine bullshit.

Eugene looked briefly confused but hid it with a turn back into the driver's seat.

"I agree. So, what do you think we should do next?" Doe could tell Eugene was playing for time, hoping to catch up with what was going on.

"Just like you said, I guess. We'll see if he knows any names then we'll cage him and leave him. Someplace safe until we have more time to deal with him properly."

Doe turned back around to face his prisoner, 'Never ask them a question' he heard from his training, 'Give them a choice.'

"I don't know fella," he jabbed a finger at the guy on the back seat, "Got any information about your pals that it would be worth our while extracting from you now? Or should we just dump you somewhere quiet and pick you up after we've dealt with the rest of them?"

The guy did an exaggerated roll of his eyes. Doe could have waited but wanted to look like the angry local cop.

"Oh right, I get it. You'll never tell us anything. You're a tough guy."

The guy in the fisherman's sweater snapped.

"There is nothing to tell you cretin. I don't know any of them. I don't need to know any of them. They need to know me. They are here for me, they are here to kill..." He was so angry spittle flew through the metal grill between him and Doe.

Now that his prisoner was talking it was just interrogation room crap for Doe. He didn't even look at Eugene. He just sat back down and made like he was ignoring the guy.

"Yeah, sure. You're the sergeant or the captain or whatever you sail-boys call each other. You all come ashore in your little rubber boats and meet up. Except you get yourself caught. Of course, they are here for you. If they are, they must be wondering what the fuck they have gotten themselves into."

The guy's range of movement was limited. His hands were shackled behind him and the back seat of a police cruiser is not designed to be a place where you can throw yourself around. He did a decent job though, rattling the wire mesh with his head and kicking out at the back of Doe and Eugene's seats.

"You fucking pricks don't know what the fuck you have on your hands you fucking morons!"

Doe took on his most patronizing of bored cop voices.

"Yep, sure, you're the Osama bin Laden of the herring fleet."

The assault on the steel protecting the back of their seats increased a notch.

"You imperialistic, shit-for-brains, fascist, know-nothing, shit-for-brains..."

Doe turned to Eugene, listening and talking at the same time. Trying to look like he had heard it all before but knowing that the guy's language would tell him a huge amount.

"He's OK back there. Let's roll."

*

Eugene started driving. He headed out of town towards the two waiting pickups. The guy in the back was still leaning forward. His head was resting on the metal mesh between the two sections of the cruiser. He had his eyes up as high as he could get them, looking down the road. He saw them getting closer to the two pickups and he started to smile.

Eugene dabbed his brakes a couple of times. The guy's head rocked back and then cracked into the mesh. Twice. Doe and Eugene shared a smile for the benefit of the guy in the back. He settled back onto the bench seat and looked like he was going to explode as they got closer and closer to the waiting trucks. A couple of streets before they got to the edge of town Eugene took a left. Doe watched the guy crane his neck to watch the pickups peel out of view. They stopped the car a couple of yards further down the road. Eugene did a K-turn in the road and parked up facing back towards Main Street. Doe got out and walked up to the back door, opened it and sat down next to their guy.

He worked out what he could get away with on the walk. It needed to be close to the truth. It needed to play with what the guy thought he knew. It needed to withdraw all hope and replace it with the certainty that he was alone now. It needed to do all these things, but it needed to sound fake. He needed the guy to worry for a while. He wanted him to wonder whether he really was screwed, but then he wanted him to decide that he wasn't. He wanted him to decide that his captors were fools. That his rescuers were still on their way. If he thought that he was really in trouble he would clam up. The look in his eye when Eugene had hinted at torture had told Doe that he only had one way to deal with threats. Doe's best chance was to get the guy to brag. If he could get him good and angry and if the guy still felt safe, then maybe he would say something revealing while he was trying to prove what fools they were.

"We know you threw your H&K tactical into the water. We have most of your pals. We got them at the road block. We spotted the two trucks. Those were our guys sitting in their trucks. We have all eight of them. They're sitting in the back of a truck on the other side of town with their hands cuffed behind them just like you. It's over. So why don't you tell us what you're waiting for?"

The guy outdid himself. Doe couldn't tell what the primary motivation was. He was clearly very angry, but he was also very happy. He squirmed and jerked and threw himself around the back of the cruiser. It must have hurt. He was bouncing around with his hands chained behind his back. He had little control and the handcuffs would be chaffing.

"You fucking morons! There are way more than eight of them. There are dozens of them. They will find me. They will..."

"Yeah, yeah, yeah... 'cos you're the Osama bin Laden of people smuggling..."

"They will find me!"

Doe turned and looked directly at the guy.

"Why?"

"Because I'm the rocket man!"

It made no sense to Doe. Some macho, self-deprecation nickname bullshit, but he didn't care. The guy was answering questions. There was a golden window now where he wouldn't be able to stop. How long the window remained open depended on how well Doe asked his questions and how well trained and how aware the guy in the fisherman's sweater was.

"Yeah, yeah. So how long do you think you'll be staying with us Mr. Rocket Man?"

"I'll be on your mainland by dawn tomorrow!"

"Light aircraft?"

"Helicopter."

"And where's the bomb?"

The guy looked at Doe for a moment. He was still in the spell, but something had spooked him. He wanted to answer but he didn't understand the question. Something wasn't right.

Eugene tapped him urgently on the leg. Doe looked forward. Through the windshield. He saw the two pickups from the road block flash past the end of the street and he jumped out of the car.

"They're on the move." He banged on the roof and screamed through the passenger's side window. "Go! Get him somewhere safe!"

ELEVEN

Doe knew that running away would worry Eugene, but he didn't know him well enough to know how he would react to that. Doe knew that if it had been him, he would have struggled. If his colleagues were behind him and about to be attacked by a bigger, better armed force, then leaving them and heading in the opposite direction would have been torture. He also knew that it right now it was the only choice they had and he thought that Eugene understood.

There had been no time for them to switch drivers. It would have been much easier on Eugene if he had been able to head back to help his colleagues while Doe drove the prisoner away. It would have been easier on Eugene, but it would have wasted valuable seconds and anyway, Doe didn't know his way around town. It needed to be Eugene so that he could find somewhere safe to hide the guy.

Doe backed his abilities as highly as he would any military personnel, even an Army Ranger. He would be able to do at least as much as Eugene could to save the lives of the cops at the Police Department. He turned away from the cruiser and banged heavily on the roof. He had more than three blocks to run before he could engage the enemy.

They had to get the prisoner away. There was no way the Police Department would be able to resist the raid for any length of time but equally, there was no way they could let their prisoner escape. It was in a cop's DNA. You couldn't just let a prisoner walk because someone threatened you. If someone pulled a gun on you, you shoot back. You don't just raise your hands and let them walk away with your prisoner and the guy in the back of Eugene's car obviously wasn't an ordinary prisoner. He was extremely important to a group of extremely violent guys. In Doe's mind, that made him a very dangerous guy indeed. Far too dangerous for Doe to risk letting him lose in the continental United States.

There was a serious problem with removing the guy from his prison cell and it was worrying Doe. The gang were professional, determined and they only had one job. Their focus would be to breach the building, reach the cells, recover their asset and leave. Anyone in the way would wind up dead, but they wouldn't hang around afterwards. They would be looking to get in, get out and get away. Once they found the cell empty that would all change. If their guy wasn't where they expected him to be, they would have to go looking. They would start by searching the entire building. They would have no choice. They needed to find him and they needed to be able to say that they had checked every room, behind every couch, inside every closet. Since the guys in the building would be trying to stop them, there would be a lot more killing than there would be if they could just snatch him up and run.

It's what the cops had signed up for and Doe expected that they would do it well, but it still bothered him. His plan to save them only worked if the gang were convinced that their guy wasn't in the building or if the cops knew that they didn't need to defend the empty cell. Doe either needed to tell the gang that their guy had been moved, or he needed to tell the cops to roll over and wait for the gang to leave. He turned onto Main Street and pushed his speed up to his fastest sprint.

*

Doe was not a sprinter. He was built to do pretty well at everything, not to do extremely well at any one thing. He was stronger than most, tougher than most and quicker than most but he wasn't going to win any medals over a hundred meters, or over ten thousand. He kept a constant speed for the first two blocks and slowed for the third. These weren't city blocks. The streets were wide, the buildings were low. There wasn't much cover and the lines of sight were long. He reached the block before the Police Department and dropped into a crouch.

Ahead he could see three military-grade Humvees lined up outside the Department building. He could see three men in three gun turrets, but so far, he could only hear small arms fire. Maybe the gang weren't sure exactly where their guy was. If he was locked up in his cell at the back of the building, then he would probably be safe from the big guns on top of the Humvees, but if he was being moved or if he was in an interview room, then their rounds could smash him to pieces along with the cops around him.

To Doe's trained eye the guns in the turrets looked like M-60's and as far as he was concerned they were unnecessary. They had plenty of men, they didn't need cannons on top of the trucks. It was a sign of strength that was also a sign of weakness. It meant they had planned the attack on paper and they were going to go through with the plan regardless of what they saw on the ground.

Doe could see half of the main force from where he was crouched. Fourteen men and four Humvees. The men were heavily armed and well deployed. They had an assault team and a mop up crew and covering their backs. There would be a total of eight Humvees lined up with eight M-60's, eight gunners and eight drivers. Doe knew that he could only see half their force because he knew how many people he had seen at the forest camp and he knew that any commander worth the name would deploy everyone they could on the raid. They had eight Humvees so they would send eight Humvees. Each Humvee could carry five people so they would send forty people. They would add the four guys from the roadblock and make forty-four, and then they would leave two in each Humvee, a driver and a gunner, and they would attack the building with twenty-eight men.

Doe could see fourteen. There was no doubting what their intention was. There was no chance that this was some kind of peaceful representation from local landowners with second amendment issues. These guys were in ex-military Humvees and they were dressed in current military fatigues. They had long guns in combat holds and vests with grenades and ammunition hanging from it. The equipment was indicative of trouble but the way they moved was absolute confirmation of it. They weren't marching toward the front of the Police Department with a letter of grievances and a designated spokesman. They were crouched or running or hunkered down behind cover.

The cops weren't just sitting there, waiting to find out what the gang wanted. Doe figured some kind of warning had been issued but by now everyone was firing at will. The windows at the front of the Department Building were all smashed. It was dark inside. Doe could only see occasional shadows moving within but whenever the attacking force moved he could see and hear the answering fire. The civilian trucks parked up outside the Department building were starting to look the worse for wear. There were smashed windows and holes in the doors and fenders.

The bad guys had deployed well. All eight Humvees were parked across the street facing in toward the front of the Department building. The two end gunners had swung their turrets around so that they were facing down the street. The one closest to Doe was pointing his gun almost directly at him. They were covering the rest of the trucks from any type of flanking maneuver. Any cops who were out on patrol would have to face down the big gun before they could mount any kind of rescue. The other six Humvees were arrayed in a semicircle with their guns converging on the front of the Department building.

Doe couldn't see an easy way to attack them, but he knew he had to. So far, the guys he could see were just mustering. They hadn't started the attack yet. They were using the Humvees and the civilian vehicles parked along the side of the road as cover and they were getting ready to hit the main doors. The cops only had their service pistols to fire and that was making little impact on either the trucks or the parked cars. Doe hoped that men were racing for the Department's gun room, breaking out the rifles and the shotguns. They didn't have anything to match the bad guys' weaponry, but they could do better than pistols.

Doe inched his way forward without the slightest idea of what he was going to do once he got within range of the action.

*

Doe huddled in the shelter of the last parked car. If he went any further forward the gunner, high up on the top of the first Humvee, would be able to see him moving. He checked his weapon and wracked his brain for a better plan. It would be nice to attack the trucks from the rear. To emerge from the buildings opposite the Police Department and target the backs of the Humvees. With a big enough force, you could probably take out the trucks and sweep past to attack the guys on the ground, but Doe didn't have a big enough force and he was on the wrong side of the street. If he tried to cross he would get mown down by the M-60 gunner in the turret of the first Humvee. The only way to get to the other side of the street would be to head back out of town for a half dozen blocks and make a mad dash for it. Even if he made it, the guy in the end Humvee would have spotted him. He would have to work his way house to house, back toward the Department building. Every time he broke cover they would let loose on him with the M-60. It would take hours. The entire attack would be over before he got back within a few blocks.

Try as he might to think of one, there was no other way. He was going to have to hurdle the hood of the only sedan on the street and charge the barrel of a turret-mounted M-60 machine gun. He couldn't think of a more pointless action, but he also couldn't imagine a way to be who he was and to leave those cops in the building to die without even trying to help. If he could get inside he could tell the cops that their prisoner was gone. He could tell them that they didn't need to try to defend the building. They could all fall back and let the bad guys check the building. That they could let them find out that the place was empty and leave without anyone getting killed.

He said what probably passed for a prayer. A small repetition of a probably apocryphal exaltation from a marine sergeant to his World War Two troops. Then he started to stand. As he straightened up he heard the whine and saw the trails as two rockets emerged from an upper story window of the police department and detonated above the street. The flares faded in the bright sunshine, but it was enough to make the turret gunner duck and turn slightly. Doe took his unexpected chance and was on the hood of the sedan and diving for the side of the Humvee before the gunner turned back around and started firing. The three vehicles behind Doe danced and jerked as the shells hit them but Doe was too close for the big gun to be effective. The barrel was nearly two feet long and Doe was only a foot away. He was winded, holding on to the side of the truck with one hand and firing up at the gunner with the stolen pistol in his other.

*

It still wasn't easy. Or it shouldn't have been. He shot the man in the turret cleanly in the face, avoiding the combat helmet and the ballistics armor. It was a lucky shot. Doe couldn't really aim from where he was, hanging on to the side of the truck, but he had been trying to shoot the guy and Doe found that the more time he put in on the range, the luckier his shooting got.

He hauled the corpse out of the gunning position, but was left lying prone on the roof of the truck with a single two foot wide hole to access the interior of a vehicle. The driver was down there and now that the legs of his gunner had disappeared up through the gun turret, he would know that something was happening.

The Humvee isn't a tough vehicle to drive. The guy down there wouldn't be some specialist without much combat experience. He would be one of the regular complement of soldiers. Armed and trained. He would be driving through some quirk of seniority. Either it was a reward or it was the punishment detail. Either the guy was being rewarded with a safer role or he was being punished by being kept away from the action. Either way he would still be perfectly capable of shooting Doe dead as he tried to climb through the hole in the rood of his truck.

To Doe's left there was a second Humvee and a second gunner already behind his own M-60. The street was noisy but not so noisy that the other gunners wouldn't have heard the M-60 on Doe's truck. They knew that something was happening down the street. The guy hadn't looked around yet but when he did he would see the empty turret and blow Doe off the roof of the truck.

It should have still been almost impossible, but fortunately, they were still working to some straight-from-the-manual, predetermined plan. They hugely outnumbered their opposition. They were prepared and they were taking the cops by surprise. Doe would have equipped each of his personnel as specialists. The gunners would have been equipped differently to the assault team who would have been equipped differently to the drivers and the mop up crew. When the gang had planned it out their commanders had gone a different route. They had assumed a dynamic situation. They had tried to cover every eventuality. They had considered the possibility that the National Guard would be there or that the cops would have been tipped off or that a local biker gang with survivalist fetishes might get involved. They had assumed the worst. They had given everyone exactly the same equipment. They had set it up so that any of their guys could fill any of the roles. It might have been a good plan when they made it, but it was awful now.

There was no reason for the gunner that Doe had just killed to be carrying the same kit as the guys who were lining up ready to storm the Department Building. He was never going to be required to leave his turret and bolster the assault team. A good commander would have changed his plans when he saw the conditions on the ground, but these guys hadn't changed a thing. Doe pulled a stun grenade from the vest of the dead gunner, dropped it through the hole in the Humvee's roof and then followed it down and shot the driver in his seat.

*

Doe had control of the Humvee but, in itself, that didn't help the guys in the Police Department. Through the windshield of the truck he watched the assault team move across the parking lot toward the building. To his left, he could see the second Humvee but the third, fourth, fifth and sixth trucks were completely hidden. They had parked in a semi-circle. He could see a portion of the seventh and eighth trucks, further down the street but most of the Humvees were covering each other. He could get back up into the turret and use the M-60 on the other trucks but he wouldn't be able to hit them all and he wouldn't be doing anything to stop the assault team that were lined up right by the Department doors

He could swing the M-60 around to target the twenty-eight men forming up around the doors but if he fired on them he would also take out anyone in the southern half of the first floor of the building. The gun wasn't a precision weapon. Once he started firing everyone in front of it would die and the guy in the second Humvee's turret would start to fire at him. Doe figured there was only one thing to do, but before he did it he could level up the odds a little for later in the day.

Doe pulled the dead driver from his seat and stripped him of weapons. He dragged the body to the back of the vehicle and stacked his liberated weapons on the passenger seat, then he stepped up into the gun turret and turned his M-60 until it faced the only Humvee he could see. He swept his gun from the turret of the second Humvee to the driver's window and back again with his finger clamped on the trigger the whole time. He knew that there was nothing in the armor of the other vehicle that was capable of resisting the M-60. That wasn't the way the US military worked. The US military had the best equipment but there was a hierarchy. The Humvees could take a hit from an infantry weapon and an armored vehicle could take a round from a Humvee and tank could take a shell from an armored vehicle, but a US tank could take out a US tank and a Humvee could take out a Humvee.

Once he was sure that nothing and no one could have survived in the second Humvee, he dropped back through the turret and hustled into the driver's seat. He buckled himself into the seat extremely carefully and stuck the truck in gear. He jammed the gas pedal flat to the floor and the Humvee lurched into motion. As soon as he cleared the cover of the second, dead Humvee he felt the rounds start to hit him from the third and then from the fourth truck in line. It was a scary feeling but by then he was already hunkered down behind the dashboard, braced for the moment when the big truck slammed into the front wall of the Police Department. It was a heavy truck, but it was old and its acceleration had never been astounding. It hit the front wall slowly but with a lot of momentum. It punched through the wall and got jammed up as the reinforced turret assembly ground against the second story. It came to a halt half in and half out of the building. Doe opened the passenger's side door and stepped out of the vehicle. He was shielded from the main force entering through the department's double doors by the whole body of the truck.

*

Doe grabbed the driver's and gunner's rifles and looked around. The cops had already taken a beating. The squad room was a mess. They appeared to have tried to form the desks into a makeshift fort, but the thin wood and metal hadn't helped them much. There were bodies sprawled across the overturned desks. A group of guys was firing from behind the furniture in the center of the room and there was sporadic fire coming from the top of the stairs.

The bad guys had formed into two disciplined groups. They were stationed just inside the front doors of the building. One group was preparing to move diagonally across the room, past the desk fort and into the cell block at the back corner. The other group had taken defensive positions and were laying down covering fire. It was a good deployment, but it had already been shaken by the appearance through the building wall of one of their own Humvees. A couple of the covering-fire team were swinging around to target the truck but like good soldiers, the majority were sticking to their original roles. Doe went to the first of his captured rifles and fired across the room towards the doors.

The assault team dived for cover and the guys behind them turned all their firepower on the Humvee. Doe covered his head with his hands and waited for the first onslaught to peter out.

*

Upwards of twenty men all firing fully automatic weapons in a single direction makes a hell of a noise and if you happen to be the direction in which they are firing then time essentially stands still. Even tucked in behind the V8 block of the Humvee's engine, Doe was utterly incapacitated. He couldn't move, he couldn't hear, it was a major effort of will to keep his eyes open. Eventually the rate of fire dropped. Some of the assault team were reloading, some had gone back to returning the sporadic fire coming from the cops.

Doe took the second of his captured rifles and stepped around the front of the truck. He knelt, braced himself against the truck's grill and aimed across the front passenger tire. He kept low and fired careful three round bursts at specific targets. The Humvee was built to be tough. In addition to the armored front wheels, there were all sorts of big chunks of metal associated with the drive train and the suspension. They were all protecting Doe from the return fire. He took down three of the suppressing-fire team in a couple of seconds and started waving frantically to the cops trapped behind the little fort of desks.

The assault team had retreated a little to find better-sheltered positions, but preparations were still in hand. They were still seconds away from moving into the room and across it toward the little cell block. The desk fort was almost directly in the way of that advance. Anyone caught behind it when the bad guys started to move was going to end up dead. Plenty of cops had died already and the whole thing was pointless. The cell block was empty. The guy was in the back of Eugene's car. There was no need for the gang to attack the Department and no need for the cops to protect it. Even if the cops had had stood the slightest of chances, the smart move would still have been to retreat and regroup. All Doe needed to do was let them know.

As Doe winged a guy in the act of pulling some kind of grenade from his vest, he saw Mathers' head pop up from behind an overturned filing cabinet. Doe signaled to him, trying to convey the fact that the cells were empty. Mathers looked stunned to see Doe there and then he looked as if he had worked something out and swung his arm around and started to fire at Doe. Doe ducked back round the front of the Humvee, out of the line of fire of both Mathers and the guys by the door. He waited for Mathers to stop firing and then stood up and fired back, not toward Mathers but across the room at the group forming up at the office doors. He fired six shots and took down another two attackers, then he ducked back down and moved once again to the front of the truck. He was still covered from fire from the doorway, but he was completely exposed to Mathers and anyone else behind the desks.

He kept up his rate of fire, but he had to let his accuracy drop. He was firing in order to keep the bad guys ducked down, behind their cover now, rather than choosing specific targets. He was looking over at the desk fort whenever he could. He was still trying to catch Mathers' eye if his head popped up, but he also hoped to get a little warning if they were going to start shooting at him again. Doe didn't see Mathers looking over, but he could imagine the cop's confusion. Doe had badly injured one of their colleagues while escaping custody. He had been, until a few minutes previously, their Public Enemy Number One. If they'd had time, his photo would have been on posters in the post office. On the other hand, they clearly had more immediate enemies to deal with and Doe seemed to be fighting that same enemy. All in all, Doe figured he had given them a no-brainer. Life behind the Humvee would be a whole lot better than life behind the desk fort.

After a few seconds, a ragged line of officers emerged from the fort. The majority headed for the strong-room door at the back corner of the building, but a few zig-zagged their way across the room towards the Humvee. Last among these runners came Mathers. He was dragging a wounded colleague by the collar.

The assault team sprang into action as soon as the cops started to move. They moved swiftly across the room, not toward the retreating deputies but directly towards the cell block. The two groups of men passed each other at a distance of about forty feet exchanging fire. A few from each side went down. Some got back up again, their vests or body armor saving them from serious harm, but a couple on each side went down and stayed down. Amongst them was Mathers.

*

Doe picked off another couple of attackers before they reached the cell block and then he took cover. He looked over at Mathers and the other fallen cops. They were almost all completely still. Mathers had lost part of his jaw and the bleeding was already starting to slow but the guy he had been dragging was still moving. It looked like he had a leg wound. He was scrabbling around on the smooth, low-pile flooring, trying to drag himself forwards with his hands and push himself along with his one good leg. He wasn't making much progress. He was hopelessly exposed, triangulated between the rescue team huddled around the entrance to the cell block and the suppressing-fire team at the door. He was stuck right out in the center of the room with just a few sticks of overturned furniture as cover.

Both the attacking teams ignored him and so did Doe. The guy was more use to the enemy alive than dead. He appeared to be unarmed and was certainly no threat to them. As long as he was alive there was a chance that one of his colleagues would do something stupid and try to rescue him. With the amount of ordnance flying around the room there was always a risk that he would get hit in the crossfire, but that was true of all of them to a greater or lesser degree. Doe turned his fire to the guys around the cell block doorway and the bad guys split theirs between the three groups. The cops at the top of the stairs, those at the vehicle yard doors and at Doe and the couple of cops who had made it to the Humvee from the desk fort.

TWELVE

Doe turned to the one of the cops sheltering next to him in the protection of the Humvee.

"Is there any internal communication? Do the office phones still work in here?"

The guy just stared at him. He had 'Brel' stenciled on a faux brass name badge on his chest. Doe tried to stay calm. He could understand the cop's reaction. The guy's whole world had exploded in just a few minutes. Friends and colleagues had died and the man he had been hunting was now, apparently, his ally. It wasn't that he was struggling to decide whether or not to trust Doe, it was just that his brain was failing to deal with it all. He wasn't trying to work out whether to answer Doe, he just couldn't process the question

"Quickly!" Doe couldn't give Brel time to recover. People were still dying and any time now the rescue team were going to notice that the cells were empty and come hunting. "Is there any way that we can talk to the people upstairs?"

There were overturned desks all around them. The nearest was lying on its side. Its contents were scattered around on the floor by Doe's feet. Doe vaguely remembered hitting it as the Humvee had smashed through the outer wall. He had an image of a 'World's Best Dad' mug flying past the windshield as he was jerked forward in the seat harness. The desk phone was a big thing with lots of speed-dial buttons. It was upside down with the handset a foot or two further away at the end of a long, tangled, coiled wire. Brel's eyes moved towards it.

"Yes! The phones! Are they still working? Can we call upstairs?" Doe resisted the urge to grab the guy by the shoulders and shake him. "Do the internal phone lines still work?"

The guy nodded. Doe swung the butt of his rifle out and hooked the coiled cable and pulled the phone toward them.

*

Doe looked around the room. The attackers at the door were still maintaining a low level of suppressing fire. The rescue team were clustered around the entrance to the cell block and were shooting when they saw a target. The majority of the cops he could see were clustered around the yard door. They could leave any time they wanted to. All they needed to do was head out into the yard and scale the back fence. All Doe needed to do was tell them that there was no reason to stay and they could be out and safe in a few minutes.

There were five surviving cops huddled with him behind the truck. Provided he could get them to listen to him, and provided they were capable of understanding, then Doe could get them out through the smashed front windows and down the street to safety. The back of Doe's Humvee was jutting out into the street. If he and the cops hugged the Department Building wall they could use it as cover all the way to the corner of the block.

It was the cops and civilians upstairs that worried Doe. They were trapped. There was an unknown number of them and they couldn't walk out of a door. They would have to jump out of the window. Doe figured that some of them would be able to do what he had done earlier in the day. Some of them would be able to leap from the window, over the fence and get away, but mixed in with the fitter cops there would be civilian staff. There would be older, portlier detectives and there would be visitors and maybe a few guys who were already injured from the initial assault. They wouldn't be able to make the jump or climb the fence. They were really trapped.

They probably didn't realize it, but the clock was about to run down for the guys on the second floor. Any minute now the rescue team would find out that the cells were empty and the first thing they would do would be to head upstairs. Doe couldn't work out what was taking them so long. Maybe they thought their guy had managed to hide somewhere in one of the bare eight-by-eight cells. Maybe they were blowing the locks on each of them and checking under the inch-thick plastic-coated mattresses.

Whatever the hold up, soon they would be out of the cell block and then they would head upstairs. They would drive the cops and civilians into the shelter of the offices that surrounded the upper room and then they would check each of those rooms in turn. They would kill everyone they found in each of the rooms and then they would come back downstairs and check the empty rooms on the first floor. Unless Doe could get them out, everyone left upstairs would die.

Doe seated the phone handset back in its cradle and then picked it up. He turned toward Brel.

"These guys are looking for the guy who was in the cells with me. They won't stop until they find him, but they won't find him because Sergeant Eugene took him out of here to give you guys a chance." He thrust the handset into the guy's hand. "They're going to go upstairs next. They will kill everyone up there in order to find this man. Dial a number and get me on the line with whoever is in charge up there."

Brel looked uncertain, but at least that meant he was thinking.

"I can still get them out of there, but we have to do it now."

Across the room a figure emerged from the cell block and shook his head. The two attacking teams switched roles. The group near the cell block started to fire at the Humvee and at the guys huddled by the yard door. The men by the front doors started checking and stowing equipment, loading weapons and gathering ammunition. They were preparing to storm the stairwell.

*

Brel pressed some buttons and said a few words and then handed the phone back to Doe. Doe put the handset to his ear.

"Hello, who's this?"

"Detective Floyd."

"You're in charge up there?"

There was a pause.

"I guess so. As much as anyone. The Chief is dead."

Floyd sounded reasonably calm. Doe guessed that the man was in control more by dint of his ability to deal with the situation than because of his rank.

"OK." Doe shifted the handset to his other ear and took a look around the front of the Humvee. "They're here looking for one of your prisoners. He isn't in the building, but they don't know that. They can't leave without being certain. Do you understand?"

The team by the doors were ready now. They increased their rate of fire and directed it all up the stairwell. The top of the staircase was peppered with bullet holes and the wooden rail alongside the steps was a shattered mess of pale wood.

"I think so." Floyd's voice was still calm. Doe waited a beat. "They're coming up here."

Doe couldn't tell whether Floyd was reporting what he was seeing or explaining his understanding of Doe's words.

"And?"

"And... they're going to try to kill us."

Doe liked his use of the word 'try'. In Doe's book that was the right attitude.

"More importantly Detective Floyd, there is no reason for you or any of your colleagues to try to stop them. They will check every room and they will not find their man, then they will come back downstairs and leave. There is no need for any of you to die up there. You have nothing to protect."

Doe waited an agonizing few seconds. The first two men from the rescue team were at the bottom of the staircase firing directly up into the second floor.

"I guess we have." Floyd sounded both resigned and determined. It was some kind of macho, Alamo shit to Doe but he guessed that if the guy really thought he was trapped then it wasn't the worst attitude. "We can't all get out through the windows. There's a couple of kids up here and Ms. James is over eighty and a few of the guys have been hit."

Despite himself Doe allowed a small pause.

"So, I think we do have something to protect."

"No, listen. We can get you all out, you just need to do what I tell you." Doe outlined his plan and hung up. He hoped that the people up there would follow Floyd and he hoped that Floyd would trust him, but most of all, he was really hoping that they wouldn't all decide to be heroes and die up there.

*

Doe turned to the five cops by the Humvee and told them that he needed them to leave, but that they couldn't sneak through the window and head off down the street. He told them that he needed their help to get the guys out of the second floor and that the first thing he needed was for them to make a break back across the room towards the door to the yard. They didn't like the idea. They looked at him as if he had suggested they storm the Kremlin armed with peashooters. Doe explained his plan. He explained why he needed them and he told them that he was going to give them some serious covering fire to give them a chance of making it. Then he stepped away from them and headed back, further into the cover afforded by the side of the truck. He stayed low until he got to the hole in the Police Department wall and then he stood up, preparing to scale the side of the truck. He was hoping that the M-60 mounted to its wrecked turret was still operational. As he set himself, ready to jump up onto the side of the truck, he heard the sound of a V-8 engine being revved hard and the entire discussion was rendered moot.

Doe glanced to his left and saw the third of the gang's Humvees ram the second Humvee. It hit the truck that he had raked with machine gun fire, shoving it a little to the left and then it revved its engine and pushed. The dead truck rocked back on its suspension. Its fat tires gripped the street surface and did their best to stop the vehicle from being pushed to the side. The third Humvee kept revving and kept shoving. Its own tires were slipping on the asphalt, fighting for traction. There was a grinding and squealing as the big truck was pushed out of the way. As the dead truck moved backwards the other one crept forward and Doe saw a gun turret start to swing into view.

He yelled a warning to the other cops and set off, running across the room to the safety of the yard door.

*

It was a nightmare run. The guys by the cell entrance must have communicated with the Humvee. They had been waiting for Doe and his guys to move but when Doe spotted the truck moving it had sprung the trap a little early. Doe emerged from the cover of his wrecked Humvee and felt bullets start to swing through the air around him as the guys across the room opened up. The gunner in the turret of the Humvee outside was still unsighted. The light-arms fire was scary enough but within seconds, while Doe was still only halfway across the room, the truck's M-60 opened up. At first it could only fire into the back and side of Doe's Humvee, but as his driver pushed the dead truck further out of the way, the M-60 gunner's angle opened up and he started to fire into the room itself. The wall alongside Doe started to disintegrate into splinters of baton wood and clouds of drywall. Light fittings exploded. The ceiling started to fall.

Doe hoped that the gunner was struggling with the elevation of his gun. He would be firing from a position slightly higher than the height of the squad room ceiling, so he would have to fire downwards to try to hit the lower story. He would be trying to keep the stream of bullets as parallel as possible, hoping that his guy was holed up somewhere, curled into a ball on the floor. The bullets would be coming in through the front wall and tracing a path through the room, dropping all the time. If he fired too high to start with he would hit the floor of the second story or fire over the heads of the running cops. If he fired too low and his guy was lying on the floor at the back of the building, then the gunner would run the risk of killing very guy he came to rescue. The math passed through Doe's mind as he ran for the back of the squad room, but he knew that it all meant nothing. He had no way of knowing what the gunner was thinking or what his capabilities were. There was nothing Doe could do except run and hope.

The arc of M-60 rounds raced towards him. Thankfully, the race was not about the speed of the projectiles. The race was all about how quickly the gunner's Humvee could shove the dead Humvee out of the way and open up the angle for the gunner to target Doe and the other cops and thankfully that was not a battle in which the tide was turning. The tread on the dead Humvee's tires was huge, it was being worn down and torn away by the lateral movement across the road surface, but there was lots of it and it was being torn away slowly. It was still doing a good job, still gripping the pavement. The mass of the vehicle wasn't changing either, so the big truck wasn't getting any easier to move.

The gunner's angle across the squad room unwound almost in slow motion and Doe and three of the five cops reached the corner of the room and dived for the big steel door leading into the corridor heading out into the vehicle yard. Doe looked back to see one of the slower cops go down. The fifth, frozen into inaction, was staring mutely from the rapidly disappearing shelter of the side of the jammed Humvee. Doe shoved the defending cops back into the corridor and grabbed a handful of collar on two of the cops who had followed him through the door. He waited for the third guy to scramble through the entrance and then he slammed the heavy steel door shut. A few seconds later the Humvee gunner got a clear sight and whole door started to vibrate as over five hundred rounds per minute started trying to punch their way through.

Doe breathed out and turned around in the wide corridor. He found himself facing six angry and deeply suspicious cops.

*

Doe pushed through the knot of cops and out into the yard. Brel had made it as far as the corridor and after his moment of shock behind the wedged Humvee, he seemed to be dealing with things well enough. Brel outlined Doe's plan to his colleagues and got them to join Doe in the yard. The fact that the reinforced steel door to the squad room was starting to buckle under the sustained fire could only have improved his powers of persuasion. No one in their right mind would want to be in the corridor when that door failed.

As soon as Doe cleared the exterior door he looked up. There was movement in a second story window a third of the way down the building. Doe heaved a silent sigh of relief. The guys on the second floor were following his plan. He looked around the yard and breathed a deeper, longer sigh. There were three cruisers parked up nose in at the end of the yard.

"OK." There was only one guy in the yard with sergeant's stripes. Doe picked him and Brel and pointed to them. "You two, get two of the cars lined up under the windows to the middle three offices."

He turned to the other cops.

"Give me first run and then get up on the roofs and smash any window you can see. No women and children first crap, let the guys in the room sort all that out. You don't have time. Whoever gets to the window first, get them out and then get them off the roof. If they don't get off there quickly throw them off. Better a few broken bones now than people still in the room when the gunmen burst through the door. A fall from the car roof won't kill them but those guys certainly will."

Everyone nodded but Doe knew that when they were up there it would prove harder to do than they thought. There would be screaming and jostling. People who didn't look like they needed help would barge their way to the front. There would be people frozen in corners. There would be people who stepped out of the window and just stood there in the sunlight, stopping anyone else from getting out. The guys on the outside would have to put everything else to one side. They would have to forget about fairness and chivalry. They would have to grab and haul people they knew. They would have to manhandle the people they thought of as strong as well as the people that they had always thought needed looking after. There would be the inhibition built up by years of civilized contact, morning coffees and kind words on birthdays and holidays. There would be the inhibition build up over millennia of evolution, group dynamics and hierarchies wired into their primate brains. And then there would be the inhibition born of the fear of future recrimination. It's hard to push your boss or a 98-pound, nineteen-year-old receptionist, from the top of a police car roof. Even if you save their life, you're gonna worry that they might take you off their Christmas card list.

Doe watched the two vehicles line up under the windows. Brel and the Sargent were scraping and smashing the side mirrors against the concrete of the Department Building wall in an effort to get the cars closer. Doe lined himself up for the run and took off through the yard. He pumped his arms hard, gaining as much speed as he could and hurdling his way on to the trunk of the last car. He just about maintained his momentum as he stepped up onto the roof and then he immediately had to decide whether to try to jump from the roof of the rearmost vehicle to the trunk or roof of the other car. Doe wasn't sure whether he would have been able to make it, but he did know it would have been a bad time to gamble. He took the reduction in momentum, dropped off the roof onto the cruisers hood and then accelerated again, onto the trunk of the second car and up onto the roof. Once he was on the roof he pushed himself harder. He had stayed as far from the wall as he could and now he ran a couple of steps, diagonally across the roof and hurled himself at the side of the building.

He hit the wall with his left arm wedged on the sill of a window third from the corner. He swung his right hand across and grasped the ledge under the penultimate window. He hung there for a moment, winded and stuck between two offices and then he pulled himself upright, wondering what to do.

*

He decided to try for the penultimate window. He was only one story up. If he failed the fall wouldn't hurt him much and it wouldn't hinder the escape attempt, but if he succeeded then being further toward the corner of the building could majorly improve his chances of success. For Doe, reward was usually worth some risk. He levered himself up level with both sills and then scrabbled his feet back across the concrete until he was leaning toward the further window. There was pain in his right wrist and he felt himself starting to fall. He let go with his left hand and reached it across toward the second sill pushing with his legs as he let go and he just about made it. His left hand caught on the recess lining the office window and he held on while the rest of his body swung across. He used the swing to push one foot up over the window sill and paused to gather his breath.

He had one elbow on the sill and one leg hooked over into the room. His other hand was gripping the concrete around the nearside of the window and he could feel his grip starting to fail. He looked into the office. It was empty.

He hauled himself through the window, sat up and peered across the room. He was on the floor, behind the desk, looking toward the office door. Doe had never wanted a job where you needed to put your desk facing away from the window. He understood the psychology. It told everyone coming into the room that you were focused solely on them. It made business sense, but Doe was sure that everyone sitting behind one of those desks really wanted to be facing the window.

From behind the desk he saw a closed door and an empty room. He stood and walked carefully to the office door. There were little foot wide windows either side of the door. They had venetian blinds closing them off from the reception room. Doe trusted the soundproofing of the office glass, so he creased the pressed metal blinds to make a hole to see through. It was better than swinging the whole blind out of the way and looking past it. Sometimes people would notice sound, sometimes they would notice movement. The rescue squad would be making noise and wearing comms sets underneath ballistics helmets. Doe could make a fair amount of sound without them being able to tell, but they would be alert to movement.

He peered through the gap in the slats and saw nothing. He moved a little to the right. His line of sight swept through an arc of the room. The back of the last man in a line of armed men swung into view. They were lined up to hit the office next to Doe's. The office Doe had decided not to climb into. One office further along and people would be streaming through the windows onto the roof of one of the two cruisers. Their colleagues would be helping them. Or forcing them off the roofs and into the yard and then over the fence and away to safety. People one office closer to Doe would have no help. They would face a biggish jump to safety and they were about to be interrupted by a group of armed and murderous men bursting through the door behind them. Doe hoped the office was empty.

Doe waited until the first two men stormed the office and then, silently, he opened his door and grabbed the last man in line and jerked him back through the door into his own room.

THIRTEEN

Doe had simply opened the office door a fraction of an inch and peeked through the gap. The rescue team had been lined up in front of the door to the next office. They were all facing away from him, completely focused on the door to the next office. A couple of guys had been kneeling down, facing further down the row of doors, covering the doors of the offices they hadn't yet checked, but they had already checked all the offices behind them. They had been in there. They knew they were empty.

Doe had opened his door, stepped out, put his hand over the mouth of the last guy in line. He slipped his hand between the guy's mouth and the microphone on his comms kit and pulled him back into the room. Doe used the hand he held over the guys mouth to pull him in close to his chest and he ran his other hand down the front of the guy's uniform pushing his rifle out of his grip and onto the floor. Without breaking stride, he strong armed the man across the office and around the desk, unbuckling the guys belt as he went. The guy had a side arm in a holster on the belt. The holster had multiple little clips and devices to stop anyone except him from accessing the gun, but his belt had a single, quick release buckle and when it hit the floor it took his gun with it.

Doe reached the open window and shoved the guy head first through it. There was no way he could have interrogated the guy in the room without bringing the entire rescue team smashing through the door and he couldn't keep his hand over the guys mouth forever. He watched the guy sail out of the window and start to windmill his arms as he headed for a two-story fall and a face first impact with the concrete of the vehicle yard. He watched long enough to see Brel and another Deputy break his fall and pin him to the floor. He saw them start to cuff the man. Doe glanced to his left. There were still people climbing out of all three office windows.

Doe turned back into the room. The bad guys were probably already lining up outside the nearest of the occupied offices. He needed to buy the people in that office some time and he wanted to level up the numbers a little for later. Doe picked up his prisoner's assault rifle and checked it over.

*

The rifle was another Heckler and Koch. It looked like a 416 to Doe, which would make sense. It was another special forces favorite. It was set to fully automatic and the stock was a little short for Doe, but it would do. He ejected the clip and checked it. It was a thirty-round magazine and was completely full. Either the guy had just reloaded or he hadn't had to fire yet. Doe replaced the magazine, brought the gun up to his shoulder and stepped over to the door. He stopped for a heartbeat at the door and then pushed it wide open.

Doe stepped out into the central room. He started firing as soon as he was clear of the door. He was close to the men he was shooting at, just yards away. The distance meant he could target necks and groins. He knew they were wearing body armor and helmets so there was no point aiming for chests and heads. He had thirty rounds in the gun. That gave him ten three round bursts and he intended to make all of them count.

The men in front of him were good but they were totally unprepared for an attack from the rear. They had personally swept the through the rooms behind them, they were certain they were empty. They had a second team downstairs covering the stairs. They knew no one was going to make it up from the first floor. They knew it in their bones, through all their experience and all their training, that they weren't going to be attacked from the rear. They had no defense and no reaction when Doe burst out and started shooting.

After the first few men went down, Doe started to walk carefully backwards as he fired. The movement opened up a wider angle and allowed him to pick new targets, but it also moved him further and further away from the safety of the open office door.

It was all going well until the sweep team came back out of the other office. They had followed the stun grenade through the door and they had found the room empty. They had checked behind the desk and behind the filing cabinets and then turned around to leave and then they had heard shooting. They were a three-man team and they weren't stupid. They had no idea how anyone had gotten up there, but they knew that they were under attack. They came out ready and they returned fire immediately.

Doe was seven bursts into his ten. He had seven downed bad guys and he was hoping to get another three, but the sight of the figures emerging from the office told him that it was time to leave. The new opponents were every bit as close to him as their colleagues had been. Doe would be every bit as easy for them to hit as Doe's targets had been for him and Doe wasn't wearing body armor. Then there was the math. There were three of them and only one of him.

Doe feinted towards the stairs back down into the squad room. Taking them would be suicide. The covering team were down there and most of their guns would already be pointed at the stairs ready to take out anyone who made it past the rescue team. They would cut him to pieces before he made it halfway down the steps. He had no intention of taking the stairs, but by heading toward them he hoped to draw the three guys fire toward the stairs. His ruse worked. The men started to fire ahead of him and Doe stepped back and to his left and went into exactly the same office as he had used to escape earlier in the day. Gunfire followed him as he ran towards the already open window and jumped out of it and onto the roof of a third cruiser.

*

Brel got out of the driver's side door and Doe jumped off the roof and joined him in running pell-mell for the back corner of the Department building. The window above them was filled in seconds. Uniformed figures were firing at them but they both made it safely around the corner. The windows above the two parked cruisers were empty. The cops were helping the last of the people from the upstairs windows to get over the chain-link fence at the other side of the lot. They had blankets and jackets draped over the razor wire and they were helping the smaller people, the civilians and the receptionists up onto the wire from the hood and roof of yet another cruiser.

Doe looked over at Brel.

"You got my prisoner safe?"

"Yep, he was one of the first over the wire. He swore a bit but didn't struggle too much."

Doe nodded. He imagined himself being snatched from a totally secure position and thrown face first through a second story window. Going from being in total control to a swan dive onto a concrete floor in a matter of seconds. They guy hadn't known that Doe had arranged for the two guys to catch him. As far as he had been concerned some malevolent force had scooped him up and thrown him to his death. Doe figured that if that had happened to him, there was a good chance that he wouldn't have struggled much either.

"We need to move fast." He turned to Brel, "They're going to be in those windows very soon now. It's no part of their plan to shoot at us from up there but I think I pissed them off. I think they'll shoot at anything they see down here."

Brel nodded. He wasn't the fittest cop Doe had ever met and he was already breathing hard. They set off along the yard, hugging the building wall just in case. The last person dropped over the fence as they neared the cars that were parked under the escape windows. One of the cops, Doe thought it was the guy with the sergeant's stripes, was hanging on the wire, waiting to help them. They reached the shelter of the car and then the jackets and blankets on the top of the fence started to shake and judder as bullets fired from the first-floor window hit them. The cop on the wire dropped down and Doe was relieved to see him stand and run off down the road to safety.

Doe and Brel looked at each other.

"Are there any secret trapdoors I don't know about?"

Brel shook his head.

"Do you fancy sticking around here?"

Brel shook his head again.

"It might be OK if we did." Doe had been thinking about it. He didn't think the rescue team would think that they had stashed their guy in the vehicle yard and that they had then all run away, leaving him there on his own. He figured they already knew that their target was gone because they knew that the cops wouldn't leave if he was still there. If they really believed that, then there was no real reason for them to come out into the yard.

"We could climb into the trunk of the cruisers and wait them out."

Brel just turned and looked at him the way you would look at a cat that had managed to open a cupboard door. It was a mix of 'did you mean that' and 'no that is wrong'.

"Yeah, OK, I agree." Doe looked up at the fence. "Do you think there's any better or worse time?"

Brel considered this.

"I guess we could wait a spell. Hope they move off and start looking through the other upstairs offices."

It was Doe's turn to nod.

"But not too long 'cos their friends will be coming through the door over there any minute now."

"So, you're thinking sometime around now?"

Brel smiled.

"I think that would be about right."

Doe touched Brel's shoulder.

"Go across the roof. Hit the fence near to the door. They'll be expecting us to take the shortest route. I'll be right behind you"

Brel nodded and looked over, acknowledging the advice and Doe's sacrifice.

"Thanks for getting them out of there."

Doe squeezed the cop's arm and they put their backs to the concrete wall and prepared to run.

*

Doe let Brel go first. They were going to have to hit a relatively small section of fence and before that they would have to step up onto the trunk of a squad car. Doe didn't think that they would be able to manage it side by side and one of them could end up barging the other, knocking him over and getting him killed. So Brel set off across the little yard first and Doe went second. Doe had struggled to work out which position would be safer. If you went first you would be out in front, exposed, but you would also be over the fence earlier. If it came down to reaction time from a shooter in an upstairs window, then you had a slightly better chance.

If you went second, then there was the chance that the shooters would all be targeting the guy in front of you and wouldn't be able to adjust their aim until you were already over the fence and away. Doe couldn't work it out, but his gut told him that the first man out was the safest. He let the bigger, slower, Brel head out first and then he set off after him. As they ran the few steps across the yard Doe couldn't help picturing that final scene from Butch Cassidy and the Sundance Kid. Running in slow motion and then the world freeze framing, their fate never explicitly shown but everyone knowing what happened.

He pictured it that way, but he didn't experience it that way. If anything, events seemed to speed up a little. He saw Brel leap up onto the trunk of the cruiser and reach out for the fence. He heard shooting from the opposite side of the fence. A few cops had stuck around and they had seen something in the windows behind Doe that they didn't like. They were putting down some scattered fire to try to give Doe and Brel a chance. Doe felt, rather than heard, the shooting coming from the guys in the upstairs windows. Their bullets fizzed through the air and sparked off the concrete of the yard.

He saw Brel jerk and start to crumple and then Doe was up, on the trunk of the cruiser alongside the cop. He jumped for the fence and made a desperate grab for the back of Brel's collar as he passed him.

He felt the tough material of the uniform collar and he held on tight as he hit the coats and blankets lining the razor wire on the top of the fence. The weight of Brel spun Doe in the air. He hit the fence sideways but with enough momentum that he rolled over the top. His body fell over the fence leaving him wedged across the top, his body and legs were on the street side and his left arm and Brel were stuck on the Department building side. Doe's head stuck up over the top of the wire like a coconut on a coconut shy. He could feel the blankets and coats shuddering as rounds aimed at him and Brel smashed into them.

Doe didn't know the world record for a bicep curl, but he couldn't believe that it would approach the two-hundred and some pounds that Brel weighed. He tried just once to bend his arm, bring his clenched fist up to his shoulder and pull Brel over the fence by pure strength. He couldn't make even the smallest movement. He tried to reach over with his other arm and get a hold of Brel, but he couldn't get close. His fingers brushed the guy's hair but there was nothing he could get a grip of. He couldn't see any obvious increase in the accuracy of the shots being fired at him. There was no neat line of holes in the fabrics draped over the fence, moving inexorably toward him, but he knew they would be getting closer all the time. It was hopeless, but Doe refused to let go of the cop until he was sure that either Brel was dead or until he was physically unable to hold on.

He tried levering himself backward, pulling his feet up under him and bracing them against the fence and then pushing backwards. He felt his shoulder start to dislocate and his elbow hyper-extend. Brel moved a little off the trunk, but it wasn't far enough, and Doe couldn't push any harder. He was about to relax his legs and slide his body back toward the fence when he felt it shudder and sensed a presence next to him. A uniformed arm reached past him and grabbed a handful of Brel's hair and together they hauled him up high enough to grab him under the arms and pull him over the top.

The three of them fell twelve feet to the ground with Brel landing on top. Doe lay for a moment winded, feeling Brel's warm blood on his legs, then he noticed the bullets slamming into the ground around them and rolled out from under the two cops and dragged Brel along the fence-line to safety.

FOURTEEN

Doe's rescuer was a little slower to get up than Doe, but he wasn't dragging Brel. They both made it around the side of the building at roughly the same time. Doe dropped Brel and collapsed to his knees breathing hard and shaking from the exertion. His elbow and shoulder burned and his left hand screamed with pain from gripping the cop's collar so tightly for so long. They were relatively safe. The shooters in the second-floor windows of the Department Building were out of sight behind the two-story block that housed the yard door and all the bad guys were either in the Department building or in the Humvees.

There were still six operational Humvees and they were just around the corner to their left. Doe didn't doubt that their commander would sanction a chase, but it wouldn't be simple. There was still a wrecked Humvee blocking the street between his main force and the block that the cops had escaped along. It had taken long minutes to shove the second Humvee just a few feet. It would take it a lot longer to push it far enough to allow them to drive down the street. They could bump up onto the sidewalk so that they didn't have to move the big truck quite so far, but then there would be all sorts of street furniture to negotiate. The Humvees were big trucks but not big enough that streetlights, mailboxes and fire plugs wouldn't stop them.

The smart move would be to send the furthest Humvee, the one at the extreme other end of the line. Nothing was blocking it and it could drive around the block and come at them from the right. As soon as it moved the next in line would be able to follow and then another one after that. They could send six vehicle-mounted M-60s to chase down the fleeing cops if they wanted to, but they couldn't do it quickly. It was a tiny mistake on their part, but it was going to save a lot of lives. All eight trucks had been parked pointing toward the Department Building. The Humvees didn't have skid steering. They would have to reverse the trucks across the street and turn and then pull forward and turn and then reverse and pull forward again. Depending on the width of the street and the turning circle of the trucks they might have to reverse multiple times before they were facing along the street and pointing in the right direction. They should have parked the last two Humvees facing along the street, ready to move quickly if they needed to.

It was a small error but Doe was extremely grateful for it. They were safe but not for long. The Humvee is a fast vehicle and at the same time as it was turning around a group of guys would be hustling out of the front of the Department building and coming along the sidewalk in the opposite direction. If they hung around they would be caught in a pincer movement.

Brel was bleeding from multiple leg wounds and he was starting to look pale. The cop from the fence took a quick look at Doe kneeling on the floor and then he hoisted Brel onto his shoulder. He beckoned Doe to follow and set off across the street. They jogged a couple of blocks to a dive bar called 'Lou's'. Doe smiled. He figured that other people or other geographies would have placed them in a sports hall or a community center, but he chose to like the guys for meeting up in a bar. The choice had a few practical advantages too. It was big enough, the cops knew the layout, and there were big metal shutters on the street windows which the officers had closed.

It was dark inside because of the shutters. There was a big guy in a faded Seahawks shirt and over-sized basketball shorts behind the bar. He looked nervous and he didn't look like he was the kind of guy who was often nervous. Most of the tables had been dragged across the room and lined up alongside the bar. The tables were full of bleeding cops in various states of repair. Most of the injuries were minor but some were also multiple. In the rush to get out into the vehicle yard, to escape the M-60 and to rescue the guys from the second story, there hadn't been time to grab any of the injured from the squad room. If they hadn't been mobile enough to get themselves out of the door and into the yard, then they had been left there. The guys who got out would be heading back at some point and they could only hope that the injured would still be there, that they could play dead and wait out the bad guys. Doe wasn't hopeful. It's tough to play dead with a gunshot wound big enough to prevent you moving. Anyone who could do it either had an exceptionally high pain threshold or was so badly injured that they might not survive until the Department building could be reclaimed.

*

The guy carrying Brel shooed a guy with a patched-up arm wound off of the nearest table and lowered Brel onto it. He looked around and frantically gestured to a guy at the back of the room. Doe took off his belt and tightened it around Brel's left leg. The other cop watched him and then took off his belt and cinched it around Brel's right leg. Doe could see five obvious wounds, two on Brel's right leg and three on his left. They were a mess of blood but they were starting to seep rather than bleed. Brel had lost a lot of blood. They had applied the tourniquets high up near his groin. They were high enough to make sure that Brel wouldn't lose any more blood, but Doe had no way of knowing whether Brel would be able to keep going with however much blood he still had pumping around in there. It depended how much blood was left and how fit Brel was, and maybe, in Doe's opinion, what sort of guy Brel was. How much he wanted to live.

The guy from the back of the room made it over to their table. He moved quickly, but wearily. Weaving through the bar like a waiter looking for a big tip, but at the end of his shift. He was wearing latex gloves that were covered in blood and a calm, but extremely hangdog expression.

"This is Sam, our medic." Doe's savior looked like it was all finally catching up with him. He started to sit down then turned around to see if there was anything behind him to sit on. He found a stool and started to sit down again and then stood up and stuck out a hand. "I'm Benny."

Doe took his hand.

"Thanks Benny, I think you saved my life."

Benny just shook his head and sat down. Doe turned to the medic.

"We put the tourniquets as high up the legs as we could get because I can't tell exactly where the wounds are. When you find out you should probably replace them lower down. You might be able to save him a couple of stumps. That can make a big difference with prosthetics."

The medic looked angry then confused. He was used to trying to save limbs. He thought Doe was callous or stupid for sacrificing them without a fight.

"He's lost a lot of blood and he isn't going anywhere any time soon. There's no radio so there will be no medevac. No one is coming for him and there is nowhere for you to take him." Doe looked around the room. "Unless you have a lot of extra equipment around here somewhere you will have to settle for keeping him alive."

The guy sagged a little but nodded.

Doe looked around the room again.

"They're all minor wounds, right?"

The medic shook his head.

"Mostly. But a few got hit running away after they got over the fence. We've got one head shot and two arterial bleeds. One of the bleeds is the daughter of one of the detectives. She came in to bring him his lunch."

Doe nodded. It was a reflex. It was intended to look businesslike, to help the guy move on rather than dwell on the situation. Doe usually managed to pull it off without looking like a thoughtless prick.

"It's going to be five to eight hours minimum before you get any kind of professional help. You have to focus on keeping them alive and, if you can, get them ready for transport. Anything else is a bonus or a luxury. This isn't medicine, it's survival. Do whatever you have to. They will thank you afterwards if you do. And if you don't, they'll be dead and then they won't be able to."

Doe watched the man carefully. His earlier, brief, deflation was entirely understandable, but if he sagged again now, then Doe would need to find someone else. This guy might be the best trained, he might be the most talented but if he wasn't capable of doing what needed doing then he wasn't the best guy for the job. There was no point ending up with a lot of corpses who would have had great medical prognoses if only the ambulances had arrived a few hours earlier.

Sam's posture didn't change at all. He didn't straighten and stick out his chin, but he didn't sag either. He just pulled a pair of shears from his back pocket and started to cut away Deputy Brel's uniform trousers.

*

Doe looked around the barroom. He spotted the cop with the sergeant's stripes who had helped Brel line up the squad cars. He was having his arm patched up and grimacing. Doe walked over to him and asked him where their prisoner was but the guy just looked blank. He could have been acting or he could have been in shock or he could have had no idea what the hell Doe was talking about. Doe didn't have time to find out. He needed to talk to his prisoner. He had gone to a lot of personal trouble and not a little personal risk to get the man out of that second story. He wasn't going to hang around looking for him while some angry cops had themselves an informal lynching out the back of a bar.

He scanned the room again. There was a guy in a brown sports jacket in one corner. He had a cluster of guys in uniform around him and he seemed to be issuing instructions or orders. Doe took a small gamble and walked over.

"Detective Floyd?"

The guy in the sports jacket looked up and nodded a fraction. Doe stuck out a hand.

"We spoke on the phone."

Floyd waited a second, assessing. Doe guessed that he never did anything much without waiting a second and assessing. Doe didn't think it was the worst trait in the world. Floyd had moved pretty quickly once he got going during the escape and to Doe's mind it was better to hesitate a fraction and then act decisively than to move instantly and then change your mind. Getting the hesitation down until it looked like you were acting instantly was the trick. Floyd was a long way from managing that, but eventually he stuck out his hand and shook Doe's.

"You're the man with the plan."

Doe nodded and shrugged. Floyd looked back at the Deputies around him.

"I was just getting these guys to take the civilians to safety. Can you think of any reason why they wouldn't be safe in their own homes?"

Doe shook his head.

"They'll be as safe there as anywhere you can get them. I don't see the gang spending time or effort trying to track down witnesses."

Floyd nodded, paused for his customary second and then turned back toward his men. He didn't need to tell them what to do. He just nodded and they moved off, rounding up the uninjured secretaries and office staff and the members of the public who had been caught up in the shooting and shepherding them out of the bar's back door.

Floyd sat back down on a bar stool. Considering what needed doing next.

"Do you know anything about one of theirs that I threw out of an office window back there?"

Floyd nodded and looked up.

"Yep. Brel told me about it. We got him over the wire in the first wave."

"Is he here?" Doe scanned the room again.

"Yep." Floyd gestured behind him with a jerk of his head. "He's in the men's room with a couple of my guys."

There was a steel in Floyd's eyes that made Doe wonder whether he had misjudged him. Maybe Floyd and his buddies had acted a lot more quickly than Doe had given him credit for.

"Is he the one they did all this for? The one you say they're looking for?"

"No. He's just one of the grunts." Doe gave the detective one of the looks he used during interrogations. The one that meant - *I want the truth but think carefully about your future before you answer this.* "I want some information from him. Is he OK?"

Floyd managed a wry little smile.

"He's fine. I think everyone here is too busy and too shocked to care about revenge right now, but I thought it prudent to have him somewhere safe with a couple of guys I trust. You know, just in case."

Doe nodded. A grateful and appreciative nod that Floyd seemed to understand subconsciously even if he didn't pick up the whole thing.

"I'm going to go in there and ask him some questions in a minute. You'd be welcome to tag along." Doe left the 'but' hanging in the air. It was a just an inflection, a response that was implied by the sound of those last few syllables.

Floyd's pause was a good two seconds longer than normal. He stared straight into Doe's eyes, but then he looked around the room and shook his head.

"No thanks. I'll leave one of my guys in there with you... to help, you know." He caught Doe's eye again and managed the wry smile. "But I think I better get on with things out here."

*

Doe was itching to get into the men's room and ask his questions. Time was running fast again and they needed to know what the bad guys would do next. Doe couldn't see them just accepting defeat and packing up camp and leaving. They were serious guys and whoever had hired them would have given them some serious incentives not to fail. Positive incentives in the form of big pay packets and bumper bonuses on completion, and negative incentives in the form of threats or promises of violent retribution if they failed.

Doe could only see two possible courses open to the gang now that the raid on the Police Department had failed. Either they would split up and start quartering the town, going door to door and rooting through cupboards and spare bedrooms at gun point, or they would take some hostages and demand that their guy was brought to them. Doe knew which one he would favor. If he needed to get the job done to earn a retirement in the Seychelles and to avoid losing an eye, then he wouldn't waste time trying to search a town that was sitting on the edge of fifteen square miles of ancient woodland. The gang had been pretty sure they would be able to hide an entire camp out in those woods. They weren't dumb enough to expect to be able to search them and find a single man.

Doe liked Floyd and he wanted to help. He wanted to help the guy as well as help the situation, so rather than issuing orders he asked Floyd what he planned to do next.

"Tool up as best we can and head back to the Department Building, I guess. See if we can help any of the guys we had to leave behind."

Doe was impressed that Floyd wanted to head back to help rather than because he wanted to take another swing at the bad guys. It wasn't a great indication of his tactical ability that he wanted to head back into the face of that overwhelming firepower, but the fact that he wanted to do it to try to save the lives of the fallen cops rather than to crack some bad guy skulls or make some arrests bought him some of Doe's respect. The why was irrelevant though. It was a hopeless plan whatever the reasoning but it was the type of thing that the kind of guys who join the police and the armed services were programmed for. They didn't like being on the back foot, they hate running away. If they ever have to retreat, they would get just far enough away to feel safe and then they would convince themselves that they are back on top and head straight back into the cannon fire. It's one of the things the Army try to train into their recruits as soon as they get hold of them and it's the very same thing they try to train out of them when they get to Officer School. It had always proved easy to do the first and nearly impossible to achieve the second.

Doe shook his head. Floyd seemed like a decent guy. Doe needed to stop him from leading his men into another massacre.

"They'll still be there, and they still have the men and the weapons and the Humvees. Either they're loading up or they're still finishing their search. If you attack they'll wipe you out. You need to give them another ten minutes and then send a couple of scouts to check the street. If the Humvees are gone, they're gone."

Floyd nodded but looked uneasy. Like he knew that Doe was right but that he also knew that he and his men weren't going to just sit there with their thumbs up their asses for ten minutes while colleagues bled to death on their squad room carpet.

Doe knew he hadn't convinced him, so he went on.

"Plus, you have a couple of other things to get done first and they are way more important."

*

Doe glanced at the men's room door and then looked back at Floyd. He didn't seem like the kind of guy who had a whole range of expressions. In Doe's experience that didn't necessarily mean that he didn't have a whole range of emotions. Sometimes it just meant that his emotions didn't show on his face. Floyd's face wasn't showing much, but there seemed to be a little bit of hope mixed in with a little bit of puzzlement. Maybe there was a little bit of something approaching expectation mixed in there too. Doe was struck again by the guy's first words to him,

"You're in charge up there?"

pause

"I guess so. As much as anyone."

It was like one of those guys who get bit by snakes a lot and didn't get poisoned. Just because you could do something didn't mean you wanted to, and it certainly didn't mean you enjoyed it.

Doe sat down on the stool next to Floyd.

"The first thing you need to do is get the worst injured, the ones that can be moved and the ones who are going to die anyway. You need to get them into cars and get on the road to Heath Haven. You've got about five minutes to do it. Those guys had a roadblock three miles out of town and they were shooting everything that tried to get out but they brought the guys closer in during the raid. They're in town right now. I think you have about five minutes before they get sent back out and everyone is trapped again. Tell the drivers to stay off Main Street until you get right to the edge of town and then hit the gas. You need to send only the injured that might not make it until tomorrow and the drivers should all be volunteers.

"The drive will be dangerous. If they decide to give chase they'll be doing it in Humvees and they can get up to highway speed on that road and take out two cruisers with the M-60's. It's pretty much exactly what they're designed for. It'll be hard on the injured too. It might finish some of them off and that's a hard thing for the drivers to deal with but the only injured you'll be sending will be the ones that will die before morning anyway. Tell the volunteers that they can either stay here and watch them die on a table or take them on the drive and see one or two of them make it."

Floyd nodded but his eyes seemed to say that hard as that would be, he could get it done and head over to the Department building too.

"The second thing you need to do is start squirreling people away." Doe looked around the bar again. There weren't an awful lot of cops still standing. Most of them had some kind of wound and Doe figured that they had left about a third of the department strength lying around their Department building. Of the rest, another third was being treated here. "You have no chance of protecting them. You have to hide them."

Floyd looked of puzzled.

"Hide who? These guys? The injured"

Doe shook his head.

"Do you have a kids' Saturday Club or anything here? Help for working parents? Somewhere they can leave little Johnny for the morning? Are there Little Leagues? Choir practices?"

Floyd nodded.

"There's softball practice, a couple of craft clubs I guess. I think there's a rummage sale at the church."

"You need to get to every place where there might be a group of children or young women. You need to scoop them all up and spread them out and give them what protection you can. You need to get word out to parents. Kids and young women need to start hiding themselves."

Doe looked over. Any admiration or expectation on Floyd's face was gone, replaced by what might be fear or horror.

"They expected to have their guy by now. They'll be on a timescale. You can't lock down a town like this for ever and you can't cut off the communications for long either. People on the outside will be trying to reach you as well as you trying to reach them. Sooner or later someone will start to ask why no one seems to be able to get a phone call into Seal Harbor and then someone will try the radio and then they'll send someone out to investigate. They can keep a lid on the whole thing for a while but not for ever.

"They expected to be leaving by now but instead they're still looking for their guy. They're back to square one except that now it's worse than it was before. Before the attack they knew where he was. It was just a matter of going in and getting him. But now they don't know where he is and they don't have time to go looking. Their only choice is to make us tell them, or better still, get us to bring him to them. The easiest and surest way to do that is to start rounding up bargaining chips and threatening to kill them. You guys are the only ones who can stop that happening. If they get a group of twenty kids and line them up on Main Street with guns to their heads every cop in town will walk through me and grab the guy and hand him over on a silver platter."

Doe stood up and started toward the men's room door. Floyd paused his second and then stood abruptly.

"Oh, shit! The Senior Center."

Doe half turned. He was trying to mimic the wry little smile that Floyd had flashed him earlier but then he saw that the guy was serious and sat back down.

"Forget the Senior Center. No one ever takes seniors hostage. No one ever made any concessions to save the life of anyone over the age of about twenty-five. Certainly not to save the lives of seniors. Thirty seniors get shot in a massacre and people say, 'isn't it terrible... but of course... they were old'. If anyone ever takes hostages in an old folks' home there's no negotiation. Either the cops storm the building or they just wait them out. What's the worst that could happen?

"You don't need to worry about men over the age of consent either. If they get killed people subconsciously think that it's at least partly their fault. They think that the men should have risen up and wrested control from their kidnappers. Cops wouldn't abandon them, but they wouldn't make many concessions either. Nobody gets a plane to Cuba that way."

"Concentrate on kids and young women, especially pretty, white, middle class women and smart little middle-class kids. They get threatened and everyone jumps. They get killed and all sorts of shit starts to fly around. If these guys are going for extortion, and I'm sure that they are, they're going to be going for your playgrounds and your cheerleader squads."

*

Doe left Floyd sitting on his stool. He hoped that the detective's inaction was just an elongated version of his habitual pause to assess, but even if it wasn't, Doe was unable to help him any further. He was worried for the kids and cheerleaders of Seal Harbor, but he was a lot more concerned about what the guy in the fisherman's jersey would do if he made it to safety on the mainland. While the guy was still on the island they had a good chance of tracking him down whatever he did but if he made it made it to the US proper there would be a million places to hide him. Doe wouldn't stop looking and he wouldn't stop hoping, but he was a realist.

Doe stopped at the door to the men's room and knocked. He felt stupid as he did it, but he knew that it meant that when he opened the door Floyd's guys inside would both be looking in his direction. It meant he could stand to the side as he opened the door and that meant that both of the cops inside would see Floyd. Floyd sitting by the bar directly behind Doe would show them that Doe was in the clear. They would think, 'Well, he came past the boss. The boss must be OK with him being here'. It was terrible security protocol, but it usually worked. It just fits so well with human nature. Being inside a place didn't mean that you were allowed to be inside that place but most people thought deep down that it did.

As it happened, Doe was supposed to be there. Floyd knew it and would back him up, but both Floyd and Doe had things to be doing. Doe didn't want to waste even the couple of minutes it would take for one of the guys to walk over and ask and then come back. So, he knocked on the restroom door, stepped inside. He walked over until he was standing between the two detectives, drawing their attention with him. It brought all the decisions into the room, away from the bar room and Floyd.

"Floyd says one of you should stay to make sure I don't kill him and one of you should go and help out there."

They looked at each other. It was called the illusion of choice. In one sentence Doe had shifted them from wondering whether they should allow Doe to talk to the prisoner and onto which one of them should stay and which of them should head back out into the action. The older one shrugged. To Doe the shrug could have meant either that he was leaving and the younger man was staying or the absolute opposite, that he would stay and let the other guy would leave. For an outsider it was impossible to tell. The two cops had obviously worked together for a spell. They knew each other well. The younger one nodded and headed for the door.

"I'm Doe." Doe stuck out a hand.

"Brown."

It seemed the Detective was a man of few words. Doe assumed he was telling him his name. He waited a beat to see if there was anything else to follow and then he turned toward the man he had last seen when he threw him out of a second story window. Their prisoner was sitting on the john in a stall with the door jammed open. He had his hands cuffed behind his back and he had an angry bruise growing on his forehead and an angry look in his eyes. Otherwise he looked fine.

Doe walked right into the stall and squatted down in front of the man. He felt pretty safe. On a normal chair, the guy might have tried a headbutt or maybe even a roundhouse kick aimed at Doe's jaw. Having his arms handcuffed behind his back would have hindered him but he could have rocked backwards and then rammed his forehead into Doe's nose. He could have let his momentum carry him forward and fallen on top of Doe as he went down. Or he could have leaned back and grabbed the back of the chair and then kicked out and tried to get his foot high enough to do some damage. It would have been a low risk strategy. He might not hurt Doe but unless Doe decided to exact some vengeance for the attempt, it would have been a plan that wouldn't have caused the guy much pain.

On a toilet that was impossible. Everything around the guy was slippery porcelain. He couldn't rely on friction to hold him in place and he couldn't brace himself because he couldn't use his arms. If he lost his balance he couldn't put his arms out. There was nothing to grab onto because the cistern behind him was slippery porcelain too and the seat under him was curved at the edges and was made of shiny white plastic. If he moved too far in any direction he would fall forward or slide to the side and crack his head on the wall of the stall. Then he would fall into the gap between the john and the wall and get wedged there until Doe helped him up. It would be painful and very undignified.

The guy could probably stand up, but that's surprisingly tough for a tall guy sitting down with his hands behind his back. He would have to put in a lot of effort and that would make him slow and obvious. Even if he managed it, Doe would just shove him in the stomach and he would fall back onto the john. If he was lucky he would end up sitting back down, exactly where he started. If he was unlucky he would end up wedged in the gap between the toilet and the wall, waiting for Doe to pull him to his feet and hoping that the dampness seeping into his pants was just water.

*

Doe started slowly. Like he had all the time in the world.

"What's the backup plan?"

The guy went for the only act of defiance he had. He spat.

Doe dodged it and felt it hit the side of his cheek. It wasn't the first time he had been spat at. It wasn't even the first time that week. Most of the times the provocation had been professionally induced. It didn't hurt him.

"What's the backup plan?"

He was going for relentless. It usually worked for him eventually. People find it difficult not to talk. Ask the same question often enough and people will answer. They might lie, they might grunt, but they will answer. The trick is to make them know that you are going to keep asking forever.

The guy said nothing, but he didn't spit again. Either he had decided that it didn't bother Doe, or he had recovered some composure. He just sat as still as he could and stared at Doe.

Doe didn't have time for the relentless tactic. The way the guy was behaving made him think that it would take a long time to work, so he headed straight for the next most effective method, threats.

"There is no plea bargain here. Nothing you can say will reduce your sentence. I might be able to do something if I really wanted to, but who knows? This is pretty serious. Lots of dead cops. Interference with the phone lines. There probably isn't anything even I could do." He paused. He was pleased with the word 'probably'. Without having to get into a big discussion about credentials, he had implied that he had huge reserves of influence. It had set him up as the man to deal with. Someone a step higher up the ladder than the local guys.

He wouldn't be able to crouch there forever. The pain was starting to build in his thighs, but he liked his position. He could stare right into the guy's eyes from a little below him. It was telling the prisoner that Doe's position was so dominant that he could take the low ground and still win without risk or damage.

"But I don't want to help you. Not that way. What you need to think about is where and how you want this to go down."

Doe held the crouch for a long couple of minutes and then stood up and pushed the guy back against the cistern. He let him slide a little off the seat and then grabbed a handful of battledress material and set him back in place.

"I'm not local. I can pick where you go to trial. Where you get held before you go to trial. Where you serve time. I can choose whether you serve your time in general population or whether you spend the rest of your life on death row."

The guy was still projecting anger and confidence, but he hadn't been expecting this. Doe took a punt.

"I could get you re-enlisted."

The man couldn't help himself. He managed not to yelp, but his eyes went wide.

"The worst case for you..." Doe pushed further, "I leave you here pre-trial. You know what you did back there. The survivors will be your guards. There'll be a lot of attention so I don't think they'll cripple you but there will be accidents, lots of indignations..."

Doe stretched his thighs carefully, hoping that the guy wouldn't notice, then he crouched back down.

"Then we go somewhere very public for the trial. Probably Texas. They have the death penalty and they have some big cities. All the media outlets work out of Houston and Dallas. no one that you have ever met would fail to see you die. Everyone you ever knew, anyone you have ever cared about would know what you did."

Doe leaned in even further.

"And then... and trust me on this... by then I would know what you feared most. If you were scared to die I would let them carry out their sentence right then but if you weren't, if there was something you were more scared of than that, then I would find it. I could hand you back to the Army and let you rot in Leavenworth. I could make it my job to tell every MP in the service what you did and what I thought of you. People would be transferring in just to get a shot at you. CO's would consider it a reward for their most determined officers, the guys who had been out front too long. The ones who needed a break, the ones who needed something to work off their anger on."

He stood up again.

"I know the answer to my question by the way. It's the only game in town. But I want you to tell me."

The guy was still sitting on the on the john, ram rod straight. Whoever had drilled him had done a great job, but his eyes were flicking around the stall now. They were still angry but now they were also looking for a way out.

"So, tell me. What's the back-up plan?"

It was almost a whisper but it was loud enough for Brown to hear and it told Doe that all he needed was time.

"We round up hostages. Kids or girls, and we get you to bring him to us."

Doe nodded and crouched back down.

*

"I won't give you anything about the guys I was working with."

Doe nodded. He wanted to say, 'That's fine because we'll get that from their dental records after I kill them'. Instead he said,

"Are there any sensors on the wire?"

The prisoner looked up quickly and then looked back down.

"No."

"Mines or booby traps inside the wire?"

The guy considered for a while then came to a decision.

"No. But it won't help you anyway. They have eyes on the whole perimeter. All the time. Even when we came here. And the guys they use are good. Ex-Rangers."

Doe stored the extra information and moved on.

"And inside the camp? Are there regular patrols? Dogs? Any machine-gun posts? Bunkers?"

The prisoner shook his head.

"No, nothing like that. Why would there be? No one knows we're there and even if they did, it's just a load of local cops." He looked confused, "I told you, you can't get in there and even if you do, there are forty-eight ex-army guys in there."

Doe gave him a smile. There weren't going to be forty-eight guys in there, not any more.

"OK. Tell me about the money."

"What?"

"Who hired you? Who bought the plane tickets? What currencies are they using, which banks?"

The guy shook his head, not refusing, just uncomprehending.

"It was all just 'up the line shit' you know. A sergeant I used to know in the service called me. A guy he knows called him. Some lieutenant called that guy. They know what we'll get paid. They tell us where to go. The money goes into my bank a bit at a time over the next five years so that I can hide it. It'll come from a number of different accounts so that it doesn't look like any one company is paying me a lot of money for anything. It's a system we've used before. We always get paid. The sergeant has never stiffed me yet."

Doe's heart sank.

"OK then, how did you get here?"

The guy shook his head again

"Commercial airline to Seattle. My sergeant picked me up at the airport and we came in together."

"What about the ticket? Did they mail it to you? How did you know where to meet him?"

"He told me to go to the ticket counter at my local airport. The tickets were waiting. They were paid for and in my name. The ticket was for Seattle, so I went to Seattle. When I arrived, there was an announcement over the PA. It said my uncle Sam was waiting at the Hertz counter. A little joke you know? So that he didn't have to use his name in public."

Doe nodded.

"OK. Then what? What about the truck? Did you see him rent it?"

The guy shook his head.

"It wasn't a rental. We met there and then went out to long term parking. The truck was just sitting there. It was already muddy and the tank was a quarter empty. We drove it here and handed it over to some guys who have been driving it around town the last couple of days."

Dead ends. Doe guessed they might be able to pick some of it apart given time, especially if they could get hold of the sergeant or one of the lieutenants but it would probably all lead back to middle men and shell companies. Whoever had organized this had gone to a lot of trouble to build in cut outs right down at the bottom, right down amongst the soldiers. Anyone who did that would have other protections in place higher up the food chain.

Doe took a step back, drawing the guy with him and adding some extra tension.

"OK. Think carefully. Get this right and I'll take Leavenworth off the table." Doe paused purely for effect. Despite the risk of falling off the toilet seat, the guy couldn't help himself from leaning even further forward, toward Doe. "Where's the cash coming from? How are you dealing with local expenses? Gas and food and stuff?"

The guy was desperate now.

"I don't know. I never saw anybody handle anything over a few bucks. They haven't been buying much. Everything seems to be already there, at the camp. There could be suitcases full of fifties in one of the containers or a bank of safes in the CO's office. I've never seen any. And if there is a bundle of cash in there, they certainly haven't been spreading any of it around"

Doe took a step back. Not intentionally, not as a tactic this time, but out of sheer frustration. Cash always leaves a trail. Individual notes tell huge and convoluted stories of deposits and withdrawals. Each bill has a unique number. They pick up pocket fibers and grease and DNA from the hands they pass through. Businesses scribble little notes on them when they are cashing up, and every bill starts out from the same place. You can track them from both ends.

Large bundles of cash are even better. Whenever Doe saw a TV show or a film where the bad guys ask for an astronomical sum of money in small unmarked bills his eyes rolled up into his head. For most people, large sums of cash money are very difficult to get hold of and you almost never have a legitimate reason to need them. ATM cards have daily limits, bank accounts have rules. To get at your cash you need to make an appointment. You have to go into a branch and stand around with about a million cameras focused on you, and then you have to sign bits of paper and enter codes. The more money there is the more hoops you have to jump through and there just aren't that many times you would need to do it. Most people carry more money on a piece of plastic in their wallet than they do in their checking account. Big ticket items are bought on cards. Cars and houses are bought by money transfers. Yachts and islands are bought on computers.

There are illicit businesses that garner large volumes of cash in small denominations, but these tell a story too. The type and condition of the notes could tell a good detective a whole lot about the criminals who had collected it. Muggers and housebreakers end up with crisp notes with a single bend. They have been taken out of respectable wallets and pocket books or out of bedside draws or cheap wall safes. Drug dealers have grimy, tattered bills that have been scrabbled for and then clenched in dirty hands before being handed over. Generally speaking, the advice to cops to 'follow the money' was always good. Physical, paper money in large quantities could give you an awful lot of evidence to work through.

Doe was getting nothing. The guy wouldn't give him names and he didn't care about them anyway. There wasn't going to be much in the way of a trail to follow and he already knew as much about the camp and the gang's plans as he needed to. He started to turn, ready to leave.

"Wait!" The guy nearly fell off the toilet trying to stand and follow Doe. "Are we cool?"

Doe considered. He didn't care one way or another. He had no intention of making the guy's life any easier, but he wasn't concerned about making it more difficult either. He had caught the guy. He was going to be punished. Doe didn't much care what happened next. He was aware that the investigation wasn't over. There might be more that he needed from the guy.

He was about to say, 'We'll see', when the restroom door opened and Eugene walked in.

FIFTEEN

Eugene looked stunned. Doe figured that the ex-Ranger had expected his days of walking though makeshift hospitals filled with his colleagues to have ended when he left the Army. When he joined the police, he would have been expecting some violence. He would probably have prepared himself to lose some colleagues during the course of a long police career, but he wouldn't have expected to walk into another field hospital and to see more of his co-workers losing limbs or their lives.

Doe stepped out of the stall and hustled Eugene out of the men's room and into the bar.

"Where is he? Where did you put him?" Doe tried to keep his voice calm and respectful, but it was a struggle. What he really wanted to ask was 'Why the hell did you leave him?"

Eugene looked around the room like he was seeing it for the first time. There was no way for him to have reached the restroom door without walking through the bar. After a second Eugene's eyes seemed to lose some of their incredulity and return to an appraising, working stare.

"He's in the car. It's parked up, off the street, locked and safe." Eugene gestured to one of the cops who was walking up and down the line of injured. The man had one arm in a sling but looked otherwise uninjured. Eugene beckoned him over.

Doe grabbed Eugene's arm.

"He's definitely not safe. These guys won't have come here with eight Humvees and no support. They will have all the bases covered. They will have other plans. Take me to him."

Eugene looked over at Doe and then back towards the approaching cop.

"Relax. He's safe. His hands are locked together. The car is locked. The garage is locked. We can go get him after we go back to the Department."

Doe tightened his grip on Eugene's arm and pulled him closer.

"He is not safe. Wherever you've stashed him is probably not safe, but even if it is, he is an incredibly dangerous man. Probably the most dangerous you've ever met. He's going to get out of any restraints you put him in, it's only a matter of time. Floyd is in control here. He knows what to do. The only thing you need to think about is making sure that we keep control of that man. Take me to him right now."

Eugene's eyes took on a glint of anger.

"They need me here. I can't just abandon them. I missed..."

Doe interrupted.

"It's under control here. He isn't. If you won't take me to him right now then tell me where he is and I'll go alone. But if you do that, my advice would be to hand in your badge and get a teaching qualification or something. If you expected this job to be different from your last you were wrong. It's still about doing the right thing. It's still about putting the job ahead of your safety or that of your men."

Doe waited. He wanted Eugene to make the right decision, but he also recognized the futility of making a gesture such as walking for the door when he didn't have any idea where he was headed.

Eugene waited until the deputy he had called over arrived and then he angrily waved him away and led Doe out of the bar.

*

Eugene took off down the street at a fast jog, Doe hustled to catch up.

"Where did you stash him?"

"In the garage of a pal. The car is locked. The garage is locked. He's handcuffed and there's a metal mesh cutting him off from the front of the car. He's safe"

"Put your gun away and slow down." Eugene had his handgun out in a combat hold. He slowed slightly but kept the gun by his side.

"This isn't your town anymore." Doe reached out to touch Eugene's shoulder, but Eugene jerked away. "There are still more than twenty bad guys in town and you guys have, what? At most ten guys active and on the streets? And that includes us. If we run across them it'll be them finding us, not us finding them."

Eugene looked up and down the street and then reluctantly holstered his gun.

Doe slowed to a fast walk and Eugene did the same.

"We're going to beat them, but we have to be clever about it."

Eugene nodded but Doe couldn't read his meaning.

"I couldn't just leave them."

It was Doe's turn to nod. Just acceptance, not agreement. He had known that Eugene was going to struggle with the idea that his colleagues were taking a beating and he wasn't helping them. He could empathize. Eugene wasn't the kind of guy who would hide in a corner when the shooting started. Doe had known from the start that there was a serious risk that Eugene would stash the guy and leave him and come riding to the rescue. For all Doe knew the guy might really be safe.

"We might get split up. Tell me where he is."

Eugene looked at him and waited a moment but then he gave him directions. Two blocks east and one block north, a house number and the location of the garage. They were real directions, but that didn't mean they were the directions to the real place.

The last piece of information was pointless anyway because when they turned into the right street the garage was sitting there close up alongside the house. It gleamed white in the sunlight and had a big, double width roller door standing open. Their guy might still have his hands locked behind him. The car might still be locked, but the garage most definitely wasn't.

*

Eugene broke into a run. There were fifty yards left to reach the garage doors and Doe was sure the cop would beat him over that distance every time, but Doe had no intention of running straight there anyway. Call him crazy but he made it a rule never to run directly towards an open door where he knew there had been at least one bad guy. He jumped the small rail separating the neighborhood gardens from the sidewalk and ran up to the sides of the house. He ran close to the front of the buildings until he was alongside the garage. He hoped to find a window. He wanted to check the interior of the garage before he decided how to enter, but by the time he got there Eugene was already inside kicking hell out of the rear door of his cruiser.

Doe stepped around front and into the garage. He watched Eugene carefully. The driver's door window was smashed and the door was standing open. The metal grill between the front and rear seats had been peeled back. To Doe it was clear that their guy hadn't escaped. If he had made it out of the car on his own it would have shown. He would have needed to lean back and put his feet up on the grill and to have slammed them repeatedly into the metal, aiming for the corners as much as he could. The car was converted from civilian use to national standards. The grill would not have given up easily. If the guy had been kicking at it from an unsighted, awkward position, it wouldn't have peeled neatly away in the neat way that it had. If the guy had smashed the grill off from inside there would have been a big dent where his feet had hit the grill. The mesh would have bent and stretched well before the frame gave way. Doe guessed that, left on their own for long enough, an unaccompanied prisoner could escape from the back of a cruiser, but if they did, the results would look very different to this.

There was one obvious conclusion, the cavalry had arrived for their prisoner. They had arrived, smashed the driver's window, put a pry bar under the edge of the grill, peeled it back and freed their man.

Smashing the rear window wouldn't have worked as well. The doors were all locked and the back doors couldn't be unlocked from inside the back of the cruiser. If they had smashed the back window then the guy would have had to slide out through the smashed window, probably still with his hands cuffed behind him. It had been much easier for them to smash the driver's window, open the door and then take a crowbar to the grill. Their guy climbed out through the hole in the grill and out through the open driver's door.

The inside of the front of the car was a mess and Eugene was doing his best to make the outside look just as bad. He had put several big dents in the driver's side rear door and now he was hitting the roof with his clenched fists. Doe looked on. Eugene certainly looked angry. Doe looked around for Eugene's gun. It wasn't anywhere that he could see. Even at a full run Doe knew that Eugene wouldn't have entered a possibly hostile building without having drawn his weapon. He must have holstered it sometime between realizing that the garage was empty and losing his temper so badly that he started trying to beat up a car. That might not mean anything either. Eugene had been a soldier for a long time. A good one. In an elite unit. Doe figured making your weapon safe after you stopped needing it was probably second nature. Not something you thought about. Just something you did.

Eugene spotted him out of the corner of his eye. He stopped pounding on the roof of the cruiser and took a half step backwards and started to turn towards Doe. Then he stopped and aimed a last, vicious kick at the side of the car and walked right over to Doe.

"OK. Get it over with!" Eugene was almost foaming at the mouth. "Say it!"

Doe took a deliberate step back and put his right hand on the gun in the waistband of his pants.

"OK." He said, "Did you let him go?"

Eugene started to shake his head and then stopped and looked angrily into Doe's face.

"What!?"

Doe pulled the gun slowly and dropped his hand to his side, resting the gun against his leg.

"I said did you let him out. Is this little bit of vehicular battery just a smokescreen to keep me in the dark?"

The anger had looked real enough to Doe and the hurt and bewilderment did too, but Doe had been wrong about that kind of thing before. He didn't trust people who thought that they could always tell when someone was lying.

"It would make perfect sense." Doe took another step backwards. He knew that Eugene had been expecting him to say something different, but he had no interest in saying 'I told you so'. "The guys who were after your prisoner were spending lots of money. If you're willing to spend enough you can almost always buy somebody in almost any police department."

Eugene was settling back into anger. A fierce, cold anger. Doe tightened his grip on his gun.

"They'd be pretty stupid not to try to get someone on the inside if they could afford it, and if they couldn't afford it, then this must be one helluva well-paid department."

Eugene was mad as hell now but Doe was pleased to see that his fists were clenching by his sides. If his fists were clenching then he wasn't making an attempt to reach for his gun.

"And your behavior hasn't exactly hurt them so far has it?"

If Eugene was going to burst, then that would be the statement that would do it. If he was going to go for his gun, either out of innocent rage or because he was working with the gang, then he would draw his weapon then. If he didn't, then Doe could lead them into a question and answer, accusation and rebuttal. He could start to work out the truth. He didn't know if Eugene was working with the gang or not, but he didn't want to have to shoot him before he found out.

"First you get Burns sent out to get shot. If you hadn't done that then the whole department would have kept on trying to find a way to fix the radio. Maybe someone would have tried to take a boat around the island or to find out if the signal was being jammed." Eugene hadn't exploded. He was gradually getting a grip on himself.

He was taking his anger and squashing it down inside himself, using it to cover up the grief and the shame and the fear that he was feeling. "And then when I turn out to be a spanner in the works you make sure you keep close to me, keep me under observation..."

"That's not true! You called me." Eugene wasn't shouting anymore. His voice was quiet and the words were clipped short.

Doe nodded conceding the point.

"But then you found me and went along with a very unconventional plan. As you said yourself..."

"That plan was our best hope!"

"And you tried your best to convince me that we had time, that they wouldn't make their move until after nightfall..."

"They shouldn't have. They should have waited. That's what we would have done!"

"Then there was your little performance in the car. When you decided to make the guy think we were both Dirty Harry a day away from retirement."

"What performance? I was trying to give you an angle."

"By threatening to torture him? He's a probable terrorist washed up on your beach. He hasn't come here from a spa resort in the south of France. Chances are he's lived in some very dangerous places." Doe checked Eugene's hands one more time and then risked stepping forward, toward the center of the room. "You gave him one of the very things that he could relate to. Probably something that he either knows he can deal with or believes that he can deal with. He visibly relaxed the moment you put it out there."

Eugene was shaking his head. There was nothing to deny at that point. He was shaking his head like a big dog with water in its ears. Like a man trying to take the past back.

"I thought it would scare him. It usually scares them."

Doe filed the 'usually' away for later.

"And then you take him out of the cells and as soon as I'm not around you leave him and he's gone."

The shaking slowed and Eugene's chin dropped. The regret and bewilderment were pushing their way back around his anger.

"I couldn't just leave them there... I could have helped..."

Doe stepped in closer and made sure he had Eugene's full attention. If Eugene was going to be able to convince him that he wasn't involved, then this would be the only opportunity. If he didn't convince him now, then even if Doe couldn't prove that Eugene was dirty, Doe would be on his own. He couldn't risk working with a man that he didn't fully trust.

*

Doe looked around the inside of the garage and up and down the street.

"OK, he was locked up in here, right?"

Eugene nodded.

"Out of sight of anyone unless they opened the garage door or looked through the window at the side?"

Eugene nodded again.

"And the glass from the driver's window is on the driver's seat."

Doe hadn't checked but it was the only thing that made sense. Their guy couldn't have escaped on his own and he had escaped, so he must have had help. If he had help then they would have been the guys who had smashed the driver's side window. The glass would have to be inside the car, on the driver's seat. If the guy had escaped on his own, he would have smashed the window from inside the car. The glass would be on the garage floor.

Eugene looked momentarily surprised and then looked inside through the smashed window and nodded.

"So, it was smashed from outside and the metal grill was peeled back using tools that the guy we left in there didn't have."

Eugene stopped nodding and looked at Doe.

"He had help."

It was Doe's turn again.

"Yes." He nodded. "And since you were the only person who knew where he was, the question is, how did they find him?"

Eugene's head started jerking around, his eyes checking out random parts of the building. If he had been a character in a sci-fi film smoke would have started coming out of his ears. It would have been the point of the film where we found out that he was a robot. The door was behind Doe, but Eugene wasn't looking for physical escape. His brain was desperate for answers and that triggered a physical reaction.

"You didn't tell anyone where you put him, not even me. Between the time you left me and when you walked into the bar restrooms there was less than thirty minutes. None of the rest of the garage doors are open. They didn't find him by chance. Not in thirty minutes. Not even in a town as small as this."

Eugene's eyes were still darting around but crucially, his hands were staying away from his gun.

"If you didn't tell anyone where he was and if he didn't escape on his own," Doe stepped back and tightened his grip on his gun, just in case, "then how did they find him."

*

If Eugene was acting he was a superb actor. His head stopped moving and his shoulders sagged.

"I don't know."

The body language was compelling, but Doe was discounting it. There was too much at stake. He couldn't trust the man with his life based on the fact that he didn't believe he could be that good an actor. When he went after the guy in the fisherman's jumper, when he took on the guys who had attacked the Police Department, he wanted to have Eugene behind him with several loaded weapons. He couldn't do that unless he was absolutely certain that Eugene wasn't a bad guy.

"OK, relax. I believe you." Doe tucked his gun back into the waistband of his pants.

It was like the guy hadn't heard him.

"You can go back to beating the crap out of your car if you want."

A little of the anger sparked back to life.

"You can't believe me. I've got nothing. I can't explain how they knew where he was. I can't explain any of it."

"Exactly." Doe walked around the car and opened the passenger door. "If you'd been the guy you'd have come up with something." He sat down, his ass on the seat and his feet outside the car on the garage floor. It had been a long couple of hours. "I gave you plenty of chances."

Doe twisted around, leaving one foot on the floor and pressing his back into the seat.

"If you wanted to cover your tracks you'd have said that you told someone when you first came into the bar. Then you would have said that you'd stopped for a while out there helping or chatting while I was interrogating the guy in the men's room. There would be no way I could have known whether that was true or not. Maybe there would have been time for someone to get a message out. How could I have been sure?"

Doe flexed his feet inside his boots. The soles were stiff and the uppers were made of hard leather but there was a little movement and it eased the ache if he curled his toes.

"Or you could have said that you thought you might have been followed or that you had seen something odd in the street when you were dropping off the car."

Doe arched his back and stretched out his legs and then he eased himself out of the seat.

"Or you could have suggested that they did it the way that they did probably do it."

Eugene still looked blank so Doe tapped the top of the car with his left hand.

"Department vehicles are tagged, right? GPS tracking? I had to tell the cops in the Police Department that there was no prisoner to protect. Otherwise most of them would have stayed there and tried to protect an empty cell. I had to practically paint it in foot high letters on the squad room wall. 'Sergeant Eugene has the guy in his car'.

Doe walked towards the garage door.

"The chances are, someone in the department told them that you had their guy. Then they tracked your car by its GPS signal."

Doe was already out on the street. Eugene still seemed dazed, but there didn't seem much point staying in the garage.

"It could still be a double bluff. Maybe I told them."

Doe shook his head.

"I doubt it. That would be a lot of trouble to go to and anyway, it would be more like a treble bluff. There's another reason I know it wasn't you."

Eugene looked over at him.

"You never went for your gun. It's chaos around here. I doubt that anyone could say for certain that I was with you and most people still think I'm an escaped prisoner. You could have shot me and headed back to the bar. You could have checked with Brown and loosened the tourniquets on Brel's legs to make sure he died. You could have spent the next fifty years convincing everyone that I was someone you had wanted to arrest not someone you had wanted to help."

Doe knew his way back to the bar. It was a short walk.

"If you were their guy and I had convinced you that you were the only person in the world that could be their guy, you would have killed me and dumped me in a ditch. If you were smart you would have done it in the street and messed with the timeline. Any witnesses would have said they saw you shoot me, but they wouldn't have been able to say whether we were walking toward the garage or running away from it. You could have said you told me where you'd stashed him because you thought I was a good guy. You could have said that I took off and freed the guy. You could have told everybody that you caught up with me too late to stop our guy escaping, but in time to shoot me."

*

A truck passed the end of the street they were walking on and they both instinctively dropped their heads and stepped to the side of the sidewalk.

"But if you were their guy you should have done it way earlier. Everything I've done and everything I told you proves that I'm a danger to their operation. You had me in the back of your cruiser, just you and me. You could have driven me out into the woods and shot me in the leg and left me to crawl away. Fifteen miles out and with a shattered femur, I'd have never made it back. I'd have been a mystery."

They were approaching the bar.

"But you didn't. Your hand never went near your weapon. You didn't even think about it. As far as I'm concerned you are clear and free."

They opened the bar door. The room was almost empty. The cops were gone.

SIXTEEN

The bartender was perched at the end of the bar and there was a scattering of injured cops but otherwise the room was empty. The barman looked up as they walked in and started to wave them away.

"Sorry folks, we're... Oh, it's you." He reached for a glass "You missed them, they all went back to the Department building."

"Well, almost all." The medic, Sam, came out from the back of the bar and walked towards them.

Doe stepped across the room and met him halfway.

"What about the detective that was guarding our prisoner? The guy in the restroom? Are they still here?"

The medic shook his head.

"Brown took off with the rest of them."

Eugene stepped up next to Doe, and they exchanged a quick, desperate look and turned towards the restroom door.

"Relax. I just checked on your prisoner. He's fine." Sam stepped between them, brushing past Eugene on the way through.

"I'm expecting the first of the guys to get back any minute now. There's going to be lots of new casualties." He looked tiredly towards the door. "At least I hope there are."

Doe and Eugene practically jogged over to the men's room door and pushed their way inside. Their guy was still sitting on the john. He looked pissed but otherwise fine. His hands were still cuffed behind his back but otherwise, he was free to move. Doe guessed that the man thought that the whole room outside the toilet door still was jammed with cops. There was no way for him to know that all there was out there was the walking wounded, a medic and the bartender. The prisoner figured he would have to fight his way through a couple of dozen armed and angry cops so he hadn't even tried to escape.

Doe tried to put himself in the guy's shoes. The soldier had gone from being part of an invincible team to being a prisoner in a few short minutes. He had gone from routine attack to absolute helplessness in the blink of an eye. He had been disarmed, thrown headfirst out of a window and then interrogated. Doe guessed it would knock some of the air out of you, but he also knew that if he had been in the same situation, once he was on his own he would have at least glanced outside the restroom door. If anyone had left him as poorly guarded as the cops had left their prisoner, then Doe would have been gone. He would have made his way out of the back door of the bar and taken his chances on the street, cuffs or no cuffs.

The fury in Doe's eyes wasn't meant for Eugene but Eugene looked away anyway. There was shame in his body language.

"They have friends lying there." He tried to excuse them by explaining, "When you all left the Department building they just left their friends behind and ran."

Doe tried to nod but he couldn't. He understood. He didn't need the explanation and to him no reason would be enough of an excuse.

"I'll stay." Eugene walked over to the prisoner. "I'll make sure we do our job this time."

Doe thought for a second or two. He knew that Eugene was desperate to be at the Department House. He needed to try to help some of his fallen colleagues and he needed to see the whole thing for himself. It was an important part of the coping mechanism for a lot of people, to confront the aftermath of a disaster head on, to see the worst, to put it into some kind of context and then take action. It would be worse for Eugene than for his colleagues. He had missed out on the attack. He only had his imagination and the scraps of information he had been given by the other cops to go on. Some of what he was imagining would be much worse than what had really happened but most of what had happened was way worse than he could ever imagine. He needed to see it for himself.

But Eugene had other needs right then as well. His department, and Eugene personally, had been humiliated throughout the day. The gang had been one step ahead of them from the moment they picked up the guy in the jersey. They had lost their communications, they had failed to spot the surveillance of their Department building. They had failed to prevent Doe's escape and they had failed to prevent the attack. Eugene had lost the one guy that all this was about and now his colleagues had left their only other prisoner in the care of a single deputy and a civilian. He needed to make amends. He felt the need to restore some dignity for himself and the whole of the Seal Harbor P.D. He needed to restore some professionalism, both personally and collectively.

Doe finally managed his nod.

"OK, but don't be long. The first detective or deputy through the door gets chewed out and then gets guard duty. We need to get the department house under control quickly and you and I have a lot of work to do."

Eugene nodded. Doe knew that it wouldn't be fair for the first guy back to get all the blame for leaving their prisoner but bawling him out would make Eugene feel better. In the long term the rebuke would rattle around the entire department until everyone felt like they had personally been the butt of Eugene's lecture. For every cop that piped up that it was unfair, there would be two who would quietly tell him that Eugene was absolutely right. It would help them to start to get back on track, to start doing their jobs again instead of running around like kids chasing a ball in a playground.

"I won't be." Eugene crouched down and then collapsed into a sitting position with his back against the wall between two hand basins. "But you be careful out there too. Whoever tracked my cruiser for them is still out there."

*

There were a few cops straggling back towards the bar as Doe hustled along the sidewalks toward the Department building. There weren't many of them and none of them looked injured. Doe didn't think Sam was going to get his large number of casualties.

He turned the corner onto Main Street. The Humvee that Doe had raked with machine gun fire was still sitting out in the street and the Humvee that he'd commandeered was still wedged through the Department building wall, but the other trucks had all gone. The third Humvee had shoved the dead truck far enough down the street to make the nearside lane passable, but the opposite lane was still completely blocked. It was the kind of situation where you expected to see a uniformed cop in a high visibility vest directing traffic around the smash, but there was no cop and no traffic to direct. The town was mercifully quiet. What traffic there was had presumably been put off by the carnage and by the sight of their Police Department standing there, empty and part demolished.

Doe wanted to get into the Department building. There was no wall separating the department's parking lot from the sidewalk. Doe could have cut across the parking lot but he didn't. He walked the full distance down the sidewalk to the parking lot entrance and then he followed the sidewalk into the lot and across a short, raised crossing and up the path to the Department's main doors. He purposely didn't step off the sidewalk at the corner of the block and cut diagonally across the asphalt, and he definitely didn't go anywhere near the smashed windows. There were angry and scared cops inside the building and Doe wanted to give them plenty of time to see him and realize that he wasn't a threat. He wanted them to see someone approaching in exactly the way they would expect someone to approach if they meant no harm. He didn't want them seeing movement in the corner of their eyes or shadowy figures silhouetted in the wreckage by the wedged Humvee. He didn't want to get shot by the good guys while he was climbing into the building through the window.

The squad room looked even worse in the aftermath than it had when Doe was running for his life toward the rear door. The little forts made out of furniture had been imbued with a level of heroism when all hell was breaking loose, but now only the futility and the stupidity remained. Some of the furniture was practically unrecognizable. Desks had been reduced to matchwood and mangled metal tubes. File cabinets had been reduced to giant sculptures of industrial cheese graters. Their metal sides forced into ragged cones and serrated edges.

There were bodies littering the floor. To a casual glance it looked as if every item in the entire room, including the people, had been smashed and dumped on the floor. A few heads turned to look as Doe opened the shattered front doors but no one stopped what they were doing or tried to stop him. Doe spotted Floyd in the corner near the cell doors and walked over.

Floyd was standing over the bodies of two of the bad guys. Doe was pretty sure they were two of the guys that he had hit as their team made their run from the door toward the cell block. Floyd looked up at Doe as he approached and then he looked back down at the bodies.

Doe stepped up next to the detective, shoulder to shoulder, so that he could look out across the squad room.

"How's it going Detective?"

Floyd looked up, following Doe's gaze out across the room.

"It's been better. We're on our last sweep. We're just re-checking the offices upstairs. We've found no survivors."

Doe knelt down next to the two dead gang members. Their weapons were missing and their webbing, with their grenades and spare magazines attached, had been cut off and taken. He could see little scraps of nylon and loose fibers from where they had hacked at the belts.

"No survivors at all? None of theirs, none of ours?"

Floyd shook his head.

"No. They must have taken them with them. There's nobody here but the dead."

Doe had a sudden, nasty and new thought.

"But everyone's accounted for?"

Floyd looked confused but then worked it out.

"Yes, sorry. All of our guys, everyone on duty, they're all accounted for. They haven't taken any of the injured hostage."

Doe took a breath of relief.

"I just meant that they must have taken all of their injured with them." Floyd gestured downwards toward the bodies on the floor, "The only bad guys we have here are dead."

"I'm surprised they left even them."

"I think they must have been interrupted. There are no dead bad guys upstairs." Floyd turned and looked up through the stairs towards the upper story. Doe couldn't tell whether he was imagining them carrying their dead down the staircase and loading them into the back of the Humvees, or whether he was reliving those desperate minutes holed up at the top of the staircase waiting for them to attack. "Down here they left the bodies and took the guns."

Floyd looked directly at Doe for the first time since he had walked into the Department building.

"You shot people up there, right? We should have found bodies?"

Doe nodded.

"Yep. Seven down, at least five dead."

Doe stood and walked toward the table fort that Mathers had sheltered behind.

"So, they took their dead and injured from up there but left the bodies that were down here." Floyd followed. "They had time to cut off their webbing but not to carry them to the trucks."

Doe nodded. "Yep, you're right. They must have gotten a call. Found out they needed to hurry along."

Floyd took his couple of seconds.

"Did you retrieve your guy? The one this was all about?"

There was nothing in his voice. It was as flat and dead as if he had been reading the questions in a math quiz.

Doe hid his pause by shifting some of the splintered desk, looking underneath.

"No. We didn't." Doe stood up and looked Floyd up and down. He thought about Eugene's reputation and he thought about the fact that the bad guys had been able to track Eugene's car. "He escaped. He forced his way through the grill between the front and back seats and smashed the window."

Floyd took the news pretty well. His fists and jaw clenched and he missed his usual two second buffer and uttered a single curse, but otherwise he seemed calm.

Doe moved on, around the fort, watching the floor, looking. His description of the escape was no more convincing when he described than it had been when he had seen it. Floyd was a detective and he would know the department cars well. It seemed unlikely that he hadn't spotted the inconsistencies but there could be multiple reasons for him not to raise any concerns and Doe certainly didn't want to open that can of worms.

"How many men do you have left?" Doe had rivaled a Floyd pause trying to find a more tactful phrase, but his vocabulary wasn't working the way it normally would and he didn't think Floyd was the kind of guy who would notice that kind of thing anyway.

"Sixteen of us completely uninjured, another five walking-wounded. Two of the injured guys are driving the emergency cases to Heath Haven. Or at least I hope they still are." The last was almost a whisper, definitely not intended for Doe's ears.

It was hardly good news. Floyd was working pretty well. He had the department operating, albeit mostly to Doe's instructions, but he was struggling with some of the responsibility and with the possible consequences of his actions. By Doe's estimate there were at least nine cops dead or dying, but the bad guys had taken a bigger hit than that. Doe had killed four of them in the two Humvees and at least five upstairs. There were the two dead down here and the two from the first sentry truck. They might have found the second sentry truck and freed the two guys that Doe had tied to the steering wheel, but they were at least thirteen men down.

Doe took another few steps and then spotted what he was looking for. A couple of feet in front of him a Deputy was fitting the corpse of a cop into a body bag. Doe stepped forward to check, but he didn't have any doubt. It was the cop that Mathers had tried to drag from the furniture fort to the safety of the Humvee. The cop who had tried to crawl the rest of the way when Mathers got hit. The cop who had been alive and well when Doe had hightailed it for the vehicle yard.

"Your guys are mostly out and about getting the kids and young women to safety?"

Floyd nodded.

"We got to the groups first. They're all dispersed now. We tried to get them back to their families but if there was going to be any delay we moved them first and then took them home afterwards. We used the other bars in town." Floyd looked proud about this and Doe guessed that he probably wasn't much of a drinker. "We figured that they wouldn't go looking for kids and wholesome young women in the bars."

Doe thought that it was likely that the gang might think that cops might use bars as a safe haven, but Floyd seemed proud of the idea. It was way too late to change the plan anyway so Doe did an admiring nod and moved on.

"They are mostly home now and we've got guys moving around the neighborhoods. Anyone with a child under nineteen is heading for the hills." Floyd got pretty close to an actual frown. "There's going to be hell to pay afterwards. We're scaring the shit out of people."

"Don't worry about that, Detective. It's not your problem. In twelve or eighteen hours from now you're going to be inundated with help." Doe knelt down by the cop's body and put his hand on the deputy's arm to stop him zipping up the bag. "Excluding all of that, how many men do you have on hand?"

Floyd looked around.

"Erm, four. Two upstairs, two down here... and me. Five in total I guess"

"OK., you might need to get a couple of the others back here. You have a couple more jobs to do." Doe beckoned the detective to squat next to him alongside the body bag. "If you have anyone out there who has a military background, you need to call them in.

"You need to get a guard posted outside this building and another outside the bar. They definitely know that you are here and it makes sense to assume that they might know about the bar as well. If they decide to come back and finish you all off, you need to have a little warning."

Floyd nodded and started to look around for officers that he would trust to protect the two buildings.

"But before you do that you need to start the investigation here. And that's where you need the ex-military guys. You need to document everything. When we get these guys, I want them to go down for everything they did. We can't let them get away with anything just because we didn't collect the evidence or take the right steps."

Doe tapped Floyd on the forearm and then reached into the body bag. He put his fingers on the dead cop's jaw and rolled his head to the side. There was a neat bullet hole in the back of his head and the hair around the wound was singed and blackened.

"Some of this stuff is going to look a lot more familiar to them than it is to you."

*

Doe hung around near the cells trying not to get in the way. He was trying not to look too closely at the bodies of the gang members. He didn't think that the retreating bad guys would have left any of their guys behind if they were alive, but he wasn't certain. He didn't want to check their bodies in case some of the cops had engaged in a little extra-judicial execution. The retreating soldiers had finished off the injured cops with a bullet to the head. If the cops had overstepped the mark and done the same to any injured gang members, right then, Doe didn't want to know. He trusted Floyd to find and preserve any evidence and he didn't want to get bogged down in the investigation himself. There were other things he needed to do.

He trusted Floyd to do a good job because, even if Floyd was the one who had helped the gang to find Eugene's car, there would still be no reason not to do a good job on the Department Building investigation. If there was any evidence against the gang then their mole might be under some pressure to suppress it, but he wouldn't have any reason to mess about with evidence of police brutality. Doe wasn't relying on Floyd or anyone else to bring the gang to justice. Doe was going to do that himself.

Doe was waiting for Eugene and he spent the time running through his memories of the battle. He was trying to tally up his own list of dead and injured. By his count he had seen ten or eleven of the attackers fall during the squad room firefight. He had shot eight of them himself. He knew that one of his hits had only been a flesh wound, but he thought the rest were fatal or debilitating. Eight dead and three injured on the first floor was a reasonable estimate.

The tally upstairs was easier to assess. The bodies themselves were missing but Doe had been the only shooter and he had been extremely close to his targets. He was certain of seven hits and he knew that each and every one of those seven was either dead or too badly injured to hold a gun. As Doe finished up his calculations he saw Eugene step in through the smashed window by the wrecked Humvee. Doe figured it was ingrained training. Never use the door if there was an alternative method. Avoid the expected. It was still stupid, but Eugene got away with it. The room was emptying. The cops that were left looked up at the unexpected figure in the room, but they recognized Eugene before they reached for their guns.

Eugene made a show of walking directly across the room toward Doe. He looked down often enough to avoid tripping over the debris and the body bags, but he didn't linger. He wanted Doe to see that he was back in control. That he was all business again. Doe took the cue. He met Eugene halfway across the room and steered him towards the back of the room.

"Floyd's got this and he'll do a good job, even if... He has guys out rounding up any potential hostages and getting them to safety. They have two cars taking the injured who have nothing to lose out to Heath Haven and they're posting a guard outside the bar..."

Eugene nodded.

"Yep, I saw him on my way out. It's a guy called Benny. A good kid."

"Floyd's organizing it all and he's going to start the investigation here as well. He'll make sure that the evidence is gathered and protected."

Eugene looked around.

"Where are the injured?"

"There aren't any. They shot all the casualties before they left."

It was shocking news and Doe gave Eugene a minute for it to settle but Eugene didn't need that long. His whole body tensed and he unholstered and reholstered his side arm and then asked Doe what he wanted him to do.

"You need to show me where they would have done the vehicle tracking."

*

Eugene and Doe stepped over and into the nearest office.

"They could have used pretty much anyone's desk." Eugene sat down in the chair behind the desk. "The software is on every PC and all the computers are linked. You just need to log on, open the program and type in the password."

"So, who has the password?" Doe followed Eugene around the desk and watched him log on to the computer.

"Pretty much anyone. It's not considered to be a very sensitive program. There's no personal data, nothing of interest to defendants. It just tells us where everyone is."

Eugene double clicked on an icon and entered a password and a map of Seal Harbor appeared on the screen. Bright red dots ringed with a red circle indicated the positions of the tracked cars. The majority were close to the Department building either in the yard or in the parking lot out front. There were a few more scattered around the town including Eugene's abandoned cruiser. Doe figured the others were the cars of off duty officers. Cars that had got left at home when the officers had responded to the emergency call.

At the edge of the map there were two moving dots. Doe breathed a sigh of relief. He touched Eugene on the shoulder and pointed to the screen.

"They're still moving. The cars with the injured guys made it out of town."

Eugene scrolled the wheel on the mouse and the scale of the map shrank. The moving dots jumped back towards the center of the screen and slowed down. Heath Haven appeared at the bottom left of the screen and the road that the dots were following looped around and met it.

"They're about halfway there."

"Anything much they can do when they get there?"

"If Heath Haven has a working radio or phones they can contact the Sheriff at Soukous. They have some SWAT there. There's a lot more at Burlington. Maybe they could get choppers with Feds from Seattle or some National Guard."

Doe clicked the computer off.

"So, it'll be six hours minimum before we see any serious help."

Eugene sat at the desk, blank screen in front of him and his hand still on the mouse.

*

"If we went around the other offices would we be able to see which computer was the last to log on to the tracking software?"

Eugene shook his head.

"If you don't do anything the whole computer logs you off after a few minutes. You have to put your password back in to get back on. There might be a way to do it, but I don't know what it is."

"OK. In that case you and I need to hit the armory."

"Bullshit! We need to find out who sold us out!"

"And we will, but first..."

Eugene look completely nonplussed by Doe's lack of interest.

"No! The first thing we have to do is find out what's going on!"

"We know exactly what's going on."

"We need to know who it is. We can't let him run around loose."

"It doesn't matter."

"It mattered half an hour ago. It mattered when you thought it was me."

Doe turned at the door.

"Yes, it did."

"But it doesn't matter now?"

"No, it really doesn't." Doe wanted Eugene by his side more than he wanted the weapons in the Police Department armory. He had access to the bad guys' guns and he was willing to bet that they would be better equipped than the cops. Given a few minutes inside the logging camp he could pull together enough weapons to start a small war.

"There's going to be a big investigation. They'll find out who it was. They'll go back through the servers and shit. They'll find out whose password was used when we were all out of here and they'll tie the password to the person who used it. Floyd will dust the keyboards for prints, the tech guys will find out which terminal was used last."

Eugene still wasn't standing up.

"You don't get it. Floyd might not find out shit! Maybe it's Floyd that fed them the information!"

"No. It's still you that isn't getting it. He will. He can't hide the evidence even if he wants to. There's too much of it. There will be server logs. He can't delete them without someone here noticing."

Doe took a deep breath. Ready to try one more time.

"And any way, it doesn't matter."

"Of course, it matters! He sold us out. People have died. We have to catch him."

Doe was getting impatient. He hadn't expected Eugene to understand right away but he had spent the whole day not only dealing with the bad guys but also coaxing the good guys.

"They will catch him. Afterwards. There's plenty of time for that. They'll identify him. He's not going anywhere. The only place he could run to is the logging camp."

Doe turned to the door.

"What we have to do is stop the rest of them from getting away with their prize."

*

Eugene half rose from his seat, muttering under his breath.

"You weren't so forgiving back in the garage."

Doe had had enough.

"You want to know why it doesn't matter to me whether Detective Floyd traced your car? It doesn't matter to me because he is now locked into investigating this crime scene. He has to check it all out. He might manage to hide some evidence but this place is dripping in it."

Despite himself Doe took a couple of steps toward the desk and Eugene.

"This is not what they were expecting. We have a live prisoner, we have their equipment, we know how they did it and they have left evidence everywhere. They're going to have to leave without any effective clean-up. I know exactly where their camp is and they're going to have to go straight to their emergency evacuation. I bet they planned to spend days breaking camp and shipping everything away. They'd have planned to take most of the stuff they brought with them away with them and without that stuff to point us in the right direction the rest of it could have rotted quietly away for decades.

"They didn't camouflage everything out there because they were worried about you spotting them before the attack. There was no reason why you would be looking for them then. They camouflaged everything so that they would have a couple of days to move shit out while you guys tried to hunt them down with a couple of spotter planes and some choppers.

"They expected to walk into the Police Department, shoot some holes in the roof, maybe kill a couple of guys if you cut up rough and then stroll out with their guy. I'm not saying that would have gone unanswered. You would have gotten state help. Extra cops and specialists and some equipment. Planes and dogs from the mainland. Questions would have been asked, resources would have been allocated but it would have been another local, backwater incident. They have been relying on a half-assed local response and believe me, they are not going to get that now. Even if we didn't know where their camp is we would find it. We'd have drones and satellites combing the island. They'll know that. They'll have moved onto plan B by now. Onto plan 'get the fuck out of here in the hours we have before all hell rains down on us.'

"So, their camp will be a treasure trove of evidence. They'll probably try to burn it, but even if they succeed, huge amounts of evidence will survive. We will comb the whole place for DNA. Fibers and scraps of paper will go through microscopes and computer programs. There will be hundreds of agents here. Thousands upon thousands of man hours will be used."

Doe remembered himself and turned back toward the door.

"They were supposed to be in and out with no one ever knowing what it was all about, but we've punched a huge hole in that. The whole thing will unravel. There is no doubt that they will find the guy who traced your car. They will also find the guys who did the shooting. Everything one who was here today will be caught eventually.

"What those hundreds of agents can't do is be here right now. What they can't do is stop them finishing their job and getting that bastard out of here. And I have a feeling that once he's out of here he'll be in the wind and we'll never hear of him again.

"They'll find the guys who killed your friends but they'll never catch the guy they did it for."

Doe looked back over his shoulder.

"One morning you'll wake up and switch on the news and there'll be mangled buildings and dead kids or there'll be a downed plane or a poisoned city and you say to yourself, 'I wonder if that was...'. It might get to the point where you can't watch the news after a while."

*

They hustled along to the small armory. Doe could tell that Eugene had accepted what they had to do but that he still wasn't happy. Doe took it for as long as he could, but he knew that if he didn't deal with it before they left the building he would have to leave it until the whole thing was over.

"OK. What is it?"

"What's what?" Eugene had the key to the gun room in his hands.

"Something is still pissing you off." Doe ushered him with his hands, "You can talk and unlock, by the way."

"I accept your assessment. The priority is the apprehension of the guy who washed ashore. The remainder of the investigation can wait." Eugene unlocked the thick steel door and opened the gun room.

Doe knew that the investigation wasn't on hold. Floyd and his team would be working on it. It was a kind of vanity on Eugene's part to think that because he wasn't involved in it the investigation wasn't happening, but after the day Eugene had had, Doe figured it was excusable and it certainly wasn't a point he had time to make.

"But?"

"But what?"

Doe stopped the cop in the doorway. He was still angry. He was still short of his usual tolerant, understanding demeanor.

"But why the hell have you still got you panties in a wad? Why are you still pissed at me?"

Eugene looked him up and down. He was in control. There was no risk that he was going to hit Doe but that didn't stop him really, really wanting to.

"It mattered about me! You put me through the wringer. You let me think it was my fault. You let me think that the evidence showed that I was the traitor and then you don't give a shit about it being anyone else." Eugene stepped into the gun room, "It mattered about me!"

Doe relaxed. His shoulders dropped, the creases in his forehead disappeared. He put out an arm and touched Eugene on the shoulder, turning him around. He looked Eugene in the eye for a long second and then pushed past him.

"Oh, that." He started to sort through the police weaponry, "There's a major difference between them and you."

Doe picked out a shotgun and turned back towards Eugene.

"I don't care who it is because whoever they are the worst they can do is a little bit of mischief back here." He held Eugene's eyes for another long minute. "I needed to know it wasn't you because you're coming with me. It doesn't matter about them because I'm not trusting them to stand behind me with a gun."

SEVENTEEN

Doe looked around the gun room. They were a well-equipped department. There were racks of automatic rifles and hand guns and some long guns and a row of shotguns. For what Doe was planning, police weaponry was never going to be the best, but it would do the job. He would have preferred a few minutes access to a military armory, but they could make do. He could see Eugene was making the same assessment so Doe let Eugene have the captured HK 416 and he took a department MP5 for himself. He was happy with his USP Tacticals and was pleased to see a couple of Mossberg 590A1 lined up with the shotguns. He took one and handed Eugene a Remington 700P rifle. Eugene rustled up a couple of black nylon kit-bags and they loaded the ammunition and the rest of the equipment. Doe wasn't going to get much better camouflaged than his dark work-shirt and black jeans but Eugene changed out of his uniform into a pair of loose fitting black pants and stretchy long-sleeved black shirt that he kept in his locker. They each checked over their guns and hoisted their kit-bags to their shoulders and Eugene headed for the vehicle yard exit.

Doe called him back.

"We need to split up."

Eugene looked around the squad room. no one seemed to be taking much notice of them, but he was keen to get out of there before someone saw them and started to wonder what they were up to.

"No, we need to get a squad car and get away from here before our mole notices what we're up to and calls it in."

Doe shook his head.

"We can't take a squad car. It would never get up that logging track. It's bad enough in a truck."

"OK. We can take my pickup. Come with me, my house is on the way."

"We can't go without telling someone what we know. You go and get the truck and then come back and pick me up."

"We absolutely cannot tell anyone!" Eugene was incredulous. "If the guy was willing to trace my car for them he'll certainly call them up and let them know we're coming. It would be suicide to tell anyone."

"Nonetheless we've got to do it. If we go out there and we fail then we might not make it back to town. We need to be sure that someone else knows where their camp is so that they can get out there quickly, before the trail goes cold."

Eugene looked around desperately.

"We could send an email."

"Not to anyone outside of Seal Harbor we couldn't. The phone lines are down. And if we manage to send an internal email then what's to say that we don't send it to the wrong person and they open it right away and we end up tipping them off anyway?"

"We can leave a note then. Stick it in the department safe addressed to the head of the rescue force."

"Same problem. If we tell someone where we hid it or if we leave it out in the open, then your traitor might find it and open it straight away. It's exactly the same result. On the other hand, if we hide it and don't tell anyone where it is, then it might not get found in time and the gang might be over the water and clear before anyone finds out what we know."

Eugene was still desperately glancing around the wrecked room.

"But they'll be waiting for us."

"Not if we're lucky. We tell one person and we tell him just before we set out. Even if we tell the wrong person, even if they have a means of contacting the camp despite the phone jamming and even if he finds time and space to make the call, even then, we can be through the logging road and on foot, in the woods, on our way to the camp well before they can respond. They are under strength and busy. As long as we have time to get off the road there's a limit to what they can do. Even if they increase the number of patrols I'd back us to get past them in the woods."

Eugene's shoulders sagged.

"So, I pick up the truck and meet you..."

"Back here, yes." Doe nodded.

"Who are you going to tell?"

Doe headed back across the squad room.

"Floyd. There's no point trying to guess who not to tell. As long as he isn't the mole then I trust him to use the information."

Eugene looked like he wanted to tear the thick metal door from its hinges and throw it across the gun room.

Doe smiled.

"Hey, relax. You've got to trust someone right?"

*

Doe couldn't find Floyd at the Department building so he had to jog back to the bar to catch up with him. Floyd eyed Doe's kit-bag suspiciously but he said that he wouldn't do anything with the information Doe gave him until the cavalry arrived from the mainland. Doe's instinct was to trust the guy but that wasn't the reason he found it easy to put his fears to the back of his mind. He had a difficult job to do and worrying about whether Floyd was going to sell them out or not wouldn't help one way or the other. They had to tell someone. Floyd was the obvious choice.

The detour to the bar put him behind schedule so he sprinted back to the Department building and found Eugene sitting outside in a three-year-old Honda Ridgeline. It seemed like Eugene's travel with the army had left him with more pragmatism than patriotism, at least as far as vehicle choice went. From what Doe knew it was a fine vehicle and a good choice. Eugene was drumming his fingers on the steering wheel as Doe threw his kit-bag in the back and he took off up Main Street before Doe had even got the passenger door closed. They sped through the deserted streets and the speed with which Eugene took the logging road caused Doe to make a mental note to ensure that he got compensation from the state for wear and tear to the truck. The suspension and underside of the pickup was going to be wrecked. In a little over twenty minutes they were approaching the abandoned house halfway along the logging trail.

*

Doe wanted to push on. He wanted to drive straight past the house and get in amongst the trees a little further up the track, but Eugene said he couldn't do that. He said that he had to look for the homeowner and try to get him to safety. Doe told him that there was nobody home, that he had already checked, but Eugene said that that was impossible. He said that there was only one way out of town from here and that was through town. Old Man Budd couldn't go anywhere without the whole town knowing about it.

Doe figured he had asked enough of Eugene to allow him a little of his own way and Eugene promised that even from here it was still only a little over a mile through the trees to the camp site. He assured Doe that if they got interrupted at the house he could lead them both a little way up the road to a place where they could cross and head toward the logging camp through the trees. He knew the country. He was an Army Ranger. It was a low risk detour and one that Eugene wouldn't skip.

They parked in almost exactly the same spot as Doe had earlier in the day and approached the building in much the same way. There was no need for Doe to make his weapons safe and hide them this time. There was no prisoner tied up in the back of Eugene's truck. Doe simply left the rifle and the shotgun in the load-bed of the pickup and tucked the two hand guns into two spare belt holsters that Eugene had produced from his locker. Eugene took his liberated H&K. Doe guessed it showed their different training. Doe's was primarily on handguns. Eugene was more familiar with heavier firepower. They were going to be mostly indoors so Doe thought that his choice made more sense. Rate of fire and long-range accuracy weren't likely to be factors. Short range accuracy and ease of movement were, but then Doe guessed that he would think that way. It was part of his training.

Eugene led the way. They ducked under the front windows and moved quickly up the steps and across the porch. Eugene gestured Doe toward the side of the door and waited for him to take up his position. The moment Doe was in place Eugene swept in through the front door and cleared the kitchen and moved on into the parlor in a single fluid movement. Doe hustled to catch up and by the time he entered the second room, Eugene was already halfway up the stairs and the door to the closet under the stairs was standing open. When Doe joined Eugene on the second floor, the bed was on its side and the bedroom closet doors were standing wide. Eugene was standing by the side of the rear window, looking out over the yard and the outhouse.

*

Eugene nodded at Doe and then took off back down the stairs. Doe caught up with him again in the back yard. Eugene gestured toward the outhouse door. Doe took up his position again and watched as Eugene crashed through the three-quarter length, bare plank door.

"Told you."

Eugene shushed him immediately and pointed with his first and second fingers spread apart, simultaneously indicating both the corner of the house and the old veranda along the back of the building. Doe shrugged and followed as Eugene checked the last corner of the house.

"See..."

Eugene silenced Doe again and moved toward the veranda, his eyes blazing and the whole of the flat of his hand pressed against his mouth in an urgent, exaggerated hushing signal. Doe looked around the yard, intrigued. It hadn't changed, the same packed dirt floor swept mostly clear of needles and leaves, the same pile of dining chairs and crates and fire wood on the same dilapidated back porch.

The same chest freezer. Eugene stepped up close to the freezer and raised his rifle. He got it pointed down toward the freezer lid and then reached out with his free hand and slowly raised the lid.

Doe stepped forward and peered over the lip. There was an old man in a red check fleece shirt and faded blue denim coveralls crammed into the bottom of the freezer. Eugene let the lid fall open against the side of the house.

*

"I knew something was wrong." Doe was embarrassed. He wouldn't let it affect him for long, but he knew that he should have checked the freezer. "The whole place felt empty and it felt like it had been empty for a while, but I knew something was off. I should have looked around more thoroughly."

He had been too busy worrying about bad guys jumping out of closets to concentrate on collecting evidence or looking for civilians. "How long?"

"He's been dead for days." Eugene moved away and lowered his gun. Doe stepped in and checked for himself. He was relieved to see that Eugene was right. His mistake hadn't cost the man his life. He hadn't been lying in the freezer dying as Doe stumbled around in his house and yard just feet away from saving him. The guy had been dead for days and he had died instantly. He had been executed, like the injured cops in the Department building. There was a single bullet hole in the middle of his forehead.

"There was a window open and water in the sink and a radio still plugged in on the shelf above it." Doe stepped over toward Eugene. "I've been hearing about a storm blowing in all weekend. It seemed stupid that someone would leave the radio where a big storm could blow it into the water. It seemed like someone who lived all the way out here would have known that it could be a fire risk and would have been used to closing a place down before leaving. Someone living in a big town might not think about it, but out here you'd need to be self-sufficient. Out here you couldn't afford to make mistakes like that."

He looked up at Eugene.

"I'm sorry. I should have known. I should have looked."

Eugene set off, back toward the truck.

"It doesn't matter. He was already dead. Nothing you could have done."

Doe jogged to catch up.

"There was nothing you could have done either. He was dead before our guy even set foot on the beach. There was no way for you to know."

Eugene approached the truck. Nothing in his demeanor to hint at anger or shame.

"We were supposed to protect him. Protect the town. Not knowing that he was in any extra danger doesn't help. We still failed. He's still dead."

Doe scooted around the front of the truck and opened the passenger door.

"I'm supposed to do that for the whole country. The organization I work for tries to stop this kind of thing from ever happening."

Eugene shrugged. "That doesn't make it any better for me."

"No." Doe conceded. "It doesn't."

Eugene put the truck into gear and pulled out onto the track.

"Or for me." Doe whispered.

*

Doe looked ahead, up the track. It was empty for as far as he could see, but that wasn't all that far. He buzzed the window open and listened, but he couldn't hear anything over the sound of their own motor. He settled back into the seat for a short journey, but Eugene pulled the truck right across the road instead. He jammed the front of the truck up against a tree and left the load-bed jutting out across the track.

"We can walk it from here." Eugene pulled his kit-bag from the back and set off toward the trees.

Doe took a look at the truck. It was blocking the road very effectively. There was a slight turn a hundred feet up the track that would stop anyone from backing up and then building up speed and smashing Eugene's truck out of the way. The front fender was pressed up to the side of a two-foot-thick pine tree. You could pull the truck back across the road, toward a wider part of the track and try make space to creep around it, but it wouldn't be quick. Or, if you had enough torque you could put your fender against the back corner of the truck and push until it span around, pivoting against the tree, and gave you a clear road, but that would be even slower. Even in a Humvee.

Doe grabbed his bag and followed Eugene into the trees.

EIGHTEEN

Doe caught up with Eugene in a few quick strides and put his hand on his shoulder.

"We should make a plan for the infiltration."

Eugene shrugged tensely but stopped. He turned towards Doe, his look was frustrated. Patient and a little amused.

Doe waited a second for effect.

"Oh no! This is your area of expertise Sargent. You tell me."

Eugene looked a surprised but then relaxed a little and turned back towards the wood.

"OK. We sneak up on them. We find a place with good cover and lie down quietly and wait for full dark. Then we storm their place and shoot everyone who doesn't surrender."

Doe shook his head a sad little shake and stepped past Eugene and turned around, putting himself between Eugene and the camp. Eugene shrugged again but it was less tense, maybe a little resigned now rather than patient.

"OK. We go single file. You follow me. We need to go north-nor-east and we have about a mile to travel. We move quickly but quietly and we walk over or through anything dry and around anything wet. If we contact the enemy we freeze. We stay still and we wait until we are sure that they've seen us before we engage them. The moment we start shooting we move from the infiltration phase and onto the attack. And we don't want that. If they don't spot us we give them a full minute to leave the area before we start moving again. All clear?"

Doe nodded. It was a simple plan, but it was good to get the simple things agreed and it had taken Eugene's mind off of the body in the freezer.

"OK. No talking until we hit the perimeter."

Eugene set off, further into the trees.

*

They were at the wire in a quick fifteen minutes. Eugene had stopped them once, raising his hand and melting into the shadows, but it had been a false alarm and he covered the flat ground with a fast, silent march that Doe struggled to match. He concentrated on putting his feet exactly where Eugene had stepped, trusting that if he could manage to do that his footsteps would be as silent as the Rangers had been. Doe spotted the familiar lightening of the horizon a little before Eugene gestured for him to slow down. They walked the last few yards side by side and then dropped to their bellies and crawled to the edge of the tree-line.

Eugene took a pair of black, rubber-covered binoculars from his bag and scanned the camp. Doe just used his eyes again. He wasn't looking for detail. He was just checking that everything was roughly the same as it had been the first time he had seen it.

Some of the discipline that had been evident during Doe's first visit was missing. There were a couple of Humvees out in plain sight. They had been parked sloppily, only partly under the cover of the camouflage netting. There were also a few small piles of equipment out in the yard between the shipping containers and a few doors were standing open. They were rattled and working fast, but the fence was still there and the two sentries in their sniper nest were still there and they were both still working diligently. Doe could see the glint of their optics as they swept the perimeter. Looking to his left Doe could see the big fork truck at the gate. He could tell that the block of concrete was down, blocking the entrance. Doe settled himself in and waited for Eugene.

He had described the set up to Eugene, but he hadn't expected such an experienced guy to simply take his word for it. The ex-ranger quartered every blade of grass in the compound. He scanned the wire perimeter inch by inch and he checked out every building, every lump and bump and all of the people and all of the equipment that he could see. After a long ten minutes, he put down the binoculars and turned to face Doe.

"There's no way in. It's not an infiltration from this point. It's an attack. We wait for dark and then I take out the two snipers and we hit the fence and split up. You head for the buildings alongside the road, I'll head along the fence toward the radio mast." He stowed the binoculars in his kit-bag and started switching equipment in and out. In went anything that he could do without during the attack, out came the weapons and the ammunition. "There'll be stiff resistance and you'll have to deal with the guys behind you at the gate as well as the guys in front of you from their camp, but you'll have the cover of the buildings. I'll swing around when I reach the edge of the camo netting and attack from inside. You work your way through the buildings and we'll meet up by the vehicles and go room to room through their huts until we find him."

Doe nodded. It looked like the only way and Eugene made it sound possible, but it would be a suicide mission. They were two men up against thirty or more. They would have a lot of ground to cover and even if Eugene took out the two guys in the sniper's nest with his first two shots, everyone in the camp would know that they were coming. If he missed with one or other shot, then they would be under fire from one or both snipers. They would be lucky to get far enough into the compound to split up but if they did they wouldn't be working their way towards a rendezvous by the Humvees, they would be running and hiding. They would be being hunted by the much bigger force. They would be trying to pick the enemy off one by one without getting shot themselves. It would be a short and bloody game of chess. Doe and Eugene would be trying to dismantle the opposition piece by piece and with nothing of their own to sacrifice. Doe wasn't a good chess player, but he was better than that.

"I have another plan. But first I need a promise."

*

Doe would have liked to be facing Eugene. He wanted to look him in the eye. He wanted to assess his responses and he wanted to allow Eugene to see his eyes and follow his body language. Doe wanted him to know that he wasn't bullshitting him, that he could pull this off if he was given the chance. Anywhere else and Doe would have turned to face Eugene, but right then they were in enemy territory. Facing each other just wasn't an option. Doe propped himself up behind the nearest tree, facing into the woods, looking for patrols, and Eugene wriggled his way into the forest floor and kept an eye on the wire and the sentries on top of the old mill building. They spoke in low voices, not whispering. Whispering tends to raise the pitch of your voice. It adds a sharpness that carries.

"I have no idea what all this is about but I know deep in my bones that this guy is really dangerous."

Eugene looked comfortable. He looked like he could lie there for days and keep up the conversation and know everything that was happening in that compound all at the same time. He didn't look like he gave a shit about what Doe was saying.

"I've been around some pretty bad guys and this guy takes the top spot for setting my hairs on end."

Doe shifted his rifle slightly, his eyes sweeping a semicircle through the green and browns in front and to the sides of him.

"I know that when we get in there you're going to want to bring this guy in for what his gang have done to your friends..."

Eugene nodded but he looked bored.

"...but that just isn't going to happen."

A bird shot from a tree to their left screeching and flapping its wings madly. Doe moved his rifle in a slow arc and held it pointing in the general direction for a while. Nothing happened.

"I could lie to you. I could tell you we're going in there to arrest him."

Eugene didn't move a muscle. There was no reason for him to.

"But it would be a lie."

"You have orders to kill him?"

Doe didn't laugh. He was trying to stay quiet but that wasn't the reason.

"No. No one knows I'm here. I'm not under orders. I'm just in the right place at the wrong time."

Doe's mind was threatening to wander. He spent his life trying to find unusual crimes and here he had simply stumbled into one. He couldn't work out whether it was dumb luck, serendipity or whether some combination of tiny clues had subconsciously led him here. He forced himself to move his head in microscopic jerks though his sweep of the forest, forcing himself to concentrate on the job at hand.

"I'm not going to kill him and I need your commitment that whatever happens, neither are you."

*

Eugene was too professional to turn or even move his eyes from the camp but his shoulders tensed a little.

"I don't mean intentionally. Although we both know it happens." Doe was keen to keep the urgency out of his voice. He didn't want an argument with Eugene and he didn't want his voice to rise and alert any passing patrols.

"Not by any Rangers."

Eugene was plenty experienced enough to know that it was a stupid thing to say. He looked up at the sniper's nest.

Doe had to decide. He didn't want to do it to hurt the guy. If he told him, it had to be for a good reason.

"The guys up there watching the wire are ex-Rangers."

He let it hang there.

"The guy in the bar restroom told me."

There was a silence. Eugene eventually had to fill it.

"I won't kill your guy."

Doe shuffled himself away from the tree and crawled his way toward Eugene.

"I know. That's the easy part." He made his way alongside Eugene and looked over at him long enough to make the ex-soldier look over at him. "I need more than that. Anyone else in there is fair game, but I need you to do whatever you can to keep the guy alive. If you have a target and he comes anywhere close I need you to disengage. I need you to tell me that he won't get shot. Even by accident."

*

"You think it's that important?"

Doe took a look out over the logging camp and then crawled his way back to lean against the tree.

"You tell me. Why do you think they're going through all this? It's costing someone a fortune."

"Some people have money to burn."

Doe knew that Eugene was just going through the motions. It was wait-out bullshit. Soldiers with lots of time to kill and something to avoid thinking about.

"And the people they were willing to kill."

"These guys kill for a living."

"No. This guy's serious. I've spoken to him. The money and the trouble they're willing to go to to get him ashore are just confirmation for me."

He was sure of Eugene now but it didn't hurt to make absolutely certain.

"There are countries in the world where the number of people they killed today is matched by the number of children killed in their homes every day. Matched or doubled or tripled."

He knew that Eugene knew this. Eugene had been to most of those places.

"I don't mean through disease or family abuse, I mean bombed or shot. And I do mean children. Not civilians. There are many, many more civilian deaths. There are people out there who blame us for that." Doe looked out across the camp.

"Then we have local ideologues, psychopaths, pecuniary motives and shadowy power conspiracies. There are people who feel displaced or dispossessed or repressed or morally offended by our society. We have a country that many people think is founded on the concept that radical action should be taken to protect our individual freedom. Not *can* be taken but *should* be taken. Action that should be taken however obscene or ridiculous everyone else finds it. Action that should be taken to protect rights that they don't even think are important. The important part has become that simple concept. The idea that someone is trying to take something away from them. Even if the thing being taken away is something that no sane person would ever want and something that is only ever used for evil."

"With all those people out there trying to hurt us, almost no number of deaths will ever surprise me. Everything I have seen and everything I feel tells me that this guy could produce something truly terrible."

Eugene raised a hand in surrender. Not the hand that held his trigger finger but the hand that was steadying the gun. It was the first significant movement Doe had seen Eugene make since he had put down his binoculars.

"OK, OK. I get it." Eugene shuffled a little in the dirt. "You need him alive."

Doe settled in beside him, scanning the perimeter wire again.

"It's going to make it very tough." Eugene was thinking out loud. "We don't have the right equipment or the manpower for a snatch. I don't see how we can do it."

"We can't. I'm not suggesting we do. I don't need a plan that keeps him alive, I just need your commitment that once we're in there you will do everything you can to avoid killing him. If he dies in the first attack, before we get some kind of control, then I'll just have to live with that. It will still be way better than him reaching the mainland."

Eugene smiled. Doe could tell that Eugene didn't have much confidence in their chances of getting to a point where they had any kind of control. It was still going to be virtually impossible just to get beyond the first few feet of the wire. Eugene was planning retribution. He wasn't expecting to return, but Doe felt that once given, Eugene would keep his word.

"Do I have your word?"

Doe turned and looked at Eugene. They locked eyes for a fraction of a second.

"You have my word that if we get in there and get to a point where we are choosing targets rather than just fighting for our lives, then I will bring him out alive."

"Good enough." Doe turned fractionally toward him, "So, listen up. This is how we're going to do it."

NINETEEN

Ten minutes later Doe was skirting the perimeter wire just far enough into the trees to be invisible to the two snipers on the roof of the old mill. He had already passed the logging camp buildings and the newer shipping containers. He was jogging alongside the wire near the camouflage netting. His destination was a point where he would be in direct line with the radio mast, the camp and the main gate.

The sun was setting behind him. The camouflage net hooked to the radio mast was obscuring his view but he could just about see through it and spot the camp road leading straight away from the center of the camp. It drew a straight line, up the incline and out past the big concrete block and the fork truck before curving away into the trees.Doe stopped, checked his guns, stowed his gear and waited for it to get fully dark.

Eugene checked the time. They hadn't bothered synchronizing watches because split second timing wasn't going to be an issue. There was no way for Doe to be sure exactly when he would be ready. He needed to wait until it was dark in his half of the bowl before he could even start and Eugene had to wait until Doe was well into the camp before he could join in. Eugene knew pretty accurately when the sun would go down. He had been living on the island for a couple of years. Sunset and sunrise changes moved with a reassuring regularity that had been absent from his life as a soldier, but he couldn't be certain how the light would fall through the trees and into the bowl. The angles and the clouds and the density of the foliage on the tops of the trees would all make a difference. Doe needed full darkness if he was going to have any chance of pulling off his end of the plan.

Eugene had argued for waiting a couple of hours, into the night, to make sure that the darkness was complete. That way they could agree a time and synchronize their attacks, but he had to agree with Doe. They were on a short timescale. Now that the bad guys had their prize, they were unlikely to be sitting around and waiting for morning. The longer Doe waited, the longer their enemy had to regroup and start their withdrawal. Two men with hand guns and rifles attacking a fortified camp might be difficult but two men attacking an armored convoy would be virtually impossible.

The sun was almost down behind the trees in front of Eugene. There was diffuse light coming through the topmost branches and the eastern half of the camp was still bathed in weak sunlight, but the camouflage netting was dark and a curving line of shadow was creeping slowly across the bowl. Eugene figured he had another half hour before he could begin to think that Doe might be on the move. Half an hour until it started and then another twenty to thirty minutes before he would need to be ready to act. He settled even further into the dirt. That's when he heard the slow, steady thump of distant rotors.

*

Doe heard the rotors a fraction of a second later than Eugene. They were coming in from the east, the direction of the mainland. Doe was marginally further away from them and heard them marginally later. They were too far away for him to make much out from their sound. He glanced across the bowl toward where Eugene was waiting, pressed into the dirt of the forest floor. They were almost opposite each other. Doe at twelve noon and Eugene somewhere near five o'clock. He knew that Eugene would have heard the chopper. What he wondered was how that would make him react.

Doe looked at the curve of shadow reaching out toward the first of the huts and shipping containers in the center of the camp. He tried to work out how much time he needed to wait before he could move. It was already dark enough for him. A third of the bowl was in shadow and, at least to begin with, that would be the area he would be working in. He would be heading toward the wire from the west, but he had to time it so that the bowl in front of Eugene would also be in shadow. Eugene would be heading in from the eastern end of the camp and the area in front of him needed to be dark enough to give him a chance to cut through the wire and make his way in. If Doe went too early, Eugene would be lit up by the setting sun, but if Doe waited too long then the chopper would get to their quarry before he and Eugene could. Doe waited and listened and tried to work out what kind of rotors he was hearing.

*

Five minutes later the shadows were fifty feet from where Doe knew Eugene was hiding and he could make out the sounds of two separate helicopters. They sounded like small machines moving fast. Doe tucked the shotgun and the rifle to his side and rolled down the slope and came to a stop when he hit the wire. The camouflage netting was pegged to the ground fifteen or twenty yards in front of him and rose up to meet the radio mast. It was dark and the netting was hiding him, but he knew the guys in the sniper's nest would be using night vision or thermal imaging. He hoped that the combination of cover and darkness would hide him from those as well. He used a pair or bolt cutters to snip through the wire mesh and squeezed through the gap.

He crouched and fast jogged his way over to the edge of the camouflage netting. Once there he should be safe from the snipers. They wouldn't be able to tell whether his heat signature was one of their guys inside the netting or an intruder outside of it. His problem when he got there would be the guys milling around inside the netting. The guys who might look through the loose mesh and wonder who the hell he was.

Getting inside the netting wouldn't be difficult. The pegs holding it down would pull up easily in the soft, loamy soil, but Doe wasn't aiming for the interior of the netting.

For now, he needed to stay outside. He had to head for the sides of the net and that mean he would be out in the open. Out where the snipers or the men busily breaking camp could see him. Doe would need to work fast. He took a deep breath, thought again about how long he needed and how long it would take for the sun to dip over the trees. Then he listened out for the low thumping of helicopter rotors and tried to work out how far away they were. Doe crouched down and moved to the corner of the camouflage net. He waited a couple of seconds and then stood up straight and walked out into the dusk.

*

Eugene listened to the whomp of the helicopters and watched the sun creep its way toward the treetops. He followed the line of the shadow edge as it worked its way along the side of the bowl. It looked like it was going to be a close-run thing. He shifted slightly in the pine needles and stowed his weapons and pulled out a pair of pocket wire cutters. He relaxed back into the hard ground and settled in to wait.

*

Doe walked onward, toward the camp and stopped when he reached the first of the guy wires. There were six wires holding the radio mast in place, stopping it from toppling over or being blown over in a storm. There was one in front of him, at two o'clock if the camouflage netting were a clock face. Another one in the center of the parade ground, twelve noon. Four more at four, six, eight and ten o'clock. Doe bent down as if to tie his boot lace and cut through the thick wire with the bolt cutters. He stood up and walked back the way he came, heading for the wire at four o'clock.

The third wire was out back, behind the camouflage netting. He didn't need to worry about being spotted back there so once he was out of sight of the camp he crouched and ran. He cut the wire and continued his run to the wire at eight o'clock before standing up and walking out towards the fifth, and for him, final wire.

The first wire had been taut and tough to cut. It had broken with a ping and jumped away from him to smack into the side of the net. Doe had looked around a little wildly hoping no one was paying enough attention to notice. The second and third wires had still been tight but after that they started to get looser. Doe looked up at the mast as he cut the last couple of wires. He had hoped that it might start to topple when he got to the third or fourth wire, but it still seemed to be rock steady. It stood tall in the center of the net. No sign of a wobble. Doe cut the fifth wire.

The mast was only held in place by gravity and the single wire which was anchored right in the center of the camp. Doe sighed. His whole plan relied of the mast coming down. He intended it to act as both a signal to Eugene, to tell him that Doe was in place and he should begin his assault and at the same time it would provide a distraction which would mean that Eugene had a chance to get into the wire without being spotted. If the tower didn't fall Eugene would have no idea when to breach the wire. He would sit there waiting and waiting, wondering when he should snip his way into the compound.

Doe strung the two longer guns more securely across his back, pulled out one of the pistols and walked over to the side of the camouflage net.

*

The helicopters were close now. Eugene figured they would be running dark. There would be no lights to give away their position. They were coming in from behind him. Miles of forest blocked his view. The only way he could guess at their position was to concentrate on the sound, so he kept his attention on the logging camp and the sentries in the sniper's nest and tried not to worry about the choppers.

The shadows in front of him were pretty long now, curving away from him along the bowl with the tip of the darkness hitting the trees about ten yards to his right. If the mast were to fall now he could elongate his run and reach the wire a little further along the perimeter, where it was already dark. If Doe waited much longer he would be able to step straight down the slope in front of him.

*

Doe pulled up three of the bent metal pegs that held down the camouflage netting and rolled underneath. It was dark inside the netting and Doe figured that no one outside would be able to see him but there was some activity around the Humvees near the front. Anyone inside there with him might be able to pick him out in the gloom. People were moving around, taking items from the trucks and stripping the weapons from the turrets. Doe stood up slowly and then walked casually toward the center of the net. Casually for a soldier on active duty that is, which is to say quickly but not furtively. It was the same principle he had relied on when he had walked over to the first and last of the guy wires. He was hoping to pass for one of the gang. They were all in uniform and he was in street clothes but there was no kind of night vision equipment that would be able to easily pick out the differences. He would look just like they did, a pale blob of face and hands and a dark body against a dark background.

With any luck, anyone who saw him would be a grunt. They would busy with their own tasks. They wouldn't be in possession of a detailed enough knowledge to know if he was supposed to be there or not. In the absence of orders or detailed instructions he was happy enough that they wouldn't challenge him.

An officer would be an entirely different proposition. Thirty to forty men is a big enough group that very few people would know exactly where everyone was supposed to be, but if Doe was spotted by someone who did, he would need to be ready to tuck and roll and come up firing.

Close up, the radio mast looked impossibly tall. Four wrist thick metal tubes stood at each corner of a two-foot-wide square with thinner metal tubes zigzagging between them to stiffen the structure. The bottom of the mast was bedded into a massive concrete plinth. The tubes rose uninterrupted for about six inches and then there was a thick piece of metal acting like a hinge. Above the hinge the rest of the mast disappeared into the darkness at the top of the netting.

Doe looked ahead, out through the entrance to the netting, toward the compound gate. When they had erected the mast, they must have driven the thing up from the coast in sections. The would have wanted to avoid the town. Driving all this crap through Seal Harbor would have been a dead giveaway. Doe guessed that they had brought it all in by small boat at night and that the plan would have been to move it back out that way. There was no time for that now. Anything that they couldn't get out by helicopter in the next few hours was going to get left behind.

It looked like they had driven the mast into the old logging camp and laid it out alongside the road. They had placed the sections end to end and assembled them where they lay. Once it was complete they lifted the bottom end and walked it forward until it met up with the hinge and then they had rammed in a big steel rod to join them together. Doe didn't have the skills to work out whether they had cast the plinth first and the dragged the mast in and aligned them perfectly, or whether they had just dumped the mast and then precisely positioned the plinth after they offered it up. Both seemed to have their problems and their advantages. Doe figured the Army Corps of Engineers would have a whole manual on the subject.

Once the mast was connected to the plinth all they had needed to do was to pull it upright. The rim of the bowl would have offered a perfect vantage point from which to site a winch. If that had been the case the mast would have aligned precisely with the main street through the center of the camp. Maybe offset a few feet from the road but exactly parallel with it, but there must have been some kind of issue. Either the ground at the edge of the bowl had only been firm enough in certain places or only some of the trees had been big enough. The plinth was not precisely in line with the road. The mast did not point directly back down the road. It was only offset by a few degrees, but that was a few degrees that might make a huge difference if Doe was ever able to get it to fall.

*

Eugene was used to waiting but he couldn't remember ever being quite so tense on an operation. He had once spent two days waiting in a damp hole in the ground only to be told to return to base when the operation had been aborted. At no point had he found that wait as difficult as this one. He knew that the effect of the mast falling would be easy to detect. He wouldn't need to actually see it happening. There would be plenty of noise. He could lie there safe and invisible with his face pressed into the dirt, but instead he had taken to glancing down into camp every ten or fifteen seconds.

He recognized the indulgence, but he allowed it. All he really needed to do at this point was to make sure that there was no obvious change in the routine of the sniper sentries. It wasn't a task that was taking up much of his time. He had to watch the snipers closely because Doe was most probably moving around in the camp by now and if anyone spotted Doe moving about then the snipers would be the thing he most feared. Even one man against thirty, on the ground in the camp, Doe would have a chance to pull himself back to the wire and disappear into the trees, but if the snipers got a clear shot at him he would be dead before he could react.

If everything went to plan then Eugene couldn't take out the snipers before the mast fell, but if they looked like they were going to start shooting into camp, then the whole plan would be aborted. At that point it was Eugene's job to take them out and give Doe a chance to escape.

*

There was an inch-wide steel pin at the back of the mast to holding it in place. It was hammered over at one end to form an L-shape and even in the absence of the five of the six guy lines, it was stopping the mast from falling back toward the camp.

Doe needed that mast to fall. He was in the bowl and under the netting. Both were stopping the sound of the approaching helicopters from reaching him, but he knew that they were still coming. He couldn't be sure how many choppers there would be in the first wave, but it didn't matter. The guy in the fisherman's jersey would be the first man on the first helicopter. As soon as one landed the whole thing was over.

Added to that, Doe was certain that the mast was instrumental in whatever was blocking the radio and telephone signals in the town. If he bought the mast down then maybe the radio would spring back to life. There were injured men to evacuate and reinforcements to request. Doe needed the mast to fall so that Eugene would know that it was time to start the attack but there was also an awful lot more at stake.

The hinge was pinned by an inch-thick piece of bent steel and the pin was being held in place by the weight of the mast pushing down on it. With the guy lines removed the whole mast was sitting back down on the plinth and pushing on the pin. Doe tried pulling it, but he knew that was stupid so didn't waste much time on the attempt.

He took a deep breath and wedged the handle of his bolt cutters behind the pin. He placed the soles of his feet flat against the side of the plinth and put all of his weight and all the strength of his legs into the effort of pulling the pin loose. It didn't budge.

Doe dropped the bolt cutters and stepped back into the shadows behind the mast.

*

Eugene checked his rifle again. It was a good weapon. The temperature was dropping around him but not enough to affect it. He had made mistakes before and some of them had been serious, but he had never yet thought that a weapon on which he was relying was loaded when in fact it wasn't. Despite that, he had already checked the gun twice. He allowed himself to go through the motions one more time and then he resolved to push himself into that hyper focused state where he wouldn't move a muscle for hours.

The shadows pushed their way further around the edge of the bowl. Maybe there was another ten minutes before he would be forced to do something. Even if Doe didn't bring the mast down. He had to consider the fact that Doe had run or that he had tripped over a tree root and snapped his neck. If Doe didn't start this soon then Eugene would.

*

Doe opened the jaws of the bolt cutters and looked at the pin holding the mast in place. He was sure that if he could get rid of the pin the mast would fall. There had been six wires holding the mast in place, five of them were gone. As far as Doe knew, the way those guy-lines worked was that you put them all under tension. They all pulled the mast in different directions and that kept the thing straight and upright, even in high winds or if some prick tried to push it over. If that was the case then the one remaining wire was now trying to pull the whole mast over. It was the only one left in place and it was tightened to hold against the other five tight wires. Right now, the weight of the mast and the pin were stronger than the tension in the wire but if Doe could release the pin then the tension in the wire would win out.

The jaws off his bolt cutters were just about wide enough to take the width of the pin but the blades were made of a similar material. Even if he could apply enough pressure he couldn't be sure what would give. Either the bolt cutter jaws would blunt themselves against the pin or they would cut it, but even to have a chance he would have to generate a huge amount of pressure. He was no Hercules, so he would need to find a big lever, if he could lengthen the arms of the bolt cutters by enough and if the steel of the blades held then he might have a chance.

Doe looked around the darkened interior of the camouflage netting. Discarded scaffolding pipe would be perfect. It took him an embarrassing couple of seconds to stop himself. He wasn't going to be able to cut the pin with a pair of bolt cutters. They weren't up to it. They were like the M-60 armed Humvees. They were a fine tool but they weren't made to attack anything as big as the pin. But more embarrassing than that, cutting the pin wouldn't help at all. He didn't need to cut it, he needed to remove it.

*

The line of shadow was close to Eugene now and by the sound of it so were the choppers. They were going to be there in minutes. He would need equipment he didn't have if he was going to try to bring down a helicopter. He would need a rocket propelled grenade at the very least. Eugene guessed he could put a few rounds from his rifle into the rotor mechanism or the engines, but the chances of taking out two helicopters with three-oh-eight Winchester cartridges were remote at best.

The mast stayed resolutely upright and the choppers got imperceptibly closer and Eugene decided it was time to act.

*

Doe opened up the jaws on the bolt cutters as far as they would go and wedged the side of the tip of the blades into the point where the metal of the mast met the metal of the plinth. There was one guy wire left, pulling the mast toward the camp, trying to lift it away from the retaining bolt. If Doe could give the force coming from the wire a hand he might be able to release the pressure on the pin. If he could slacken the pressure on the pin sufficiently he might be able to pull it out.

His first few attempts just resulted in the bolt cutters slipping out of the tiny groove between the plinth and the mast. Eventually he found a rock and tapped the blade into place as quietly as he could. That gave him enough purchase to grab the bolt cutters handles and pull hard. He gave it the full weight lifting method, bending his knees and straightening his back and pushing with his legs and pulling with his upper body, but the mast didn't move. He shifted position. He put his back against the mast and tried pushing it backwards while he pulled up on the handle. Still nothing.

Doe stepped away from the mast. He had tried everything. He couldn't put any more force into it. If the pull from the guy line wasn't enough then he was going to have to abandon the mast. He would have to emerge from the camouflage netting fast and hope that Eugene would react quickly enough and take out the two snipers before they could shoot him. Without the signal and the distraction, it was going to be difficult and very dangerous. Doe forced himself to think about it but whichever way it came out he kept coming back to the same conclusion. Stopping the guy in the fisherman's jersey from reaching the US was important enough to warrant the risk.

Doe stepped back up to the mast, checked his weapons and ran through his first few moves in his head.

*

Eugene waited for a gap in the sentries sweep and then he jogged down to the wire. The slope was relatively steep at the top and his first few steps were more like long bounds, but the ground was firm under his feet and he controlled the run well. He had the wire cutters ready in his hand and he was counting down in his head. He was willing to make a few trips to the wire and back in order to cut a big enough hole for him to crawl through. When the countdown in his head told him that the sniper's relentless sweep of the perimeter was coming back around towards him he scrambled back out of the bowl and collapsed, panting between the trees.

The choppers got closer and the hole in the fence got bigger and the bowl got darker and darker.

*

Doe looked across the bowl. The sun was setting behind him. There was a crescent of light still around the opposite side of the camp. He could see the gap in the fence where the gate stood. He could see the spot where Eugene was holed up, waiting for the signal that would never come. The trees looked as if they were glowing. At the top of the trees, the sky was an imperceptibly pale blue, almost white and then it darkened quickly to the deepest of purples. The inside of the netting was in deep shadow. Doe looked up. A sliver of the guide wire glinted silver, lit up against the dark background. It looked like it hovered in the air, alone and desperately trying to pull the mast over, straining against the retaining pin but failing to break it. Failing to pull the mast against the hinge and topple it.

Failing to pull the mast *against* the pin! The reason that the pin couldn't be pulled out wasn't because the weight of the mast was holding it in place, it was because the pull of the guy line was pulling the mast upwards, squeezing the pin tighter against the mast. Doe had been trying to loosen the pin by pulling up on the mast. What he needed to do was loosen the pressure by pulling the mast back down!

He picked the bolt cutters off of the floor and jammed them between two cross members at waist height. He angled himself toward the bent end of the retaining pin and placed his stomach across the bolt cutter handle and lifted his feet off the ground. The mast groaned a little and Doe felt the bolt cutters shift slightly. He reached out and grasped the pin and pulled. It shifted a little under his hand.

*

The bolt moved, but all it did was rotate. He could turn the bent end of the pin towards himself or away from himself, but he couldn't wriggle it out of its slot. He was pulling at it whilst lying flat on his stomach. He pushed until his shoulder muscles and his biceps burned but the pin didn't budge.

He needed a better angle. He needed to be pulling against the bar and he needed to bring the strength in his legs into play, but he couldn't. If he got off the bolt cutter handle to get a better position, then his weight wouldn't be pulling the mast back toward the upright and the pressure would be back on the pin. He already knew that without his weight pulling down on the mast, he couldn't move the pin. It was a catch-22. If he stayed laying across the bolt cutter handle then the pin was loose enough to move but he didn't have the angle to pull on it. If he got off then the pin was too firmly held in place.

Doe eased himself gently off of the bolt cutters and stepped back. It was a two-man job. Two people should be able to do it. One would lie on the bolt cutters providing the weight to counter balance the pull of the guide wire and the other would pull on the pin to free it. But he was alone. No second man. He would have to find a way to do it himself.

*

Doe repositioned the bolt cutters. He put them as low as he could and he grabbed hold of the mast and sat down on the handles. He felt the mast settle and he felt the bolt cutters thrum slightly under the strain and then he raised his feet off the ground and braced one against the pin and pushed and kicked at it. With the soles of his boots. It sounded noisy to Doe and it hurt like hell. He clung on to the mast and pushed and kicked and stared at the pin.

Very slowly it started to jerk free of its slot.

*

It was probably the last trip. Eugene snipped through a last few strands of wire. The hole was big enough for him to creep through. If the mast didn't fall soon he would continue to creep down and widen the hole for a few more trips but he would do it every two or three sweeps by the sentries rather than every sweep. He would widen the hole so that it would be easier and quicker to get through when the time came but he would do it more slowly so that he could rest up between the frantic forays into the bowl, so that he could get his breath back and be ready when the time came.

The countdown in his head reached the critical point. Eugene stowed the wire cutters in his pocket so that he wouldn't lose them in the mad scramble back up the slope and he turned and headed back toward the shelter of the trees.

*

Doe realized he had a problem when the pin was about halfway out. His position had been perfect when the pin was fully home but now that it was half out the head of the pin, the bent over section at the end was too far away for him to reach. He eased himself off the handle and stood up. The mast twisted a little and creaked alarmingly. Doe heard a couple of shouts from over by the parked Humvees. He hurriedly repositioned the bolt cutters and got back on-board kicking and pushing the bolt the last few inches hoping to get it finished before someone decided to come over and see what was going on.

Luckily, he didn't have to push the pin the whole way out. It had been slotted into thick metal tubing. The first six inches of tube were welded onto the plinth. The next foot was attached to the bottom of the mast and the last six inches were part of the plinth again. Together, the pin held the three sections of tube together but as soon at the pin cleared the central section, the back of the mast was free of the plinth. The mast was only connected by the hinge on the camp side of the plinth. Doe felt the mast lurch as his last kick pushed the pin the remaining inch and then the pin rattled, loose in the last six inches of pipe. The bolt cutters shifted under him and Doe stood quickly. Without his weight on it the mast started to swing over, pulled by the tension in the one remaining guy wire.

The mast creaked its way over by about five or ten degrees from the perpendicular and ground to a halt. The tension in the wire was exhausted. The wire held the mast steady once again, counteracting the pull of gravity that wanted to tug the tower back into place on the plinth. Doe sighed. There was definite shouting now from all around the camp. He needed to move the mast further and he needed to do it quickly before his distraction became a signal to the guys in the camp rather than a signal to Eugene. He picked up the battered bolt cutters once more and jammed them back into the mast at the corner nearest the hinge.

*

Eugene was halfway up the slope when he heard the faint sound of the mast groaning and the louder sounds of the camp coming alive. He scrambled the last few yards out of the bowl and spun around to face the camp, struggling to control his breathing and his heart rate as he did so. The top of the mast, glinting in the last of the sunlight, seemed to have shifted a little and that was good enough for Eugene. It was go-time.

He pulled the Remington to his shoulder and slid the bolt.

*

Doe felt like all he had done for most of his life was push or pull on the handles of that particular pair of bolt cutters. The mast was light but it was tall. He wasn't trying to move a huge weight but all of that weight was pushing almost straight down. Doe could hear the sounds as people began to realize what was going on. He bent his knees, straightened his back and heaved. The first bullets tore through the netting to his left. The guys in the sentry tower were firing at him. They must have realized that there was something wrong with the mast. Maybe they could see him with their night vision or maybe they had simply guessed. It didn't matter, they weren't taking any chances. Doe found a little more resolve and pushed even harder with his screaming leg muscles.

*

Eugene's first two shots missed. Not by much but they missed. It was the run up the hill. He was out of breath and his heart was hammering. He settled himself back into the slight imprint left by his body, slowed his breathing and heart rate and took aim.

*

The mast was moving. Not by much but it was moving. Doe had no idea how far he would have to shove it. He knew it had something to do with its center of mass. It was tall and thin so it wouldn't need to move far before gravity switched from being his enemy to being his friend but his breath was coming hard and all the oxygen he had was needed in his muscles so he didn't spend much time trying to think. Instead he started to count. There were people on the ground headed his way and the snipers on top of the old saw mill would be getting closer and closer with their shots. He would give it five seconds and then move back to plan B. Plan B was simple. Plan B was to survive and try to move into the camp rather than away.

*

Eugene's next shot missed as well. It was getting embarrassing. He was a Ranger for fuck's sake. He could see that his third shot had rattled them though. Up to that point they had been at the far end of their nest firing into the camp. Now they were turning. Looking to line up their fire on him. That was good news for Doe but unless Eugene could get himself back on track it could be very bad for him.

*

It seemed to happen very suddenly. Doe didn't notice any graduation in effort. One minute he was giving it everything and nothing was happening, the next the mast was falling. He stepped backwards and told himself not to watch as the metal structure accelerated its way toward the ground but he found it difficult to tear his eyes away. When he outlined his plan to Eugene the only purpose to taking down the mast had been to bring the town's radios and telephones back on line. The distraction and signal had been worked in as an added advantage but the moment Doe had seen that the mast didn't line up exactly with the road through the camp he had realized that there would be a third, massive benefit to taking down the mast.

The mast fell through the line of parked Humvees. It didn't have enough mass to damage them much. It crashed across them and bent itself slightly and carried on. It hit one across the windshield and smashed the glass but otherwise the trucks looked relatively undamaged. It would take a bit of doing to get two or three of them out from under the wreckage but if you could manage it they would run.

The mast continued to fall. It didn't fall into itself, like a brick tower being demolished, it fell like a pencil balanced on its end. It fell a little to the north of the single remaining guy line. The direction of the fall determined not by the guy line but by the hinge at the bottom of the mast. The mast must have gone in before they built the rest of the camp because the mast fell in a line that smashed it into the little quarter circle of huts they were using as offices and bunk houses. It was a glancing blow and that was just fine by Doe. A direct hit probably wouldn't have done much more damage to the buildings than it had done to the Humvees but a glancing blow meant that the mast caught the edge of the nearest two huts and fell across the front of them blocking the doors and windows. The third and fourth huts were angled across the path of the falling mast. It hit the third and buckled, the narrower cross-section nearer the top of the mast bending and once again falling across the front of the building. The fourth building was at an even steeper angle but it was also even further away. The tip of the mast fell against the roof of the building and snapped. The structure thudded finally to earth blocking all access in and out of all four huts.

Doe wasn't the only one who seemed to have stopped to watch the mast fall but as the dust started to settle in the bowl bullets started to fly. Thankfully the snipers had stopped firing at him and there were god-knows how many people trapped in the offices and bunk houses but there were still plenty of other people at large in the camp and they all had a pretty good idea where he was. Doe reached for his rifle and his shotgun and fought his way out of the collapsed camouflage netting.

*

Eugene's fourth and fifth shots were perfect. The sentries in the guard tower had managed to get a few shots away but they weren't certain where he was and he was well tucked in to cover and close to the ground whilst they were upright and silhouetted against the lighter sky. He put one bullet into each of their centers of mass and then reloaded and waited two full seconds to see whether they came back up but they didn't. He trained his binoculars on their nest and tried to confirm the kills but he couldn't see them. The might be lying dead on the floor but if they had been wearing body armor they could be tucked down, behind the rail, waiting to stand up and start firing again.

A bigger team would have left someone in Eugene's position, scrunched down in the dirt with a rifle, to wait them out, but Eugene didn't have anyone to leave behind and he was needed in the camp so he swung the Remington onto his shoulder, picked up the Heckler & Koch and headed for the hole he had cut in the fence.

TWENTY

Doe was using the shotgun. It didn't have the accuracy or the rate of fire of his MP5 but he was trying to clear a path not take out specific targets and the shotgun made one hell of a big bang. He had it loaded with double-aught buckshot and every time he fired eight lead balls the width of his fingernail scattered out in front of him. It was like firing eight handguns in eight different directions and he could fire them as quickly as he could pump the action. There was a downside though. It took him longer to load than to fire so he couldn't lay down a wall of fire for any length of time. He fired his first few shots across the collapsed camouflage netting toward the parked Humvees. He knew there were people over there and if he could hit any of them he would be happy but mostly he just wanted the effect that the rounds all hitting the side of the trucks would have. Then he fired a couple of shots across the parade ground in the center of the wrecked semicircle of huts. He wanted to send as many people running for cover as he could before he moved out of cover.

Doe reloaded the shotgun before he came out from the side of the netting. He stepped out into the open and set off toward the side of the nearest hut. He took a long, fast stride, not quite a run but faster than a march, and he fired the shotgun as rapidly as he could. He needed to make it to the next piece of cover before he had to reload or he would be running alone while a couple of dozen men tried to take aim at him.

He reached the side of the first hut and reloaded. He was on the wrong side of the mast. He had moved to the right to duck out under the netting and that meant that the mast was between him and the parade ground. It had jammed up on some concrete paving slabs that acted as the steps up into the first portacabin so in front of Doe there was a foot-high gap then two feet of mast. He needed to get over the barrier before he could move on into the rest of the camp. All around, he could hear the sound of the gang regrouping. He toyed with the idea of some kind of parkour running jump. His foot would hit the side of the hut at speed and he would bend into the impact and push off and up twisting as he leapt until he landed one-footed on the top of the mast and pushed off onto the ground and across the parade ground.

He liked his chances of making the jump but he wasn't sure about the mast. It hadn't been built to take the kind of stresses it had just been subjected to. It had snapped and bent in a number of places during its collapse and Doe wasn't sure what would be the effect of a point load impact of one hundred and ninety pounds coming down through the sole of his boot. If it gave under him he would be off balance and there was a chance that his ankle would brush against jagged, broken metal as it dropped through the wreckage. He was also aware that there were an unknown number of people trapped inside the hut and while they couldn't get out through the door they could easily fire through the walls and he didn't really want to wake them all up by kicking the wall.

The problem with tucking the guns under his arms and scrambling under the mast was that when he came out of the other side he would have to stand up and start moving again and while he was doing it he wouldn't able to shoot. He took a deep breath and stood up. He emptied the shot gun firing across the yard and trying to hit each of the shipping containers and then aiming at any movement he could spot, then he dropped to the floor and shuffled his way under the mast. When he stood up on the other side he was carrying the MP5. He wasn't heading anywhere now, he was exactly where he wanted to be.

*

Eugene wasn't where he wanted to be. He was through the wire and half way to the back of the first of the old logging buildings. He was moving in his combat run. He had been trained well. It was fast but not so fast that he the only thing he could do was fire blindly in front of him. The run was just fast enough that he could still aim before firing. He was moving slightly more slowly than he would usually because he needed to check periodically for movement in the sniper nest. Once he was in the shelter of the buildings he would be safe from them but Doe would still be out there and he would be somewhere near the shipping containers by now. Even if he could survive a concerted effort from the surviving members of the gang Doe would be a sitting duck if one of the snipers on top of the mill building was still alive.

Doe's trick with the mast seemed to have drawn all resistance toward him. No one even seemed to have noticed that Eugene had taken out the snipers but he kept his rifle up at his shoulder and he covered all the gaps between the buildings as he ran and he fought his impulse to drop the gun sight, look at the floor and sprint for the parade ground.

*

Doe sprinted across the yard. He was out in the open now and he felt it. Every hair on his body was standing up. He could hear the shooting and he knew they were shooting at him. It was a long ten yards to run but it was dark and he was moving fast. He fired as he moved, picking targets in the shadows where he had driven the gang with his shotgun. He hoped he might have winged a couple more guys but mostly he just hoped that he made it to the shipping containers in one piece and he hoped that he was right and that the guy in the fisherman's jersey was holed up in one of them waiting for the chopper that would take him to the mainland.

Doe didn't think the guy would be waiting in one of the portacabins across the yard. They had all looked to be in constant use when he had reconnoitered the place that afternoon and Doe couldn't see the guy sitting on a bunk with his buddies from the rescue team. The guy Doe had met thought he was something special. Even if they hadn't prepared a bunker for him he would choose to sit on his own in a supply container rather than in a room full of grunts. He might deign to sit in the camp commander's office but that would be the limit.

Doe expected that they would have prepared a bolt hole for him anyway. They would have provided somewhere that he could sit and feel safe. Somewhere hidden and somewhere the officers in charge of the operation could feel secure in the knowledge that he hadn't strolled off or gotten himself killed. The last thing they would want would be for them to do all the hard work and get the guy to the camp and then for him to pick a fight with the wrong comrade or wander off into the woods and get himself eaten by a bear. Their employers weren't the kind of people to pay up on a plea of 'it wasn't our fault'.

A couple of bullets dinged off the corner of the shipping container as he reached its side. That was bad. It meant they were starting to outflank him. When the mast started to fall, they had all moved to get out of the way. Then it fell toward the west of the parade ground so instinctively most of the gang had moved east, away from the danger. Once the mast had landed, Doe had driven them further out of the circle with his pump action. It had bought him the time he had needed to move up to the side of the first shipping container but now they were moving counter-clockwise, along the front of the collapsed camouflage netting, toward the fallen mast, moving around to flank him. There would be guys moving in the opposite direction as well, creeping clockwise around the back of the shipping containers. Doe had fired six shots on his way across the parade ground. He briefly debated reloading but that would leave him with a part empty magazine for later in the day. If twenty-four rounds couldn't get him to the container door then he might as well fail early as late.

*

Eugene reached the buildings on the street furthest out from the main road into the logging camp. Out here the buildings were little more than shacks and the weather hadn't been kind to them. He put his back against the plank wall out of pure reflex, it wouldn't have protected him from a marble thrown by a toddler. It felt right though, having some kind of protection at his rear. He stepped forward, through a hole rotted through the wall and then moved across to the open front of the building.

He could hear small-arms fire from the direction of the parade ground. He looked left and then right, up and down the dirt track between the abandoned saw mill buildings. The street was completely empty. He looked right one more time and then he stepped out of the building and turned left, away from Doe and the parade ground, away from the fight. It wasn't easy, but he had a job to do and a soldier knows how to follow orders.

*

Doe swung around the corner of the shipping container and fired three controlled bursts from the MP5, each burst of three shots. Nine more rounds from his emptying clip. There was a little answering fire from in front of him but the men who were creeping around the back of the containers clearly hadn't had time to set up yet. He had time to rush forward and pull the big metal handle holding the massive doors closed. The door was unlatched but it wasn't open and he couldn't step around it and haul it open from the side the way you would normally. The guys behind the containers might not be in position yet but he didn't want to spend long seconds with his back to them walking slowly into their field of fire. He did what he had to do. He pushed the door open far enough to make enough room for him to slip inside and then he poked his head into the gap to make sure that the container was empty. He could see enough of the interior of the box to know that there wasn't a firing squad waiting for him inside so he slipped through the gap and pushed the door the rest of the way open with his back.

The container was empty, or at least there was no one in it. There were two lines of crates stacked floor to ceiling, one of them hugging the left-hand wall and the others piled down the center of the container. They had rigged racking along the right-hand wall and at the back-right corner there was even a weapons cage. It took Doe less than three seconds to realize that his quarry wasn't there and he turned and prepared to leave.

*

Eugene cleared every building on the row moving from the building nearest the big mill building in the center of the bowl to the ones where the camp petered out near the slope up to the trees. They were all completely empty and had been for decades. Doe had insisted that he check every single building. It was possible that the gang had placed the portacabins and shipping containers only as a deception, to draw attention away from the old buildings that they were in fact using for everything important. Eugene thought that is was unlikely but Doe seemed pretty insistent that these guys liked to use misdirection and disguise.

Eugene had been more inclined to believe that the buildings were empty but that the guy they were hunting might have taken refuge in there for that very reason. He wasn't part of the camp. He wasn't part of the crew. Either before or after the shooting started it made sense to Eugene that he might have decided to get away from their camp and hole up on his own until it was time to leave.

Eugene hugged the wall of the end building and then slipped across the street. There were still lights and movement at the gate but no one had spotted him. Eugene set off, back along the row, building to building on the opposite side of the street, heading back toward the fire fight he could hear up ahead.

*

Time was clearly of the essence now. Doe was being flanked on two sides by a larger force and he had no reason to expect any reinforcements. Eugene had to check six rows of buildings including several multi-floored buildings and then he had to climb a ladder or staircase up to the sniper nest on the roof and check that their quarry hadn't taken sanctuary there. He wasn't going to be entering the fight any time soon. To Doe's left there were men trying to cover the gap between the two shipping containers but they couldn't get to him because the open door of the first container was shielding most of the gap. The thick metal door clanged every now and then as shots hit it but Doe felt safe enough behind it. To his right there was more of a problem. Men were rushing across the parade ground trying to get a firing position. They were moving quickly but warily, aware of his shotgun and rifle.

Doe took a split-second decision and sprinted for the corner of the container. He swerved the wall and slipped out into the yard. They reacted quickly. Bullets came his way almost immediately, but they came from behind and to the right of him which told him he had a chance. They weren't in position yet. They hadn't made it across the yard and they didn't have men in front of him. If he could keep ahead of them they wouldn't be able to pin him down. Not yet anyway.

Doe put his head down and ran for the corner of the second shipping container.

*

Eugene reached the last building in the row. The one that butted up against the big saw mill. He walked up to the back wall and found a spot where cold winters and wet summers had reduced the wood to a papery shell. He kicked his way through and out into the gap between the two rows of buildings. The building in front of him didn't lean against the side of the saw mill the way the one behind him had. There was a small gap between the two external walls. Eugene squeezed into the gap and walked out toward the street.

From that point on, he zigzagged back and forth across the dirt street until he had covered every one of the buildings on the eastern side of the main track into the camp. He stopped by the wall of the mill building and looked into the parade ground. He could see movement ahead of him. Figures were creeping across the central yard toward the shipping containers on the eastern side of the camp. His trigger finger crept from the trigger guard, but he was forbidden to engage them. His job was to slip across the main track and head back toward the gate house. His job was to clear the rest of the buildings. He looked longingly across the bare earth and then ducked down and scuttled across the gravel road.

*

They had Doe virtually dialed in by the time he reached the corner of the second container. The flanking maneuver was complete. The guys outside the circle were in position. They fired directly into the gap between the two boxes the moment he ran into it. The guys behind him had his position marked pretty well too. They were still chasing him, but they had been shooting at him for a while now and they were getting close.

He had to endure a hail of bullets as he turned the corner. He had no choice but to swing open the heavy steel door and slip inside without checking. There was no firing squad lined up inside waiting for him. Doe kept the door slightly ajar and took a deep breath. There was no way he would be able to head back out into the parade ground. If the guy in the fisherman's jersey wasn't in this container, then Doe had some serious thinking to do.

Bullets slammed into the metal walls in front of and around him. Doe crouched for a second and thought and then he pushed both doors open so that they formed a corridor most of the way between his container and the back of the third container. The first door provided protection from the gunmen outside the circle and the second covered him from shots fired from the parade ground. The metal would stop most small-arms fire and it also stopped the guys chasing him from seeing what he was doing. They would have to slow down and approach carefully, because for all they knew he could be kneeling in the center of the gap with the MP5 on fully automatic, ready to unload on them when they made their move.

It would slow them, but it wouldn't stop them. They could climb onto the roof of the two containers and rush him from up there, and if they had grenades or flash-bangs they could throw them over the doors and come in and pick him off or pick up the pieces.

Doe checked his magazine and turned to investigate the interior of the container.

*

Eugene was on the western side of the main street. He had cleared two more rows of buildings, there was only one row left. There was a lot of shooting coming from the parade ground now. Eugene knew that Doe was alone. Doe wouldn't be firing any more often than he had at the beginning of the skirmish. Most of the increased shooting had to be coming from the bad guys. Doe was clearly already under a lot of pressure and that pressure was increasing rapidly. The shock of his initial distraction had worn off and the gang were finding ways around the disruption the falling mast had caused. They were getting organized again, reacting to the new geography.

Doe was a sitting duck. A fish in a barrel. His only chance had been to buy some time and then keep moving once the shooting started. Shoot and move was a pretty simple tactic, but Doe's movements had been limited from the outset. Out in the woods Doe could have kept the game up pretty much indefinitely, but in the bowl around the logging camp he was hemmed in by the wire and the steep slope.

If Doe's only job had been to stay alive he would still have had a decent chance. He would have been able to move in unpredictable directions. He could have headed for the shadows and for cover and then emerge shooting. He could have holed up and waited for the gang to overtake him and then come out behind them or he could have circled round and tried to get behind them that way. He could have picked his positions and his targets and he could have led them on a chase of his devising.

If his only job had been to stay alive he could have tried every trick in his book but staying alive wasn't Doe's only job. He couldn't do anything clever because Doe was doing exactly the same thing that Eugene was but in the other half of the camp. Doe had to check the parade ground buildings in a methodical manner, just the way Eugene was checking the old logging camp. He had to sweep through the shipping containers and the prefabs looking for their guy. It was a tough job. In Eugene's estimation, it was one of the toughest things he had ever seen anyone attempt. Doe needed help and he needed it quickly and Eugene was the only man within ten miles who could offer it.

He still had a row of buildings to clear. He glanced left and right, checking the dirt track ahead of him and then he crouched and ran across, into the first of the buildings on the opposite side of the street.

*

The front of the container was empty but two thirds of the way toward the rear there was a stud wall partition with a single unpainted wooden door. Doe sighed and checked the corners of the container before striding across and kicking the door with the sole of his boot just about where the handle sat. Neither the wall or the door was designed to withstand a good hard kick. It was thin chipboard sheet pinned to pine batons with inch long nails. It looked like they had used a nail gun. Both the door and the frame failed under Doe's boot and he stepped through.

He didn't wait to check the room before entering. He figured that if there were armed men in the container then they would have waited for him in the main body of the box. The front doors of the container were far harder to open than the little wooden door and they offered a lot more protection for the ambusher. If there had been anyone in there with a gun they would have waited for him in the center of the main room with their gun trained on the door. They would have started shooting the minute the door started to open. They didn't need to hit him, they just needed to keep him outside and let their colleagues catch up with him. If there was anyone left in the container then the only reason they could have for being in the back was to hide.

There was no one in there. It was fitted out with racking and it looked like the racking was full of medical supplies. The supplies weren't valuable but there were probably drugs in there, so they had separated them out from the rest of the stores and put a lock on the door. It wouldn't have stopped any serious thieving, but it was enough to stop petty pilfering and to keep unauthorized drug use to a minimum. The lock wouldn't stop you getting in but kicking the shit out of it would certainly alert your superior officers.

Doe walked back across the container. He slowed near the entrance and peered out. The little courtyard he had created between the two boxes was empty. They hadn't organized themselves for an attack yet, but it was only a matter of time. He couldn't move either door without facing half a dozen men and he didn't expect them to be taking prisoners. In front of him there was a solid steel wall eight and a half feet high and behind him there was a solid steel box.

He could probably stay where he was. Eugene was coming, and with the mast down Doe guessed that communications would be restored in Seal Harbor. As long as Floyd wasn't the mole, it was only a matter of time before the cavalry arrived. If he could keep them out of the container for a few hours he would probably survive but the gang would have the guy in the fisherman's jumper out of there and safe in well under half that time.

Even if the choppers were unwilling to land now that there was a firefight, and Doe very much doubted that, he was sure that they would have a back-up plan. They would probably spirit the guy away through the woods to a fast boat to the mainland. Sitting in the container waiting for rescue would be the same as letting their guy go.

Doe looked across the gap between the two shipping containers. A song from his childhood ran through his head, 'We can't go under it. (we can't go under it). We can't go through it. (We can't go through it). We'll have to go...'

*

Eugene cleared the last of the buildings. They had all been completely empty. He hadn't even seen a rat. Eugene stood at the door of the last building and turned his head to the left. Five rows of buildings tackled in a zigzag, all the way up one line of buildings then a dart across the street and back all the way along the other side of the track to clear all the buildings on that side. It had left him way out at the edge of the camp, a couple of rows back from the main track and the ramp up to the camp gate.

Eugene glanced right and then worked his way toward the main street. He stopped at the corner and looked up at the gate. He couldn't see any movement. As far as he could see the sentries had all left to join the fight at the parade ground. It was a dumb move. They had no reason to believe that there weren't more cops out there in the trees, ready to move in once the mast fell. Now that the gatehouse was unmanned there was nothing to stop Eugene from starting up the fork-truck and moving the giant hunk of concrete that blocked the road. If he had a small army of cops in trucks waiting around the bend he could let them in.

It was a nice thought and the fact that Eugene and Doe were completely alone didn't make the abandoned gate house any less of a disgrace. Eugene looked up at the sniper's nest again. There might be ex-Rangers in the camp but they weren't good ex-Rangers.

Eugene thought that it was possible that Floyd would saddle up and head out to help them. Once the communications had been restored and he had gotten some help on the way he could leave a few officers to carry on the investigation and bring the rest out on a rescue mission. It's what Eugene would do in his place, but it would take some time to organize and even longer to negotiate the dirt track and the ten miles of distance. Eugene wasn't expecting the cavalry anytime soon. He left the fork-truck where it was, but in the absence of sentries he also abandoned skulking from building to building. He turned left and fast jogged down the center of the main street.

*

There was a foot-wide lug welded to the back of the steel wall in front of Doe. It was just a strip of metal welded to the back of the container. It was tacked on at one end, bent out a couple of inches then across, parallel to the wall. A foot or two later it bent back in was tacked back onto the wall. Doe had no idea what it would have been used for. Something had hooked into it or something had been kept an inch or two away from the back of the container. As far as he could see it was the only one. It sat about three feet from the ground and about dead center of the wall. Doe figured that he would have been tempted by it even if he hadn't been in a position where he had no choice. It was like a boy with a catapult finding an empty coke bottle on the top of a fence.

Doe looked at the lug a couple of times and practiced the moves inside the container, the way he had seen high jumpers do it at the Olympics. Two strides across the gap, jump up, lead foot high, knee bent, land with instep on the lug, straighten the leg. A lot depended on his performance and a lot depended on his footwear. If he slipped off the lug he would hit the wall and fall to the ground. He probably wouldn't lose much more than a couple of teeth and the tread on the front of one boot, but he would be left in the hole between the two containers, bleeding, on his knees and running out of time.

He took two deep breaths and raised each knee to his chest in turn. It was another thing he had seen the jumpers do on the TV. He did it partially for his own amusement, a lifelong habit of diffusing tension that he recognized and nurtured. He also did it because he thought that the people he had seen were well-trained and successful athletes. Whatever they thought was working for them might just help him.

He took one more look and then launched himself across the open space. His foot hit the lug and the tread on his boots held and he made the push with his knee well enough to launch himself upwards instead of forward. His head cleared the top of the container by a surprising distance and he was on the way down before he realized that he should be reaching out and holding on to the roof. He landed heavily but with his elbows bent. It was relatively simple to lever his legs up onto the roof and roll onto the flat surface. He could feel warm fluid and cold air on his right forearm, but he was up and there was a chance that the guys shooting at him didn't know that.

*

Eugene reached the end of the street. The road he stood on was old, compacted earth with gravel and concrete and chalk bedded in. The road ahead of him was new. Perfectly graded with a simple gravel surface and an inch deep, inch wide drainage ditch at each side. A European supercar could have driven that new street. The construction was completely unnecessary for a road built primarily for Humvees and pickup trucks. It was like the guys who had planned it had read a book that told them what the road into a military camp should look like and then they had hired guys to deliver it.

The firing in front of him had slowed a little over the last few minutes, but there was neither the complete silence nor the noisy jubilation that he would have associated with Doe's death. He chose to assume that Doe still needed his help. He checked his weapons and then looked east and west, into the buildings on his left and right. He wanted to be in the parade ground. He was sure that was where he needed to be, and he was sure that nothing else was going on in the camp, but he had promised Doe and he was a professional. He still had one last job to do. He turned to his right and stepped into the old mill building.

*

Doe weighed it up in a couple of seconds while he got his breath back. He could worm his way across the top of the container. Silently, hoping the bad guys would think he was still in the container behind him. It seemed the safer option, but he didn't know how close or how brave his opponents were. They could be climbing the sides of container as he lay there thinking. They could be planning to creep back towards the second container hoping to take him by surprise.

If they emerged onto the container roof while Doe was creeping across it then it could get very tricky. On the other hand, if he took off across the roof at a run they would be taken by surprise. They would have to react. They would need to work out what was going on and aim and hit a moving target. They would need new tactics and they would have to put it all into action before Doe could cover the forty feet to the front of the box.

He raised himself slowly. He didn't want to wave any flags and give them extra thinking time. Once he was ready he set of across the top of the container at a run, the stiff soles of his boots making booming noises with every step.

*

Eugene crept up the stairs to the second floor of the mill. He had checked the second floors of all the other buildings that had them, but he hadn't checked the roofs. None of them would have had the strength to hold the weight of a man. Eugene moved quickly. He wasn't worried about the sentries any more. If they were up there then they had been hiding for more than ten minutes. Sitting there against the sniper's nest's walls, refusing to help their pals in the parade ground. Waiting for him to arrive. If that was the case he was going to die, but that wasn't going to be the case.

He covered every blind turn but he knew that the only person who could be up there now was the guy in the fisherman's jersey. He might be armed and he might be good but he would certainly be wary. Eugene had to be careful, but in his heart, he knew it was a wild goose chase. It would take a seriously weird mindset for someone to take refuge up in the sniper's nest. If he was up there now then either he had been up there from the beginning, when Eugene had shot the two sentries, or he had crawled up there afterwards to hide.

The first option took a strong stomach and a tough skin. The second was plain stupid. The second meant that the guy had climbed two flights of stairs to put himself somewhere he couldn't escape from except by climbing back down those stairs. It didn't seem likely, but it wasn't impossible, so Eugene took all the precautions, but he moved as quickly as he could. He knew that it was going nowhere useful and he knew that where he really needed to be was in the parade ground.

*

Doe wondered what he would do if the guy he was looking for wasn't in the third container. His boots slammed down on the thick steel and drummed out the words of the old nursery rhyme, a kind of call and response song his mother had sung.

'We can't go *around* it (we can't go *around* it).

We can't go *through* it (we can't *through* it)."

And if he had to get to the fourth container he would be able to add,

'We can't go *over* it (we can't go *over* it).'

It had worked in the song, as far as he could remember, but he couldn't see how he was going to make it work in practice not second time around. So far, they hadn't spotted him, but he couldn't imagine himself making it all the way across the roof without drawing attention and once he had pulled the roof trick once, they would be ready for it.

'We'll have to go... *under* it.' He couldn't see any way to do that. He guessed he might get really lucky and find an oxy-acetylene torch in the third box but realistically he knew that his luck was already stretched as far as he could reasonably expect.

They figured it out when Doe was about half way across the top of the container. He had to concentrate on staying alive as bullets started flying around him. He put his head down and all of his energy into the run and he headed for the end of the container.

*

Eugene poked his head through the trap door. The snipers' nest looked empty. The gang had covered a small square area by rooting two-by-fours through the shingles and nailing a platform to it. The two-by-fours continued upward, well over head height and they had topped the structure off with a tar-papered roof. Waist high, chipboard walls made the whole thing feel less exposed. The walls wouldn't stop a bullet, but they offered some concealment and stopped you stumbling over the edge and falling onto the parade ground below.

Eugene spotted the two dead infantrymen before his shoulders had cleared the platform floor. They were both slumped in the same corner and their weapons were lying beside them. Training told him to check that they were dead even though common sense told him they certainly were. Professional detachment let him notice that he had hit one on the helmet before he hit him in the face, and that the other had died from a neck wound that would have taken some time to kill him. The plywood barrier was three feet high. The roof of the saw mill was flat and it stretched a block and a half. It was dark. There were protuberances. Eugene stepped over the low wall and headed off, across the roof.

*

Doe's guy was in the third container. He must have been spooked by the sound of Doe's boots hammering down on the steel roof. The sound must have reverberated around on the inside of the metal box like being on the inside of a huge cowbell. The guy came bolting out of the container like he thought the fifth army was on the roof. He was yelling as he ran and he slammed into the back wall of the fourth container trying to take the turn into the parade ground but was carrying too much speed. Fortunately for him the guys on the ground were all firing upwards at Doe. By the time they had readjusted their aim, reacting to the new threat, they had also worked out what was going on. Doe hadn't fired a shot in several minutes and he wasn't about to start now. He wanted the guy alive. He didn't want him killed in crossfire.

Doe skidded to a halt. His boots slipped out from under him and he hit the steel roof on his side. He twisted around and came back up, purely by accident, in a sprinter's starting position. He took off back the way he came, shadowing his guy but eight and a half feet higher off the ground.

It was getting dark. Doe couldn't tell if the guy running through the parade ground was still wearing his borrowed fisherman's jersey, but it was definitely his guy. He was running crazy for the edge of the parade ground where the camouflage netting had stood. Doe had a decision to make. The guys on the ground had been distracted by the sudden emergence from the container and by Doe's sudden change of direction, but they were getting back on track again. Doubling back on himself had put the gang behind him again and they were still shooting upward. Up on the roof Doe was a tough target to hit, but in order to stay up there he would have to leap the five-foot gap between each box. On the ground he would be an easier target, but he would be able to run uninterrupted.

Doe had been less than halfway across the third roof when the guy he was hunting had come popping out like a rabbit from a hole. The end of the container was coming up fast. He had to decide now. Should he jump to the ground and take his chances chasing the guy on the flat? Or should he try to hurdle the gap between the boxes and risk missing his jump?

*

Eugene worked his way across the roof of the mill slowly. There were air ducts and fans and chimneys all over the place. It was dark, the shadows were deep. It was tough to tell how big the structures were until he got really close to them. He had to take each patch of shadow as if it could be hiding a squad of bad guys.

He reached the end wall and turned. He was done. He had checked everywhere. Their guy wasn't in the old logging town. Eugene could finally join the fight. He sprinted across the dark roof, avoiding the lumps and bumps mostly from memory, and hopped the chipboard wall. It was time to get to work.

The choppers were low now, and close. Eugene had been right, they were running dark. There were two helicopters. No lights on the outside of either, but there was still a little light in the sky and there was instrument glow in the cockpits. Eugene could pick them out, dark shapes above the trees at the edge of the bowl. They were moving slowly. Looking for a safe landing zone. The pilots would be combat veterans. The shooting around the containers was worrying them, but it didn't mean they were about to turn tail and leave. It slowed them down because it meant they couldn't land in the parade ground, but they would find a place to set down. A little shooting wasn't going to stop them from getting the guy away.

Eugene leaned the Heckler & Koch against the half wall of the sniper's nest and swung the Remington from his shoulder.

TWENTY-ONE

Eugene sighted on the glow from the instrument panel of the first helicopter. If he could hit something important enough, something either human, mechanical or electrical, then maybe he could bring the chopper down. Bringing the machine down in flames would be a magnificent bonus. All he really expected to do was to hit it. Military pilots land under enemy fire all the time, but they need to be extremely motivated to do so under sniper fire from a range of less than three hundred feet. If he could hit the helicopter he might make it turn around and leave. That would force the bastards who had killed his colleagues to try to take themselves and their arrogant prick of a prize out of the area the hard way.

Eugene slipped his Heckler & Koch through the hole in the roof and dropped it to the floor below. If either helicopter was armed he would be leaving the roof extremely rapidly. A door gunner with an M60 would make the roof of the mill building a death zone in seconds. He took a deep breath, stared into the dark, tucked his Remington tighter into his shoulder and fired his first round.

He knew the bullet hit. He knew because the sight on the rifle didn't waver and because he knew the rifle to be accurate over an equivalent distance. The two dead snipers behind him were testimony to the effectiveness of the gun. A fraction of a second after he fired he saw the glow coming from the cockpit windows twitch and move. It wasn't an uncontrolled spin toward the tops of the trees, but it was a definite forced maneuver. Eugene kept his finger on the trigger and watched for a second. He needed to know why the pilot was moving. If he was swinging around to let a guy hanging out of the side doors open up with a cannon, then Eugene would need to run for the trap door and he would need to run fast. On the other hand, if the pilot was reacting to the bullet or turning tail, then Eugene needed to stay exactly where he was and fire again.

The maneuver looked instinctive to Eugene and no deadly hail of lead peppered the sniper's nest. He worked the bolt and fired seven further shots at the first chopper. He fired slowly enough to make sure of a hit with every shot but quickly enough to let the pilots know that he was good and then he threw the rifle through the hole in the roof and followed it as quickly as he could. He didn't need to fire at the second helicopter. He had shown what he could do and his muzzle flashes would show where he was sited.

Eight shots had been a calculated choice. It was a strange number of bullets to fire. It wasn't impossible that eight rounds represented the entirety of the ammunition available to him, that it was safe for the helicopters to land, but that was highly unlikely. Eight shots might also mean that he was picking his shots. That maybe he was waiting until one or other helicopter was closer, maybe just feet from the ground. Maybe he was waiting, ready to fire into the cockpit or the engines or the rotor assembly.

Eight shots implied that even if he allowed the chopper to land, he could sit up there and pick off the guys on the ground as they ran to get on board. Eight shots was a code. It was intended to tell the two pilots that they weren't going to be able to land and that even if they did, they couldn't be sure of getting their cargo on board.

Eugene dropped through the hole in the roof and took the ladder as quickly as he could. He scooped up his Heckler & Koch and headed for the stairs. He knew that there were no gunners in either aircraft. If there had been the wooden building would already be disintegrating around him under the impact of six hundred rounds a minute. Eugene wasn't running away. He was running because he knew he had done enough to make the helicopters turn and head for home. He was running because he wanted to get into the parade ground and take on some of the guys who had killed his colleagues. He was running because he was worried that Doe might not have much more time left.

*

Doe decided to try the jump and he made it, but only just. The toe of his lead boot caught the edge of the container. Doe felt it scrape across and then off the metal before his other leg swung past. He leaned forwards as he felt himself start to fall backwards into the gap between the containers. His second foot hit the top of the container. It was way short of the mark he had expected to hit but his foot was down solidly and he hauled the rest of himself after it using the strength in his thighs. He pulled his first foot high to clear the edge of the container and just about managed to continue his run but there was no way he was going to be trying the jump again at the end of this box.

The guys on the ground were getting organized. They had a few men shooting up at him while they ran. They weren't really trying to hit him. They just wanted to make sure that he needed to run hard. They didn't know what he was trying to do. They wanted to make sure that he couldn't stop, aim at the guy in the fisherman's jersey and shoot him as he ran.

The rest of the guys in the parade ground were sprinting to get alongside or ahead of Doe. They weren't going to manage it before Doe made it to the corner of the second container, but it wouldn't take much longer. Doe would have to jump down into the parade ground. He was definitely tiring. There was no way he was going to be able to leap further on his second attempt than he had on his first. He had made the first leap by the skin on his teeth, if he tried it again he would fail.

Knowing that he didn't have to reserve any energy for a massive leap, Doe pushed a little more into his legs and managed a little acceleration. Sparks flew ahead of him and to his side as bullets skimmed off the steel. He looked ahead and down, trying to pick a landing spot that might give him a little cover or a slight advantage. The parade ground was a dark, empty circle. He couldn't spot anything helpful. He would just have to keep his acceleration going and hope that they would expect him to make the same move he had made before. He had to force himself to keep breathing as he got close to jumping. The tension was gripping at his lungs and trying to make him hold his breath. He forced breath out and focused on the point from which he would jump.

*

Eugene was in his element. Everyone was concentrating on Doe up on the roof of one of the containers. No one was under cover. They were out in the open, on the parade ground, facing away from him. He could see the remains of the radio mast where it had come to rest against the fronts of the buildings on the left of the parade ground. Eugene guessed that some of the enemy force was probably trapped inside.

He took down three men who had been shooting up at Doe and he moved on to engage a group who were setting up a little further forward. They were still facing away from him, shooting across the parade ground. He was perfectly safe as long as he could keep everyone moving away from him. He had used nine shots taking out the first three guys. He had twenty-one left. He ran forward and counted out the next fifteen shots. Another two guys fell and Eugene headed over to the cover between the second and third containers, emptying his clip indiscriminately as he ran.

Eugene sheltered against the steel, ejected the empty clip from his rifle and reloaded.

*

No one was shooting at Doe by the time he reached the corner of the container. He figured that Eugene must have finished sweeping the old logging buildings. There were gunshots behind him but whatever was happening, he didn't waste any time turning to look. The guy in the fisherman's jersey was still in front of him and he was still moving fast. He was the whole reason that Doe was here, the whole reason for the multiple risks he had taken. He didn't care about the guys behind him. He only cared about the one ahead.

Doe planned to jump from the roof of the shipping container and hit the ground a little to the side of the corner and he landed in the parade ground just a couple of inches short. His knees buckled and he turned the fall into a roll and used the momentum from the roll to propel himself upright and back into a run. He scooped up the guns he had thrown ahead of him and panicked for a moment when he looked up and couldn't see the guy, but then he picked the man out. He was standing by the side of one of the Humvees. Doe sprinted for the end of the container. He saw his guy pull on the door of the nearest Humvee and climb inside and a few seconds later he heard the big engine spark to life. It left Doe with yet another decision to make, but his rule was simple. If you have to think, keep doing whatever you are already doing until you have worked out what to do instead. If you are sitting, then stay put and figure it out, if you are moving then keep moving. Doe kept moving. His first plan was probably the best plan anyway.

His options were to stay where he was and try to ambush the Humvee or to head to the netting, steal another Humvee and give chase. The chances of successfully stopping the Humvee without killing the driver were low. The man had nowhere to run to but if Doe failed to stop the truck then he would have to take one of the Humvees anyway. Chasing a truck capable of hitting sixty on the graded track into town would be pointless on foot. It would also mean running back through the firefight that was developing between Eugene and the rest of the gang. Doe gritted his teeth and headed for the netting.

The Humvee's tires spun and the guy in the fisherman's jersey fishtailed out from under the collapsed netting. Doe smiled. Whatever else the guy was, he wasn't an expert driver. The netting was draped over the back half of the truck and it was a tough net. It was military grade, designed to be abused by quartermasters and shipping clerks and combat engineers and to still work. It was over-engineered because if it failed people died and expensive equipment got destroyed. The net was tough but the Humvee was tougher. A couple of the aerials got bent and something small and black ripped off the side with a small pinging sound like an expensive cellphone alert, but the Humvee moved on into the parade ground and the netting stayed where it was.

The guy pointed the Humvee at Doe and floored the gas, but Doe was running close to the side of the shipping container and the guy chickened out well before Doe did. He yanked the steering wheel and accelerated off across the parade ground toward the road, the gate and freedom. Doe looked across at the remaining Humvees. There were at least two that still looked serviceable, but they were both parked at ninety degrees to the road. They were facing out, past the containers and the road, toward the fence.

*

Eugene was fully reloaded. He put a few shots around the corner of the container and then followed them out into the parade ground. He was moving fast. He headed straight across the open ground toward a group of guys massed near huts on the other side of the square. He was acting on training mixed with personal motivation. He didn't want to let the bad guys settle. He didn't want them to find safe firing positions and start taking aimed shots at him, but more than that he wanted to keep himself on the front foot. He was going to be the one dictating the pace of the battle, not them. He wanted to hit them hard and to do it quickly. He spotted them as soon as he left the shelter of the container and took the first guy down with two three round bursts, moving toward the others as he fired at the first.

He moved halfway across the space, winging another gunman and scattering the rest. He had twelve rounds left in the magazine, four short bursts. He ignored the two guys on the floor and moved to follow the runners, counting down the shots in his rifle.

*

Doe reached the side of his chosen Humvee. He was under serious fire. As soon as he had left the shelter of the final shipping container, the guys who had been outside the parade ground, behind the containers had spotted him. They were back among the shadows with the collapsed netting right in front of them and they were all shooting at Doe as he ran the last few feet and reached the shelter of the trucks. The Humvee that the guy in the fisherman's jersey had taken had been parked facing into the parade ground offering perfect cover. They hadn't been firing at him but if they had been then the big truck would have protected him. He could have scooted over to the side of it, opened the passenger door and then climbed over all the equipment and into the driver's seat. It would have been risky, but it would have been way favorable to what Doe had to do.

Doe's chosen truck was parked face on to six or seven rifles. They were all firing at him. All trying to kill him. He had to make his way to the front doors. He couldn't run to the back of the truck and climb in through the trunk. There was probably a hatch back there, but Doe couldn't be sure and even if there was he might not be able to get it open. Military vehicles don't lock the way civilian cars do. There just isn't the need. They are usually parked someplace where you have to get through a gatehouse and twenty to thirty armed men if you want to steal one. Even if you do manage to steal one they tend to stand out on the highway or around a city. You can't just give a military grade Humvee a spray job and a change of tags and pass it off as a legal ride.

When they are out in the field it's even less likely that you would want to lock them. Their legal operatives might need to get into them in a hurry. If you are under heavy enemy fire you don't want to be fumbling in your pockets for a key or a remote fob. If you need to get into that kind of vehicle in a hurry your hands are likely full of the weapons you are firing. So, the doors don't lock and the handles are big and easy to use.

Military vehicles also have plenty of hatches and lockers on the outside, but when you aren't using them you keep them stowed tight. The rear hatch might not exist, or it might be too small for Doe to climb though or it could exist and be big enough but be secured from inside the truck or blocked by equipment.

Doe didn't waste any time looking for a way in. He knew how to get in. He was going to use the doors. His tactic was exactly the same as it had been in the gaps between the containers. Get there fast, get the door open and hide behind that. It was a good tactic but it didn't make for a fun couple of minutes.

*

Eugene still had ground to cover when his rifle clicked empty. It didn't actually click empty. He stopped pulling the trigger when he fired his last round. He knew the gun was empty. He didn't need to pull the trigger to confirm it. He had three guys down and two still up and shooting. He was pretty sure that two of the guys he had hit were staying down, but the third might still be able to get up and surprise him. He dropped the Heckler & Koch and it fell away from him, swinging back on the strap across his shoulder. He had the Remington across his other shoulder, but it would be cumbersome to use and it didn't offer the rate of fire that he needed, so he reached for his belt and pulled his Glock. It gave him a further fifteen shots.

He changed the angle of his run slightly. He was still heading toward the fallen mast at the edge of the parade ground, but now he was running toward the guys he had already hit and firing toward the two that he hadn't. He counted his shots carefully. He would need to have a few left when he arrived.

*

Doe got to the door of the Humvee. He got it open and squeezed his way into the cab. He wormed his way across into the driver's seat. Things were better but still not great. The shell of the truck gave him some protection, but it wasn't what the uninitiated called bulletproof. Bulletproof implied that you could pour bullets at something and nothing would get through. Bulletproof implied that you could sit behind something and feel completely and permanently safe. In practice nothing was truly bulletproof, nothing would ever keep you completely safe forever.

It always came down to weight and thickness and cost. If you build a wall thick enough it would stop any bullet but at the same time if you made a sharp enough, heavy enough bullet and you fired it fast enough, it would be able to penetrate any wall. It all came down to how thick and strong you could build your wall and how massive and fast they could make their bullet. There are practical constraints on both sides. The Humvee needed to be fast and maneuverable and it needed to not use more fuel than could be easily supplied in a hostile environment. That all meant that the truck had to come in under a certain weight and that, in turn, dictated the thickness of the steel protecting those inside. You could be clever with the materials and careful with the placement and design of the protection, but ultimately the thickness of the wall was constrained by the amount of weight the designers were allowed.

It was the same for the bullets. They needed to be small enough to be propelled by a charge that could fit inside the casing and in turn the casing needed to be small enough the fit into the gun. The gun and the ammunition needed to be portable in large enough quantities to be useful and they needed to be simple enough to be reliable and field serviceable. Finally, the bullets needed to be cheap enough that armies could give them out to their soldiers like candy and they needed to work every single time.

Doe remembered a myth that had circulated when he was growing up. The idea was that the way to breach bulletproof glass was to fire twice in rapid succession at the same place. The second shot was supposed to shatter the whole sheet of glass like a window tapped with an ice pick. The glass would craze and then collapse into a pile of glittering pebbles. It was a scenario that might have some truth if the bulletproof glass that you were firing at really was glass but in real life it would be a thick sandwich of glass and a tough plastic film. The glass would resist the bullet and take the brunt of the force and then the plastic would try to catch it. Like a stretchy net. Depending on the thickness of the sheet and the number of alternating layers of glass and plastic, the same windshield might take multiple hits in the exact same place.

Doe was extremely pleased that the myth wasn't based in fact. He could feel and see the physics in action. The pentagon wasn't stupid. They worked in huge numbers and to very tight margins. The bullets being fired at his Humvee were very well matched to the task of punching through the steel of the truck and ripping him apart but the armor of the truck was also very well designed to resist them. It all came down to time and luck and minute differences and imperfections in the metals or the build.

There were sparks flying off the heavy steel at the front of the truck and the windshield in front of him was popping and cracking as bullets and shrapnel and ricochets hit it. Doe fired up the engine, praying that nothing important had been hit badly enough to stop it working. He put the transmission in reverse.

*

Eugene had made sure that none of the three guys he had put on the ground were going to be getting back up again and reached the cover of the radio mast. He loaded up both the Heckler & Koch and his Glock. He had plenty of spare clips for the rifle, they were literally littering the floor around him. The whole gang were using the same rifle, so they were all using the same ammunition. The parade ground was covered in it, dropped or still attached to the bodies of the guys he and Doe had killed. He wasn't going to run out of magazines for the rifle, but he was running low on clips for his Glock. Either he was going to need to take rounds out of the bad guys' magazines and feed them into the empty clips from his pistol or he would have to take one of their guns and do without the handgun he preferred.

He didn't want to spend the time emptying and loading magazines and he didn't want to switch to a gun that he didn't know and which hadn't kept its user alive, so he stowed his empty pistol clips, scooped up a couple for the rifle, and set off again. He was chasing the two remaining guys on the parade ground. The three of them were heading south toward the cam netting and the parked Humvees.

*

The truck fired up first time and Doe backed it away from the firing in front of him. The camouflage netting was tangled up on the ground beneath him, but the trucks tires were big and the transmission and the axles were up high. Doe figured it would take a lot for the netting to wrap itself around anything important enough to stop him. He felt the back of the Humvee hit the downed radio mast. He turned the wheel, took the truck out of reverse and pulled out into the parade ground. The bullets kept coming but they were hitting fresh steel on the side of the truck now. It still wasn't bullet proof but it was a lot less damaged than the armor on the front.

Doe considered stopping and climbing up into the turret. The thought of swinging the M-60 around on the guys who were shooting at him was attractive, but up ahead the other Humvee was already reaching the last of the shipping containers and heading onto the newly graded road. Doe could get up into the turret in a couple of seconds and demolish the end shipping container within a couple more, but the escaping Humvee could cover a tenth of a mile in that time. Doe figured that his guy only had one plan. He was going to run and keep running. He would stay on the road all the way through Seal Harbor and all the way to Heath Haven if he could. He would only stop there because the road would run out. He was rattled and he wanted to stay in the big safe truck and he wanted to keep moving and to move fast. The Humvee was a good vehicle, but it wasn't going to make much progress off road through these trees and it wasn't inconspicuous enough for the guy to get on to the ferry at Heath Haven or for him to park up somewhere and hope to stay hidden.

Doe thought the guy was running scared but there was always the chance that he was still thinking. If his plan was to try to get far enough away to be able to dump the truck and melt away into the trees then there could be trouble. With enough of a head start, tracking a single man in that terrain could be tough. Doe didn't think the guy would make much of a survivalist. He didn't look like he was going to set up camp and make a life in the forest for a year or two, and Doe was certain he wasn't going to make some bark canoe and paddle to the mainland, but Doe wanted to be certain. It wouldn't be enough for him to think that the guy had died of exposure somewhere out there. He wanted to be sure. Doe needed to keep the Humvee in sight so that if his guy got out he could follow him into the trees.

Doe ignored the people shooting at him, gunned the engine and took off across the parade ground. The Humvee ahead of him turned slightly to hit the main road and disappeared for a moment behind the side of the mill. Doe held his breath, but he didn't really think the guy was going to park up and hide out inside the camp. He had been much closer to those buildings when he started running. If he was looking to hide he would have tried it then. Instead he had chosen to head back toward Doe and back into the firefight. The guy had really wanted one of those Humvees. He wasn't going to abandon it almost as soon as he had gotten in to it.

Sure enough, as Doe cut the corner onto the newly repaired road and felt the big tires bite into the new gravel, he saw the other Humvee a hundred yards ahead. It was still moving and nearing the end of the buildings. A few more yards and it would hit the ramp that would take it up and out of the bowl. Doe glanced further ahead and grinned. The fork truck was there at the gate. The big concrete block was down, in place. The guy in the fisherman's jersey had nowhere to go. He was trapped. He would have to stop and move the block or swing the truck around and come back into the camp.

Doe stepped on the gas and rocketed down the narrow road, maxing the truck's highway speed.

*

The truck ahead of Doe didn't slow. Perhaps he was a better driver than Doe gave him credit for or perhaps he was desperate. Either way, he barreled on toward the blocked gate with his foot on the gas and the pedal to the floor. He reached the last building on the block and swerved a little to his left. He misjudged the maneuver and caught the corner of the last building in the line. If he had hit the corner of the Police Department at that speed he would have crippled the Humvee, but the old logging shack barely slowed him down. It was like hitting cardboard. The dried-out, rotted wood of the logging building wall offered no resistance at all. Doe saw a little puff of gray smoke and then the guy's Humvee was through.

The driver swerved again to get the truck back in line with the ramp and it bucked a little as it hit the slope. The truck slowed as it climbed out of the bowl, but it was slowing because the engine couldn't maintain its speed while it was going up the incline, not because the driver was stopping as the concrete blocking the gate at the top of the ramp got closer. The right-hand wheels of the Humvee were on the graded track and its left-hand wheels were on the slope at the side. The Humvee powered up the slope cantered over at an angle but without breaking stride. It was designed to traverse a forty-degree slope or climb a sixty-degree incline. The edges of the road were unprepared but the chunky tires coped like they were supposed to. The driving was tough but the truck was operating well within its design criteria.

At the top of the ramp the perimeter fence came to within a few feet of the fork truck and the concrete block. The guy in the fisherman's jersey pointed the front of the truck at the fence and kept his foot to the floor. The fence posts were a lot sturdier than the side of the logging shack, but they were still no match for the front of the Humvee. The driver instinctively swerved and tried to hit the pole over the passenger's side of the truck, but Doe couldn't see whether he was successful or not. All he saw was the fence post bounce off the roof with a sound like a hard-boiled egg hitting a thin sheet of ice.

A few yards later the truck hit the top of the rise. The right-hand wheels were still on the shoulder of the graded road. The left-hand wheels hit a three-foot bump where the side of the road angled down into the bowl. The Humvee wheels cracked against the banked earth and then dug in and spun and gripped and the steering wheel twisted under the driver's grip. The back of the truck was pushed sideways by the impact and the driver found himself on top of the bowl but facing away from the road. He had a steep drop to the left and big tree trunks to the right and Doe barreling up the track out of camp straight toward him. He only had one way to go so he slammed on the brakes and selected reverse and inched his way backwards, toward the road to Seal Harbor.

*

Doe watched it all, tried to take notes and followed as closely as he could. He hit the logging shack a little deeper to give himself a slightly better angle. His narrow windshield fogged with pale gray dust and then he was through the cloud and turning a more measured curve to the bottom of the slope. He slowed a little before the start of the slope and accelerated the whole way up with one hand on the wheel and the other bracing himself against the tilt of the truck's cab. He didn't need to worry about the fence, he didn't even need to worry about the fence post. It had been snapped in two by the Humvee's bull bar and then thrown over its roof. It was still attached to the wire of the fence and it had swung around in an arc and landed well away from where Doe's truck was powering up the incline. The bump up onto the rim of the bowl was still an issue so Doe lined himself up dead straight to the lip and gave the motor everything it had. The wheel bucked under him when he hit and he kept his thumbs outside of the wheel just in case it started to spin. When he felt the front tires bite he yanked the steering to the right and ended up on top of the lip. One wheel was spinning in the air over the bowl, but he was facing the right way.

He could see a pale face behind the wheel of the other Humvee as it reached the road. Doe selected first gear and roared off along the top of the bowl. He was only a couple of dozen feet away from the lead Humvee by the time it reached the camp entrance and Doe really thought he was going to be able to end it right there but the guy pulled out an inch-perfect turn. He swung the rear of the big truck toward the concrete block filling the gateway and then turned the wheel and accelerated off down the road toward town. Doe had a simpler maneuver, he was facing forward and only had to turn onto the road but by the time Doe hit top speed the other truck was a good forty or fifty yards ahead.

The road that had looked so straight and level on the little Sat Nav map was completely different at ground level. It curved and climbed and fell. The long slow curve toward the camp entrance was more of a snake and the trees lining it were so tall and so dense that the truck in front of Doe kept passing in and out of view. The disappearances were frequent but only lasted for a few seconds at a time. Doe was confident that if the guy chose to ditch the truck and hit the trees then he would be able to mark the spot and follow him in.

Doe's truck's speed was maxed out. They were identical vehicles. They had identical top speeds. There was no way that Doe could close the gap unless his quarry made a mistake. The road wound around on a large scale but it was an easy drive and the ride was smooth. Doe fixed his eyes on the back of the other Humvee and settled in for a long chase.

*

When he knew that he was getting close to the abandoned house Doe sat up a little straighter behind the wheel. The foot on the gas pedal stayed glued to the floor, but his other foot drifted over and hovered over the brake. He kept two hands on the wheel, fighting against the big truck's suspension and the occasional vagaries of the otherwise well-built road. He tried to stay calm but he tensed slightly. He was ready to brake sharply or to brace for a crash.

He had an inkling, a half memory, that the road would curve close to the house. He thought he remembered looking up the road from the house and the track either disappearing into the trees after a few dozen yards or dipping down and out of sight. Sure enough, the chase Humvee disappeared from sight for a final time and when it came back into view it was parked up hard against the side of Eugene's truck. The driver's door was open. The house was off on Doe's left and Eugene's truck was parked across the road with its front fender hard up against the pine tree.

Doe checked his guns were loaded and slipped across the transmission tunnel and out through the passenger-side door. He crouched by the side of his truck and then he stood up and walked across the track toward the house. He moved briskly but he didn't run and he didn't crouch. He was on the hunt. The other guy was running and Doe didn't expect any accurate fire to come his way. He wanted the guy to glance over his shoulder and see him as relentless. He wanted him to run. He wanted him to try to hide.

TWENTY-TWO

The house and the woods were very nearly silent. The paint on the overlapping wooden slats of the wall of the building were still peeling and from the eastern corner of the building the porch and the front door were still to Doe's left. Doe swung his rifle onto his back and pulled out his handgun. He took a slow, controlled breath. He was angry and he was elated. He was close enough to the body in the refrigerator at the back of the building for his anger to be rekindled and he knew that he was into the end game. He knew now that he was going to prove to be better at this than the guy in the fisherman's jersey. Whatever that guy's specialty was, it wasn't going to be infantry style close quarters fighting. If that had been his specialty then his employers wouldn't have sent forty ex-special forces mercenaries to help him get onto the mainland. If the guy had any of those skills he would have brought himself in and neither Doe nor Eugene nor anyone else would have known anything about it. Doe had natural talent and a lot of training that was going to be very helpful indeed.

He took a few seconds to slow his heart rate. He was still buzzing from the exertion needed to bring down the mast and the adrenalin from both the firefight and the chase that had followed. He knew that he needed to get himself under control before he went any further toward his quarry. He stayed in the shelter of the side of the house until he was happy that he was ready and then he set out, not to his left, not toward the front door of the house, but right, toward the yard at the back.

*

Doe didn't know whether the guy had holed up inside the building or made a run for the trees, but he had a good feeling that he would be inside the building. If he had chosen to hit the trees, then he might have gone into the woods on the opposite side of the road. Doe could be wasting time heading in completely the wrong direction. It was a possibility but Doe wasn't worried. He had seen the way the guy had run. He had come out of the shipping container like the devil himself was on his tail. He had run hard the whole way here and he hadn't stopped because he wanted to. He had stopped because Eugene had had the forethought to block the road.

The guys driving had been panicky, the glimpses Doe had of him behind the wheel were of a pale face and wide eyes. People that close to the edge of their abilities and under that much pressure rarely made decisions. People in those circumstances made plans and when the plans went awry they reacted. Doe's guy had heard the sound of Doe's boots on the top of his shipping container bunker and he had decided that he had to move. He had made a plan. He would run underneath his pursuers, back toward them rather than away from them and in doing so he would find himself a mobile bunker. He would swap the shipping container for a truck capable of keeping him safe and getting him away from the battle raging around him. He would risk everything to get to the Humvee because the Humvee would save him. He had doubtless seen them on newsreels and possibly in person. In action on the ground. Rolling in huge armored columns and victory parades. To him the Humvee, quite literally and quite wrongly, represented safety.

Doe could relate to the delusion. The truck seemed so big, so solid. He had sat inside the thin steel shell feeling invulnerable even while he knew that it wasn't really going to protect him. He had destroyed an identical machine with his M-60 and then he had rammed one into the front wall of a well-constructed modern building. He had done all of this despite the fact that he knew that even after they had been up-armored the Humvees were not all that safe. Soldiers had died in them in their thousands.

But to the Guy in the fisherman's jersey, the Humvee had represented escape and safety. Then the truck he risked so much to get hold of let him down. He had turned a corner in the road and seen Eugene's truck blocking the road and he had realized that this fantasy of security wasn't going to save him. He had opened the driver's side door and fled. Doe couldn't imagine a guy who had made such bad decisions up to that point suddenly slowing everything down and deciding to skirt the truck's hood and head into the trees on the opposite side of the road. He couldn't see him calmly bypassing the house and heading into the trees behind it either.

In the man's mind he had been running forever and he had followed his plan. He had been running since he had left the shipping container. He had run to the truck and then he had run in the truck to the gate and he had managed the slope and then he had run from the top of the slope to the road and then he had run from the gate to the house. In his mind, he had made plan after plan after plan and now he was done. The plan was over. The plan was dead. It was time for a new plan and a new plan needed space, it needed time. So, he would be drawn into the house. He might not stay long. He might be out again in a few minutes, but he would go in. He wouldn't have a choice.

*

Doe moved around to the back of the old house and ran across the yard toward the rear door. He stopped outside the door, glanced quickly at the chest freezer and then ran at the side of the building and jumped. He caught the sill of the second story bedroom window. He had opened the window and left it open on his first visit just so that it would be available if he ever needed to use it. He pulled himself up onto his elbows and wriggled his way in. He hit the floor with a bang. He knew that the noise would mean that no one in the building would be in any doubt that there was someone else in there, but he was on his feet in a few seconds and moving toward the open staircase. He got to the top and spotted his guy. He was standing frozen, halfway up or halfway down the stairs. Doe clicked the slide on his gun making an entirely pointless audible snick and the guy in the fisherman's jersey dropped his arms and dropped his shoulders.

Doe marched the guy out into the yard and made him lie down in the dirt with his hands behind his head and then he frisked him. He frisked him hard and carefully. He had no idea what this guy's skills were. For all he knew the guy was some kind of escapologist. Maybe some Las Vegas billionaire was bringing him in for a tour of Caesar's Palace and trying to avoid immigration or taxes. Doe wasn't going to underestimate him.

The man was clean. His pockets were entirely empty. There wasn't even lint in there. There were no weapons taped to his body or concealed in his garments. He was clothed, but otherwise he was physically as innocent as a newborn babe. Doe left him lying in the dust and walked over to the freezer. He stopped a dozen feet from the freezer, spread his legs, braced his arms and fired four shots through the side of the metal box. He aimed high up and to the left of the center and spaced the holes widely enough that they wouldn't weaken the structure. Doe holstered his weapon and then opened the lid of the freezer. He walked back to his guy, turned him with his toe and motioned him to his feet.

The man stood up and allowed Doe to shepherd him over toward the back porch. Doe watched the guy carefully. He showed no reaction when Doe motioned for him to get into the freezer. It didn't get him much credit in Doe's eyes. It meant that he didn't know that there was a body in there. no one could be that uninterested in being asked to climb into a small metal box with a corpse. The guy might not have been directly involved in the homeowner's murder but in Doe's eyes he was just as culpable as the man who had pulled the trigger. He was the reason for the man's death and Doe was certain that he would have ordered it if he had been around at the time.

"Get in."

The guy still looked unwilling. He obviously didn't know there was a body in there but he wasn't keen on being locked in a freezer even if he thought it was empty. He didn't like it but Doe pointed the gun at his face and he moved to the side of the freezer and leaned forward. He put his hands on the metal edge keeping his eyes locked on Doe. He turned away from Doe and looked down into the freezer and took a fast step back when he spotted the corpse at the bottom. Doe jabbed him in the back with the barrel of his gun.

"Get in."

The guy looked into the freezer again.

"You can't be serious."

"Rarely more serious." Doe shoved him again. It wasn't revenge. He needed somewhere that he could stash the guy and be sure that he wouldn't escape. There wasn't a room in the house that he could trust. Doe could have ripped his way out through the walls of that house if he had needed to and there would be no reason to. There were windows in every room and no way to block them up.

Doe had considered the closet under the stairs but the wall was just thin planks, the door barely stronger. Doe wouldn't trust it to keep a puppy out of trouble. He wasn't going to trust it with his prisoner. He might have tied the guy up but he wasn't arrogant enough to think that his knots would be escape proof. If he had a couple of Eugene's plastic restraints in his pockets he might have risked it. He could have found a water pipe grounded deep into the foundations of the building or secured the guys wrists and ankles around a two-foot-thick tree trunk.

Doe needed to head back to the compound and help Eugene deal with the rest of the mercenaries. It would take a little time to get the Humvee turned around and then more time to drive it back to the compound. If he got there and found that Eugene already had the gang under control, he might be back to reclaim his prisoner inside half an hour. If not, it could be hours. With a few hundred pounds of junk and furniture piled on the top of the freezer Doe could be sure that his guy would still be there whatever time he got back. He might even pull the power so that the guy didn't freeze.

"But he's..."

"Get moving. I doubt he's the first corpse you've seen and it's because of you that he's in there." Doe dug the gun into the man's kidneys, upping the pressure and aiming to cause pain. He knew that he was still in control but he also knew that he couldn't let the conversation run. Eugene was fighting for his life and the longer they talked the more likely it was that the guy would recover. The more likely it was that he would attempt an escape or an attack.

"It's still not..."

"He's fresh, he's been on ice."

Doe pushed him in the small of the back again, letting the point of the gun slip upwards and scrape against his spine.

"One way or another you're joining him in there. It's up to you whether you need the air-holes or not. I don't mind wasting five bullets."

The guy looked at the four holes in the side of the metal box and did the math. He looked at Doe one more time and then he climbed into the freezer. He placed his feet as carefully as he could, either through respect or squeamishness, and he set himself down, hunched up near the dead guy's feet. Doe closed the lid. The pile of junk and furniture was still there on the back porch and Doe picked up every piece and placed it on top of the freezer. He paused and looked at the result and then he headed into the house and pulling out everything he could find and piling it on top of the furniture. He even pulled out the armchair and the closet. He found space for the chair on top of the lid, but he set the closet down about three feet from the freezer and then tipped it over so that the top was leaning on the edge of the lid.

*

Doe stepped back and looked at his handiwork and tried to work through the physics. The lid was hinged and it opened toward the wall of the house. He thought that with the TV and some tools and a vice that he had found, he had about three hundred pounds of weight piled up on top. If it was him that had been trapped inside, Doe would lie on his back and use his legs to push on the roof. He would have been able to lift that weight. He would have been able to move it, but unless he could lock out his legs he wouldn't have been able to hold it for long.

The hinge would both help and hinder him. It would mean that he wouldn't be able to press his legs out evenly. One would move further than the other. It would make the press harder, but it would also mean that the pile of furniture would be pushed over toward the wall of the house. Maybe the junk would jam up against the wooden wall. Maybe Doe would have to push hard enough on the lid to smash the chairs and side tables before he could get out. Or maybe it would all move sideways as Doe lifted. Maybe items would be dislodged. Maybe they would start tumbling to the floor. Maybe he would be able to lie on his back and repeatedly push the lid a few inches. Maybe he could shake the whole pile lose. If he could knock enough stuff off the lid he would probably be able to sit up and lift the lid open with his arms.

Doe had just about convinced himself that he would need to go back into the house and somehow manhandle the dining room table out into the yard when he heard the first engine.

TWENTY-THREE

Doe went around the southern end of the house, toward the front door and the porch. If the trucks were coming from the direction of camp they were likely to be filled with bad guys. If that was the case Doe wanted to give himself the best chance possible of approaching them from behind while they weren't looking. If they drove up as close to Eugene's roadblock as they could get then a single truck would be parked up half the length of the house away. If there were two trucks Doe would still be a little behind the last of them as he emerged from the southern end of the house. He doubted that Eugene had left enough men up and active to fill three trucks.

Doe swung the MP5 off of his back as he crept along the side of the house. He reached the corner and squatted down low, following the barrel of the rifle around the corner and pointing it toward the track from amongst the rails of the veranda. He could see two Humvees blocking the track. They completely hid Eugene's truck, but they were the two Humvees that he and the guy in the fisherman's jersey had arrived in a few minutes earlier. There were no other vehicles behind the two Humvees. Doe kept the gun pointing down the road and turned his head left. The tall trees on either side of the track made it difficult to tell which direction the engine sounds were coming from.

They were loud. They were either coming from small engines nearby or large engines still some way down the track. Small engines nearby would be good. Small engines nearby would have to be coming from trucks on the other side of Eugene's roadblock. There were no small trucks in the enemy camp, only big trucks.

Doe tried turning his head. He tried cupping his ears. He tried cupping one at a time and then he tried cupping both together. He still couldn't tell what the engine sounds meant. He took another good look around and then he moved. If he couldn't tell what was going on from the sound he was going to have to use his eyes.

*

Doe turned his back on the house and moved out, toward the corner of the porch. He could only face one direction at a time. He wasn't going to go running across the front of the house spinning around and trying to watch every angle. If the bad guys were coming then they were coming from the direction of the logging camp. It made sense for him to face that way. Unfortunately, there was no reason for Doe to assume that the good guys coming from the opposite direction would recognize him immediately and hold their fire. If the cops came past Eugene's truck on foot and spotted a figure up ahead with a gun, then the most likely scenario was that they would start shooting.

Doe kept his back to the porch rail all the way to the steps up onto the veranda. The hairs on the back of his neck were sticking out. It was some kind of primitive fright response. Some ancient piece of him was trying to protect him from danger by making him look marginally bigger, marginally more dangerous to attack. Doe didn't think the hairs would make one jot of a difference to a nine-millimeter round fired at his back.

He made it to the corner, turned around and ran for the cover of the two Humvees. Feeling safe inside a Humvee might be naive, but the inside was still a lot safer than the outside and the outside offered a lot more protection than a porch rail. Pressed up alongside an armored vehicle you can be completely invisible to anyone on the other side of the truck and you have double the amount of steel between you and them if they start shooting at you. The outside of a stationary, lightly armored vehicle was a lot safer than the inside in Doe's view.

He kept low and let the truck cover his back and he checked back up the road one more time. It was still completely empty, so he moved forward, along the side of the vehicle, toward Eugene's roadblock.

*

They were parked right out in the open. In the center of the track, nose in against the side of Eugene's truck. There were two pickups full of uniformed Deputies. Floyd was in the first truck. They were sitting ducks. Doe sighted down the MP5 and swung the gun in an arc across the front of the two trucks. If he had pulled the trigger he would have taken out the drivers and passengers for sure. They were in the process of backing up the two pickups to get them off the road. A couple of the cops were standing around at the side of the road with rifles resting on their knees. Doe shook his head.

He stepped further back into the cover of the Humvees and then shouted out,

"Detective Floyd. This area is secure. I'm armed and I'm coming out."

It sounded terrible and he blushed a little at the clichés, but he hoped that it would sound authoritative enough and official enough to keep the cops' fingers off their triggers. Doe shook his head again when he heard the inevitable scrambling for cover and readying of weapons that followed. He raised his rifle high into the air and stepped around the hood of the abandoned Humvee with both hands in plain sight. The cops were suddenly all business. He was triangulated by a half dozen rifles. He stepped around the front of the vehicle and walked toward Floyd. Floyd waited his customary couple of seconds and then lowered his weapon and gave a half nod. There even seemed to be the shadow of a smile at the corner of his mouth.

Doe stared at the other cops until he saw every one of the six weapons trained on him had been lowered to the ground and then he dropped his arms to his side and jogged over to Floyd.

"Good to see you."

Floyd inclined his head.

"You too."

Doe nodded toward the house.

"Let's get everyone under cover."

Floyd nodded and blushed a little. He glared at the guys by the side of the track and motioned them all over to the side of the building. They lined up along the side of the house. There were eight of them including Doe and Floyd. Doe took Floyd by the elbow and led him out into the yard. They stopped by the ramshackle outhouse, far enough from both the freezer and the cops to make sure they weren't overheard.

"What's the deal?"

Floyd looked around the packed dirt yard.

"It's all under control back there. The radio came back on so we reported everything. We left enough guys back there to look after everything and then I grabbed everyone with any combat experience and came out here to help."

Doe looked back at the guys grouped around the side of the house and wondered what constituted combat in Floyd's experience.

"I can use two of them here, but you should send the rest back to town."

Floyd tried to nod and shake his head at the same time.

"Yes. I know. I know they look bad... But no. The way they were acting when you found us... I know they look useless... but that was my fault." Floyd looked up at Doe. "We saw the Humvees and panicked... well, reacted. Once we worked out they were empty we relaxed."

"It was a terrible reaction. I know that. But if you'd got there a couple of minutes earlier we were text book."

Doe gave him a hard stare and knew that Floyd realized that what he had said meant nothing at all.

"If I'd wanted to I could have killed half of you before you'd even raised a gun." One of the guys Doe was looking at glanced over at them. Doe couldn't decide if the look of fear on the kid's face was a good thing or a bad thing. "If there'd been two or three of us we would have got you all."

Eugene nodded again.

"They're better than that I promise."

"It only takes a moment. There are plenty of you dead already. I don't want any more. And there's no room for error here."

"They all volunteered. They can all look after themselves. They just need direction and action."

Doe looked deep into Floyd's eyes and saw, or hoped he saw, some truth in there.

"OK, but you're all on your own. I can't babysit anyone in there." Doe knew he was being harsh. He knew that none of them wanted his help even if they did probably need it. "Do you have any concerns about any of them?"

Eugene looked away. It was enough of a tell in itself, but then he swallowed and nodded.

"Yes. Jain, Tift and Merritt. Jain looks a bit shaky and I haven't known Merritt long and..."

Doe held up his hand.

"That's good enough, I don't need to know the stories. If you're not sure of them they don't come." Doe stepped over toward the freezer on the back porch. "I need you to tell them that there is a deadly chemical weapon safely secured in that freezer over there. They will be in no danger whatsoever but they absolutely must make sure that no one goes near it. Tell them that one of our guys is in there looking after the thing and if he comes out then they are in no danger but that under no circumstances can he be allowed to leave. Tell them that he might get disoriented. Might get dazed and try to leave. Tell them that they mustn't shoot him but that if they let him leave, a massive chemical threat might leave with him."

Floyd gave Doe a look that he guessed he deserved but he returned it and asked,

"Do you think you can convince them of that?"

Floyd glanced over at the corner of the house.

"I guess so. Not for long, but I guess so."

"A few hours are all we need."

Floyd took a lot longer than his usual pause and his eyes were troubled when he met Doe's. Doe stared right back at him

"Do you think you can sell that story?"

Eugene glanced away, but his voice sounded confident when he replied.

"Yes, I can sell that for a couple of hours."

*

Doe was still worried about leaving his guy behind in the freezer. He was probably more worried about leaving the guy with the cops than he was about leaving him alone. Dragging the dining table out of the house would have been a major pain in the ass. He would have needed to tip it on its side to work it through the door into the kitchen and then he would have had to turn it again to work it out through the door onto the porch. After that he would probably have been able to lever it up over the rail and walked it around to the rear of the building. It would have been hard work and it would have taken time, but with the table upside down on top of the freezer lid and the rest of the furniture and junk piled up on top of that then he would have been sure that the guy wasn't going to get out while he was off helping Eugene mop up at the logging camp.

The cops could make sure of that as well, except that there was still the mole to consider. Someone had still logged onto one of the Department computers and tracked Eugene's cruiser. Someone had still sent a crew to bust the guy out of the back of Eugene's car. There was still no other explanation. If one of the cops that Doe left behind to guard the freezer was bad, then he could incapacitate his partners, release the prisoner, and if the money was good enough he could head for the hills with him. If the money wasn't worth throwing his life away over, he could kill his colleagues, crack his head against the side of the house and say that they were all attacked by person or persons unknown.

If any of that happened, Doe would have to start tracking his guy all over again and he would be an hour or two behind. That would be frustrating, but Doe could live with it. The guy would still be trapped on an island. It would still take him hours to reach the ferry to the mainland even if his accomplice provided him with transport. Now that the phones and radios were working again, Doe could have helicopters and planes and boats all over him before he could get any place where he would be able to melt away into anonymity. Doe even had a vague memory that there was a submarine somewhere nearby, he could probably get that involved if he needed to.

The main reason Doe hesitated wasn't a worry that the cops would help the guy to escape. The reason that he had concocted the ridiculous story about the freezer wasn't that he was worried about them being dirty, it was because he was worried about them even if they were clean. His wouldn't be the first prisoner to be shot in the back while apparently fleeing his captors. His guy had given the police department of Seal Harbor more reason than most to exact some extra-judicial vengeance. They were all pumped up to engage the enemy and instead they were going to end up kicking their heels, guarding a freezer outside a clapboard house a mile away from the shooting. If they knew the guy was in there, the temptation to pull him out and either have some fun or ask some questions was going to be tough to resist.

Doe didn't want to give them that temptation. He didn't know them well enough to know whether they would be able to deal with it. He didn't want them at the logging camp and he didn't want to ask them to start moving furniture onto the top of a chest freezer for no obvious reason, so he had come up with the most plausible cover story he could create on the spur of the moment. He stuck around while Floyd passed it on to the Deputies. He stuck around just to make sure that the detective didn't drop some hints or theatrical winks and let his guys in on the secret and at the end he tried to impress them with the importance of their job. He talked about the heroism of the agent guarding the weapon, about the potential for him to become disoriented, about the importance that they keep him at the house whatever he did and whatever he said. He tried to make the job sound vital and perilous and he tried to keep the presence of his prisoner secret. The fact that in order to do so meant that he had to involve some kind of contortionist and hitherto never-seen agent squatting in a chest freezer on a crumbling porch and hugging a dangerous chemical weapon, embarrassed Doe, but he guessed he could live with it.

Doe turned to the men that would be accompanying him to the logging camp. He was far from certain about their ability, but he couldn't just send them home. They probably wouldn't go even if he did. They would head off until they were out of sight and then they would turn around and follow him to the camp and then they would try to join in the action from behind. There's only one thing worse than having guys you don't trust alongside you and shooting and that's having guys you don't trust behind you and shooting.

Despite the timescale, he spent a few minutes preparing them. He checked their guns. He made sure that they all had a rifle and a side arm. He checked that they hadn't made stupid mistakes in their keenness to get out there. He purposely slowed down and as he walked he talked. He told them about the camp. He told them about the strength of the geography and the expert methods that had been used to make the logging camp into a fortress. He walked them through his earlier progress across the camp and the efforts that Eugene had undertaken. He quieted them all with the scale of the task and the risks that he and Eugene had already taken and then he headed toward the trucks and he switched tack. He talked about the fall of the mast and the battle in the parade ground. He told them about Eugene's arrival and the mad chase to reach the Humvees. He let his voice soar.

It was all about selling at that point. He had tried to take the assurance from them and replace it with confidence. He wanted them determined and sure of their ability, but not feeling invulnerable and convinced of their victory. They needed to be focused on what they needed to achieve and on the risks that were involved. They would fight better. They would be safer, and most importantly of all, whatever happened Doe would be sure that they had all gone in with their eyes open. He slipped behind the wheel of his Humvee and waved Floyd towards the second. Men mounted up behind them in quiet, but not grim, determination.

Before they left he tapped a few shoulders and squeezed a bicep or two. He made meaningful eye contact with as many of the guys as he could and then he gave a theatrically military winding up gesture with his left arm.

"Gentlemen, let's ride."

*

It took them a little longer to get back to the gate than it had taken Doe to get out to the house. They hustled, but it wasn't the hell for leather dash that the guy in the fisherman's jersey had made and that Doe had pushed hard to keep up with. Doe dabbed the brakes hard a few hundred yards from the fence and then released the brakes and accelerated. The Humvee behind him squirmed as the driver reacted to the unexpected braking and then he straightened up when he saw that Doe's truck wasn't getting closer. They didn't have radios. Doe knew that they were running in close formation and that there would be a reaction time for the driver. If he had simply pulled up in front of the fork truck there would have been a risk that the truck behind him would have slammed into the back. He didn't want to spend thirty seconds slowing down and giving the guy in the second Humvee plenty of warning, so he dabbed the brakes to wake him up and then drove to the gate with his own foot welded to the gas pedal.

"We have a gatehouse coming up," The road was straight. Doe could afford to look sideways at the guy next to him and then backwards at the two guys in the rear of the truck, "are any of you guys comfortable with a fork truck?"

Both of the men in the back of the truck raised their hands. Doe allowed himself a little smile. Self-reliant people. Neither had asked him what kind of fork truck it was or what he meant by 'comfortable'.

"OK. The gate is blocked by a big concrete block on a fork truck. When I stop I need one of you to jump out and start the fork truck and get that block up out of the way. Once it's gone I'm gonna accelerate as much as this heap will allow and try to get out of the way before the truck behind has to stop."

He looked back at the guys in the rear of the truck.

"Whoever it is that gets into the fork truck can follow along on foot, but I'm not going to stop for him to get back in, OK? My priority is to get these trucks up close to Sergeant Eugene."

His priority was the turret mounted guns not the trucks, but the simplification was acceptable given the circumstances. Doe slowed almost to a stop and the smaller, wirier of his two rear seat passengers jumped out and ran for the fork truck. Doe let the big truck coast until he saw the guy settle in the cab and the block start to rise and then he floored the accelerator again and crunched through the gears. The truck behind slowed but then when it saw Doe accelerate away it stopped braking and followed. Doe's truck squeezed through a gap that was a foot higher than his truck and a foot and a half wider. Three feet behind him the other Humvee matched his speed. They all felt a millisecond of free-fall as their trucks tried to jump the start of the ramp, and then they were hurtling down it and toward the first dried out buildings of the logging camp.

For a crazy second Doe considered steering for the corner of the building that he and the other Humvee had hit on their way out of camp. He knew it wouldn't cost him much time and he figured he could take the whole building down with one more good hit. The memory of the cloud of gray dust came unbidden but he put it down to the adrenaline and an adolescent desire to destroy. He kept his hands steady on the wheel and steered straight down the central street and into the parade ground.

*

Doe spotted Eugene as soon as he cleared the old mill building. He couldn't see the ex-ranger, but six crouched figures were making their way across the empty parade ground and they were all pointing rifles and headed toward a single point. Doe slammed on the brakes and pushed himself out of the driver's seat in time to see the second of his rear seat passenger's legs settle into the Humvee's swing harness. Doe sat back down in his seat and watched the six guys scatter like nine pins as the M60 started to fire.

They chased the bad guys into cover and then Doe opened the door of his Humvee. He and Floyd and two Deputies stepped out of the trucks and grouped themselves at the side of the lead truck. They gathered themselves for a moment and then headed toward the containers. Whenever they saw movement the gunners on top of the two trucks fired. A fraction of a second under their fingers released a mountain of rounds. To Doe, having the guns fire above him felt the same way as it felt getting out of a small helicopter. There was the same physical sensation of air moving violently above him, and the same tingle in the back of his neck. The same knowledge that something insanely dangerous was happening just above his head.

He waved the cops apart and stopped a few dozen feet from the containers. Any closer and the guys in the Humvee turrets would be worried about hitting their pals if they felt the need to fire. Doe cupped his hands to his mouth and yelled to the hidden remnants of the gang,

"The helicopters are gone. It's three miles across country to get to the coast and much further than that to safety. You can't get off this island other than by air or boat and that isn't going to happen. It's over."

There was a sound of metal scuffing from behind one of the shipping containers and the two guns on top of the two Humvees opened up simultaneously. Doe nodded. He had been wrong about the cops. They weren't bad. They fired for a few seconds to make sure the guys behind there were keeping their heads down and then they shut the guns down so that Doe could continue.

"We have ten dead cops and I have a prisoner who is a high value target for homeland security. You are all going to do jail time. No way around that." He paused, not to emphasize what he had just said, but to emphasize what he was just about to say. "I doubt it will be the first time for any of you and these will be civilian, not military courts and jails.

"If you choose to run, I strongly suggest you run now, but even more strongly I would suggest you stay and put down your guns."

It felt a bit like one of those other western films. Not Butch and Sundance but Pat Garrett and a posse in front of a grand, old, balconied whorehouse in some nineteenth century gold rush town.

"I think you guys call it the fog of war. Who knows who killed who. I hear that military pricks like you normally fire off like a thousand rounds without hitting anyone and having met you and traded blows with you, I can believe it to be true. A good lawyer.... A favorable judge... you might do twenty years."

This pause was purely for effect.

"And that's twenty years in a civilian jail. Not twenty years in Leavenworth."

Doe checked on his cops. They were strung out in a loose semicircle, guns high. They looked alert and proficient, not skittish or angry.

"But all of that stops right here. From here on out there are only a handful of you left and you're going to be spread out. You'll be chased and watched the whole way. Any action will be easily attributable. Any deaths will be pinned squarely and individually on you. You'll get the chair if you're lucky and you won't be lucky. I'll make sure of that. I'll push for you to be tried in Arkansas. They use Midazolam there. It's the injection they used on Ronald Smith and on Clayton Lockett. They died slowly. No one knows why the drugs didn't work properly but those guys died slowly, gasping for air, strapped to a table.

"In about twenty minutes this whole place is going to be crawling with people and if you run, most of them will be hunting you. There'll be a drone up there spotting for us and we'll have dogs choppered in and the water will be packed with coastguard and navy and law enforcement. I'll probably be able to walk from here to Canada across the decks of the boats there'll be so many of them.

Doe felt movement behind him and glanced back. It was Eugene.

"You all know the drill. Leave your guns where they are and come out with your hands on your head. Stop when the officers tell you to and do exactly what you are told. The M-60's start up again in sixty seconds if you don't."

*

They waited most of, but not all of the sixty seconds and then they came out as one big group. Doe figured they didn't want to come out in ones or twos. He imagined they might be were worried about being shot in the back by their own guys. It had happened before, the Red Army had whole detachments of personnel dedicated to preventing desertion or retreat.

The guys emerging from behind the shipping containers weren't an established fighting unit. There were no unit loyalties to contend with. No personal affections built up over months or years. No debts forged in the heat of multiple battles or during physical and stressful training. Doe doubted whether these guys had known each other for more than a few days, a week or two at most, and they were facing serious jail time at the very least. Maybe one of the guys out back would decide that he would have a better chance if there were fewer witnesses. Maybe someone with a little more on their conscience from that afternoon in the Police Department building would decide that he would be better off if his comrades died before they had a chance to tell the cops who had done what. Maybe he would wait until they were out in front of him, with their weapons out of reach in the shadows between the shipping containers. Maybe he would open fire as they emerged into the parade ground.

Whatever the reason, they all came out together. Eugene and his men yelled at them until they lay down on the ground and then they yanked their hands off their heads and handcuffed them behind their heads and sat them down in a line in front of the first shipping container. Eugene sent a couple of guys to check for stragglers and then he came over to Doe.

They gave each other a brief nod of the head, thanks from each of them to the other. Doe for Eugene's arrival when he was under fire and running across the container roofs and Eugene's for the arrival of the Humvees when he was cornered and out of ammunition. Eugene showed Doe his empty guns and Doe handed over his MP5 and spare clips. Eugene smiled and headed off with two of the Deputies to check the rest of the compound. Floyd seemed happy to let Eugene take command and the rest of the guys seemed to accept it as a natural hierarchy.

All Doe wanted to do was sit down, make some phone calls and get some specialists in to deal with the clean-up. He was bone tired. Adrenaline was washing out of his system. He hadn't eaten since before the battle at the Department building. He could have laid back on the packed earth of the parade ground and stared at nothing in particular until the cavalry arrived. He could have watched the stars until he noticed them arc across the sky. He could have breathed in the pine scent and pushed his hands against the dusty soil.

Instead, he borrowed a cop's cell phone and made a single, brief call to a very secure and very secret duty desk and then he walked over to the Humvees. They found some ropes in a locker on the back of one of the trucks and hooked them up to the radio mast. Doe liberated another H&K, checked it and loaded it and then he took one of the cabin doors and stationed cops outside each of the others. He waved his arm and the Humvee pulled on the rope and the mast slid and grated its way across the parade ground. They waited. Two of the doors were opened from inside and a handful of men, mostly officers by the look of their battledress, emerged. The cops yelled them to the ground and cuffed them and walked them over to sit on the ground with their other prisoners. One of the doors stayed stubbornly closed.

It was impossible to tell whether the cabin was empty or whether some guy was in there with his rifle pointed at the door. There could be a single soldier in there, ready to go out in a blaze of glory, or there could be a whole squad of them, waiting until the door opened from outside. Waiting to sweep back out of the cabin and start a counter attack.

Doe shrugged. He walked over to the line of handcuffed men and bent down in front of one. He pulled a stun grenade from the man's vest, walked back over to the closed door, kicked it hard just above the handle and then threw the grenade into the room. Doe rolled away to the side of the door furthest from the hinge. There was a bang and a flash and Doe stepped into the empty room.

TWENTY-FOUR

Thirty minutes later Doe was sitting in the middle shipping container, the one with the partitioned off room at the back. He had lashed the door closed against the splintered lock and the guy in the fisherman's jersey was sitting in there on the floor. Doe figured it was safer and more comfortable for him than being hunched over with a corpse in a chest freezer. It was over. Doe didn't need to punish the guy.

Doe had pulled a chair over from one of the cabins and he was sitting with one foot up on a crate of bottled water. He couldn't see the stars or feel the dirt but it was comfortable and his prisoner couldn't go anywhere without walking past him. Eugene and Floyd opened the container door and Doe could hear the sounds of helicopters close behind them as they stepped into the box.

"The cavalry's nearly here?"

Eugene nodded.

"The National Guard out of Redmond."

"There'll be some of my guys too. They'll be taking him," Doe gestured to the room at the back of the container, "and some of the more senior guys out there."

Doe noted the tightening around Eugene's eyes and he watched Floyd start to open his mouth to complain. Doe stopped him with a gesture.

"You'll get those guys back before the trial."

He stood up. He always thought it was better to give bad news eye to eye.

"But I suspect you'll find that this guy was never here."

Eugene nodded tersely but Floyd just shook his head.

"I don't see how we can do that. It's going to be all over the place. We lost ten men today and they have families and friends. You can't just sweep it under the carpet."

Doe sat back down. He was still tired and all his news would be good from now on.

"Nothing's getting swept under anything. The guys out there will all get tried in exactly the way you want. They'll all go to jail for the rest of their lives. A few of them actually might even get executed. That'll be down to the politicians to decide. But the guy in there is going to disappear."

Floyd took a step forward.

"Believe me, he isn't going to get away with anything. I doubt that any of the guys out there would swap with places him. Where he's going, he is going to wish he got a trial here instead."

Doe leaned back in the chair.

"Besides, what exactly would you charge him with? He didn't shoot anyone. He'll claim he was kidnapped. He'll say he had nothing to do with all this. He'll say he was innocently sitting in your jail cell until Sargent Eugene took him for a ride and abandoned him in some garage. He'll say he was waiting patiently there for him to return when unknown men broke him out and brought him here as a prisoner. He'll say that when I attacked the camp he saw an opportunity and tried to run. He'll say that I chased him, caught him, and unfairly imprisoned him once again. He'll claim that all he's been trying to do the whole time was cooperate."

Doe looked across at the hastily repaired door.

"He might be responsible for all this but there is very little that you could prove."

Floyd's shoulders sagged.

Doe continued, "I think that what you'll find is that what happened here was some crazy militia shit. A private army trying to take the island by force. Maybe they wanted to set up a free state, throw all the tea into the sea and cede from the Union or some shit. Only the heroic actions of the island's police force foiled the plot and saved the town."

"Not that far from the truth I guess."

Eugene leaned back against the side of the container. He knew where this was going but Floyd wasn't ready to accept it yet.

"What about the press? There's a lot of people here who know that isn't what really happened."

Doe stood up again. A little bit of anger in the movement.

"Who? Who knows that? A handful of cops. Most of your colleagues don't know what the hell happened and most of those will find it easier to believe the story I just told you rather than to try to come to terms with the idea that today was all about some guy that got washed ashore in a rubber boat. A handful of you know the truth, but I really don't think you're going to want to talk to the press. You have livelihoods and careers to consider and like it or not there are a lot of agencies out there with a lot of powers these days. And they all want this kept quiet."

Floyd was very red. His fists were clenched by his sides.

"Some of us might be thinking of retiring."

Doe shook his head.

"And emigrating to a beach hut in Haiti? Taking your pensions with you in suitcases stuffed with cash?"

Floyd seemed to deflate again.

"I'm just telling you how it is Detective. They won't come at any of you like this. Not at first anyway. At first it will be promises and thanks. There'll be support for the Department and for the town. There'll be promotions for the living and hardship payments for the families of the dead. There'll be rebuilding and new community buildings dedicated to the fallen. There'll be assurances regarding the fate of the perpetrators, including the guy in there, and there will be appeals to your patriotism. And those appeals will be right because believe me, nothing will be served by letting the rest of the country know how close that man came to making it onto the mainland and a huge opportunity will be lost if he stands trial and we don't get the chance to learn exactly what he knows about our enemies."

Doe sat down yet again.

"But if you keep going down the road you're on now, eventually the threats will come and they will be very real. But I don't think any of you will let it come to that."

Floyd glared at him,

"I'm not easy to bribe."

"I hope not, but I think you might be open to persuasion."

"Not by you and not by some federal jerks in shades and cheap suits."

Doe nodded again.

"Have you ever met your Governor, Detective Floyd?"

Floyd looked confused by the change of conversation but shook his head.

"Well you might want to find your jacket because you're going to." Doe looked at his watch and looked out of the container door toward the sounds of the approaching helicopters, "In about twenty minutes I should expect."

*

After the soldiers had landed, but before the helicopters carrying the State Governor and his detail arrived. Before Doe's colleagues touched down and he started his own, long mop- up operation, Doe and Eugene took a walk back to the mill building and up the stairs to the sniper's nest. Doe left two National Guardsmen to keep an eye on his prisoner and he and Eugene walked in silence until they were standing in the chipboard eyrie looking down over the parade ground.

"Floyd seemed genuinely upset."

Doe nodded and looked over at Eugene.

"Yep. He was, but he'll see sense." Doe stopped by the gap in the roof, alongside the top of the long ladder down to the factory floor twenty feet below them.

"He sure will. He's a big fan of the Governor. He voted for him I think. He's born and bred here. He'll protect the state if that's what he thinks he's doing." Eugene leaned on the low wall, "But that isn't what I meant. I meant..."

"I know what you meant Sergeant Eugene but don't worry, Floyd isn't your mole."

Eugene straightened up and turned to Doe who continued to stare out over the parade ground.

"What do you mean? How do you know?"

Doe turned to face Eugene and pulled out the cell phone he had borrowed.

"I made some calls. A friend of mine in New York pulled in some favors and their tech guys accessed your department servers. They know whose password was used."

Eugene stepped back, away from Doe, toward the furthest corner of the wooden box. His hands swung down towards his waist.

"I'm afraid your tech guy's going to lose his job."

There was a shell casing caught up between the boards by Doe's foot. He worked it loose with his toe and sent it rolling toward the hole in the roof. It accelerated and then slowed and then it almost stopped and then tipped over the edge and accelerated again falling faster and faster until it hit the floor and bounced. Stop, start, stop, start. Faster, slower, faster, slower. Pushed by Doe's boot, slowed by friction with the wooden floor. Accelerated by gravity and then stopped by the pine boards of the mill floor. Then up and down and up and down until it settled and rolled away into the dimness.

"But other than that, your department should be fine. It looks like you're all clean."

Eugene's arms swung behind him and eased him down as he sagged onto the corner of the wooden frame.

"Do you remember an Agent Merritt? He came up a few months ago for a couple of weeks from Immigration and Customs Enforcement?"

Eugene nodded.

"It seems his computer account was never deleted. My guy says it looks like incompetence or laziness rather than corruption. He says his friends found a whole mess of un-deleted passwords and stuff in your system, dating back a couple of years. Looks like your IT guy was bypassing or ignoring the procedures."

Doe looked up from the floor and met Eugene's eyes.

"The guy will have to answer a lot of questions, of course. We'll have to make sure that he wasn't leaving all that junk behind him just to make it look like incompetence afterwards, when we started digging around after he sold you all out. He'll have to convince some people that he wasn't working on a plan for the last few years."

Doe turned away to look out over the camp and the darkening forest. The camp below him was bright with rigged up spot lights. Some had been brought in on the newly arrived helicopters, but most had been brought in by the bad guys and set up around about the time they winched the radio mast into place. The guardsmen had simply had to find the right switch and flick it. The parade ground and the makeshift buildings around it were a hive of activity, but beyond that the dark tree tops spread away to a pale blue, almost white horizon that deepened instantly into a jet black, star-studded night.

"It's possible," he continued, "but it doesn't seem very likely to me. Not out here. In a big city I guess it might make senses. Someone there might have gambled on the fact that something profitable would turn up eventually. An enterprising young man might have started to build himself an alibi and waited for an opportunity to present itself.

"But I don't see that happening here. It would be too big of a coincidence. Somewhere like this you would have to know for sure that something big was going to happen to make it worthwhile preparing for it. A guy could go his whole career out here without getting a sniff of a payday worth going to all that trouble for."

Doe dropped his gaze and looked at the heavily-armed men bustling around in the square below him, guns held tight or strapped across their chests or backs. He thought about Deputy Brel, hopefully being medevacked by one of the evac helicopters that he could see in the distance. Hopefully being raced to a mainland hospital for surgery and a long recovery. Alive but at best facing a life in a wheelchair. He thought about Deputy Mathers shot dead on that mad dash to the side of the Humvee in the squad room. He thought about Mather's injured colleague, the one Mathers had been trying to drag to safety through the hail of bullets. One of the men that the gang had shot in the back of the head as they left the Department building. He thought about the Detective's daughter who had brought her father his lunch and had ended up badly injured and miles from help.

"For it to work here they would have had to have told your tech guy to start preparing more than two years ago. There's no way they told a cop that this was all going to happen that long ago. It would be a massive risk. They've been planning this for a while. All this kit would have taken months to smuggle in. The roads would have taken longer. But even if preparations were underway more than two years ago, only a small handful of people would have known. They certainly wouldn't have confided in some unknown, rural cop who could get busted or have a change of heart at any time."

Doe looked back over at Eugene. He seemed to be recovering and he would work the whole story out for himself anyway eventually, he was a smart guy. Doe figured it was always best to get as much of the shit as possible out of the way early and he liked Eugene. He felt he owed him some respect.

"They might have targeted you because of him though. They might have heard rumors about some slapdash practices at a Department in roughly the right location with roughly the right geography. They might have looked at your neighbors and picked you out because they thought they could get an advantage here because they could get at one of the guys that had left over the last couple of years. They might have known that they'd be able to bribe someone to give them a password that they hadn't used for years and they might have known that password would still be on the system because your tech guy was lazy or incompetent. They might have figured it was an extra little safety feature. If they had to go to a fall back plan they would have access to your computers. It might have tipped the balance."

Doe looked beyond Eugene, the opposite direction from the parade ground view. The trees spread away from him in exactly the same way as they did on the other side of the bowl. There was no brief, implausible white glow, the sun only sets on one horizon, but the trees and the blackness of the sky and the pinpricks of the stars were just the same.

"There are thousands of miles of coastline around here. Any one stretch would have been pretty much as good as any other. Personally, I doubt he was a major factor in their decision, but it might have been in the mix. He'll have to live with that I guess."

Doe stepped away from the rail, ready to change the mood.

"Now Agent Merritt... he's a got a whole heap of nasty coming his way."

He had felt that Eugene, and the Department as a whole, deserved to know that they probably hadn't been betrayed by one of their own. He felt that after all they had been through, they could live without the internal suspicions, the division and fear that the rumors of a mole would bring, but now Doe wanted to get back on the front foot. He wanted to get back into the action and he was aware that his ride wasn't far away. There were helicopters everywhere and the one that was coming for him would be among them soon. He hoped that Eugene would follow him off the roof and get back to work himself, but he guessed that was up to Eugene. Doe turned toward the ladder, but Eugene was shaking his head.

"Our tech guy won't be answering your questions. Our tech guy was Deputy Mathers.' Eugene pushed himself off the half height wall and gripped his rifle tightly. "He never wanted the job, never liked it, but there was a pay bump. He had a couple of kids and an ex-wife. New family, old expenses."

Eugene walked past Doe and turned at the ladder.

"Our tech guy died trying to pull a colleague out of the firefight in the squad room and I hope to hell it never crossed his mind that it might have had anything to do with him."

Eugene climbed down the ladder. Doe stood on the roof alone for a moment and then shrugged and followed. There didn't seem to be a lot more to say.

*

"Any chance you're going to tell me what this was all about?" Eugene took the stairs two at a time, in front of Doe. Doe appreciated the fact that Eugene didn't turn around. That he didn't try to force some admission with an emotional look or by trying to stare Doe down. Doe figured he would be able to resist, but he took Eugene's restraint as a courtesy.

"I doubt the government will ever tell anyone below the level of Mayor. Probably not even that low. And anyone they do tell will be sworn to secrecy with dire threats and portents." Doe smiled. "But then, this weekend, in this part of the country, I'm no part of the government, right?"

He waited for Eugene to turn and look at him.

Eugene smiled, just a little smile but it looked like a real one. It looked like it was a reaction to the humor not a sign of appreciation or one of those wry lip curls.

"So, if you did hear anything, strictly off the record, it couldn't possibly have been from me because I was never here, right?"

Eugene nodded.

"I can't talk for the entire town, but I think it would be reasonable to assume that no one in Seal Harbor is ever going to be telling anyone anything about anyone who matches your description for a long, long time."

It was Doe's turn to smile. It wasn't the way he had planned to win his little wager, but he thought he could accept the victory.

"Well, who knows then? I can't be responsible for what speculation a non-existent man might pass on, right?"

Eugene fell in alongside Doe as they stepped out of the old saw mill into the cool night and turned toward the parade ground.

"Before we talk about anything else I need to apologize." Doe was taking a slight liberty. He wasn't really apologizing to Eugene. He didn't care that he had misled him. "The two guys from the first sentry truck are way back in the trees about two and a half miles out of town. I think you should be able to spot where I left the road pretty easily, I crashed the truck through the trees. If you look closely I'm sure you'll be able to see all sorts of broken branches and tire tracks and stuff. One of the guys is dead but the other probably needs help. Look after your own guys first, but I'd appreciate it if you'd get around to him as soon as you can. He's had multiple concussions and his nose is busted good. He's almost certainly not breathing well and he's been in there for a long time now."

Doe did the thing that Eugene had been unwilling to do and looked the guy in the eye, hoping to leverage some added co-operation.

"It won't kill me if he dies like that, but I'd feel a lot better if he didn't."

Eugene nodded.

"OK, anything else?"

Doe looked away.

"One thing. It's not important but it has been driving me nuts."

Eugene showed no interest at all. Doe's problems didn't seem to worry him one bit.

"When you first pulled me in, when I asked for a phone call..."

Eugene smiled a little, like he knew what was coming.

"You knew that the phone lines were down then, right? I wasn't going to be making any phone call?"

"No, you weren't."

"So why did you tell me I was? Why did you move me? If you'd kept me in the cell..."

"Then you'd never have escaped and...."

Doe smiled. He didn't usually respond to such challenges, but he was tired. He figured he could indulge himself and he guessed they were at the beginning of a relationship that might be able to take a little strain.

"I'm not sure about that. I'd have found a way out. There was always plan B."

Eugene looked across, part question, part challenge.

"Whatever."

"So why? Why did you pretend I was getting a phone call? You must have known that as soon as I picked up the phone I would have known you were pulling something."

Eugene shrugged.

"We couldn't think of a reason to say no without admitting that we were cut off. And we thought we might learn something. We have a reverse directory. We figured we would leave the cuffs on you and ask you what number you wanted us to dial. We figured we could run the number through the database. If you phoned a lawyer then maybe you were legit, if not..."

Doe mulled it over. It made sense. Nothing clever, nothing meaningful, just a snap decision made by people under stress and seized upon. They walked on, into the parade ground.

*

"OK, thank you." Doe turned a little toward Eugene as they walked toward the very center of the parade ground. Guardsmen hustled around them, working in that way soldiers have when a VIP arrival is imminent. "I guess it's my turn. You know none of this of course, but I sent through a photo..."

Doe pulled out his borrowed cell phone.

"By the way, I think I'll need to buy this phone, I'm pretty sure my tech guys won't want to run the risk of someone recovering that file. Can you tell the guy? I think it's safe to assume he'll be happy with the price we'll give him."

Eugene's smile became a little wry. One of his colleagues was going to get a thousand-dollar bonus and while Eugene wasn't upset about that he knew that the socially expected response was a roll of the eyes and a wry grimace. He was operating well enough to give both.

"The evidence isn't good enough for court yet, but then again, I doubt it'll ever need to be. His name is Errol Goodman, AKA about a hundred things. He's a US national by birth but he's been out of the country for a decade. He's got a heap of weird ideas and a much bigger heap of money. He's worked for pretty much every terrorist organization in the world and he charges a lot." Doe stepped around Eugene and led the way, moving faster now, nearly finished and nearly done. "He's on every list we have and he'd be hard to hide too. He got into trouble here before he left the US. We have his fingerprints, we even have his DNA. There was no way he was making it through an airport or even through Immigration at a fishing port. If he flagged a computer in Bunukiport MA it would trigger a drone strike. If he tried to get through LaGuardia he'd never leave."

Eugene didn't know whether to believe the drone strike or not.

"So, what was he doing back here?"

Doe turned and rolled his eyes.

"Believe it or not, it's his mother's birthday!" Doe strode off toward the parade ground. Eugene waited too long, stunned, then rushed to catch up.

"Seriously!?"

Doe smiled.

"No. He's a bomb maker. More importantly he's a missile expert. He works with pretty much everything, up to and including cruise missiles."

A sleek, black helicopter landed right in the center of the parade ground and Doe made straight for it. It was a small, corporate machine, dwarfed by the gigantic troop carriers that had made the more difficult landings at the edges of the camp.

"So, what was he here for?"

"No idea." Doe nodded toward the side of the parade ground where the guy who had previously worn a fisherman's jersey was being escorted toward the helicopter. "But, knowing the guys that he's about to meet I'd be very surprised if we don't find out."

Despite himself Eugene's eyes got wide. He shook his head and jogged on, trying to catch up with Doe again.

"OK, but what do you think? Why do you think he's here?"

"What do I think Deputy Eugene?" Doe ducked into the down draft of the helicopter's rotor blades. "I think you and your colleagues delayed a missile attack on the United States of America today, maybe even prevented it altogether. Probably a small missile fired from inside the US, but I really can't work out whether that would be a better or worse event than a big one fired from outside. And I think its only optimism that makes me say that anyway. There's really no reason why they couldn't have been planning something much bigger."

Doe paused at the side of the chopper and reached one hand toward the door and one hand toward Eugene, looking to shake his hand.

"Thank you, Sergeant Eugene, let's stay in touch."

Eugene looked at the door and then looked at Doe. The guy who had previously worn a fisherman's jersey was being loaded into the back of the helicopter.

"Shouldn't you wait for the governor to get out?"

Despite the whirling rotors, Doe couldn't help looking up. He pointed upwards, careful to keep his fingers below his head.

"The governor has been hanging around up there for the last fifteen minutes, circling, waiting for us to land and take off." He leaned in toward Eugene and in a shout that mimicked a whisper in the din of the rotors he said, "Don't tell Floyd."

End

Printed in Great Britain
by Amazon

58591154R00199